Frole

Silver Tears
Book 4

By
Daniel J Strait

This is a work of fiction. The events and characters described herein are imaginary and are not intended to refer to specific places or living persons. The opinions expressed in this manuscript are solely the opinions of the author and do not represent the opinions or thoughts of the publisher. The author has represented and warranted full ownership and/or legal right to publish all the materials in this book.

Frole
Silver Tears Book 4
Copyright © April 2020 Daniel J Strait
V 3.5

Edited by:
Heather C. Wentz

Daniel J. Strait

ISBN: 978-0-578-80608-2

For my wife and daughter. They are the lights in my life and I'm truly honored to have them in my life. I Love you so much,

Ruby and Precious.

In loving memory of the best mother-in-law,

Carmen Pascua (Duldulao).

We miss you every day.

The Prophecy

From a time long since past
Shall the Future be told
Beyond our time when many have Forgotten
Five there will be, Strangers All
United Four will Stand
Further than Any have ever been
The First will bear the Mark
The Second from the Darkest Wilds
The Third from an Ancient race
The Fourth Royal Blood it Will be
The Last the future He can See
This it must Be or an end to the Dark
There Will Never Be

Preface

Four out of five members of the prophecy have been found. The first, as she is sometimes called, was Nakiata, who comes from the planet Trouganda. She's about eighteen years of age and stands four feet, three inches tall with jet black hair and a slightly pale complexion. She is quite the beauty with her exotic, royal blue eyes.

She was trained in the martial art known as Shadow of Thought. Shadow of Thought is not only a martial art, but a discipline in which Trougandan men train themselves to alter their bodies to allow light to pass through them. This renders them almost completely invisible, with the exception of their eyes, which give off a faint glow due to their concentration. Nakiata outdid her male counterparts, and she is capable of reaching the purist level of SOT. She can become completely invisible. She is now a Shadow of Thought master, or SOT master. She is the first person mentioned in the prophecy. We know this because she was born with the birthmark that it described. We followed her when she was sent out to finish her final test, during which she found herself being immediately confronted with hardship and danger, and it seemed that at every turn people wanted something from her.

Finally, she was nearing the end of her journey that would enable her to finish the final test, and that's when she discovered that her true adventure had just begun.

Next we were introduced to Dravone, who is about thirty years old and a Morphan who was living on the planet Trouganda. He stands a bit taller than average at a height of six feet. He's slightly cherubic, with dark brown hair and blue eyes, at least while he is in his normal-state.

His people, the Morphans, are similar to werewolves. The have the ability to change at will into large, fur-covered humanoids with claws and mouths full of sharp, canine teeth. The Morphans are not originally from Trouganda. The location of their home world remains clouded by mystery.

As fate would have it, Nakiata and Dravone met in the most agreeable way possible, at odds with each other. Nakiata was trying to get to a Black Door, something she knew nothing about, but was told that it held the secret to finishing her final test. Dravone and the other members of the Morphan council had made the ruins, which contained the Black Door, their den.

It was a swift battle and bittersweet defeat for Dravone. In the end, he decided to swallow his pride and save the remainder of his people from Nakiata's wrath.

Nakiata realized that Dravone fit the description of the second person mentioned in the prophecy. From that moment on, they joined forces and headed out into the universe to locate the rest of the members that they were destined to find.

The two of them stepped into the blackness and into the unknown, ending up on another planet, Zondura, which is where *Zondura: Silver Tears Book 2* began.

They quickly found out that the people of Zondura were ruled by a ruthless matriarch known as the Prowess of Prosino, and it was her ultimate desire to have every last Morphan killed in the most gruesome way possible. The duo was left with no choice but to fight their way out of the castle and make a run for their lives.

The Prowess, however, was going to stop at nothing to get her prisoners back. She was not going to hold back, so she summoned the best warrior tracker, who just so happened to be her daughter Ka'tia.

Ka'tia, who's about six feet tall with reddish-orange hair and beautiful green-grass-colored eyes, and is in her mid-twenties. She had a somewhat tan complexion, which for anyone from Zondura was a bit darker than normal.

This was the first time in her life that she had a real challenge ahead of her, and she couldn't wait to hunt down the escapees.

Nakiata and Dravone were able to elude the warrior tracker Ka'tia with the help of an unexpected stranger named Reyvahn. Nakiata and Dravone followed along after their new guide until they were suddenly betrayed by him.

Just a few minutes after Nakiata had slain him did they find out that he was Ka'tia's brother. Witnessing her brother's horrific death, Ka'tia was left wide open to be captured or killed. However, Dravone stepped in between Nakiata and Ka'tia in the nick of time and suffered a mild injury. He told Nakiata that it would be better to have Ka'tia as a prisoner because she could guide them to where they needed to go, and, as a bonus, she would know if someone else was following them.

They continued on with their quest, and their journey ended up bringing them full circle back to the castle of the Prowess. It was then that they learned of the matriarch's new secret condition. That was all the information they needed to get the upper hand, which they used to ensure there would be a lasting peace from that point on.

Not having found what they were looking for, the adventurers were at wits' end when one of Zondura's best scholars made an amazing discovery. He had been researching the prophecy for months on end when he realized that our adventurers, Nakiata and Dravone, were two of the members mentioned in the prophecy. At the same time, he made the connection that the Prowess's own daughter, Ka'tia, had to be the fourth member mentioned in the ancient text because she fit the description of one who has royal blood.

Shocked by the news, Ka'tia was more than a little hesitant to join in on such a quest. She was conflicted by the fact that Nakiata killed her brother, but something deep inside her told her that this was the right thing to do. So, in the end, she decided it was her destiny and it just might lead her to the justice she was seeking.

From there, the three of them departed Zondura through a second Black Door. That is where the last book, *Vazdrag: Silver Tears Book* 3, picked up the story.

It started out with the three members of the prophecy getting stuck in a dark, underground maze. That is, until Dravone and Ka'tia unexpectedly noticed an alien creature in one of the tunnels. Unfortunately, they only saw the creature for a split second, but it was just enough to give Dravone the fortitude to change to his wolf-state and give chase.

By the time he reached the spot where he'd seen the creature, it had already vanished into thin air, but he was able to pick up on its scent. He followed it back to the main cave, where he lost it.

Nakiata and Ka'tia finally caught up to him and thought that the being was long gone, but it wasn't gone; it was just invisible. Our adventurers found out when it arbitrarily attacked, which gave Nakiata the idea of how to find the exit to the maze.

It was at this time that Ka'tia began to notice she had subtle hints of magical abilities. She was somehow able to use magic to open the invisible door that was the exit from the maze.

Shortly after exiting, the group came face-to-face with an adversary unlike any they had ever encountered, the Roarrgs. The battle itself was short-lived because the Roarrgs had something they didn't: technology.

The group now consisted of four, to include a Roarrg guide named Promnarr. From there they headed down to the planet's surface and began the trek to a stronghold being held by the enemy. Just before they reached their destination, the group ran into a few of the new enemy creatures, the Ugs.

The three faced several more battles including one with their Roarrg guide. Next they were thrust into an all new part of the galaxy where Nakiata and Dravone suffered minor injuries, but Ka'tia wasn't so lucky, she had been pierced by a large piece of metal, and her life was fading . . . fast. Just when they were about to lose hope, some aliens arrived and assisted them. They even saved Ka'tia's life.

After that they got separated and along the path to finding their lost Zonian warrior princess, Nakiata and Dravone ran into something neither of them expected to ever see in a random corner of the galaxy: a large group of Morphans.

A brief display of male dominance ensued, but Nakiata ended the charade by killing their leader, at which point the Morphans offered their assistance. The first bit of help was good news when they were told about the Ho-drooli.

The Ho-drooli are a symbiotic pair of beings: One is a large being with weapons in their forearms, and another being controls them from within. Nakiata didn't really care what they looked like, she just knew they had Ka'tia and she was not going to stop until her friend was free. So, without a second thought, she engaged them, and they fought each other.

At the end of the short battle, Nakiata ended up killing several hundreds of them before they managed to trap her in a bubble, which completely incapacitated her prior to transporting her halfway around the planet.

The Ho-drooli informed the newly reunited Nakiata, Dravone, and Ka'tia that they had to take back the key to a Black Door. The only downside was that the key was located on the Breoli planet.

With the help of their new ally, the Ho-drooli, the trio made the short trek through the solar system and arrived on the Breoli planet. As soon as they landed, a fight ensued, and somehow Nakiata was fatally wounded. Out of nowhere, an Ug showed up, picked up her body, and vanished.

Another battle ensued and they managed to get the key back. The three of them made their way back to the Ho-drooli planet, were they immediately used the key and were able to return to Vazdrag. Nakiata knew exactly what they had to do, and, as circumstance would have it, the Roarrgs didn't hold any grudges, but in fact were ready and willing to assist them. They quickly realized that the Roarrgs had become their greatest ally.

The Roarrgs gave them a new task, one that was going to prove even more dangerous. They had to somehow rescue Promnarr, who was being held captive by the Ugs in a remote, extremely cold region on Vazdrag. On the way, each of them were given specially designed suits of armor that were genetically coded to them. The suits not only could protect them from all sorts of weapons, but they also protected them against simple things, like extreme temperatures.

Once suited up, the trio made their way into the Ug stronghold and managed to rescue Promnarr from the clutches of the beast, which turned out to be a mere child. They fled before the beast's mother could get to them.

The returned to the Roarrg council, where they finally learned the information they'd bargained for. They were told that they had to find the Sodaran, who'd been living on Vazdrag longer than most of them could remember. The council insisted that Promnarr join the group and lead them to the Sodaran's lair.

They went back down to the planet's surface, and made the long trek across the dry, barren area of Vazdrag that led to the beast's lair. The group entered the lair, and before long they encountered the Sodaran. Everyone in the group, except Nakiata, started to laugh when the saw the beast, who barely stood just over three feet tall. He had the appearance of a red-scaled kobold with the usual hands and feet, along with a pair of wings.

The laughter enraged him, and that's when he showed them his true power. He burrowed into the soft, moist ground, and a minute later he emerged, twenty-five feet tall and prepared to incinerate them with his fire.

Those that were laughing turned and ran as fast as they could for the entrance, leaving Nakiata to fight the great dragon alone. The face-off between Nakiata and the Sodaran began.

At some point the great hulking beast observed her left arm, and thus he saw her exposed birthmark. The Sodaran knew what it was which changed everything. That's when he hopped up onto the stone with her and introduced himself as Tyrog. He immediately pledged his loyalty and life to Nakiata.

Nakiata called the others back, and from there they went further into Tyrog's lair. He humbly welcomed them into his dwelling, where they soon learned even more about the prophecy, especially the part where Tyrog fit the description of the third individual mentioned in the prophecy. After getting a different, newer perspective, he was able to come to that conclusion, since he was the last of his race, and as far as any of them knew, the Sodaran were the oldest, most ancient races in the Theyan galaxy.

To help expedite their journey the Roarrgs escorted them back to the Black Door. Promnarr waited near the exit of the ship, and as they said good bye he imparted upon Nakiata, Dravone, and Ka'tia a small, unique badge of honor to each of them.

The Black Door was activated, and the four members of the prophecy walked through, arriving on the Ho-drooli planet, and after Tyrog and the Ho-drooli used their combined knowledge, they were able to locate the approximate whereabouts of the purple planet, and hopefully the last member of the prophecy.

With the coordinates locked in the control table, they activated the Black Door, and the group walked into the blackness with hopes of finding the last member of the prophecy, the one who could see the future.

Chapter 1

The group had just stepped into yet another Black Door. Tyrog was the first to make it through, arriving in dimly lit, almost always dark room. The red-scaled, three-foot, six-inch tall Sodaran had no issues seeing in the low light. His purple eyes almost had a glow as his white, cat like irises quickly adapted. Within seconds he found the glow of the control table. Before anyone else made it through he flapped his wings and flew over to the control table — which, at the time, was providing the majority of the room's light. He began operating the controls, and a moment later a huge array of lights high above turned on, allowing the others to arrive in a well-lit room.

Nakiata was the next to arrive on the other side. She smiled, reached up and moved a strand of her jet-black hair, which had managed to come out of her ponytail. *This is a first, the lights are on*, she thought. Her royal blue eyes scanned the room. Even from her vantage point of only four-feet, three inches tall, she immediately noticed that this room was much different than the others they had grown used to entering by way of a Black Door. The space was at least five times larger than normal. Normal being a rectangular room about twenty feet long and about fifteen feet wide with an old wooden door for an exit. This room was circular, and had a large, domed ceiling.

She moved her pointed, elf-like ears back and forth listening for anything out of the ordinary, but the only thing she could hear was the deep steady breathing of Dravone, who stood directly behind her. "We should get out of the way. Ka'tia was right behind me," he said looking down at her, since he was just over a foot-and-a-half taller than her.

Nakiata looked back at him and smiled. "That Roarrg armor really looks good on you," she commented moving out of the way.

Dravone looked down at his tattered robe which cover the high-tech second skin the Roarrgs had designed for them. *I hate to say it, but I have to agree with her. It does have a pretty awesome look to it. I bet it even makes me look more menacing after I change into my wolf-state*, he thought.

"There's nothing here. There isn't even a commonplace doorway which we could use just to get out of this room," Ka'tia the six-foot tall, red-haired, Zonian warrior, noted the moment she arrived.

"Maybe there is and we just don't see it. If we split up and do a quick search, we'll know for sure," Nakiata said. Dravone nodded and the two of them walked in opposite directions around the room, examining as much of the walls as possible. Sure enough, there was no other way in or out except through the Black Door in the center of the room.

Nakiata couldn't help herself as she started, "Tyrog, do you even know where we are? And how exactly do you plan on getting us out of here?"

"This is one of a few, extremely rare, places that have been nicknamed a 'hub'," Tyrog said. "And just because you don't see something doesn't mean it isn't there. You of all people should know that by now, I would think." He waved a hand over the control table. All at once, low hums began to fill the room as multiple Black Doors came to life at the same time all around the room.

"Oh, wow! There has to be at least twenty Black Doors here. How are we going to know which one to go through?" Ka'tia asked.

"Thirty-one Black Doors, to be precise," Tyrog said. "And to answer your question, any one of them will take us where we want to go, except the one in the center. That one is connected to a select number of corresponding doors. Now, if you will excuse me, I have a little more work to do here before we'll be able to leave, so I suggest getting comfortable and . . . Just sit tight."

Dravone continued walking around the room, looking at each of the Black Doors and wondering where each one could take him. He began to notice that most of them had a faint blue glow around them, while a few of the others had a red glow. He stopped next to the control table and asked, "Why do those Black Doors have a red glow to them?"

"A red glow indicates that the Black Doors to which they are currently connected could be damaged, or destroyed," Tyrog said, his eyes never leaving the control station as he continued working on various calculations. "It could even be something as simple as an obstruction on the other side, which would cause the traveler to become injured — or worse. No matter what the cause, they become red to prevent travelers from entering an unsafe or life-threatening situation. Another possible reason could be that the atmosphere is no longer capable of sustaining life. Don't worry, though; every Black Door was built with a myriad of sensors installed in them that prevent anyone from travelling into a known hazardous condition," he explained.

"How *interesting*," Nakiata said. She rolled her eyes and continued scrutinizing, "Now we know a little more, even though I doubt it helps our situation."

"If that's all the questions you have, I need to concentrate on what I'm doing. I have a lot of computations to make, so please, no more interruptions," Tyrog said as his small clawed hands tapped furiously on the controls. His deep voice reverberated, and he grumbled under his breath. *They don't understand; one small mistake and we could end up on the wrong side of the galaxy.*

Nakiata frowned because she still had no idea what Tyrog was talking about. The technology of the Black Doors was far beyond that of any found on Trouganda.

Dravone didn't seem to care that much, as he just shrugged his shoulders and kept circling the room.

Ka'tia was the only one who was fascinated by technology, which was just as new to her as the others. She sat down near the control table where she could watch Tyrog's every move.

An hour passed, and they drew closer to the control table, impatient for Tyrog to finish his computations. Nakiata decided to take the opportunity to meditate.

She let her mind lose all focus. The first random thing that came to mind was the moment back on Zondura when she held the true box of Katoh. She heard the unique soft, voice again, *"You are not far. I am waiting."* The tone and pitch of the voice changed drastically, *"Go back! Or I will have no choice but to end you! Go home!"*

"Who are you?" Nakiata asked.

"I am. We are. You are. We will be —"

"Time to go!" Tyrog's said, his voice pulling Nakiata out of her meditation. The voice faded away into soft whispers and they were gone like the smoke of a candle that had just been extinguished.

"Are you all right, Nakiata? You look really upset," Ka'tia asked.

"I'm fine! I was just remembering what happened when I found the real box of Katoh," Nakiata said, closing her eyes and spreading her hands out in frustration. "Do you recall what it did to me? I was trying to remember the vague places I witnessed while I was in the trance. I still feel like I'm missing something. I should have paid more attention."

"I'm sure it's all right," Dravone said. "Tyrog's already figured out where one of them is. See, there — you're calming down and starting to look better," he turned back to Tyrog, "So, which door do we go through?"

"Watch this," Tyrog said as he pushed down on one of the control table's blinking red lights. All of a sudden, two rows of lights — which were embedded in the floor — lit up. "Follow the lights," he said.

The lights led to a Black Door that was halfway around the room. Nakiata walked up to it and noticed that the color around the circumference was continuously cycling from blue to red, and then back to blue. She stepped forward until she was within a few inches of the blackness, turned, and asked, "Are you certain this is going to take us to where we want to go? What about that?" She pointed to the edge of the Black Door, which was still switching back and forth between the two colors.

"Curious," Tyrog said. *I've never seen a Black Door do that*, he thought while scanning the control panel for any irregularities. "I don't see any malfunctions. Yes, I'm sure it's the right door."

How come you don't sound so sure? Nakiata thought. *I guess it doesn't matter in the least. I mean, where else are we going to go?* She turned and walked into the blackness.

Nakiata had been on the other side for only a few seconds and she was already feeling . . . different. It was like she had just stepped into a steam room, but it wasn't just the heat, there was something else in the air. It was making her eyes water. *This isn't right,* she thought. *But he swore to me that he was sure.* She did her best to focus, but as usual she was having trouble seeing anything. It was, as expected, extremely dark, with the exception of the soft glow coming from the around the edge of the Black Door.

Nakiata could just make out the outline of the exit, which was located directly in front of her. She quickly moved away from the Black Door so that she wouldn't be knocked over when the rest of the group came through. She staggered out of the room and began to examine her surroundings. She noticed that some of the vegetation close to the building seemed to be giving off small amounts of light. *I think the air here is starting to affect my vision*, she thought.

Nakiata rubbed her eyes, trying to dry them out. After several attempts she was able to focus a little better, at least well enough that she could see they were in a large jungle. All of the vegetation was beyond anything she'd ever seen before. Most of what she could see were small bushes with huge, shiny brown leaves and the stems were littered with thorns the size of her index finger.

They'd only been on the alien planet for a few minutes when Nakiata began having difficulty breathing. She started coughing continuously, all the while trying to catch her breath.

Tyrog was the last one to arrive, and as soon as he was through he knew right away. "Oh no, this isn't good!" Tyrog said, looking for the control table.

"What do you mean?" Dravone asked, rubbing his eyes and trying to locate Nakiata. He sneezed twice, shook his head, and squinted his eyes. "Nakiata, are you okay?" he said when he caught sight of her standing just outside the room.

Nakiata didn't respond, and before he knew it she was falling to the ground. Within seconds, Ka'tia began complaining, "Why do I have such a bad headache?"

Tyrog glanced at Dravone. "What are you waiting for? Hurry up and go get Nakiata and bring her back so we can go through the Black Door!" he commanded.

"Why?" Dravone asked through labored breaths.

"No time to explain! Just get Nakiata and . . ." Tyrog was unable to finish his sentence. The words left his mind, along with every other thought. He felt his body hitting the ground and then his eyes shut.

Dravone's eyes went wide, and he turned his attention to Ka'tia just in time to see her fall to the ground. *What's happening?* Dravone thought, growling. His stomach felt as if it were turning over and inside out. He wasn't sure if he was about to vomit or not. He reached up and put a hand over his mouth, but it did no good. He tried to breathe in slow and steady, but the only thing it did was allow him to become extremely dizzy. He couldn't maintain his balance, so he dropped down to his knees and sat there for a few seconds, hoping his head would clear.

To make the whole experience even worse, he heard something large crashing through the jungle. Whatever it was it was moving toward them. He fought to keep his eyes open and just as he heard branches breaking at the edge of the woods, darkness overtook him.

A few hours later, Dravone was the first awake. Not long after that, his mind became coherent enough to register the pain he was feeling. *Oh, I really feel sick now.* His thoughts became reality as he vomited, clutching at his chest in an effort to relieve the burning sensation that increased with every breath. He coughed as hard as he could several times, but nothing seemed to alleviate the pain.

It dawned on him that there might be enemies nearby, so he scanned the area and was relieved to discover that they were alone, they were alive, and in the same places where they'd fallen. He tried to stand a bit too fast, and his head instantly felt like it was going to explode.

One by one the others came around. The first thing they felt was the same burning sensation in their chests, except for Tyrog, who only complained about being moderately dizzy.

Even though her head was pounding like never before, Nakiata couldn't shake the weird feeling she had. Something in her gut was telling her that they were not alone. She pushed past the pain and got back onto her feet. She searched the surrounding area, and that's when she noticed a distinctive distortion. *Am I hallucinating? Before I fell, there was nothing there, and now...* Her eyes focused much faster now and she could see that it was definitely some type of glass.

She moved a little closer and noticed that is was in fact a much larger structure. Nakiata stopped and followed it up and over her head. Now she knew, *it's a dome.* The structure appeared to be about thirty feet high, and, from what she could tell, it encompassed only the small building housing the Black Door, as well as about twenty feet beyond the building in all directions.

The entire area was now bathed in more light as dawn was approaching. *I wonder who or what put this here?* Nakiata thought. *Even more importantly, how did they do it? I mean, there doesn't seem to be a single broken branch anywhere indicating how it got here.*

Nakiata continued to slowly walk along the edge of the dome, looking for clues as to who might have put it there. *I wonder if this is like that Ho-drooli barrier, where it only looks like there's nothing on the other side. I'll bet I can push my hand right through it.* She reached out and touched it. The dome was cold and felt just like glass. There was no tingling in her hand, and the harder she pressed against it the more it resisted.

This is nothing like the Ho-drooli barrier. As she stood there with her hand against the dome the tips of her fingers began to bounce off the surface ever so slightly. "It's vibrating," she announced to the others.

Intrigued, Tyrog flew over to where Nakiata was standing and placed a hand on the dome. "You're right, I can feel it too. Now, if we can figure out who put this — dome — here, I'd certainly like to thank them!" Tyrog commented loudly.

"Why do you want to thank them?" Nakiata asked.

Ka'tia had just walked up when Tyrog started explaining, "Well, I'm pretty sure this dome, or whatever it is, is responsible for keeping us alive."

"What do you mean, keeping us alive?" Ka'tia asked.

"When we first arrived here the air was mildly toxic for the three of you, and it had an adverse effect on me. I passed out. So, whoever, or whatever, put this here, they saved our lives. I hope that was their intention, unless this dome is some sort of cage. Hmmm, come to think of it, we probably shouldn't remain here much longer, just in case. Besides, we don't know how much time we have until. . ."

Tyrog was interrupted by the sound of a branch breaking not far from them on the other side of the dome. Nakiata's reaction startled them as much as the sound, when she vanished into SOT. Everyone else froze, watching the wooded area beyond the dome. "Maybe it was nothing," Ka'tia said reassuringly.

Nakiata peered through the dome, searching through the dense underbrush trying to see what might be moving, but she was unable to detect anything. She tried relying on her second-best sense, hearing. She moved her ears slowly back and forth, and then she smiled when she heard it; something was close by, breathing slow and steady. *It sounds big, but I can't see it.* All of a sudden she noticed the four glowing orange eyes, which just appeared in the dark void behind some large leaves on one of the trees about fifteen feet on the other side of the dome wall.

Without warning, every bit of the vegetation gave way, and the dome began to shine and shimmer. It was like looking at a still pond the moment a rock breaks the surface. As the ripples expanded, two loud thumps were heard as the alien beings stepped through, stopping a short distance away from them.

She focused on the nearest creature which was a good foot-and-a-half taller than Nakiata, and far more robust, too. *You're a fat one aren't you? I'll bet you weigh at least four hundred pounds,* she thought.

She continued to examine her new prey, looking for obvious weaknesses. The thing was ugly. It had a tuft of black, spiky hair on its plump, flat-topped head. It had two arms, hands, legs, and feet. She noticed it was wearing what looked like a brown leather vest, a black belt, and dark green pants made of a material she didn't recognize. It was also wearing thick black boots, and on the belt there appeared to be tools. *So you aren't just dumb beasts,* Nakiata thought. *Well, from the look of them, they aren't weapons, and if they were, I don't suppose you'd do much damage with them.*

Upon further study, she could see that this alien's skin was a light tan color and had the same texture as the Ugs. *Perhaps these things are a distant relation to the Ugs.*

Other than its four, glowing, orange eyes, the only other prominent features that were noteworthy were the being's snout and tusks. The snout was round, flat on the forward-facing side, and had two large holes for nostrils. The tusks came out from the upper jaw, curling up and just past the snout.

The creature snorted several times, made some grunting noises, and squealed loudly. A few seconds later, two more of them showed up and snorted back. There was a pause before they started making some short grunting sounds, after which the closest one to Nakiata pointed at her and then at the building behind them. There was another pause, and she could tell that it was obviously sizing her up.

Its face contorted momentarily followed by a squeal, a snort, and a grunt, and it was waving its arms around the entire time. Nakiata reappeared and said boldly, "Are you trying to tell me something? I hope you realize that I don't understand you, and from what I've heard of your language, I never . . . ," she snapped her fingers together, "wait a sec, Tyrog do you still have that — device?"

The alien must have taken some kind of offense or just couldn't stand to smell them any longer because it reached behind its back and produced a mask, which it put it on quickly. Nakiata went to reach for her Kharak blades, but these beings were much faster than she'd anticipated. She felt the tug on her pack as it lifted her off the ground.

Nakiata finally got a hold of her blades and began slicing at its arm, but the being's skin was as extremely tough, even more so than Tyrog's.

Ka'tia watched as the beast holding Nakiata turned and headed toward them. She quickly nocked an arrow and let it loose. The arrow stuck in the leather vest, but that's where it stopped. It didn't have the strength to penetrate the being's hide.

Dravone had just enough time to finish the transformation to his wolf-state when several more aliens walked through the dome wall. These were already wearing masks and they looked like they were in a hurry to do something. Dravone sounded his battle cry with a gut-wrenching howl. When he finished, he watched as one of them rushed over, grabbed Ka'tia by the wrist, and flung her over its shoulder.

Dravone growled ferociously and was about to jump at the creature when he felt pressure on the nape of the neck. Another of the beasts had grabbed him and lifted him off the ground with surprising ease. The alien's grasp was more painful causing him to whimper like a young pup. The being snorted at him as if it were telling him to simply deal with the pain.

Tyrog wasn't sure if he should do something or wait and see what these alien beings were going to do. It was clear that they had strength and speed, not to mention their hides proved to be highly resilient against his companions' attacks. Besides, as far as he could tell, these creatures were not harming his friends, and they were only causing mild physical discomfort.

Tyrog followed them as they carried and dragged his companions all back inside the building with the Black Door. "What — do you think — they're going to do?" Ka'tia asked, struggling to get free from the alien's hold.

"I don't think they mean us any harm," Tyrog said, hopping into the room with his alien escort nudging him gently along.

"What do you mean?" Nakiata grumbled, wiggling and slashing at her captor in an attempt to get free.

Before Tyrog had a chance to answer, the aliens began throwing each of them into the Black Door. Once Tyrog was the last one they turned to face him, snorted, squealed, and motioned for him to enter the door. Tyrog gave the creatures a bow and walked into the blackness on his own.

The second Tyrog was through to the other side, Nakiata began yelling at him, "Why did you just stand there while those things attacked us? How could you just let them toss us into the Black Door? I think we should go back and . . ."

"No!" Tyrog said sternly, "There is no reason for us to go back."

"Why not?" Dravone asked.

"Because it wouldn't be safe for us," he replied.

"What makes you say that? Is it because of those beasts?" Ka'tia asked.

"No." He paused for a moment. "Do you recall what happened when we first arrived on that planet?" he asked.

"Yes," they replied in unison.

"All of us became dizzy, and then we fainted," Ka'tia said.

"Exactly, and when we awoke, you three felt a burning sensation in your chests, correct?"

"And your point is?" Nakiata asked heatedly.

"My point is this, the reason you felt that way is because the air wasn't suitable for us. I think the aliens were trying to help us. I also believe it was them that put up the dome, which was keeping us alive. If you recall, they put masks on once they were inside the dome, probably because they couldn't breathe the same air as us. Which is why they rushed to get us back here, where we'd be safe." Tyrog explained.

"What about the last member of the Prophecy? If, whoever this person is, was supposed to be on that planet, how are we going to find him, or her, if we can't even breathe?" Nakiata asked angrily.

Tyrog shut his mouth tightly, and instead of answering, he flew over to the control table and went to work tapping away on the interface. After a few minutes he became excited. "Ah-hah! That would be the reason for the variation in color, and it's also the reason we didn't go where we were supposed to have gone! I knew I should have used the Ho-drooli extrapolation formula instead of mine. Theirs is more accurate."

"Care to explain it in a manner that we will understand?" Ka'tia implored, knowing Nakiata was already furious with him.

"My apologies, Nakiata, Ka'tia, and Dravone. During my calculations, I accidentally placed a decimal in the wrong location, resulting in the four of us travelling to a planet that we should have never tried going to. Now, before you get too excited, let me try to explain a few things. Nakiata, before we left you noticed the colors kept changing around the edge of the Black Door. Well, that happened because the air was toxic to the three of you," he tapped several more times on the controls, "and the only affect it had on me was that it caused me to lose consciousness. So, the Black Door was detecting two situations simultaneously. It sensed that I would be able to survive, even unconscious, and that it was unsafe for you three. This resulted in the continuous color changes. I have re-calibrated the sensors, and that won't happen again. I also made the appropriate adjustments in my calculations. Now, we should go through this Black Door." Tyrog said, pressing on a blinking red light on the control table. The two rows of floor lights shifted, leading to a Black Door on the other side of the room.

Everyone walked over to the new door, stopped, and eyed it very closely. The color around the circumference was a steady constant blue. "How sure are you about this door? I'm just asking because I don't feel like ending up facing some obscure new beasts that want to devour ours, ya know," Dravone said.

"If this doesn't lead us to the purple planet, you can . . . you can . . . cut off my tail," Tyrog said with confidence. *It's a good thing they don't know that my tail will grow back in a matter of minutes, if they actually managed to cut it off,* he thought, grinning.

"We have a deal," Nakiata said, giving him a serious look as she walked past him and into the Black Door.

The others followed her lead, walking one at a time into the blackness.

Chapter 2

On the other side of the Black Door, they were relieved to find the room to be the same, standard, ancient place that was identical to almost every other one they'd encountered with a Black Door. However, the smell in this particular area worsened with every minute. The aroma, resembling that of old onions, was quite pungent.

Tyrog stuck his forked tongue out several times, tasting the air. At the same time, Dravone took long, deep whiffs.

"Intriguing," Tyrog commented.

"What?" Ka'tia asked.

"The air here, it's — different. It doesn't seem to be harmful, and yet there is — something — about the way it tastes, and smells," he answered.

"It just has a horrific, bad o . . . dor to — it," Nakiata said, slurring through the last few words.

"Per . . . haps we sh . . . should turn the lights — on?" Ka'tia said with a brief giggle.

"Yeah, that's a — silly idea, hahaha," Dravone added.

"Oh, dear, can this really be happening, tw . . . ice?" Tyrog asked himself.

Suddenly the door in front of them opened, and five cloaked figures entered. They quickly formed a line between them and the only way out of the building besides going back through the Black Door. The strangers before them were wearing long, dark brown cloaks that completely covered their arms, hands, and feet. The hoods of their cloaks concealed their faces in darkness.

Oh, how wonderful. Whoever these people are, they seem to be very organized, and quiet, Nakiata thought, observing the intruders, who stood in silence, clearly waiting for something.

The group stared at these new arrivals through hazy, unfocused eyes. They were starting to feel like they were slightly intoxicated. *I don't understand it. How would this happen?* Tyrog thought. *Unless . . .* Tyrog shook his head, struggling to remain focused. He felt his mind giving in to the temptations of that red, juicy, succulent substance, *I guess its fine. I really don't care right now. I wonder, did they bring some nice, fresh, meat. I would love to eat right now,* Tyrog thought.

As drops of his saliva hit the ground creating small holes in the floor, the sizzling sound, along with the smell of burnt stone, helped his mind to regain a bit of cognizance. He realized it had to be something in the air. *What if it's not? It could be something here in this room . . . which is a lovely room.* As he looked, the "lovely room" started to spin.

"Are we . . . dreaming?" Ka'tia asked, trying to stay focused. She began to feel weak in the knees, so she sat down. She squinted her eyes in an effort to force her mind to concentrate on the cloaked figures. She was barely able to put a single coherent sentence together. "What is — those are lovely cloaks, no wait. What's happening — wow my hands are so — I mean, to us? Can you . . ." she grunted and with every bit of strength and focus she managed to put three words together, which she hoped they might understand, "Please help us!"

From somewhere close by, sounds similar to a soft harp filled the room. The notes ringing through the air were high in pitch, but they were not so high as to cause physical harm to anyone.

What a lovely ensemble — that is music I hear, isn't it? Nakiata said to herself, no longer capable of forming proper words. The music stopped briefly and then started again. This time it was a much lower-toned harp playing.

"I don't think they — under . . . stand us. That music is — lovely though," Tyrog said happily.

The cloaked figure in the middle stepped forward and approached Nakiata. It reached out with its hands, everyone gasped. This alien's hands were almost completely transparent, and in one of the hands was a small glass tube containing some kind of white liquid. In the other hand was what looked like a leather pouch resembling Ka'tia's water pouch.

Nakiata was definitely not feeling like herself. Everything seemed weird to her at this point, and on top of that the sight of see-through hands was just about all she could handle at the moment. *I don't care, though; I'm not going to let whatever is happening affect me,* she thought, trying to convince herself she was fine.

The individual stopped right next to Nakiata, who was swaying from side to side. "I'm not — thirsty, thank you," she said right before she fell to her knees.

The figure knelt down and handed her the glass tube, helping to guide it up to her lips. Nakiata caught a whiff of the liquid and turned her face away. "I don't — want it!" she cried like a child.

At the same time, three of the other cloaked figures approached Ka'tia, Dravone, and Tyrog. Each of the strangers produced glass tubes, but each one had a different colored substance in it. The aliens handed over the glass tubes and waited patiently with leather water pouches.

Tyrog was the only one who didn't turn up his nose at the concoction, which for him was a green, faintly glowing, thick oozing, liquid. He quickly turned it up and gulped it down. He licked his lips and said, "That was tasty," he said just after he belched, which produced an uncontrolled miniature ball of fire. "Sorry about that."

Finally, the others stopped resisting and drank from their glass tubes. The reactions were quite different. "Yuck, this tastes horrible," Dravone said. The contents caused him to belch loudly.

Nakiata and Ka'tia were beyond words. They were on the verge of puking, and their faces had the same disgusted expression. Within seconds, the two women were grabbing for the pouches of water and drinking almost every drop. With a sigh of relief, the two women followed suit and belched.

"Pardon me," Ka'tia said, momentarily putting a hand in front of her mouth. She looked up at the hooded stranger and asked, "What did we just drink?" Her question remained unanswered.

After about five minutes, everyone was back to feeling, for the most part, normal again. The four cloaked figures resumed their original positions with the fifth stranger, who had never moved. As his head cleared rapidly, Tyrog couldn't help but stare at them. "Who are you?" he asked. Tyrog rolled his eyes at his own question because he just remembered the strangers didn't understand a word they were saying, and the only way that they were going to was with something he snuck into Ka'tia's pack just before they left his lair back on Vazdrag. Tyrog flapped his wings, lifting himself off the ground. He flew over behind Ka'tia.

"What are you doing back there?" she asked him.

"Just hold still. You have something of mine that will be of great help to us right now. I just need to find it," he replied, hovering. He reached into her pack and rummaged through it until his clawed hand came into contact with the metal object. He clutched it tightly and pulled it out. It was a small, shiny, metal ball.

"What's that, and how did it get into my pack?" she asked.

He held the object up above his head and stared at it for a moment. With a gleam in his eye and his pulse starting to race he said, "This — is an Itzuli!"

"And that's supposed to impress us, how?" Nakiata asked.

"Oh, I forget how technologically inferior the three of you are. Just watch and you'll see," Tyrog scoffed. He flew over and landed between the strangers and his companions. He pointed at the cloaked figures, then at the metal ball he held in the palm of his clawed hand. He turned to the others. "Keep your eyes on the ball," he said. He moved the object really close to his snout, whispered something that no one else could hear, and with everyone watching he tossed it onto the ground. Tyrog took a few steps back and waited.

The metal ball wiggled for a second. Everyone watched adamantly as it left the floor and rose into the air, stopping about four feet off the ground where it hovered in silence. Everyone's head jerked back a bit when it made a few clicking sounds. As they stood there anxiously watching, it began emitting a bright, green light.

The strangers' reactions, or lack thereof, was a bit unnerving, almost as if they had anticipated what the ball was going to do. They didn't move, turn away, or even flinch. "I forgot to mention it, but don't look away. Stare directly at the light," Tyrog said.

No one argued with him. They all gazed at the light and found it to be rather soothing. The metal ball quietly hovered for about two minutes and when the light faded it fell back to the ground with a loud thud. Tyrog stepped forward, picked it up, and flew back behind Ka'tia, where he returned it to her pack.

"That's it? It created a green light? I know it was nice and all, but how does that help us?" Nakiata asked.

"It did more than you realized," said a beautiful feminine voice, coming from one of the cloaked figures. The stranger standing in the middle pulled back the hood, revealing a being unlike anything they were expecting. "The light was only the medium in which it transferred knowledge, which mainly consisted of the languages you speak. It also gave you our language. Now we can understand one another. It's quite simple really, and fascinating. "

The alien could easily be described as some type of ethereal being: The majority of her body, except for her eyes and lips, was nearly transparent, allowing everyone to literally see right through her. However, her faint silhouette made it possible for them to know she wasn't a ghost or some other figment of their imagination.

With everyone's attention on her, the woman felt as though she wasn't being seen in the proper fashion so she let her skin fill with a tan-colored pigment, giving her body the substance that the group was accustomed to seeing in other, similar species. "I'm sorry for not being prepare to welcome you properly. We are not accustomed to so dealing with a variety of other species."

She looks even better than before. Even though these people don't seem to have a single hair on their entire body, Ka'tia thought.

"We are the Dia'fani. My name is Aydvina', and we want to welcome you to Frole."

"Frole? Is that the name of this planet, or the place we're in?" Tyrog asked.

"Frole is what we call our world, or planet, as you say. This place," Aydvina' moved her hands in a grandiose gesture, "is the temple of Foskota' and . . ."

"That's great, hello, greetings, and all the niceties, but what exactly did we just drink? How do you know if it was safe for us?" Nakiata asked.

"Each vial that you drank from contained a small amount of Vela'dran's serum."

"Vela'drans serum? We've never heard of it; could you elaborate?" Ka'tia asked.

"It is named after the scientist who engineered it," Aydvina' started.

"Engineered?" Dravone and Nakiata asked at the same time.

"Vela'dran was one of our greatest molecular engineers. He had a few assistants helping him who had . . . other skills. Together they created a — new form of life. These creatures are so small that they cannot be seen with normal eyesight."

"Micro biologics?" Tyrog spouted.

"Yes indeed, or at least in a similar fashion. They are actually nanorgs, or micro-cybernetic beings. Part machine and part living creature."

"And what's their primary function?" Tyrog asked excitedly.

"First and foremost, their job is to support alien life while on Frole. Once they enter the host body, usually through ingestion, which you've already experienced, they scan the host's genetic code, which gives them the vital information they need to traverse through the body and reach the lungs or whatever organ might be affected. Once they have set up and attached themselves, they begin to filter out a unique gaseous element found in Frole's atmosphere. It was that element that caused all of you to experience the dizzy, unfocused state you found yourselves in just a few moments ago. The nanorgs use the special compound as a type of fuel resulting in the byproduct, which of course, is breathable air. Don't worry, they won't cause you any pain or discomfort. In fact, you won't even know they are . . ." Aydvina' was interrupted by a sudden, blinding flash of light, followed by everything going dark.

No one knew what was happening. *I'm glad no one's panicking, especially Nakiata,* Ka'tia thought. Everyone remained motionless, listening to every little sound.

"What was that? Who's moving? I just felt something or someone as they brush passed me," Dravone announced.

"No one's moving. There is a light breeze coming in from outside," Aydvina' said.

Nakiata was ignoring everyone. She was only focused on the open door behind Aydvina', which was the only source of light — and there wasn't much, because it appeared to be on the verge of night. The edges around the doorway went dark. Nakiata took a breath and held it in. In her mind there was only one explanation for what she was seeing, something large just walked in.

"What was that?" she asked. *For a second, I could've sworn I saw what looked like the outline of an Ug exiting the room. Then again, it could be my mind playing tricks on me. It is possible that it was just some thick clouds passing overhead.*

"We can't say," Aydvina' replied.

"What do you mean, you can't? Or is it that you won't say?" Dravone asked.

"It's difficult to explain. We are not allowed — to alter the outcome. Which leaves us with few choices, and that's all we can tell you," Aydvina' said in a pleading voice.

"You can't alter the outcome? What does that mean? Either you know or you don't," Nakiata said, irritated.

A much deeper male voice spoke up, "Please, do us the honor and remain calm. Everything you need to know will be answered, in time."

Nakiata didn't like the answer she was given, but for now she didn't see any other choice. "And who are you?" she asked the man who just spoke.

The cloaked figure to the right of Aydvina' pulled back his hood, and his body immediately filled with a darker pigment. "I am . . . Tursa. Now, if you will follow us, we will take you where you need to go," he replied.

"Wait just a moment! How do you know where we need to go?" Nakiata asked.

"As I've already said, we are unable to explain that to you right now," Aydvina' said. "Please, we must go. I know we are asking you to trust complete strangers, which for most of you is not easy. So, on my life, you are in no danger from us. We mean you no ill will."

"Where are we going?" Tyrog asked.

"There is a village not far from here. You can stay there until the morning." Aydvina' turned and headed for the exit. The other Dia'fani waited for the newcomers to follow her. Once everyone was safely out, they were the last to leave. They kept a comfortable trailing distance behind the rest so that they would feel more at ease.

There's something you don't see every day, even for experienced travelers like us, Ka'tia thought the moment they exited the building. Even in the low light of the evening, she could see an impressive forty- or fifty-foot-high wall, a couple hundred feet in front of them. She looked to her left and right and noticed the two adjoining walls. *Looks like the Black Door building is completely surrounded by these high walls.* "Why such a large wall, Aydvina'?"

"Those walls were built long ago, when the Dia'fani were still young," Tursa answered.

"How far is the village?" Dravone asked.

"By the time we get there, it will be close to twilight," Aydvina' replied.

The Dia'fani pulled their hoods up and rushed past them so that they could open up a large, fifteen-foot set of wooden double doors, allowing the group to proceed down a path leading toward a large forest.

At least everything looks fairly normal here, Nakiata thought, glancing around at the grass, trees, and dark blue sky. *Wait just a sec, this doesn't seem right,* she thought. Nakiata had just remembered that the box of Katoh had shown her a planet with a purple sky. "Frole doesn't have a purple sky?"

"It does. The particulates in the upper atmosphere only appear to be blue at the moment. Once the planet approaches daylight, the color will take on a purple hue," Tursa replied.

Nakiata nodded her head as if she understood what Tursa was telling her. They were nearing the edge of the forest. She stopped and turned around to see the wall that surrounded the Black Door.

It was nothing like what she was expecting to see. The sunset had given the perfect silhouette of the entire structure. There was definitely a large, glass, pyramid-shaped structure placed perfectly above the ancient stone building. It was elevated by what looked like steel rods, which were bigger than Dravone's legs, jutting out from the walls. There were also towers at each corner, and those towers had cone-shaped roofs. She also took note that there were no other structures around, just an open field surrounded on all sides by trees. "Impressive," she commented on the alien architecture.

Tursa stopped, raised his right hand and waited. Everyone looked at him with curiosity, except Nakiata who thought, *what is this fool doing?*

Something was moving fast through the wooded area in front of them. They could hear it breaking branches as it rushed toward them. The group readied itself for another encounter. They couldn't see anything through the dense vegetation, but it was very close. A long staff broke through it and flew straight into his hand. *Whoa, where did that come from?* Ka'tia thought. She watched as he turned and pointed the staff in the direction of the wall. He began to murmur something, and a burst of purple light came out of the end of the staff, striking the glass structure at the apex.

The cone tops on the four towers began to glow, getting brighter and brighter every second. The power build-up was magnificent, but nothing compared to what happened next. Focused beams of light shot into the heart of the glass, converging in the center above the ancient stone building. A small ball of energy formed, and started swirling around, gaining momentum. It ceased all movement and a final, much larger, beam of light blasted downward.

"Wow, what just happened?" Ka'tia asked.

"The towers have been activated. They are harnessing the energy I gave them in order to deactivate the Black Door so that we don't have any. . . uninvited guests," Aydvina' said.

"Hold on, you mean to tell me that we were invited?" Dravone asked.

"Please, we cannot say any more," Tursa said, as he turned to walk down the path in the forest.

They had been walking for hours in the dark forest when up ahead the trees began to thin. They had finally reached the other side. *I hope this village isn't much further,* Nakiata thought. She was exhausted.

Just as they left the forest, they could see a relatively small village off in the distance. As Aydvina' had told them, it was already twilight, and not too far down the path there were torches on either side, lighting the way to the village. Nakiata was sure the torches were there so that any newcomers could be spotted well in advance of reaching the village. *Guess they've never encountered a SOT master before,* she thought with a smirk on her face.

Before the group reached the first torch, all of the Dia'fani stopped and moved to the sides of the path, where they knelt down. "We will wait for you here," Aydvina' said. "All you need to do is go to the largest hut in the center of the village and ask for Hura'm." The pigmentation in her skin faded until she was transparent again.

I have a bad feeling about this, Nakiata thought. "Why are you going to wait here?" she asked.

"Please, you must go. It's almost — too late," Tursa paused and looked up at the night sky. It was almost as if he was praying. He lowered his head back down. "Tyrog, could you stay here with us, just for a moment?"

Tyrog looked over at Nakiata. She gave him a nod of approval. "I would be delighted to stay," he said joyfully.

"Would you like me to stay as well?" Ka'tia asked.

Nakiata frowned, grabbed her by the hand, and said, "Come on, you're not staying."

The Dia'fani bowed and remained in that way until Nakiata, Ka'tia, and Dravone were well out of listening range. In unison the straightened up, and turned to Tyrog, who was anxiously waiting to ask, "Is this the time you tell me about your gift?"

"It is," Aydvina' replied. "Have you been able to sense it? We've never been able to figure out how you knew, even with our gift of foresight. I mean, everything that is going to happen has already been seen by one of our kind. And, before you ask, yes, our species has managed to learn, over countless generations, that the universe will unfold as it should. Some of us have also learned that if we try to change something, the universe responds quickly, and, almost every time, brutally."

"So why did you ask me to stay, since you already know what is about to transpire?" Tyrog asked.

"It's true, we know, but do you? We had you stay because you must not interfere with . . . what must happen. Don't worry, when the time is right, you will be needed. You will have to protect the others and stop Nakiata before she has an opportunity to destroy our entire world," Tursa said. "No, we cannot tell you any more than that. The reason should be obvious, even for you."

"At this very moment, there is a group of assassins in the village waiting to make an attempt on Nakiata's life. It won't go as planned."

"I'm confused, if all the Dia'fani have this gift, how is it that there are assassins trying to kill Nakiata? Wouldn't they already know that their attempt is futile and will end in their deaths?" he asked.

"We don't have time to explain all the details right now. All you need to know is that she will kill them, along with all the villagers. You will only intercede to keep her from killing Dravone and Ka'tia," Aydvina' concluded.

"How long do I have?" Tyrog asked.

"We will let you know when it is time," Tursa responded.

The village was quiet, almost too quiet for Nakiata's liking. She already had a gut feeling that something bad was going to happen, mainly because she didn't trust the Dia'fani in the least. Not long after they entered the village, Nakiata noticed five cloaked figures huddled in the dark on the side of one of the dwellings. They were the only ones out and about, so she walked up behind them. "Excuse me, we are looking for Hura'm, do you know . . ."

Before she finished, the figures ripped off their cloaks, drew edged weapons, and started their attack. "Ambush!" she yelled to the others, vanishing into SOT.

Both Dravone and Ka'tia were caught off guard by two different assassins who had been hiding in the shadows on the opposite side of the path. One of them grabbed Dravone and tried to wrestle him to the ground. This proved to be a difficult task, as he was going through his transformation. The other would-be killer seized Ka'tia and pinned her to the ground.

Nakiata wasted no time letting rage take its hold on her. In the first few seconds, she moved to the side, avoiding the initial slash that was meant to kill her. She thrust her Kharak blade forward and pierced her target's throat. She didn't stop the motion as she spun and allowed her other blade to slice open the abdomen of her next target.

These people have no clue, she thought, doing a flip and sinking her knuckle blade into her third victim. Only a few seconds had passed, and she had killed all but one of the original five attackers. She began circling the last one, watching, waiting, savoring the moment until she could see the fear and anxiety in her target.

Finally, the time had come. The last would-be assassin was looking frantically in every direction and had started backing up. Nakiata rushed in un-observed and cut him ever so slightly. The assailant began to tremble, knowing that death was imminent.

Nakiata couldn't resist temptation any longer, she had to do something she'd never done before. She reappeared directly in front of her attacker. She waited just long enough for him to realize she was there before she swung her arm, elbow out, in a rapid downward motion. She cut him from the top of his chest down to his abdomen.

He had a ghastly look upon his face as his innards spilled out onto the ground. Nakiata looked deep into his eyes as the life left his body. She smiled, and, before she knew it, her mind went blank, her rage had taken over and she was unaware of what she was doing.

At the same time Dravone was doing just as well because the strength of the wolf was more than the assassin could handle. All he had to do was flex his muscles and spread his arms while sticking his chest out. This caused his assailant to lose his grip and fall backward onto the ground.

Dravone spun around, grabbed him by the shoulders, and lifted him up off the ground so that he could look him in the eyes. Dravone's upper lip curled up and twinged, flashing his large canines, drool formed on the corners of his mouth as he anticipated the new, hopefully delicious flavor of alien blood as it gushed out all over his eager tongue.

He started to growl, and in the blink of an eye his head lunged forward, biting down on his captive's throat, ripping it out. *Oh, that's not bad,* he thought as the taste of the blood finally hit his tongue. It was much sweeter than he anticipated. *I think I want more!*

With the taste of fresh sweet blood in his mouth, Dravone wasn't expecting the excruciating pain which invaded his ears when several short screams spread throughout the small village. He growled because he already knew what was happening, and he didn't have time to deal with the out-of-control Nakiata. He had more immediate concerns, like helping Ka'tia deal with her attacker.

He turned and jumped onto the assassin that had her pinned to the ground, and he began tearing him apart with his razor-sharp claws and trying to grab bits and pieces with his mouth. *Oh, I got a big piece, yummy.* He licked his chops, but there wasn't enough left to make him happy. He looked down at his hands and claws, a smile swept across his fur-covered snout. There was just enough of the exquisite substance there, so he wasted no time as he began licking them.

Dravone gently reached down and helped Ka'tia back to her feet. As she began dusting herself off, they heard something large crashing its way through the forest just beyond the building they were facing. "I don't like the sound of that! Whatever it is, it's almost on us and we have nowhere to go!" Ka'tia said.

Dravone put his arms out to his sides, spread his hands open wide, and snarled. Ka'tia stepped back a bit and to one side. She quickly took the bow off her back, drew an arrow, and waited. "By all that is holy!" she gasped.

Dravone roared defensively in fear at what emerged from the dark forest: Two larger-than-life Ugs.

"Where did they come from?" Ka'tia asked, letting the first arrow fly. It struck one of the Ugs directly in the middle of its chest. Both Ugs stopped, and the other one reached over and pulled the arrow out of his companion. They took a moment to examine the arrow before throwing it to the ground. The injured Ug snorted and took several steps towards them.

Aydvina' looked directly into Tyrog's purple eyes. "It's time, but before you go, I would suggest that you adjust your size. After that, the first thing you'll need to do is grab Dravone and Ka'tia and bring them back here. The next task will be a bit more difficult. Once you return to the village, you have to contend with Nakiata. Please do your best not to hurt her; she is still fragile. You should probably focus more on getting her to calm down."

"I'll do my best," Tyrog said, giving her a quick bow. He hopped a few times before taking to the air, heading toward the village. A few seconds into his flight, he saw the perfect spot to consume some raw materials. As he tilted forward, he noticed two more Ugs moving in on Dravone and Ka'tia. He folded his wings in close to his body and did a nosedive, plowing into the soft ground below. He quickly ate as much material as he could. A few moments later, he burst forth, landing just behind his two companions. Tyrog blew a long line of fire, cutting the Ugs off. He reached down, grabbed his friends, and quickly returned to the skies. He glanced back at the two Ugs to see if they were following him, but he saw that they didn't stand a chance against Nakiata and her Kharak blades. She killed them in the time it took for his heart to beat once.

She stopped abruptly, turned, and looked up at him. He could tell something was different about her. She had nothing but extreme rage on her face. Nakiata reached behind her back and pulled out a small object. She managed to throw it with considerable force.

Tyrog heard the thing whistling through the air, and it was gaining on them. He didn't want to endanger his precious cargo, but he didn't have much choice. He rolled in the air, barely avoiding the Takoura of Death as it screeched past him.

Surprised by her ability, and not willing to learn if she had any other weapons that could reach them, Tyrog beat his wings as hard as he could, increasing his speed and distance from her.

Tyrog was flying faster than he'd ever tried which made for an even shorter flight back, Tyrog could finally see the edge of the clearing where the Dia'fani were still waiting patiently. *I'm not going to have enough time to do this delicately. Here goes nothing,* he thought, coming in for a quick landing. Instead of the usual soft hop, Tyrog hit the ground a bit harder than even he was expecting, making it rumble and shake. He tossed Ka'tia and Dravone down to the ground and didn't even take the time to apologize for such rough landing or throwing them down. He merely turned around and took off, heading for the village as fast as possible.

I think it will be best if I go high and try to spot her from the air. That should give me enough time to figure out how to . . . deal with her, he thought as he gained altitude and began circling the village. It wasn't long before he had Nakiata in sight. *Now how do I do this? Maybe a strong roar and the threat of fire?*

He dove and landed almost as fast as the last time. He let out the deepest bellowing roar he could, and spit several short streaks of flame in her direction. This had no effect on her at all. She smiled and started rushing at him.

Ok, how about some wind? He beat his wings with all of his strength. She was almost knocked off her feet. "Enough! Nakiata, you need to focus! And calm ... down!"

She gave him an evil grin and vanished into pure SOT. Even though Tyrog could still see her, she lunged at him. He was nowhere near fast enough, but he felt confident that his highly resilient hide would protect him.

By a random chance — a one-in-a-million shot — the sharp point of Nakiata's Kharak blades managed to slip between the scales on his right leg. The minute space that none had ever found before. She was amazed at how easily it pierced through to the soft under tissue.

Caught by surprise, his eyes went wide, and he bellowed in pain. Out of instinct he reared his head back and was about to unleash every last molecule of fire when he remembered what Aydvina' told him: *Do not hurt her.* He reached down and tried swatting her.

Nakiata evaded his every attempt to knock her down. "Ha-ha, you're a big and slow Sodaran," she taunted, watching for another opportunity to strike. She rushed back at him; this time she knew he had a weak spot. She focused on a pinpoint accurate spot between his scales. Her blades sunk just a little deeper into his leg this time.

Tyrog roared and spun his body around, slinging his tail like a whip. This time he was able to make contact. His tail hit her smack-dab in the chest. Not only did it take her breath away, but it sent her hurling through the air like an arrow shot from a bow. She crashed through a wooden door on one of the village dwellings. Tyrog spun back around when he realized how hard his tail had struck her. He didn't want to injure her too badly. To his surprise, she was already back on her feet and racing toward him.

This is not working. I need to try something different. He began beating his wings again. This time he put more force behind every beat, forcing Nakiata backwards. Once she was far enough away, he took to the sky. Remembering her aptitude for flinging deadly weapons, he watched for any weapons she might have already unleashed at him.

Tyrog circled the village. *Okay, my feisty little friend. How are we going to end this? I don't want to hurt you anymore, but you're not leaving me much choice. I know,* he thought as brilliant idea just occurred to him. *I will grab her as fast as I can and just hold on to her, at least until she calms down.*

This has to work — I'm all out of options! He thought as he soared straight up into the sky. He broke through the clouds and reached the pinnacle of his ascension, his silhouette filling the center of Frole's dark, grey moon high above. He folded himself up into a ball for a second, rotated, and then straightened out like an arrow, pointing directly at Nakiata.

Tyrog narrowed his eyes so that he was focused only on Nakiata, who did just as he hoped. She stood her ground. Tyrog reached out and opened his hand. At the last moment, he spread his wings and soared just above the ground at an incredible speed. Nakiata screamed with rage as he approached her.

He grasped her a moment later and carried her up into the air. His grip was strong, and Nakiata couldn't get free, but she still had a lot of fight left in her. She started squirming, trying her best to get at least one of her Kharak blades free to strike at his hand.

Tyrog closed his eyes momentarily. "Forgive me," he whispered to her. He began to squeeze just hard enough that it wouldn't hurt her, too badly. He flew higher and higher into the sky, reaching an altitude that was dangerous even for him.

He didn't have to remain there long. The pressure he was exerting on her and the lack of air began to affect her, and finally she lost consciousness. Tyrog folded his wings and fell at a steep angle, back down into the lower atmosphere. He made his way back to the Dia'fani and landed more gracefully this time. He gently placed Nakiata's unconscious body on the ground.

Tyrog took several large steps away from the group so that he could safely let all his fire out.

"She's not dead, is she?" Dravone asked.

"No, she's just unconscious. When she wakes up, you need to be there by her side," Tursa said.

Dravone smiled and nodded in agreement and knelt down by her side. He noticed that her hair had come undone and was covering her face. He reached out and was about to move the hair away from her face when her eyes popped open.

In less than the blink of an eye, Nakiata thrust her Kharak blade up at him, stopping where the point of the blade was just barely making contact with the skin of his throat. Dravone eased away and watched her eyes as they slowly changed from their black and gray color to the beautiful, royal blue hue he liked. "What happened to you?" he asked.

"All that I can remember is attacking one of the assassins. Everything after that is pretty much a blank," she replied with soft sobs.

"Now that we are . . ." Tursa's statement was cut short when Nakiata spun around, thrusting her Kharak blade deep into his throat. She glared at him with hatred in her eyes. She didn't need rage to enjoy watching the life leave his body.

"Why did you do that? You didn't have to kill him!" Aydvina' wailed appallingly, her voice trembling with undertones of fear. The shock of what had just happened was starting to set in as she said, "I never envisioned you doing that. I need . . . I need to . . . we mustn't stay here. It's no longer safe."

Nakiata slowly withdrew her blade, allowing Tursa's body to fall to the ground. She turned to Aydvina'. "What do you mean, 'envisioned'?"

"There's no time to worry about that right now. I think it would be best if we just moved on," Tyrog suggested. He let out a small cloud of smoke from his nostrils in an effort to redirect their focus. "Where do you suggest we go from here, Aydvina'?"

Aydvina' had no reply. She was still in shock over the death of Tursa. To everyone's surprise, Ka'tia walked over to her and slapped her across the face. "He asked you a question, Dia'fani!"

Nakiata's mouth opened wide, and she commented, "My, my, such brutality against the natives, whatever are we to do with you?" With an evil grin on her face she bowed low and gracefully.

Ka'tia looked at Nakiata with a frown, and then back at Aydvina'. "I'm sorry for my hostility. I think I am just weary and want to find some place to rest."

Aydvina' put a hand to her face, and said, "I accept your apology. We should head to the great city of Gai'daros. Once there, we will go to the Temple of Kili'dri and speak with the high priest, Tso'li."

"Is this going to be a long journey? I'm only curious to know if we will need to stop for provisions along the way," Tyrog asked.

"If we travel by air, it will only take half a day. However, I suggest we travel on foot to avoid any unforeseen problems," Aydvina' said. She closed her eyes for a minute. Her eyes seemed to shut even tighter. Whatever she was thinking about must be something horrifying. Even her skin reacted by becoming opaque. When she opened her eyes, she looked afraid. "It will take at least three days on foot, and we won't have any more complications. There will be no need to scout ahead, Nakiata."

"How did she know I was going to ask her that?" Nakiata asked.

"A three-day journey. I take it that I will be okay to scavenge for some food before we leave?" Tyrog asked, and yet he already knew the answer. Aydvina' nodded all the same. He accepted her silent approval and left with a single beat of his wings.

He was gone for about ten minutes, and when he returned, he had what looked like a large furry beast clutched in tight to his chest, which made him a little off-balance when he landed, almost toppling over. Once on the ground they could see that in his arms was not one, but several large carcasses, which he dropped to the ground. He immediately went on to separate them, unequally. Four of the largest for himself and two for everyone else.

Tyrog knew that his companions did not consume raw meat, so he blew a few short streams of fire on the two dead things. "That should do it," he announced. He collected his portion and began chomping away at them.

The group ate their fill and rested for about an hour.

Nakiata and Ka'tia were sitting next to each other looking up at the foreign sky, admiring its strange color. Both Tyrog and Dravone were busy licking their hands and fingers, which still contained small amounts of the savory juices from whatever it was they just ate. Aydvina frowned as she stood. "We've wasted enough time here! Gai'daros awaits," she said stomping down the path leading back to the small, now desolate village.

Chapter 3

Once the group passed beyond the village of dead assassins, they entered a densely wooded jungle and traveled for a day and a half before they came to a small river. Aydvina' had them follow the river for the remainder of that day. As the night sky was blooming, they approached a small inn, which was nestled not too far from perhaps the only bridge on the river. "We can cross here in the morning. We should reach Gai'daros by tomorrow evening," she said.

Before they entered the inn, she pulled Tyrog to the side. "The people inside have never seen strangers before, and especially not a Sodaran."

"What are you trying to say? That I am not welcome here?"

"Oh, no, not at all. Quite the opposite, really. I would encourage you to stay, but the food will not sit well with your . . . palate. So, I have another option for you. Not far from here is a nest of . . ." Aydvina' put a finger to her lips for a moment. "Well, you won't be dissatisfied, that's for sure," she finished with a smile.

Tyrog's curiosity was piqued. *I so love the thrill of a good hunt,* he thought, as he flew off into the distance.

He gained altitude until he could see at least five or more miles in any direction. *Now, let's put these old, keen eyes to good use.* He focused on any signs of movement from the ground below. As he circled a large area high above, he spotted a small field a short distance from the river. Something scurried across the field.

Tyrog banked and repositioned himself so that he was circling directly over the field, looking for more signs of life. *Oh, now look at you. You look very tasty,* he thought, watching another small varmint crossing underneath.

Tyrog swooped down and grabbed the next one that tried to cross the field, and he swallowed it whole. *Oh, you are tasty. I hope there's more*, he thought. Just as he was about to fly up and out, he noticed a large mound with several more of the creatures perched on top.

He circled back around and came to a soft landing directly on top of the mound. The varmints started rushing out, trying to defend their nest. He immediately began grabbing as many of them as he could, but he didn't realize that his size was increasing with every bite. Before long, he was gulping ten at a time, and after just a couple of minutes he was already reaching thirty feet in height.

Tyrog stopped eating momentarily so that he could belch. He was a bit surprised by the flame that was expelled at the end of his belch. Instead of the usual orange hue, it was a brilliant blue color. *That was pretty amazing,* he thought, spewing some more of the oddly colored flame.

I haven't felt this good in, well, I don't actually remember how long it's been. Tyrog felt stronger than usual, healthier, and more energetic. He scooped up a few more of the little creatures and crushed them with his sharp teeth, savoring the taste. *I wonder how long my energy will hold up. I guess I shouldn't sit around here waiting to find out.*

He pushed his way toward the field, knocking down several trees in the process. Once he was clear of any obstruction, he squatted. His legs were ready, but he hesitated for a second, scanning the skies above. The time was perfect, his muscles contract, thrusting his body upward, launching into the air. He flew as high and fast as he could, enjoying every second of it. He closed his eyes for a few seconds, allowing himself to experience as much as possible through his other senses.

The rush of air passing over his head was cool and moist and felt great. Tyrog shut his eyes for a moment. *All I need now is a battle,* he thought. He could feel his heart beating faster and the blood in his veins felt like a river of power. He was feeling a boost of power. The last few varmints were being digested.

An idea came to mind. *I should show them my new flames.* He opened his eyes, closed his wings, and dove for the river at an incredible speed.

The moment he reached the river, he spread his wings and glided just above the slow-moving water. He looked down at his reflection and smiled. Before he reached the bridge where the inn was located, he started turning his head from side to side trying to figure out why he felt stinging sensations all over his body. He finally looked back at his tail, and saw that he was not alone.

A large group of tiny birds numbering just shy of a hundred had somehow attached themselves to his body and were pecking at him with long, sharp beaks. *How did they . . .* he began to contemplate, when he witnessed one of the small birds fly away. *You have strong, fast wings, but can you swim?*

He dropped down into the water and felt relieved. He emerged, and the swarm was waiting for him. They rapidly attached themselves to his hide and resumed pecking vigorously. Normally, it wouldn't be a problem because his scaly hide was tough enough to withstand almost every attempt at being penetrated, except for his recent misfortune when Nakiata managed to get past his scales, not once but twice, and both were still quite tender. The beaks on these birds were just long, small, and sharp enough that they too were able to get through his hide.

His annoyance grew with the pain. He narrowed his eyes, focusing on as many of them as possible. He waited until most of them were in the kill zone. *Now!* He thought as he spewed an intense blue flame across his body. He incinerated almost all of the small pests, but to his dismay he painfully learned that his new-found flames had more damaging effects. He had managed to singe his own scaly skin.

He dropped back down into the river and came to a stop under the surface. He waited and watched as the small group of birds gathered just above him, lying in wait for him to emerge.

Not this time. He eased his snout out of the water and took a deep breath. He exhaled, releasing the rest of the blue flame, consuming the entire cloud of small birds.

Tyrog climbed out of the river and saw that he was close to the inn, which only took him a few minutes to reach. By that time, he was already feeling vastly different than he was prior to eating so many of the varmints. He looked down at the double wooden doors of the inn, which were now too small for him to fit through at his current size. He snarled at them. *How am I supposed to fit through there?* He made a fist and swung it up from his body, bashing the doors in, along with some of the stonework. Tyrog ducked down and eased into the interior of the inn.

"What's with you? You could have hurt somebody. You need to go back outside and let some fire out so you can come in — a lot smaller, and in a more civilized manner," Nakiata said harshly.

Tyrog didn't hear a single word Nakiata said. His head was spinning wildly. *What was that?* He asked himself, spinning around sharply. His tail whipped around, smashing several tables in the process. *I guess it was nothing.*

He turned back around and noticed a group of aliens staring at him. He roared and took up a defensive posture.

"Tyrog, it's us!" Ka'tia exclaimed.

Tyrog raised a fist and slammed it onto the ground so close to Ka'tia that it made her jump back a couple of feet. "I don't know who you are, or how it is that you speak my language, but I am warning you now: I'm not in the mood for this. If you want a fight, I will oblige you, because at this point my head hurts so much that I don't really care," he retorted.

"Oh, really? You want to fight? Come on, you scaly beast, I'll fight you!" Nakiata said as she grabbed her Kharak blades.

"Wait!" Aydvina' yelled, "Everyone get down on their hands and knees!" Nakiata turned and looked at her with hatred in her eyes, "You want us to do what?"

"Please, just trust me," Aydvina' said. She got down on her own hands and knees.

Nakiata shrugged her shoulders, and rolled her eyes. "Alright, you heard the Dia'fani, everyone down."

Tyrog backed up through the open doors. He hunkered down onto his belly and brought both of his hands up to his head, moaning.

Aydvina' stood back up and slowly walked past everyone. The rest of them followed her out of the inn, stopping close to Tyrog. "What's wrong with him?" Dravone asked.

Aydvina' did not reply. She kept walking, making no sudden or random moves. They all watched as she made her way down to the river's edge. She scanned the edges of the river and the moment she saw what she was looking for she smiled and said, "Aha! There's one right here." She reached down and plucked the large purple flower. As she raised it high everyone noticed that the stem was actually writhing around like a snake. Aydvina' turned her head so that she could observe the group's reaction to this unusual plant.

Both Ka'tia and Nakiata had expressions on their faces that clearly meant, *don't you even think about bringing that thing anywhere near us.* Dravone on the other hand was intrigued. Aydvina' gripped the stem with her other hand. She turned and walked back up to Tyrog.

Tyrog moved his hands down his snout, still gritting his teeth, and watched what she was doing. His lip curled when he realized how close everyone was standing to him, and even though he was maintaining his enormous size, he didn't have the strength to resist, let alone fight anyone.

Aydvina' held the flower out in front of her, allowing him to sniff its sweet aroma. He took several long whiffs, but his sense of smell was a little out of whack, but it still smelled delicious. He slid his long, forked tongue out, wrapping it around the stem. Aydvina' let go, allowing him to pull it into his mouth. He chomped on it several times before swallowing it.

"Everything will be just fine," Aydvina' said.

A few seconds later, he began to moan, and had just enough strength to stand up. He wobbled away from the inn, stopping on the bank of the river. He looked out at the horizon. A sense tranquility swept over him as the toxins from the purple flower entered his bloodstream.

The scene before him went in and out of focus, and before he knew it his eyes rolled back into his head, and he fell into the river. The water around the area where he fell began to boil. Everyone ran over to the river bank, worried about Tyrog.

"What's happening?" Ka'tia asked.

Aydvina' was about to answer when different colors of light started flashing through the bubbles. First there was blue, then red, yellow, and finally orange. The water began to settle and became still. No one moved, they just stood by and waited. None of them were even sure if there was anything they could do. Finally the water settled, becoming still.

"Where is he?" Ka'tia asked.

"Do not fear. Look there," Aydvina' pointed to a spot on the edge of the river, just a short distance from them.

Tyrog, who had reverted back to his original size, limped out of the river and plopped down on the grass.

"Are you alright?" Dravone asked.

"He'll be fine in a few moments. He ate too many Daga, and to make it worse he was bitten multiple times by the poisonous Maga'balas birds. We're lucky he has an amazing natural ability to fight off poisons," Aydvina' said.

"I hate to interrupt, but I would like to get moving soon," a new voice said near the bridge. Everyone except Aydvina' and Nakiata were surprised by the female Dia'fani's sudden appearance.

Aydvina' walked over to the newcomer and bowed. The two of them reached out with a single hand, putting their palms together. A few seconds went by, and their bodies became translucent.

As they watched, the Dia′fanis' skin changed a deep, purple hue. The two women remained motionless for almost an entire minute before a flash of white light erupted from within them. Their supernatural theatrics were now over, and the two Dia′fani walked back over to the group.

The newcomer bowed to the group and said, "Greetings. I am Liwana′. I have come to assist by guiding you directly to the Temple of Kili′dri."

"What just happened between the two of you?" Ka'tia asked.

"Aydvina′ was, out of sync, with us, so I had to help guide her back to the common path. Had she been out for much longer, we would have run the risk of losing her," Liwana′ said.

"Interesting. I don't know if I understand any of it, not even sure I believe — ohhh, my head is starting to spin again," Tyrog moaned.

"In time, you just might come to understand everything that we know, Tyrog. In the meantime, we should get moving because I've spotted another flock of Maga′balas heading in this direction," Liwana′ said.

Nakiata grimaced. *I don't know why, but I just want to rip her apart. I do not trust this Liwana′*, she thought, and for once she remained silent. Nakiata raised her hand, gesturing for the Dia′fani to lead the way.

The rest of their journey toward Gai′daros was less eventful, save for Tyrog's occasional moaning about his headache. The heavy foliage on both sides of the path began to thin until, finally, a clearing lay before them. They were now on the outskirts of a great city filled with thousands of Dia′fani.

Gai'daros was not the usual large city they'd encountered previously. There was one major difference that set this place apart. It didn't have any high walls or guard towers. *Clearly, these people have no enemies to protect against, or they are so ill-prepared and ignorant to the fact that their city is wide open to attack. Then again, they may have no idea how to defend themselves. There might be some prospect here; I could teach them a thing or two,* Nakiata thought.

They continued down the path, which turned into a neatly paved road just before entering the city. They walked down the main street for at least five minutes before turning onto a side street, then another. Zig-zagging their way deeper into the heart of the city. The buildings in the center of the city were much larger than they had seemed from a distance.

Nakiata kept herself as alert as possible. She didn't know who to trust anymore. *There are only five individuals that I trust my life with: My parents, Master Akizan, Dravone, and Tyrog. Anyone else, I would certainly question. Although, I will have to say that I might have to include Ka'tia as well. I know that she will undoubtedly never forgive me for killing her brother, and I can't blame her. I still think that if she ever had the chance, she'd probably slit my throat. I think now that we have found Tyrog I shouldn't worry about her as much. I guess time will tell.*

The group stopped at a large intersection. They watched as more and more people filled the walkways as they went about their early evening business. Ka'tia wasn't the only one to notice that there were two distinct races present within the city.

The Dia'fani, whom they'd already met, were easily identified because of their transparent skin. Even though some allowed their pigmentation to remain, giving them more substance, they still had an altogether different shape than the other race. Those whose skin had color were all similar hues of brown.

The other race of beings was not unlike the travelers themselves, except Tyrog whom could never be mistaken for anything other than what he is, a Sodaran. Yet these other people still had a distinct difference: Their skin was pale, closer to that of Nakiata and Dravone.

As they made their way nearer to the temple, Aydvina' and Liwana' hurried off ahead of the group, almost to the point where they were out of sight. All the while Ka'tia saw more of the other race going about their tasks and her curiosity go the best of her, she saw a woman walking with what looked to be a bag of food. Ka'tia reached her hand out and stopped her. "Excuse me. Are you able to understand us? What's the name of your race?"

When she didn't answer, Tyrog knew what he needed to do. "Hold on a second, Ka'tia," he said. He flapped his wings to hover in position behind her. He rummaged through her pack, searching for the Itzuli, which he pulled out a few seconds later.

He didn't toss it onto the ground this time; instead, he held it up in the palm of his hand so that everyone could see it. He whispered something, and just as before it floated up into the air, produced a soft green light for several minutes, and fell back into his hand. "That should do the trick," he commented.

The woman was just about to walk away, but she stopped after taking a single step. "I understand you," she said with a horrified expression on her face.

"You don't look all that happy about it," Nakiata scoffed.

"We've been forbidden to have such knowledge since the days of old," the woman replied. The woman started jumping up and down a little and breathing heavily. Looking around at the group, she came to a realization. She dropped the things she was carrying, turned around, and was about to run away.

"Wait! We have questions for you. We won't hurt you. Please, we just want a few answers!" Tyrog pleaded.

The woman hesitated, but she slowly turned around with a smile. "Thank you for giving me your knowledge. I wish I had time to thank you properly, but I really must hurry and share what I've learn —" But before she could finish, a searing flash of white light engulfed the woman.

Once the light's intensity faded, there was nothing but a pile of ash in the spot where she had been standing. Astounded, the group quickly turned their attention immediately skyward, where they found a Dia'fani, sitting on a curiously shaped piece of shiny silver technology. The cloaked Dia'fani sat in the middle of what looked like a throne. His hands were resting on the armrests, which had moveable grips that he was holding and maneuvering ever so slightly. Underneath the chair was what could only be describes as two large weapons similar to what Roarrgs use. On the underside of the machine there was four spots, and they were all emitting a cool blue flame. He continued to hover in the air about thirty feet high. The Dia'fani didn't say a word. After several seconds he pushed forward on the grips. The chair whisked away as quickly and as stealthily as it had arrived.

"Wow, I wonder what's going on here? I haven't seen such oppression since the Sodarans were the ruling species amongst the stars," Tyrog said aloud.

"I don't know either. But what I do know is that I really don't trust these Dia'fani. I know they are hiding something," Nakiata said angrily.

"I think we all agree on that fact, but what are we going to do about it?" Dravone asked.

"I have an idea," Tyrog said as he lowered his hand, which was still clutching the Itzuli. He was just about to toss it as high as he could when another Dia'fani man appeared out of nowhere and grabbed Tyrog's arm, preventing him from moving it.

He thrust his hand forward, reaching for the Itzuli. With a firm grip on it, the Dia'fani gently pried it out of Tyrog's hand. He started to whisper, and the Dia'fani's voice sounded like some a smooth strumming music.

The Dia'fani man held out his hand and allowed the Itzuli to float into the air. Once it finished the transference of knowledge, Tyrog caught it.

"I'm sorry if I might have startled you. But, unfortunately, we cannot allow you to do what you're thinking. The consequences would have been too severe, almost beyond imagining. So, please put the device away and do not try again. If you do, we may have to rely on harsher methods of prevention. Now, if you would continue to the temple as we've instructed, you'll find Aydvina' and Liwana' are waiting for you. It really is the best course of action. And yes, Nakiata, I do swear so on my life." The Dia'fani let go of Tyrog's arm, stepped back, and then vanished.

"Well, that was strange," Tyrog said, spitting on the ground.

"I'm not sure I follow," Dravone said.

Before he replied Tyrog noticed the look on Nakiata's face, which inwardly he accepted whole heartedly and would like nothing more than to see her ravage and destroy and it would allow him to set his own fires of destruction, but his intellect outweighed his primal desire as he began, "It seems they don't want us to communicate with the other race of beings on this planet. In all my travels throughout our galaxy, which are more extensive than most of you," he pointed at the others. "I have never come across a situation like this. I'm going to suggest that, for the moment, we do as the Dia'fani have asked."

"Fine, let's get to the temple and find this Tso'li fellow. I have a feeling he's not going to like the greeting we give him," Nakiata said aggravated.

Tyrog bowed, tossed the Itzuli to Ka'tia, and flew off in the direction of the temple. It took several minutes before they caught up with Liwana', who was moving her arms and motioning them to continue up the street. She led them into the heart of the city, which was now settling down for the night. Liwana' stopped on the edge of a small open area. "The Temple of Kili'dri is there," she said, indicating a stone structure with a large tower in its center.

The base structure was at least six stories high, with the tower extending up at least another five above that. It definitely had an air of mysticism. Massive, red spikes with an unusual upward curve fringed the top of the main building's roof, adding to the travelers' impression that this was a dark place.

"This is where we must leave you. We hope the rest of your journey goes well, and without further incident," Aydvina' said. She and Liwana' gave them a slight bow and left.

"How do you like that? They get us all the way here and then just leave us at the door. I wish they'd would just take us directly to where we need to go and point out the person we need to see. I mean how are we supposed to distinguish this Tso'li from any other Dia'fani? If you haven't noticed they all seem to look alike, especially when you can pretty much see right through them. And of course, we don't even know if it's a he or a she," Ka'tia said.

They walked the short distance across the open grass area, stopping at the base of the temple steps, where they found Tyrog pacing back and forth. "What's seems to be the problem, Tyrog?" Ka'tia asked.

"Them," Tyrog replied, pointing at the two guards on either side of the main entrance. They blocked the doors with long spears, preventing anyone from gaining entry. Both guards appeared to be members of the planet's secondary race of beings.

Nakiata frowned as she walked up the steps toward the entrance. Just before she reached the door, the guards lowered their spears, held out their hands, and made angry faces at her. "We are here to see Tso'li. Please let us pass," Nakiata said as politely as she was capable.

This came as a surprise to everyone. They were so used to seeing her whip out her blades and attempt to force her way through any obstacle. But, despite her efforts, neither guard moved an inch. It was likely that they didn't understand her.

Nakiata didn't care if they understood what she was saying. There were other ways to communicate one's intentions, and she did so by taking a step back, motioning for them to part ways. The guards remained steadfast. She cocked her head to one side, put her hands on her Kharak blades, and said, "Well, in that case, you can either let me pass, or you die — here and now." The guards looked at each other, but otherwise remained motionless. "Very well," she finished, just as she vanished into pure SOT.

Nakiata moved in with ferocity, slicing one of the guard's legs, causing him to fall to the ground. The other guard didn't know what to do. He began swinging his spear, stabbing at the air, hoping to pierce the invisible foe. He stopped swinging and his grip on his spear loosened. His expression went from determination to one of confusion. He slowly looked down at his chest with curiosity. Something was amiss. He reached up to touch his chest, and just as his fingertips made contact, it began spewing green blood. He fell to the ground and quivered for a few seconds.

Nakiata reappeared for a just a second. She watched with eagerness as the life left her victims eyes. Satisfied the guard was dead she re-entered the pure form of Shadow of Thought, becoming invisible.

The guard whose leg had been cut began yelling something, and the door to the temple opened. A priest wearing a black-hooded robe emerged. He took several steps toward the fallen guard. He was about to reach down and help the guard up, but stopped. The priest started, and Nakiata reappeared directly in front of him, her Kharak blade buried deep in his chest. "Now, there should be no more obstacles to keep us from entering this temple — or are there?" she asked the priest.

"You must not . . ." Death took the priest before he could finish.

Nakiata removed her blade and walked over to the fallen guard, who was still clutching his leg with one hand and trying to hold his spear in a threatening manner in the other. The guard attempted to spear her, but she easily side-stepped the attack, swung her arm, and cut the tip of the spear clean off.

Nakiata's demeanor shifted from displeased to anger when she knelt down close to the guard and said, "Can I help it if you don't understand me? I gave you the opportunity to not be a hindrance, but you refused to listen." She slowly pushed her blade into the guard's chest. The color in her eyes seemed to fluctuate when she began to pull her Kharak blade out even slower, causing the guard to suffer as much as possible.

The rest of the group was horrified and didn't know if they should attempt to interfere and risk being stabbed as well. Ka'tia, however, wasn't going to stand idly by. "You didn't have to kill them!" she said in harsh tones.

Nakiata spun around, glaring at her with her black and dark gray eyes. This was the first time that Tyrog had seen Nakiata in this state. "Do her eyes change like that often?" he asked.

"I haven't seen them this dark before, but they have been changing more frequently, especially when she becomes upset, or in this case, very angry. So far the worst was when she was fighting the Breoli," Dravone said.

Nakiata started to take a couple of steps toward Ka'tia when out of nowhere, bam, a bolt of green lightning struck. Half a second later another bolt touched the ground just a few inches from her. She could feel the electricity which cause all of her hair to stand on end. Within seconds there were multiple lightning strikes all around her. She tried taking a step back and another bolt struck behind her. Every time she tried to move another bolt hit in the direction she was attempting to go, preventing her from moving. Another priest, dressed in a black-hooded robe, appeared out of thin air, standing just behind Ka'tia. He waved his hand at her as if he were saying hello. The instant his hand was back at his side, the lightning ended. The newcomer mumbled something and appeared to be waiting on them.

Nakiata grumbled, but she was not deterred whatsoever. She even allowed a smirk to shine on her face as she took another step closer. Her expression changed the instant she was knocked backwards. She quickly regained her footing, dusted herself off, and composed herself to show that she hadn't lost her dignity, she was flustered by it.

She moved her eyes from side to side, assessing her surroundings. *What did I run into? I'll bet it has something to do with this new priest. Now, let's see if there is something there,* she thought, easing one foot forward while stretching out the Kharak blade in her right hand.

She didn't feel any resistance, so she took another step and reached out again. Nothing. She took a third step, and this time the metal in her Kharak blade began to react violently with something directly in front of her. Sparks began to fly in every direction. The reaction extended through the metal and into her hand. Nakiata felt a searing pain, so she retracted her arm.

"That stings!" she said, rubbing her arm.

She backed up, turned to her right, and took a step forward. She was stopped by the same invisible force. "What evil magic is this? Is this some type of magical prison? Let me out of here at once!" she commanded.

The priest drew near to Nakiata. He held out a plain-looking staff and tapped the bottom of it on the ground. A small bolt of lightning struck the staff and surged throughout his body, causing his eyes to glow for a brief second. "I will release you once you're calm."

"Who are you?" Ka'tia asked.

The priest turned and pulled off his hood, revealing the stern-looking, light-brown complexion of a weathered Dia'fani man's face. "I am Tso'li, high priest of Kili'dri, and you must be Ka'tia, Dravone, and Tyrog," he said, nodding his head after looking at each of them. He finally turned to the last member of the group. "And that leaves us with you. Not at all the least of the four, nor the strongest, but you most certainly are the most unpredictable . . . Nakiata," Tso'li said with a grander cordial bow.

"So, you know who we are? Is that a good thing, or is it because we already have a reputation that precedes us? Just so that you know, we were told to find you. Aydvina' said you would be able to help us. Is that true?" Tyrog questioned him.

"I'm sure I can be of some use to you," Tso'li replied. He turned his attention back to Nakiata, who'd given up trying to get out of the magical prison and was now sitting comfortably on the ground, and meditating.

"As I said before, unpredictable," Tso'li commented as he slowly raised his staff, gripping it tightly with both hands. He held it aloft for several seconds while muttering to it. His brief chant ended and he slammed the tip of his staff down against the ground. A lightning bolt flashed across the sky above, followed by the crackling of thunder, which rumbled through the city.

Tso'li had never seen such resolve. Nakiata didn't flinch. She was unaffected by his attempts to distract her. "Impressive," he concluded. Tso'li walked around her several times, tapping his on the ground. He was testing to see if she would react, and when she failed to even acknowledge him, he said, "You know you're free? Your captivity has already ended, and you may come with me into the temple. I give you my word, I will do my best to assist you."

Nakiata opened her eyes and stood up. *If I still can't get out of here, I am going to kill this Tso'li person*, she thought as she took a few steps toward the temple. There was no more prison. She smiled and waited for him to guide them into the temple.

Tyrog took a mental note of her behavior, which he found to be hilarious. In his mind he started laughing, which manifested externally as a hissing and clacking sound. He reached up and put a hand to his mouth, forcing himself to keep silent. He shook it off and hopped his way into the temple behind Nakiata.

Dravone and Ka'tia looked at each other and giggled at Tyrog's technique of keeping himself quiet along with his unusual noises. Dravone stopped and sighed, "If this keeps up, I might die from laughter."

Ka'tia had collected herself momentarily, but, as soon as she heard Dravone, she burst into tears and more laughter.

"What's so funny?" Tyrog's deep voice came from the doorway of the temple.

"Nothing at all," Dravone replied, grabbing Ka'tia by the hand and pulling her up the steps of the temple.

As soon as they were inside, they found Nakiata staring at the empty interior of the temple. "What is it? What are you looking at?" Dravone asked her.

This is the oddest temple I think I've ever been in, and I've been in quite a few as of late. There are no statues of whatever deities these people worship, nor are there any paintings of the previous High Priests. I just can't believe there is nothing here. I wonder who or what it is they worship here? She thought.

She also noted something else, though it wasn't as profound as some might think, and that was the absence of any other priests. "What, or who, do you worship here at the Temple of Kili'dri?" she asked.

Tso'li did not stop to answer. He simply led them down a short hallway that opened up into a large, empty room. He stood just inside the room, waiting for all of them to enter. "We do not worship anything or anyone, that is why you will find no braziers, statues, or other things related to the divine. To tell you the truth, this is a place curtailed to learning, even though there hasn't been a whole lot of that going on, either — at least, not for quite some time."

"Learning? What is it that's taught here?" Tyrog asked with excitement.

Tso'li smiled broadly and replied, "Magic is the main topic we teach here, though there are a few others."

Tyrog began to make the same hissing and clacking sounds that he had made a few moments before. "Magic? Do you really expect us to believe that the Dia'fani, a race of beings as advanced as the Sodarans, believe in magic?" Tyrog asked.

"I believe in magic," Nakiata scolded him.

"As do I," Ka'tia added in support.

Dravone looked to each of them. "I'm not sure," he said with a shrug of his shoulders.

Tso'li smiled, raised his staff, and started spinning it above his head. The light in the room diminished rapidly, and out of nowhere, a strong wind began circling the room.

Everyone glanced upwards, high above their heads. Amongst the rafters they could see actual clouds forming. After only a few seconds, the density of the clouds was strong enough to support bolts of lightning and the accompanying sound of thunder, which shook the entire building.

If that wasn't crazy enough, the lightning seemed to be drawn to the center of the floor, right in front of them.

"What's going on?" Dravone yelled above the wind.

Tso'li began to laugh hysterically as he slammed his staff down onto the floor. In an instant, everything went back to the way it was. He took a deep breath, "Yes, my Sodaran friend, the Dia'fani believe in magic, and some of us still practice it as well. I would even go as far as to say that, for some of us, it is our life's blood. When we were all children, most of us would tinker a bit with magic, but as we reach the age of young adults, we choose to follow other paths, and the magic within fades. However, the few of us that continue to use magic eventually become masters in one or more of the disciplines. The hardest part of magic is getting past the complexities coupled with the unpredictable nature of magic itself. You could ask any of us so-called masters, and each will tell you how they can only control a small portion of the chaos that can be unleashed through magic."

"But if Dia'fani believe in magic, why is there an abundance of evidence proving that you know about science and technology? Doesn't that disprove your magic?" Tyrog asked skeptically.

"Science and technology most certainly have their place in the universe, just as magic. The thing is, facts and theories are far easier to learn and manage because they are based on solid rules which are predictable and controllable. It's the path that many take. That specific group of Dia'fani certainly have their place in our society. If not we wouldn't have such things as the skyrider, the thing that looked like a flying throne. You witnessed first had what it's capable of. Let me rephrase that, you've seen what the person controlling it can do, they are known as the Dao'uda Guard. I have to admit it, I feel a bit sad on how we treat the other inhabitants of Frole, like the Ra'hisi."

"The Ra'hisi?" Ka'tia asked.

"Yes, they are the less advanced, both physically and mentally, subspecies that cohabit our planet. We have shared this world with them for as long as any can remember. They unfortunately lack the mental aptitude and control of the Dia'fani, so we have found ways to co-exist with them," Tso'li responded.

"Ways of co-existing? Is that what you call it? That so-called Dao'uda Guard didn't just resolve the issue — he flat out murdered that woman!"

Tso'li grimaced. "Now is not the time to argue the semantics. There are more pressing concerns facing us at the moment."

"Sym, what?" Nakiata asked.

"It's nothing to worry about," Tyrog assured her with a deviant smile on his face.

"Now, if everyone could form a circle, I will take us deeper into the temple," Tso'li said as he motioned with his staff.

Ka'tia could tell by the tone of his voice that he was not about to argue with her. She was however, amazed to see that Nakiata was the first to comply with Tso'li's request. After a brief period of silence, they all formed a small circle in the center of the room.

Tso'li took his staff with both hands and held it out in front of him horizontally. He closed his eyes for a few seconds, then let go. No one could believe their eyes, the staff remained exactly where it was, suspended in midair. A second later, it began to float through the air until it came to a stop in the middle of their small circle. As soon as it reached the center, it began to spin rapidly.

Tso'li raised his hands again and said, "Now, we go!" An immensely bright, blinding white light shot out from his staff, consuming them.

Chapter 4

The light faded quickly, and, as their eyes adjusted, they looked around and noticed Tso'li standing in the corner of the small room, holding his staff and smiling. After an unexpected moment of disorientation, they became aware of the fact that they were no longer in the same room. "Where are we?" Ka'tia asked.

"Deep within the temple; only now, we are several levels higher, and it's somewhere few outsiders have ever seen, until now. Of course the answer you were probably expecting to hear was that we are on the fifth level, to be exact. If you'd come this way, I have something I need to show you."

He led them down a short hallway and up a single flight of stairs. As they ascended, they reached a point where something offensive attacked their noses. It was an aggressive, foul smell and there was only one thing in the universe which produced such an aroma — rotting flesh.

For both Dravone and Tyrog, it was so vile that it forced them to quickly raise a hand and squeezed their snouts shut.

"I'm sorry about the smell. I have not had the opportunity to remove those who have fallen in the upper level."

"Those who have fallen . . . you mean, there are dead bodies up there?" Ka'tia asked.

"Yes. There is no time to explain, so please, come with me," Tso'li urged them as he finished walking up the last few steps. At the top, he paused before crossing the threshold to the upper level.

Ka'tia was the first one to enter the upper level. When she did, she gasped. "What do you see?" Nakiata asked, pushing her way past Ka'tia. "Yuck, you should really do something about these bodies. They're scattered all over the room, and they reek of decay. How long have they been up here?" she asked, pinching her nose.

"As I said before, I haven't had the time, but since I am here and I can see how much the smell is bothering you, I'll take a moment to deal with them now," Tso'li said. He raised his staff with one hand, pointing it to his far right. He slowly moved the staff across his body until it pointed toward the opposite side of the room. "I really shouldn't boast, but I say, that should just about do it."

"Might I ask you something? Do you have a problem with your vision? The bodies are still..." Dravone stopped mid-sentence when a few of the bodies on the right side of the room began to glow a beautiful, blue hue. The light intensified until the shapes of the bodies could no longer be seen. When the light subsided, the bodies vanished without a trace. After a minute or two more and more of the corpses began to glow.

The process was slow, but once the last body was gone Tso'li took his staff, swung it around, and tossed it up into the air. Just before it reached the ground, he caught it and applied as much downward force as he could, slamming it down against the floor. A subtle wind crept in and encircled the room several times before fading away.

"What was that?" Ka'tia asked.

"I sent the bodies on to a higher plane of existence. The breeze collected the smell and discarded it elsewhere."

Dravone slowly let go of his nose and took a short whiff of the air. "What a relief. The putrid smell is gone, but it still smells like an old dirty rug in here. Which I don't mind at as much."

Nakiata shook her head and asked, "So, what is it that you wanted to show us?"

"That." Tso'li pointed at a door across the room.

"A door? You wanted to show us a door?" Nakiata sounded really disappointed.

Ka'tia, on the other hand, was intrigued. She moved closer to the door and started to examine it. "Well isn't that rather peculiar. There's no doorknob. How are you supposed to open the door?"

"I don't know," Tso'li said. "The Door of Mystery, as we have named it, is the only one of its kind. We call it that because no one knows how to open the door, or what lies on the other side. We have tried using our technology, our magic, and even brute force, but nothing seems to work. The only thing we know for certain is that the answers you seek can be found on the other side. No, we don't know what those answers are. We just . . . *know* . . . you will find them on the other side. It's one of the last great mysteries on our planet."

"So, you're telling us that you know the answers we need are on the other side of the door, but there's no way of opening it?" Dravone asked.

"Wait!" Ka'tia yelled. "There's something here . . . I can . . . feel something," she tilted her head, closed her eyes, and reached out toward the door. None of them knew what she was doing but it appeared that she was reaching for something. She turned her head slightly as if she was trying to hear something coming from the other side of the door.

Ka'tia opened her eyes with a look of surprise. She was indeed hearing what sounded like very faint whispers. It was very subtle and seemed to be coming from the door itself. As she moved even closer to the door, she could feel something else. A vibration, or a hum. She was now only a couple of inches away from the door. The edges around the door started to glow a vivid red. The glow immediately changed to pulses of light.

Tso'li knew from experience what was about to happen, so he yelled, "Stand back, quickly!"

Ka'tia turned and looked at the door. She could feel the hostility emanating from it. She jumped back away and looked curiously at the door.

Tso'li was already prepared for what he thought was going to be a heinous outcome, but, instead, something else happened. Something that he wasn't able to anticipate. Nothing. At least, as far as any of them could tell.

However, Nakiata, being at a much different height than the rest of them, had a different vantage point. She caught a glimpse of a minute color variation directly in line with her field of vision. At first, she thought it was just a shadow from one of her taller companions, but as she stared at the spot in her line of sight, which was just below the center of the door, she was finally able to discern a unique shape. "Was that there before?" She asked, indicating the spot. "I think there's a keyhole there," she finished.

Tso'li pushed her aside, moving in close to the door so that he could examine it for himself. "I don't see . . ." he was bolstering in a peculiar tone as he searched. Finally Tso'li adjusted his stance, dropping down to one knee. Observing the door from roughly the same height as Nakiata, was something he'd never thought of, and sure enough, there was a keyhole in the middle of the door.

"How extraordinary. It's almost as if those who built this door, made it so that only you could find the place to put the key. I never noticed it until now, and I can assure you of one thing, no one else noticed it either. It must have just appeared," he concluded. Tso'li stood back up, keeping his full attention on the spot where the keyhole was located. He took his staff and pointed it at the keyhole. He closed his eyes, gripped his staff tightly, and began to mumble something. His staff began to shake uncontrollably, causing him to open his eyes and stop his chant.

"You must leave this place at once. You will need to travel far from here. I know of a sage who lives beyond the Baha'zi expanse, which is on the other side of Frole. You must find the sage. She is the one who can guide you and teach you the knowledge that you will need to unlock this door."

"This better not be some kind of a trick, or your attempt to get us to do your bidding, because if it is — I will kill you and any other priests I can find in this temple," Nakiata warned him.

"I have no secret motives, my feisty little friend. The sage you need to find can also show you the path that will bring you to the key that fits this door. I have to apologize; I don't have the strength to send you all the way to the sage, but I can get you close. From there, you will meet with a guide who will take you the rest of the way. Now, go."

Before any of them could ask how they were going to get there, Tso'li began to spin his staff and tossed it up into the air. The staff came to an abrupt stop directly above them. The instant it stopped; they were pulled upward into the air while the staff began emitting an intense white light.

There was something different about the light, it was causing off them to feel disoriented. It was similar to the sensation they had shortly after they arrived on Frole. The feeling increased in intensity, as did the light. It was on the verge of becoming painful.

Out of the blue, and for no reason at all Tso'li could be heard laughing like a madman. His laughter ceased just as abruptly as it started, and everything returned to normal. The sensation was gone, and the light from his staff was no more.

A split second later, they fell back down onto the ground. They found themselves on the edge of an extensive swamp. Nakiata was the first to regain her footing and examine their surroundings. She immediately noticed a Dia'fani woman standing in the middle of the path just behind them. "And who might you be?" she asked, clutching her Kharak blades.

The Dia'fani woman did not reply. She simply bowed slightly and pointed at Ka'tia. Next, the woman made a gesture, one that made her appear as though she was grabbing something and lifting it up. "I think she wants Ka'tia to get the Itzuli out of her pack," Dravone said.

Tyrog flew over behind Ka'tia, reached in, and pulled out the Itzuli. Without hesitating, he tossed it onto the ground in front of them. The device did what it was designed for, and, once it had finished, Tyrog collected it and returned it to Ka'tia's pack.

"Thank you. I will guide you to the sage now," the Dia'fani woman said.

"Who are you?" Nakiata asked.

"I am Kolia'. Please, we mustn't delay. It will be dark soon, and we don't want to be in the middle of the swamp when night falls."

"Why?" Dravone asked, sounding a bit smug. "Are there dangerous creatures lurking about? Or shady figures that seek to take our valuables? I'll have you know that there aren't too many things that we've come across that have caused us to be afraid. Usually, it is we who cause fear in others. I'm sure that, whatever is out there, we should be able to handle it."

"Until now." Kolia' paused, looked around momentarily, as if she was checking to see who might be listening. She obviously seemed tense about something as she continued, "Please, I cannot say any more, only that if you decide to remain, it will mean the death of millions on our planet alone. I implore you, if we delay much longer, it will be the reason you fail in fulfilling the prophecy."

"What do you know about the prophecy?" Nakiata demanded.

"No more time, come!" Kolia' said. She rushed down the path that led into the swamp.

Ka'tia shook her head. She was the first to follow after Kolia'. Once she'd caught up with her, she asked, "How long will it take to reach the sage? I noticed that the sun is already setting, and I am guessing it will be dark in about an hour."

"You're correct. There is only an hour of light left, and it will take at least two-and-a-half days to reach the sage, if we continue to walk." Kolia' stopped and pointed at the ground.

They were standing on an intricately carved stone circle. Around the circumference of the circle there was writing, but Ka'tia wasn't able to read any of it since she didn't know their language. In the center of the stone was an image of what resembled some kind of serpent-like creature. "What is it?" Ka'tia asked.

"This is how we are going to get to the sage before the sun sets," Kolia' replied.

"How is a stone circle on the ground going to help us? It's a stone," Tyrog said. "There are no signs of any technology that will transport us to wherever this sage is. However, I believe it's safe to say that you're going to tell us something along the lines of, oh, wait for it — magic?"

"Technology is a marvelous thing, but you must have so many things come together, bits of this, and pieces of that, the correct algorithms and so on, in order for it to do what you want it to do. I prefer a more natural solution," Kolia' said. She motioned for them to join her and Ka'tia on the stone.

Tyrog moved his upper lip, showing his teeth, before he joined them as they all gathered on the large stone. Once they were all standing in close proximity, Kolia' placed her staff in the center of the stone, closed her eyes, and muttered something in a foreign language. She let go of the staff. It remained upright in the center of the stone.

As everyone watched the staff, they noticed the image of the serpent-like creature begin to move beneath the staff, almost as if it had come to life. The creature began to writhe around the bottom of the staff for a moment before it began to shrink, like it was moving, burrowing away from them down into nothing. A few seconds later, the image of the serpent had been reduced until it was barely visible.

"Now, ready yourselves!" Kolia' said. As soon as she finished speaking, the ground started to rumble and shake, and the serpent reappeared in the image. Only now it was growing rapidly. For a brief second, all they could see was the creature's head. As it approached them, it opened its mouth like it was about to swallow their feet.

Just as the image of the serpent's gaping mouth reached the edges of the stone circle, disappearing from sight. They all thought that it was the end of the show, but they felt tremors in the ground and heard a rumbling all around them. A set of stone jaws erupted out of the ground, extending upward and reaching a height of eight-and-a-half feet, which was just wide enough to surround them, with no way out. The jaws closed completely. Everything was calm for a moment.

"This is different, and I don't really like it!" Nakiata began.

Still closed tightly, the jaws retracted, pulling them down into nothing but utter darkness.

They did not remain in the dark for long. The end of the staff began to emit a soft white light, which was just enough for them to see each other.

"What just happened?" Ka'tia asked.

Before she got an answer, the stone surface below them vanished, and they began to fall. Kolia''s staff continued to provide light as they fell through the blackness.

Ka'tia felt as though her stomach was about to violently exit her body through her mouth. She managed to take a deep breath in, but as it came out so did a scream. Nakiata jerked her head around to see where Kolia' was, because she wanted to cut her throat, just so that the screaming would cease, but she couldn't move. She was going to have to let go of her desire for blood shed. *Since I can't kill her, yet, I'll just yell at her for now.* "Why didn't you warn us about this? And, how much longer is it going to last?" she yelled.

Kolia' smiled and pointed downward. The answer Nakiata was waiting for came swiftly. The stone circle rose up out of the depths and came to a stop just beneath their feet. After a few seconds, the stone made contact with their feet. They were still falling.

The group almost lost their balance when the stone circle beneath their feet came to a quick stop. The stone jaws that had them trapped in darkness opened up, and slowly retreated back into the ground. The image of the serpent's jaws appeared on the stone. The mouth closed allowing them to watch as it writhed around for a moment before returning to its original position and becoming a solid, unmoving, stone image. Kolia' retrieved her staff and stepped off the stone circle.

The rest of the group looked around, a little dazed by the short journey. Tyrog was the first to speak. "So that was what, exactly?"

"We traveled through the belly of the stone beast," Kolia' replied, sounding impressed.

"We travelled? Where? Everything looks the same," Dravone said.

"No, she's right; we have travelled," Nakiata said. "Look, the path is different, and the sun has moved much further across the sky. The question is, where did we go?"

"We've arrived at the edge of the sage's realm. We must use caution from here on in. The sage is not fond of visitors. However, the sage is great at detecting magic. So, I am going to ask Ka'tia to lead us," Kolia' said. She motioned toward the path.

Ka'tia moved to take a step when both Dravone and Tyrog caught a whiff of an odor neither of them had ever experienced. They sniffed the air heavily. Ka'tia had learned to trust the senses of her Morphan and Sodaran friends, so she stopped and asked, "What do you smell?"

"I'm not sure. It's both pleasing and revolting at the same time," Dravone said. He closed his eyes and took in several deeper breaths. He held it in and grimaced.

"He's right. I have never encountered an odor as wonderful and revolting as this one," Tyrog said, while he, too, continued to sniff the air. Though he did not have the same facial expression as Dravone, he did squint his eyes after each breath.

Without warning, a pillar of fire erupted beneath Kolia'. Within seconds, she was incinerated, leaving nothing but a small pile of ash on the ground. An undamaged dagger slid from the remains, meeting the stone surface with a definitive "clink".

The group was awestruck for a brief moment. Out of the corner of his eye, Dravone caught a glimpse of someone or something moving not too far off in the distance. He immediately transformed to his wolf-state, crouched, and lunged forward. He rushed at whoever or whatever it was.

It only took him a few seconds before he was close enough to his target to launch his attack, leaping high into the air. Dravone spread his hands open wide and curled his fingers so that his claws were poised for contact with the flesh of his prey.

He could clearly see that his target was a person wearing a dirty, tan-colored, hooded cloak. He or she was also holding a long, black staff, similar to the one Kolia' had. The best thing was that the person didn't appear to be paying him any attention.

As he descended towards the target, he came to a complete stop in midair. As he hung there, he could feel something holding him, something like a gigantic, invisible hand. Whatever had him, it was stronger than he realized. It continued to hold him about ten feet off the ground.

Without any warning, it began to squeeze him tightly, and he immediately started having difficulty breathing. Dravone had no choice but to change back to his normal state in an effort to try and catch his breath. The second he finished the transformation, the invisible force that had him restrained in midair released him, and he fell to the ground, gasping for air.

The hooded figure's attention was concentrated on the arrow that had just been released from Ka'tia's bow. The arrow was heading straight for the person's head. Seconds before the arrow was to reach its target, the figure quickly waved the black staff, and the arrow disintegrated into fine particles of white ash.

Nakiata had already vanished into SOT and was closing the distance quickly. Not far off, Tyrog emerged from the ground, took to flight, and followed close behind her. Nakiata was about ten feet away when she leapt high into the air. She was going to couple her momentum with the force of gravity to inflict the killing blow.

Tyrog was swooping down from high above when the hooded figure slammed the bottom of the black staff down onto the ground. A blustering gust of wind immediately expanded outward in all directions, causing Nakiata to be blown backwards onto the ground and pushing Tyrog back up into the air.

The figure tapped the bottom of the staff on the ground four times, and for the fifth time, slammed it. Four bolts of green magical energy expanded from the bottom of the staff. Each bolt raced across the ground like lightning, heading straight for each of them. The moment the magic reached them, it burst upward.

Everyone took a deep breath in as they were expecting balls of flame or something just as bad, and painful. Instead they were encased in a soothing light that produce, in each of them, a sense of peace and tranquility. It took the fight out of them, it was over.

The hooded figure made a large, fast, circular gesture with an open right hand. As soon as the gesture ended, the hand closed, and the Itzuli flew out of Ka'tia's pack and came to a stop a couple of feet away from the hooded figure. Everyone watched as the Itzuli began to emanate its unique light, and, once it was done, the hooded figure waved at the Itzuli as if shooing a fly. The Itzuli flew back over and returned to Ka'tia's pack.

The figure reached up and pulled the hood off, revealing a beautiful, blue-haired woman. She looked like one of the Ra'hisi they had seen in the city earlier that day. However, she had really haunting red eyes. At first glance, her eyes gave them the impression that they had a slight glow to them. "Come with me," the woman said.

"Wait just a moment. We are not going anywhere with you. We don't even know who you are," Tyrog said sternly.

"I am the sage Melia'na. Please, we don't want to waste any more time here. Come close, I will not harm you."

Tentatively, they moved closer to her. The moment they were in position, she signaled for them to stop. Melia'na quickly went to work, drawing a big circle on the ground around them. She stopped in the center where she started muttering something. The sky began to fill with dark clouds, which blotted out a large amount of the light that was coming from the sun. A moment later, a bright flash of blue light engulfed the group, and they vanished.

It was pitch black.

"Where are we?" Nakiata asked. "I can't see a thing. Is this the result of the flash of light, or is it just dark?"

"This is my home. Where you have nothing to fear," Melia'na said snapping her fingers. A multitude of torches along the walls of a spacious room burst into flame, including a large chandelier hanging high above them.

Even though Dravone and Nakiata had already seen the dwellings of more than a few different species, they were delighted to see that the sage's home was much nicer than either of them expected. Ka'tia, however, wasn't impressed. Mainly because of her upbringing in the palace back on Zondura. Tyrog couldn't care either way, he was always comfortable no matter where he went. Though he did miss his technological niceties.

The room had a high ceiling, at least twenty feet up, and it was curiously full of couches and chairs, all varying in size and type of construction material. The walls were adorned with paintings depicting various creatures and people that none of them recognized.

"You have a lovely home, but why are there no windows?" Ka'tia asked.

"Thank you. There are no windows here in the great room because we are underground. I —"

The sage was about to say more when Nakiata interrupted. "Enough of the niceties. Why have you brought us here, and why did you murder our guide?"

Melia'na frowned. She was not used to someone like Nakiata, but she refrained from any retorts and simply answered the question. "She was not a guide. She was an assassin sent to kill . . . her. I am sorry I don't know your names just yet." She while pointing directly at Ka'tia.

"Her name is Ka'tia. The Sodaran's name is Tyrog, his name is Dravone, and I am Nakiata. Now that we've been introduced to one another, could you possibly explain how you know they were trying to kill her?"

"They don't want you learning magic," Melia'na said with a slight grin.

"Why would they care whether or not she learns magic?" Tyrog asked.

"My guess is that they might have foreseen the power she possesses, which made them afraid. It doesn't make sense to me. I know that the Dia'fani have the ability to see into the future and they also know the consequences of trying to change it. Although, there may be some out there who are misguided into believing they can," Melia'na replied.

"They can what? Are you able to see the future as well?" Nakiata asked, sounding a bit surprised.

"No, I am not like them. I am part of the race known as the Ra'hisi. The Dia'fani are the only ones who can see into the future. It's a gift that's been passed down over many centuries, since before anyone can remember. No one really knows when the first of the Dia'fani gained this ability, but, ever since they did, all of our lives have changed. The Dia'fani think of life as dull and uneventful because they seem to know what's going to happen. That is, as long as no one tries to change anything. They learned long ago that if someone tries to change the future, it ends up altering the future they'd seen, and it almost always ends in death. So, they began living from day to day, only looking into the future if there was a real need. However, there are still some that spend all their time searching the future, beyond what most care to, because so many things can change. You've already met two of them. They are part of the group known as the Kili'dri."

"How is it that you are not like the other Ra'hisi?" Dravone asked.

"Are you referring to those still living under the control of the Dia'fani? I am not like them because of an old and wise Dia'fani sorcerer. He was one of the Kili'dri's greatest, and one day when I was a small child he noticed that I had a rather unique aura. He called it a 'spark of potential', which he said was like a faint light that was shining from within me. He took it upon himself to raise me and train me as if I was his own daughter. He taught me everything he knew, as long as I promised him one thing."

"You were forbidden to share *any* of the knowledge that you learned with *any* of the Ra'hisi," Nakiata said, coldly.

"Yes, that is *exactly* what he made me promise. How did you know?" Melia'na asked.

"Control," said Tyrog. "Your race are slaves to the Dia'fani, and to keep the rest of them in line you were forced to swear an oath that would keep your people from learning the truth about who they are and what they could become. Had you broken that oath, the Dia'fani would lose their control of the others, and that might introduce chaos into their world."

"I don't know what you're talking about. What I have sworn will help my people because I have the power to free them. I have not found the right moment to accomplish this task yet, but I assure you they are well cared for right now. They have nothing to be afraid of, since the Dia'fani do not mistreat the Ra'hisi in any way. Many of them have told me that they just don't want us to get entrapped by technology and the dangers that come with it."

"Yes, you have the power to change everything, Melia'na," Tyrog said. "All it takes is one voice in the darkness to bring life to a sleeping giant. Perhaps the time has come for you and your people to go beyond what the Dia'fani want for you. Maybe it's time for the Ra'hisi to make their own way in the universe."

"I will consider your words carefully. As for now, I have other more pressing concerns. She needs my guidance."

Ka'tia was taken aback. She shrugged her shoulders and asked, "I do?"

"Yes; if you don't learn to control the magic that flows through you, it will end up consuming you and ultimately destroying you and those around you. We shall begin your training in the morning. As for the rest of you, please make yourselves at home and try not to destroy the grove or my home."

"What grove?" Dravone asked.

"You will see tomorrow. For now, I will show you to your rooms and bid you a good night." Melia'na led them down a flight of stairs, where she showed them two spacious rooms. "Here is where you can rest. I will let you decide amongst yourselves where you'd like to sleep. Good night." Melia'na lightly tapped her staff on the ground and said a single word, which none of them had ever heard before. A swirling pillar of blue-gray smoke enveloped her, and she vanished.

"We will sleep in here. You two can take the other room," Nakiata said. She grabbed Dravone by the hand, pulled him into one of the rooms, and closed the door.

Ka'tia frowned and looked over at Tyrog, who said, "Don't worry, my young Zonian friend. The room is all yours. My race does not sleep every day. We can go for weeks without sleep. I intend to explore our new surroundings to see what might be lying about."

Ka'tia smiled and gave Tyrog a slight bow. He turned and flew off, back the way they had come. Ka'tia entered the room and shut the door behind her.

Chapter 5

Ka'tia had been sleeping soundly for most of the night. She had several random dreams that had no real meaning, but then she felt a pull, not quite physical. Something had jarred her mind. Her dream was now focused and clear. *Is this a dream or could I be having a vision*? She thought. Whichever was the case, she knew one thing for certain, she was far from anything she recognized, and the scene before her caused her great fear.

She was standing on the ledge of a mountainside cliff, overlooking a valley that stretched almost as far as she could see. It wasn't that that caused her heart to skip a beat. The fog overlaying the valley was whisked away, and poised in perfect formation, an army of ten thousand monsters with glowing, blue eyes.

Feeling helpless and alone she thought, *where are the others?* At the bottom of her field of vision a shadow appeared behind her and at the same time she heard a familiar roar. Ka'tia turned just in time to see Dravone, in wolf-state, jumping over her and onto the first monster. He began clawing at it with no success. Ka'tia immediately noticed that none of the monsters had moved a muscle. They remained motionless.

She noticed a large blot as it passed between her and the sun, so she put a hand over her eyes and squinted, focusing on whatever it was. She was happy to see that it was Tyrog flying overhead. Her mouth dropped when she noticed Nakiata was sitting on his back riding him like a brolo. They were headed toward an oval-shaped, dome-roofed building on the other side of the army of monsters.

They were almost there when it looked like they crashed into an invisible wall. Ka'tia was relieved when she saw them picking themselves up off the ground. They appeared to be unhurt. However, the instant they encountered the wall, the monster army came to life. The battle was about to begin.

Ka'tia grimaced and immediately put her hands to her stomach. She felt as though someone had just kicked her in the gut. She looked down to see if she was injured, but she was perfectly fine. As she examined her abdomen she fell backwards. Lying on the ground she physically felt like someone was standing on her stomach, but no one was there. It finally occurred to her that she was indeed, still sleeping. Ka'tia woke up to see Tyrog staring down at her with his uniquely purple colored eyes.

Tyrog's eyes had a faint, orange glow to them. Ka'tia tried to sit up, but something had her pinned to the bed. Tyrog stuck his long, forked tongue out and licked her cheek. Ka'tia turned her head in disgust and tried to thrash about to get him off of her, but to no avail.

Tyrog inhaled deeply, allowing his chest to expand. Ka'tia could see the fire forming in his mouth. She closed her eyes, anticipating the extreme heat from the fire, but she felt no pain even when she heard the fire escaping from Tyrog's mouth. Curious, she quickly opened her eyes and could see that the fire being blown directly at her, but something was preventing it from reaching her.

Tyrog let out the last bit of fire and growled. He was already inhaling another deep breath when they both heard something tap twice on the floor. By the time they'd turned their attention to the sound, a ball of purple energy engulfed Tyrog and lifted him off of Ka'tia's stomach. The ball of energy, with Tyrog inside of it, hovered over her for a moment before it slowly moved over and onto the floor. The energy vanished, depositing Tyrog on his rump. He sat there wobbling for a moment. He jumped onto his feet and almost lost his balance as he stammered around for a bit. He quickly looked around the room, bewildered. "What happened?" he asked.

"You, my scaly little friend, should not eat plants unless you know what they are," Melia'na said with a frown. "You devoured the only Ois flower I've ever had. I came across it about fifteen years ago. They are one of the rarest flowers, and the chances of finding one are beyond measure. If you haven't noticed, the flowers possess certain, magical properties. Just getting a whiff of the aroma they produce is known to create lucid dreams, some of which are possible futures, unless you're a Dia'fani. I put it in here in hopes that Ka'tia would experience the effects and see a glimpse of her future. At least we now know what it does to a Sodaran when he eats it."

"I'm sorry. I came in the room to check on Ka'tia, and that's when I noticed the beautiful, soft, orange glow of the flower. As I gazed at it, I sensed it was beckoning me to come closer. I flew over to it and sniffed its sweet aroma. I felt exhilarated and instantly desired to eat it. So, I did. The next thing I knew, I was sitting on the floor," Tyrog said. He shook his head back and forth.

"Apology accepted, and to let you know the next time, I will deal with you more harshly. Now that you're both awake, I'd like you to meet me up in the great room. I am going to go wake the other two," Melia'na said. She left the room and knocked on the door to the other room. Dravone answered it, holding a sheet around his midriff.

"Yeah?" He asked.

"Breakfast will be ready shortly. Meet me and the others in the great room," Melia'na said. She vanished in a cloud of dark blue smoke.

The moment she'd gone, Dravone looked across the way and into the other room, where Ka'tia, who was wearing her black, silky night gown, stood and stretched. She turned around and noticed Dravone staring at her with an open mouth. He heard Nakiata clear her throat behind him. He snapped out of it and played it off with a yawn. He closed the door while looking down at the floor.

Ka'tia smiled, walked over to the door, and gently closed it so that she could change clothes. "I saw that," Tyrog said.

"You saw nothing! Especially if you wish to continue breathing," she said harshly.

Tyrog stuck out his forked tongue for a second, and bowed slightly. "As you wish, my lady." He took the liberty of plopping himself up on one of the armchairs in the room and began watching her every move.

Ka'tia frowned, opened the door back up, and said, "Out! I don't need you watching me as I change."

Tyrog stuck his forked tongue back out several times. He lifted himself up off the ground with a few beats of his wings. He flew out the door, and it slammed shut behind him, just missing his tail. He smiled ever so slightly as he headed up to the great room.

Tyrog entered the room and saw a table, about ten feet long, full of food. Melia'na was sitting at one end of the table. She had just finished eating. "Good, you're here. Where are the others?"

"They're still getting ready. This feast looks magnificent," he said. A small spot of drool was forming at the corners of his mouth.

"There is plenty here. Help yourself to whatever you fancy — except that." Melia'na waved her hand, and a plate rose from the table and floated over to her side. "This is specially made for Ka'tia."

Tyrog looked up and down the long table searching the food for what he desired the most, but at first glance there was nothing that had any appeal to him. He rolled his eyes at all the fruits and vegetables and was about to ask if she had any raw meat. Before the words could escape his lips, a strong, mouth-watering, aroma filled his nostrils. It was coming from the center of the table, where a rather large stack of fresh, red, raw meat had just appeared. Tyrog flapped his wings and fluttered over to the platter that was twice as big as him.

He hesitated. He didn't want to offend his host by gorging himself without her approval.

"No reason to be shy. We all have to eat to maintain the life we've been given, so don't hesitate —" Melia'na was saying. Tyrog had already understood the message and had already done a face plant into the pile of meat. He lifted his head up so that he could gulp down the large chunk, of whatever freshly slaughtered creature he was enjoying.

A few minutes later, the rest of them came into the room and sat down at the table. Dravone's eyes looked like they were about to pop out of his skull as he watched Tyrog devour several more chunks of raw meat. "This look more than adequate, thank you," Nakiata said, before she began helping herself to some of the cooked meat on the table.

"There's enough for everyone. Enjoy it while it lasts. Ka'tia, I have a special dish here just for you. I'd really like you to try it," Melia'na said. She waved her hand, and the plate of special food floated over to where Ka'tia was sitting.

"Thanks, I think. What's so special about it?" she asked looking the food over.

"It will help you get through your first day of training."

"Training?" Nakiata repeated.

"Yes, today I will begin training Ka'tia in magic," Melia'na replied, happily.

"How long will that take? And what of the rest of us? What are we to do while you and Ka'tia spend the day together?" Nakiata asked.

"You can help me," Dravone said.

"Help you what?" Nakiata said, smiling.

"Well, you can teach me how to meditate, for one, and maybe you can teach me how to fight a little better," he replied with a smirk.

Tyrog finished devouring another chunk and said, "If it's okay with our host, I would like to observe Ka'tia's training."

"It's settled then. As soon as you've finished eating, we will get started," Melia'na gestured for Ka'tia to eat her food.

Ka'tia took a bite and was a little disappointed. It tasted funny to her. She didn't know if she should say something or not, until Melia'na asked, "You can't be picky. Personally, I think it lacks flavor, but it will do the job."

Ka'tia swallowed the first bite, smiled, and said, "It's not that bad, but yes, it is a bit lacking in flavor. As far as —" She wasn't able to finish her sentence because there was something about the food. As soon as it passed over her taste buds and reached her gullet, she was overcome by the urge to finish the entire plate of food.

"And it begins," Melia'na said.

"What begins?" Tyrog asked.

"A new magical life for Ka'tia. The food she ate introduced endorphins which will help unlock those parts of her brain connected to the use of magic. In more technical terms, it has hyper-stimulated the savical membrane. It will be less painful, and her training will go more smoothly and won't take as long, at least that's what I'm hoping. The downside is that if we wait too long, there is a possibility she might lose control and destroy us all," Melia'na said, sounding overly optimistic.

Ka'tia looked up. With wide eyes, she said, "This stuff is amazing. Can we get started with my training? Right now!"

"Have the two of you had your fill yet?" Melia'na pointed to Dravone and Nakiata.

Both of them nodded. "Excellent. Let's not dilly-dally. Form up so we can travel to the grove." Melia'na clapped her hands together, and the entire table, along with the remainder the feast, vanished from sight. She stood, moved to the center of the empty space, and waited for the rest of them to join her. As soon as they came to the middle of the room, she clapped twice. This time, the chairs vanished, and her staff appeared in front of her.

Melia'na whispered, "*O-a'rkaben sumara'k.*" They were engulfed by green smoke.

When the smoke cleared, they found themselves in a small, grassy field surrounded by an extensive grove that went on as far as the eyes could see. The trees were all spaced neatly apart, but not too far that they couldn't provide the ample amount of shade.

The branches on the trees started branching out about eight feet up and the leaves were large and green. It was an ideal place for all sorts of things.

Along the edge, on one side of the field were several wooden targets. They too were positioned at different distances, allowing for all sorts of training.

Ka'tia bit her lower lip and her eyes began to appear watery. She could barely contain her emotions. "Oh, yes, I am great at target practice." She reached over her shoulder as she normally would but was surprised to find that her bow wasn't there.

"Where's my bow? What exactly am I going to learn without my bow?"

"Don't worry about your bow, it's safe in your room. I will tell you when to bring it. Now the first thing we must find out is, what types of magic you can summon and control. Once we know that, I will be able to teach you how to apply it in combat," Melia'na said.

Everyone burst into laughter, including Ka'tia. Melia'na was confused and looked like she was getting angry. Dravone walked up to her, placed a hand on her shoulder, and said, "I am going to take a wild guess that the Dia'fani did not inform you of what Ka'tia has already accomplished. She can already apply magic to her arrows, and believe me, they are not lacking in power. I will even go out on a limb to say that they might be *too* powerful, at times."

"No, they did not tell me anything about her. I was only told that she requires training in the magical arts. If I was a Dia'fani, we wouldn't be having this conversation. I would have known what skills she has and where she's lacking." Melia'na raised an eyebrow at him. "It doesn't matter in the least; she still needs to learn some of the basics that way she can control what she does, and not do it by accident, or use the wrong magic."

Melia'na stared at Ka'tia who was blushing and looking down at the ground. She continued, "I'm sure she doesn't want to be caught in the heat of the battle searching for the right magic to use, especially when lives, yours in particular, might be in danger. I will train her to know exactly what to do and when. So, if you don't mind, I am the teacher and she is the student."

Melia'na turned her attention back to Dravone and her tone of voice changed, so that it now sounded like she was talking to a small child, saying, "Besides, aren't you supposed to go off with Nakiata and learn how to meditate? Oh, and I do recall something about learning some combat skills. Now would be the perfect time for the two of you to run along and do that?"

Dravone frowned and glanced over at Nakiata. She smiled at him and said, "Come on, handsome, let's leave them to their *magic* lessons."

Dravone rolled his eyes and walked over so that he was standing beside her. The moment he stopped, she looked up at him, smiled, and before he knew it, she punched him in the gut.

Dravone almost lost his breakfast. He quickly gathered himself and asked, "Why'd you hit me?"

"Your first lesson. Never roll your eyes at me. The second is to be ready for anything at any moment of the day," Nakiata said, rather harshly. Dravone rubbed his gut while nodding. Nakiata couldn't help but smile. She grabbed his hand and led him off into the grove where they couldn't be seen or heard by the others.

"Now that those two have gone, we can get down to training you in magic. First, I need to know if you have any understanding at all on how to summon magic. I'd also like to know what sort of things you've done magically. From there, I will be able to decide which direction we need to go, and which areas we need to work on together. After that, it will be a simple matter of improving your skills."

"Well, the only thing I know I have been able to do is add magic to some of my arrows, just before I release them. Other than that, I really don't know much about magic."

"Well, that's a start, I suppose. At least you have the ability to imbue inanimate objects with magic. Normally, that is a difficult skill to master, so I am glad we won't have to work too hard on that. You're sure there's nothing else?"

Ka'tia thought about it for a minute or two. "Yup, that's pretty much all I can do. Before we get too far into all this, can you tell me a little bit more about magic? I'm just asking because I've never had any training in magic before, and I'd really like to know."

Melia'na nodded and said, "There isn't one specific type of magic out there. In reality, magic is everywhere. There are many forms and groups of magic, for instance, elemental magic which consists of three types: fire, ice, and wind. Another, more dangerous type of magic, is lightning. It has to do with all thing electrical along with the natural form, which is where it gets its name."

"I never realized it was so complicated," Ka'tia said.

"Exactly, and one of these days you'll realize that you can do things most people can't even imagine. The magic that I've learned, and will be teaching you, are ones that have been studied extensively, and it's that knowledge which allows us to become, not just proficient at summoning it, but a part of the magic," Melia'na said raising her hands up, out, and around in a large circle.

"Can I ask you, why is lightning magic the most dangerous?"

"I will explain that, in time," she could see the excitement growing in her new pupil's eyes. "We have talked long enough. It's time to get started on the basics. I want you to try some elemental magic. They are the easiest to summon and control. The first one I want you to try is fire magic. Once I'm convinced you have some semblance of control, I'll show you how to work some ice magic." Melia'na paused. "If, and when, you show me that you have become proficient with both of those, I will allow you to attempt a little wind magic."

"Sounds fair enough. Show me what needs to be done." Ka'tia said, and for once, she knew she was ready. *Besides, how bad can I mess up? I've already been trained in quite a few disciplines growing up. I was taught to read and write. How to hold a sword, shoot a bow, fight hand-to-hand. Oh, and I'll never forget my training as a tracker. It was my favorite. Having to pay attention to the smallest details. I am going to enjoy this.*

"Yes, how *does* she do that?" Tyrog asked. He said it sarcastically, but he couldn't help feeling intrigued.

"There are several ways to summon magic. Most require a certain set of motions, accompanied by vocalizing a specific word. The combination of the two calls forth the magic so that it can be used. That is the most basic way to perform magic. Another, more advanced way, involves focusing on a singular thought or precise feeling, which in turn will summon more powerful magic. There have been many instances where magic-users have accidentally created magic when they had a random thought about certain elements or unknowingly focusing on a feeling. Luckily, no one has ever caused any serious damage or harm to anything or anyone."

Ka'tia blushed a little when she said, "Feelings. Those I am becoming aware of. That's how I, as you said, imbued my arrows with magic."

"That is all lovely sounding, but I don't understand how the use of words, along with physical movements can summon magic. Is there any chance you could explain it in more detail? Or, better yet, demonstrate it?" Tyrog asked.

Melia'na rolled her eyes at him, frowning. She continued, "You may observe, but do it quietly. I will teach *her* the words, along with the corresponding motions. Together they will allow her to focus her magical energy and perform the basic types of magic. I don't want her to think that what she does is by accident. When I'm done with her, she will *know* that it's magic. Now come with me." She turned, grabbed Ka'tia by the hand, and walked a little closer to the targets. As soon as they reached a spot that was about fifty feet away, they stopped.

"The first thing I want you to do is concentrate on the meaning of the word, and not just the word itself. Let me demonstrate with a little fire magic. Pay close attention, because you're going to repeat what I do," Melia'na said. She straightened her robes and adjusted her hair slightly. She raised her hands out in front of her with palms down. "The word that we associate with fire magic is *Fotya'*." Several small sparks flashed from her fingertips.

"You see, just me saying the word, did that. Now, the only thing that should come to your mind when you think or say, *that* word, should be an image of a blazing fire." Melia'na rubbed her hands against her garments and put them back into the same position. "You might even begin to feel some warmth in your hands as you begin the motions. I think it's time I show you those. Watch closely, I will go slowly so you will be able to follow."

Melia'na began moving her arms and hands in a specific pattern. Her hands began to glow a soft, yellow-orange. "*Fotya'*!" she said, and a small fireball exploded from her hands and flew across the field, striking the target nearest to them. Upon impact it burst into flames.

"As you saw, toward the end, the magic beginning to manifest into my hands, making them glow. The import thing to remember is the moment at the end when the magic begins to swell, and you can feel it about to overtake you." Melia'na reached up and wiped a bead of sweat from her brow. "I want you to push it away, guiding it to your target or enemy."

"How important is it that she says the word?" Tyrog asked.

"In truth, it's not so much the word that will bring forth the magic. It is more her focusing on what the word means as she follows the motions. Okay, now I want you to give it a try. Just remember — focus on the meaning of the word. Be fluid in your motions, and when you feel the magic building within you, say the word out loud and unleash the magic," Melia'na said. She clapped her hands together and wiggled her body at the same time. She was eager to see what her student could do.

"All right, here goes," Ka'tia said. She closed her eyes, began the motions, and did her best to concentrate on the word *Fotya'*. In her mind, she could see a bright, orange ball of fire that swirled around and around in midair. It wasn't long before she actually felt the heat and knew that the magic was forming within her hands, making its way out to her fingertips. The moment had come, her eyes opened wide, and as she sounded out, "*Fotya'*!" a ball of fire formed between her hands. She turned all of her attention onto the closest target and pushed the little ball of fire straight at it.

The fireball streaked across the field, striking the target dead-center. It exploded violently in an intense, yellow-orange flame. Several seconds later, the entire target was completely consumed, leaving nothing but a small pile of ash on the ground.

"Excellent!" Melia'na said.

Tyrog snuck up behind them. "Yes, that was most impressive," he said. "I have a feeling that I could actually start believing in magic, based on what I've just seen. Is there any chance that I can assist her in the rest of her training?"

Before Melia'na was able to give him an answer, the sky above quickly filled with dark, thick clouds. Within minutes, the sun was gone, and the entire grove was covered in a darkness similar to twilight.

A bright flash of light burst from the center of the field. When it dissipated, a stranger appeared in the middle of it.

"Wait here, *both* of you," Melia'na commanded. She walked over to whoever it was, stopping a couple of feet away. She bowed, and exchanged a few words. She bowed again and returned to Ka'tia and Tyrog. "I must leave you for a while." Melia'na waved her hand through the air, and as she did a small blue light flashed in her hand. The light faded quickly, and they could see that she was now holding a scroll. "Take this. I'm going to assume that with your level of understanding, you shouldn't have too much trouble guiding her through these exercises. The scroll describes in detail what she needs to do, and when. Do not deviate from it." Melia'na looked back at the stranger briefly. "I should be back before too long. If anything, *bad* should happen, throw the scroll onto the ground and breathe fire on it. That will tell me that my help is needed." Melia'na handed Tyrog the scroll, but she held onto it when he grabbed it. She gave him a stern look before letting go. She gave them a slight bow and walked back to the stranger. The instant she stopped, they vanished in a cloud of black smoke.

Melia'na and the stranger materialized in a small room strewn with scrolls. In two of the corners, the scrolls were piled up almost to the ceiling. In the middle of the room was an elegant yet old-looking desk with an accompanying high-backed chair. The stranger sat down and pulled his hood back, revealing a Dia'fani with dark brown skin.

"Why have you brought me here? Where exactly are we?" Melia'na asked.

"That is of no concern right now. I have had a new vision of the future, one that is much clearer than any I've ever had before. Once Ka'tia has finished training, you must send them to Mount Voba'l. Before you say anything, I already know it is forbidden for you to go there. But these strangers are not us, and you will take them to the base of the mountain, and no further."

"Why Mount Voba'l?" she asked.

"It's the last place the lost key was seen, the one they need to unlock The Door of Mystery," he answered.

"Are you really going to send them after, a lost key? Is it even possible that it's still there? How will they know what it looks like?" Melia'na asked.

"Well, it's only been two-thousand six-hundred forty-two years since it was last seen on Mount Voba'l, so yes, they will go after it. And yes, it's there, *and* it isn't. This is what I want you to do. Tell them what we know about the locks, they keyhole, and this: the key isn't a regular key. It will stand out and they will know it when they see it," the stranger said.

His mouth opened but he hesitated as if he wasn't sure what to say. He continued, "Before you let them ascend to the top, you must convey a message to Ka'tia. Tell her that she's going to have to use poison magic on the smaller ship and after she does that, take Nakiata to the big ship," he smiled for a moment. "Trust me when I say, she will not understand you. As soon as you deliver the message you will return to your home. I will send you word when they have returned. Only then will you continue to help them," the stranger said. Before Melia'na could ask any questions, a pillar of black smoke engulfed her, and she found herself back in the field.

The instant Melia'na and the stranger were gone, the sky became clear and the sun began to shine. Tyrog looked down at the scroll he was holding and unrolled it. Inside were three words with several corresponding images next to them, depicting the specific movements for each type of magic. *Fotya'* for fire, *Convoula'* for ice, and *Jeta'r* for wind. "Well, I guess you should do the same thing with the other two words," he said.

Ka'tia looked at the word for ice. The second she read it; she could feel the air around her dropping in temperature. She began to concentrate on the word, and the more she focused the more she felt chilled. She looked down at her hands and smiled when she noticed they were slowly taking on a soft-blue glow. "*Convoula',*" she said. A ball of swirling blue and white energy appeared between her hands. Ka'tia smiled with excitement, but she did not let it interfere with her concentration. The ball of energy began to slowly increase in size, so she moved her hands up and outward, pushing the ball of energy away and toward one of the targets.

Before the ball of energy reached its target, a plume of black smoke appeared directly in its path. Melia'na appeared just in front of the target, surprised to see a ball of ice energy heading straight for her. She quickly waved her hand and redirected it to another target, which was instantly encased in a block of ice the moment of impact. "Well done!" she yelled from across the field.

Melia'na walked over to them. "I have been instructed to teach you magic that is rarely taught to anyone. It's because of the fact that if you fail to do it right, you will end up dead. The magic I am refereeing to has but one use, to kill. I myself have never had to use it. I don't necessarily approve of it, but as I said, you must learn it, and be able to use it."

"Do I have a choice? If it's that bad, I don't think I want to learn it," Ka'tia asked

"No, it seems that neither of us has a choice in the matter. I was told that your lives might depend on you being able to use . . . poison magic," Melia′na said, softly.

"Poison magic! You want me to learn about poison? I don't see how that would be of any use to us. However, you are the teacher, and if you instruct me, I will learn it. I just hope I never have to use it." Ka'tia answered.

"If you do, you will know when, and you will be prepared. Now, let's begin." Melia′na looked around for something appropriate to practice on. "Do you see that group of plants over there?" Melia′na pointed at some shrubs.

"Yes."

"Like other magic, poison magic requires a combination of motions, as well as a word, to elicit the effect. The word associated with poison is *O′tote*," she said with disgust. "Bleh, such a horrible taste now." Melia′na stuck her tongue out and smacked her lips together several times, and spit on the ground. She shook her head followed by her entire body.

"Every time I say that word it leaves a nasty taste in my mouth. I hate it," she said wiping her mouth with her hand, even though there was nothing there to wipe away. "Now, pay close attention as I demonstrate the moves. You must perform them exactly as I do. If you don't, there could be devastating consequence, like killing the entire grove and poisoning all of us."

Ka'tia frowned momentarily, but she grit her teeth and thought, *I can do this. I'm not going to kill anything except some bushes.* She watched Melia′na intently, as she began the motions. It was an eerie display. The moves made her look like she was moving through water. She came to the last movement spreading her hands apart. She whispered, "*O′tote.*"

At first nothing happened. Melia′na straightened herself, spit on the ground again, and brushed her hands on the front of her clothes.

"What did it do? I don't see anything," Ka'tia asked while concentrating on the vegetation in front of them.

Out of the ground, directly below the bushes, came a combination of black and green mist, like smoke. The shrubs began to wither and die within seconds.

Ka'tia's eyes went wide, and she exhaled heavily, from the spectacle that just happened.

"Now, do you think you can recreate what I've just shown you?" Melia′na asked.

"Yes, I believe I can do that."

"No, there is no middle ground here. No room for error. You do, or you don't, which is it?"

"I can!" Ka'tia replied determinately.

"Very well. Concentrate on the bushes over there to the right of the dead shrubs."

Ka'tia began the motions, fumbled it just a tiny bit, and whispered "*O′tote.*"

They waited and watched until a small puff of green, misty gas came up from the ground and caused several of the branches on the bush to wither and die, but the majority of the bush remained intact.

"Well, that was . . . not good. It was kind of pathetic really. I'm just glad she didn't *destroy* the grove and kill us all," Tyrog said. He hissed several times, chuckling as best that a Sodaran can.

"I noticed you didn't quite get some of the motions exactly right. I'm thankful you didn't create more of a disaster than that. I am curious, what were you thinking about?" Melia′na asked.

"Well, to be honest, I hesitated a little. I really don't want to learn magic that's only used for killing. I know that it's only some stupid bushes right now, but what if . . ." She crossed her arms and stuck her lip out and began to pout.

"So, you need help focusing. I think I can help with that," Melia′na walked around behind her and put a hand on her shoulder. She began to whisper the same word over and over again, "*Hrissfa′.*"

Ka'tia looked back at the shrubs, something was happening, and it wasn't what she was expecting. The ground beneath the plants broke open, creating a gaping hole. Ka'tia gasped just as an Ug reached out and pulled itself out of the hole. It made a horrific sound and began stomping its feet.

Ka'tia put everything out of her mind and started the motions. This time she did every single move flawlessly, and at the end she said with a commanding tone, "*O'tote*". The area, starting with the hole, along with some of the surrounding shrubs and trees which was equivalent to the size of a small house, began oozing the black-and-green colored gases, which killed all the surrounding vegetation almost instantly. The mist wafted up rapidly, and Ka'tia watched as the Ug took several deep breaths. It snorted and sneezed several times, obviously from the foul smell. The Ug looked at her with fury in its eyes. Without warning, it slumped over onto the ground, began convulsing in extreme agony, and died.

Melia′na removed her hand from Ka'tia's shoulder. The Ug vanished. Ka'tia was amazed to see that the bushes and trees were the only things to have withered and died. They had even entered a serious state of decay.

"What did you do to me? I swear there was an Ug standing there, and now there is nothing but some dead bushes."

"I made you see something that frightens," Melia'na said. "Do you think you can do it again, but without help?"

"Yes, I can," Ka'tia said, solemnly. She looked around the edge of the field and saw another group of shrubs. She let the same feeling arise within her and focused her thoughts on the single word. Within seconds, a green mist rose, and the plants began to wither and die.

"I would congratulate you on a job well done, but I believe we still need some practice. With this kind of magic, you cannot be bothered by the outcome. We must accept the magic for what it is and what it will do. I understand your sentiment, I myself feel the same when it comes to using poison magic. Can you tell me honestly, do you think you're competent at using poison magic, or should we keep trying?"

"I'm proficient enough. Besides, I'd rather not push my luck, especially the way I feel about it. It could turn ugly," Ka'tia said with a half-smile. "Can we move on to something else?" she asked as her gaze quickly changed to the ground. At the same time she started wringing her hands together.

"I'm not sure that's a good idea. How well did you do with ice magic?"

"I had just performed my first ice spell when you arrived," Katia said. "Which reminds me, where did you go, and who was the stranger?"

"We'll discuss my coming and going later. Let's not lose focus on the task at hand. Repeat the ice several more times while I watch, and then maybe we will finish the day with you trying some wind magic," Melia'na said, sternly.

Ka'tia frowned and did as she was asked. For her, ice magic was the easiest. It just felt right to her. She went through the motions and froze two targets with a single blast, and by her third attempt she had it down pat.

"You are doing better than I expected. That was almost perfect. One more time should suffice, and I think we will try a bit of wind to finish our day," Melia′na instructed.

Ka'tia smiled momentarily and complied with her instructions. She sent the perfect swirling ball of ice magic over to the target. A second after hitting, it shattered into a million small ice particles.

"It's time to hand Ka'tia the scroll Tyrog. She's going to try wind magic now," Melia′na said, knowing he was standing behind her, still studying the document.

He hissed very softly and handed it over to his companion. Ka'tia looked at the open scroll and focused on both the word and the meaning. This time she couldn't feel anything. She heard a small breeze pass through the trees and nothing else.

"That's what I expected," Melia′na said, sounding disappointed. She looked around at the remaining targets.

"I don't understand," Ka'tia said.

"It's quite normal. Every magic user tends to have strengths and weaknesses in certain areas of magic. I myself have problems with fire magic. The magic is what —"

Melia′na didn't finish. When she glanced back at Ka'tia, she noticed that she was still concentrating, as if she couldn't let go of her thoughts. Melia′na was about to interrupt her, before she could hurt herself, when Ka'tia's entire body went rigid. Her skin changed color, becoming ashen.

Both Melia′na and Tyrog jumped back the moment she blurted out, "*Jeta'r!*"

Out of nowhere, a funnel cloud appeared, touching down in the middle of the field. The small tornado moved this way and that way, working its way around the edge of the field, destroying each of the remaining targets. As the last of the targets broke up into fine particles, the funnel cloud dissipated into nothingness. Ka'tia immediately regained her color and was able to move again.

"I must admit, I am a little astounded," Melia'na said. "In all my life I have never heard of a single magic user, who could perform magic, so competently from more than two of the elements. Especially on the first day. It usually takes half a lifetime before they even attempt a third element, and even then, it's never one that they will use quite so well. I was taught that each magic user will have a strong affinity for two out of the three elements, along with several other non-elemental types of magic. I suppose the Dia'fani were right to be afraid of you."

"I think I've had enough training for today. I really feel exhausted now," Ka'tia said, sitting down on the ground. Tyrog hopped over to her side and began to examine her.

"Yes, that is enough training for today," Melia'na looked up at the sky. "And look, the sun has begun to set. We have been at it for hours," she said. "I wonder if your friends, Nakiata and Dravone, are ready to leave as well. Tyrog, escort my pupil back to her room? Make sure she goes straight to bed. I want her well rested before we set out to train tomorrow." Melia'na tapped her staff on the ground twice.

Tyrog was about to respond when the two of the two of them were consumed in a swirling cloud of dark blue smoke. Melia'na turned and headed into the grove in search of Nakiata and Dravone.

Chapter 6

Nakiata found a perfect spot in the grove. It was a small, circular clearing, about ten feet across. "Let's stop here and meditate."

"Why here?" Dravone asked.

"Why not? It seems to be as good a place as any to meditate and learn some moves," Nakiata said with a smile.

"What kind of moves are we talking about?" asked Dravone, blushing a little.

"First, we'll concentrate on learning to meditate properly. I'll need you to have a seat and cross your legs like I'm doing. Once you're in a good position, but not too comfortable, close your eyes and try to clear your mind of everything. That will be the hardest part for you."

Dravone sat down, crossed his legs, and asked, "Why do you say that?"

"Because of your heightened senses. It's much easier to let go of the outside world with all of the sounds and smells if you've been properly trained. I don't expect you to get too good at it just yet. Just try your best, and we'll see what happens."

"Fair enough. So, I've got my eyes closed. Now what?"

"Clear your mind. Try not to think of anything. Let your mind become a blank slate. Let the emptiness drown out all sounds and connections with the physical world around you. Once you can do that, meditation will have been achieved. I must warn you, though, while meditating you may have visions. These visions can come from anywhere. Sometimes they might come from far out in the universe, or from deep within yourself. The main thing to focus on is their meaning."

Dravone found it difficult to block out all the sounds of the grove. His people were so used to listening to every little sound and knowing what it was. He took a deep breath and slowly allowed his mind to go blank. He heard something small jitter across the ground, and he opened his eyes to see what it was. He grunted at his lost concentration.

That's when he noticed Nakiata in deep meditation. She looked more peaceful than he'd ever seen her. He closed his eyes and tried again. It took several more attempts just to clear his head. Finally, he began slipping into a meditative state. The sounds of the grove began to fade into oblivion.

As he sat there, blissfully unaware of the world around him, he began to have his first vision. At first, everything was blurry. He tried to focus as hard as he could, but that only seemed to make it worse. He was becoming frustrated, when he finally remembered that all he had to do was just let go.

He settled and let the vision come to him. The vision became clear, and he could see a small city of Morphan people. The city was surrounded by a grand green jungle, the likes of which he'd never seen before. He began having a sense of Deja vu: He felt as though he was at home, and there was nothing to be afraid of. There was nothing but peace and tranquility.

As he was pondering an idea popped into his mind. Could he actually be observing the Morphan home world? Seconds after this thought entered his mind, he tried to concentrate on the specifics in his vision. However, the vision became blurry again and started to fade rapidly. Something even stranger began to happen. In the small span of time before the vision was gone, he could've sworn that he saw Ka'tia turn around, holding a child who was smiling directly at him.

Dravone was so disturbed by his vision that, the moment he opened his eyes, he simply fell over backwards onto the grass and found himself looking up at the canopy of the grove.

"Are you all right?" Nakiata asked.

"Yes. I will be fine in a moment. You never said the visions would be that powerful," Dravone said, still blown away by what he'd seen.

"Well, as soon as you've recovered, I would like you to refresh my memory on the lesson of lovemaking," Nakiata said as sweetly as possible.

Dravone's eyes widened. He looked to his right, but didn't see her anywhere. He replied softly, "Where are you?"

Nakiata appeared, lying right next to him, and she was completely naked. She smiled, snuggled up close to him, and looked deep into his eyes for several, long, minutes. She gave in to her desires the moment she moved in and began kissing him.

Dravone's heart was pounding in his chest, and in a matter of minutes they were deep into passionate lovemaking. Their passion lasted for a while, and when they had finished, they lay on the grass and stared up at the grove's canopy.

There was a light breeze blowing through the trees. It was calming to listen to. Their peace was broken when a twig snapped not too far from them. Both Nakiata and Dravone were on their feet in seconds, at the same time realizing that they were still naked and had no real defense, unless Dravone transformed.

Melia'na had never been put into such a situation, which is why she was blushing. "I would ask you to please put some clothes on before we return to the house. If you want, I can turn around?" she asked.

Nakiata frowned at Melia'na for disturbing them in the first place. "Yes, if you don't mind. And how long have you been standing there?"

Melia'na shook her head and faced away from the two lovers while they got dressed. "Long enough," she started, "I never thought it possible, for two such as yourselves, to do what you were doing. The entire thing was . . . beautiful."

Now Nakiata was the one who was blushing. Dravone was speechless as usual. "Shouldn't you be somewhere else? Perhaps training Ka'tia how to use magic? Instead of spying on us?" Nakiata questioned her.

"We are done for the day. Ka'tia needs plenty of rest at the moment. She needs to recover her strength. Tyrog is looking after her, and he should be putting her to bed right about now. As for me, I was just coming to see if the two of you had finished your *training*. If you'd like I could always come back later?"

"Nope, no need. I think we're done for today," Dravone said, quickly.

Nakiata gave him a rather stern look, and said, "We'll continue with his training tomorrow. You may turn back around now." Nakiata had her hands crossed over her chest and she looked really annoyed. "We are ready to go."

Melia'na turned, walked over to them, and tapped her staff on the ground. They vanished in a cloud of dark blue smoke. The moment they were back, the first thing they saw was Tyrog sitting on the edge of several large, potted plants. Their sudden arrival startled him as he turned around, still stuffing his mouth with some green-colored flowers.

"You scaly little devil. Shoo! I told you not to eat any more of my —
you . . . you ate all of my tha'lassa flowers! When I get my hands on you, I'm
going to throttle you severely!" Melia'na was outraged. She immediately gave
chase, running after Tyrog, who took to the air the moment she called him a little
devil. He maneuvered as quickly as he could through the large house. He even
turned his head every so often to spew a small stream of flames, to keep her just
out of reach. Melia'na waved a hand, dispersing the flames before they even got
close to her. After several minutes, she stopped, clearly out of breath.

Tyrog looked back at her and smiled broadly. As he turned his head
around, he slammed into a wall that was closer than he'd realized. Melia'na
began to laugh as his body slid down the wall onto the ground. He was picking
himself up, and shaking his head when he heard her say, "Serves you right, little
devil. Now, stay out of my garden!" And to make sure he got the point; she
tapped the bottom of her staff on the ground and lightning flashed from the tip. It
struck dead center on his tail.

The jolt surged through his body, and a glass shattering shrieking sound
erupted from his lips. Tyrog turned, smoke bellowing from his nostrils. "I get the
point!" he mumbled, grabbing for his tail to check it. He looked back up at
Melia'na and glared at her while he spit on the ground, making a hole in the
floor.

Melia'na tapped her staff on the ground a little harder. "And stop putting
holes in my floor!" A stronger jolt arced across the floor and hit him in the leg.
This time the blast knocked him unconscious.

Nakiata, Ka'tia, and Dravone all came running up behind Melia'na. She turned to face them, and with a smile she said, "Now, if someone would like to take our scaly friend to his room, I will see to dinner. Ka'tia you need to return to your room and go to sleep. If you're hungry, I will have one of your friends bring you something in a few minutes."

"I'll take him to his room," Nakiata said, while eyeing Melia'na. "I won't be eating dinner tonight, I'm not really hungry. I *will* see you in the morning for breakfast. Good night." She bowed slightly before picking up the limp Tyrog and carrying him off toward the bedrooms.

Melia'na looked at Dravone with an innocent, unapologetic look. They stood there in the hallway in silence for several minutes. She kept staring at him, and it seemed as if her gaze was changing fast. It was quickly turning into an awkward moment, because he was sure she was viewing him with desire in her eyes.

Dravone didn't know what to do. He wasn't exactly sure why she was looking at him in this manner, so he thought of a way to diffuse the situation. As graciously as he could, he said, "I think I'll call it a night as well." He skulked out of the room with haste, leaving Melia'na alone.

The next day came much faster than any of them wanted. Ka'tia was the first to awake, feeling refreshed and ready for the day's lesson. She felt rather anxious to get to the day's lesson, so she hopped out of bed, changed clothes, and grabbed her bow. Just as she was about to head out, she heard some unfamiliar sounds coming from behind the armchair.

Ka'tia walked over and peered behind the chair. There she found Tyrog sprawled out, looking like a dead, furless, miniature Poun-poun. She let a giggle slip out, but quickly put a hand over her mouth to keep herself from making any more noise. She stepped back away from the chair and left the room. As she closed the door behind her, the door to the other room opened up, and Nakiata came out.

"Good morning," Nakiata said. "Did you sleep well? I did, even after all the commotion with Melia'na interrupting . . . zapping Tyrog with some kind of lightning bolt. You seem to be well rested."

"Yes, I did sleep rather well. You said something about an interruption?" Ka'tia asked.

"I just figured you were already asleep when we returned and the noise woke you up, is all."

"Oh. I was almost asleep when I heard them making a ruckus. Now, I'm really hungry, and hope there is something to eat. Care to join me?" Ka'tia asked.

"I'll join you. I could always do with a bite to eat. It helps to start the day out right. That's what my mother always said to me," Nakiata said. They headed up to the main level.

Once the two of them had reached the main floor, they found the room completely empty. As they walked through the wide, open space, Ka'tia caught sight of a piece of parchment lying on the floor. She reached down to pick it up, but hesitated.

"What is it? What does it say?" Nakiata asked.

"Nothing. It's blank," she replied.

Nakiata walked over to pick up the parchment when Ka'tia said, "Wait! Don't touch it."

"Why not? It's just a —"

"No, it's not. There's something not right about it, I can feel it." Ka'tia grabbed Nakiata and said, "*Convoula'*!" The parchment immediately began to glow a bright white, and ice formed over the floor and walls.

"*Zesou'j*," Melia'na said, as she appeared in the center of the room. The glowing parchment vanished, along with all of the ice. A few seconds later, all the furnishings, including the long table filled with food, reappeared.

"What was that?" Nakiata asked.

"Nothing much. A simple test, and Ka'tia did adequately. Now, we can eat." Melia'na said.

Nakiata didn't reply. She simply frowned, sat down at the table, and began to eat her breakfast. Biting down on a piece of bread and tearing it while glaring at Melia'na.

"Melia'na, I'm curious. How was I able to feel the magic coming from the parchment? It's just a scroll. And yet, somehow, I knew I had to use the ice spell to keep the magic bound to the paper. I guess it's good that ice is particularly easy for me, or was I missing the whole point of it?" Ka'tia asked.

"I imbued the parchment so that it would explode when opened, and only ice could keep it from doing just that. You did well, thinking on your feet when lives could have been in danger. I'm also glad to see that you are becoming more in tune with detecting magic around you," Melia'na replied. "Every magic user is different in what they can do. You, on the other hand, are not like them. You have a real knack for magic, all forms of it, but don't let that go to your head. Even the most experienced practitioner can cause devastation with the most mundane spell, if not properly trained."

The three ladies ate the rest of their meal in silence, and as they sat there enjoying a nice, warm cup of spiced water, Dravone and Tyrog showed up. Dravone took a seat opposite Nakiata. He still had a blank look on his face, as if he were not fully awake yet. He closed his eyes and inhaled the various aromas coming from the large amount of food still left on the table.

Tyrog had perched himself in his usual spot toward the end of the table, where there was plenty of raw meat. He didn't wait for anyone to speak as he began to devour the meat.

Finally, Dravone seemed to wake up. He asked, "Have you already eaten?"

"Yes, sleepy head, we have already finished, and as soon as you're done, we can get started with today's lesson," Nakiata said, sarcastically.

Dravone shot her a scornful look as he grabbed a handful of food and began devouring it. Disgusted by his attitude, Nakiata left the table and went back to the room to get some of her things.

"Must you eat like an animal? You know she only does it because she cares about you, and maybe you could show her a little more respect and acknowledge what you two have for each other," Ka'tia said, sounding a little disappointed.

"That's enough," Melia'na said. "I think it's time we got started. Tyrog are you joining us again today?"

Tyrog lifted his head from the pile of meat he was still trying to consume, grabbed a huge chunk, and tossed it into his mouth. He grabbed another handful before he flew over and landed next to Ka'tia. He nodded, and continued chomping on the food in his mouth.

"Dravone, when you and Nakiata are ready, tell her to hold your hand and then one of you will place a hand here on the table. You will be instantly transported to the grove," Melia'na said. She pointed a finger at a clean spot on the table.

Dravone nodded his head. He reached for another handful just as they vanished in a cloud of black smoke.

Nakiata returned several minutes later and immediately asked, "Where is everyone?"

Dravone held up a finger while he finished swallowing a mouthful of food. "They've gone to the grove already."

"Well that's just great. I guess we are stuck here," Nakiata moaned. She eyed Dravone up and down the same way he looks at a nice juicy piece of meat. "I'm sure we can find something to do with our time, don't you think?" she asked. Nakiata bit down on her bottom lip and nudged her head in the direction of their bedroom.

He smiled, blushed, and swallowed hard. "There is a way to get to the grove, if you feel like putting me through another day of punishment, I meant training."

"How are we supposed to get there without Melia'na?"

"That is the easy part, Mistress Nakiata," he said, bowing his head.

A seductive grin crossed her face. "Please, enlighten me."

Dravone stood, went to her side, and took her hands in his. He placed one hand against his chest and walked with her to the end of the table where the clean spot was. He eased her other hand just above the table, and said, "Just put your hand here." The moment her hand touched the wood, a cloud of black smoke spewed from the table, swallowing them up. In the blink of an eye, they had arrived in their favorite location, deep within the grove

"Punishment it is," Nakiata repeated looking deep into Dravone's eyes.

Chapter 7

After several weeks of intense training, Ka'tia had proven her mastery of fire, ice, wind, and poison magic. She even proved to Melia'na that she could imbue arrows with two of the elements and poison. She was even allowed to experiment with some of the more difficult magic, like *Ei-yee-a'* magic, which focused on physical healing, and *Off-ksa'* magic, which is the ability to make things grow. Now she was ready to move on to something new.

Tyrog was the astute listener, and he never failed to observe with enthusiasm. "Are you going to try again today?" Tyrog asked, hopping around her in circles

"Yes, I think I will finally able to pull it off. I've memorized the words, and now I just need to try," Ka'tia said, just before Melia'na teleported them to the familiar field they'd been using day after day to hone her skills.

"You may be anxious about today, but that is no excuse to lose focus. I have taught you to use caution when trying something new, so I expect discipline. This is going to be . . . a type of magic that only a few have ever been able to perform, and even more disturbing is the fact that it has never been mastered, by anyone" said Melia'na. She raised her eyebrow and watched Ka'tia's reaction.

"What magic are you referring to?" Ka'tia asked.

"It's called *Hisi'k*, the power to command pure energy, otherwise known as lightning magic," Melia'na said.

Tyrog's eyes flashed, "Wait, I know for a fact that several of you have demonstrated the ability to use, *Hisi'k* magic. You yourself did so when I was caught eating your plants, or have you forgotten?" he questioned her.

"Tyrog is correct, I have been able to cast similar spell, but those are minute in comparison to what Ka'tia is about to learn," Melia'na said.

Tyrog seemed to perk up. He glanced at Ka'tia hoping she felt the same way.

Ka'tia let slip a brief smile, which she retracted quickly. She bowed to Melia'na, and him, saying, "I will do my best."

She lifted her head expecting her teacher to begin the lesson, but Melia'na didn't say anything. She didn't even appear to be paying Ka'tia any attention. Confused by the silence, Ka'tia asked, "What do I need to do? I'm sure there's a special word that I need to focus on, or perhaps a feeling? Tell me what I must do to perform *Hisi'k* magic, please."

"There is one problem with you request, I don't have the knowledge to teach you, there is one on Frole, who can assist us."

"So, if you don't know how, and there is only one person on this entire planet that can teach her, how is she expected to learn?" Tyrog asked.

"You would do well to learn some patience Tyrog!" Melia'na said. "There have been some, who were able to summon *Hisi'k* magic, however, there are even fewer, that have survived to pass on what they learned." She saw the concerned look on their faces so she continued, "That is why we do not teach it to every would-be magic user. The ones that cast it . . . at least once, and survived, died long ago, but there is hope. One Dia'fani found several scrolls, which he later deciphered all on his own. With the knowledge he gained from them, he managed to do the impossible. He should be here soon."

"At least once? What does that mean?" Ka'tia asked, sounding more nervous.

"It means that the few who've tried casting it, without being taught, usually ended up incinerating themselves, or, worse, themselves and anyone around them. Therefore *Hisi'k* magic has been deemed extremely dangerous and not to be taught. It is just too hard to control." Melia'na paused to look around the grove. "He's late! I thought he would have been here by now," she said, almost to herself. "Wait here for a moment." Melia'na waved a hand and vanished in a cloud of black smoke.

Ka'tia looked down at Tyrog, frowned a little, and shrugged her shoulders. As a reply to her non-verbal gesture, Tyrog cocked his head to one side, stuck his forked tongue out for a second, and then flew off to one side of the field, where he disappeared into some waist-high grass. Ka'tia watched with curiosity.

A couple of minutes went by when Tyrog finally stood up with some type of little, furry, long-tailed animal, which was currently squirming in his mouth. He chomped on it a few times, swallowing it in large pieces. He noticed Ka'tia was watching him. He smiled with pride and dove back into the grass in search of another little beasty to eat.

It didn't take him long to find an abundance of the small rodents scurrying about. This time, he thrust his small, clawed hand down, skewering one creature while grabbing another with his other hand. He tossed up the one, savoring the moment it fell into his wide-open mouth. Tyrog didn't bother chewing it, he just swallowed it whole. He looked down at the one still skewered on his claw. In a violent jerking motion, he bit it in half.

Ka'tia could tell he was enjoying the flavor, but the entire scene sent a slight shiver up and down her spine.

As they sat enjoying the moment, the sky above began to rapidly fill with dark clouds. In the middle of the field, a pillar of black smoke appeared and the moment the smoke cleared, Ka'tia could see that Melia'na was standing next to the same person that had appeared several weeks ago. *I don't really know for sure. I just know that this individual and the stranger from before were both wearing navy-blue-colored robes with silver trim, a black sash, and a black hood. How many people would have the exact same set of clothes? I guess I wouldn't know that either. I have no idea how the Dia'fani go about buying and selling their clothes,* she thought while staring at them. The hood kept the person's facial features hidden in darkness. Ka'tia smiled and felt her heart skip a beat when she noticed Melia'na motioning for her to come join them.

For the first time in a long time, he was torn between his curiosity and his desire to gorge himself with more of the highly tasty varmints. He sighed. His desire for knowledge and understanding outweighed his carnal instincts, so he flapped his wings, flew over to the middle of the field, and landed just behind Ka'tia. "Who do you think that is?" he asked her.

Melia'na overheard the question and responded, "This is Kola'gram. He *is*, the only one on Frole who has ever performed *Hisi'k* magic . . . and survived."

Ka'tia's facial expression became fixed. Her mouth and eyes were wide open, and her pulse started racing. "That's especially good . . . for him. I'm not sure how that helps me. I could still end up dead or killing us all while trying to use *Hisi'k* magic," she said, sounding a little distressed herself.

"No, you will not die, Ka'tia," Kola'gram said with a raspy voice.

"And how do you know that?" Tyrog asked.

Kola′gram reached up and pulled his hood back, revealing a somewhat familiar Dia′fani form. At the moment, his skin had no pigmentation, and yet it wasn't transparent like many of the other Dia′fani they'd seen on Frole. "I know because I have had many visions, and in every one of them I saw Ka'tia using and controlling *Hisi′k* magic. Her skills went far beyond those of anyone who's ever tried."

"Well, in that case, I will give it a try. What's the worst that can happen? I blow up?" Ka'tia chuckled. "Nonetheless, I still need you to show me what I need to do."

Kola′gram motioned for her to follow him. At the same time, he put his other hand up and said, "Tyrog, Melia′na, I will need you to go to that side of the field and wait there. I don't want to risk either of you getting, accidentally, struck by the magic." He pointed in the direction of the grove, "You'll be safe over there." He turned and led Ka'tia to the middle of the field.

"Now that the other two are at a safe distance, we can begin. *Hisi′k* magic is the most powerful of all magic. To summon it, you will need to focus on an energy that is as strong as life itself. Once you've found that intense feeling, allow it to build within you. Once you feel that it is about to overcome you, you will need to move your body and hands exactly as I am about to do. That will focus the energy of the *Hisi′k* magic through your hands and to your target. Now, watch closely."

Kola'gram began to move his hands. At first, he put them together as if he was praying, holding them close to his chest. Keeping them together, he moved them straight out. Next, he slowly turned his hands, palms facing up, and moved the up above his head. At that point he continued, "Once you have your hands in this position, the energy should almost be at your hands. You should also be able to see some of the energy in the sky above you. It's one of the reasons they call it lightning magic. What they don't realize is that you are drawing energy from all around you. I have speculated that, based on the conjurer's strength, the power can come from far out into the universe, but that's just a theory."

Ka'tia looked up and smiled. She could see rapid streaks of lightning as they crossed the sky horizontally, and what made it more impressive, there were no clouds around.

"Once you've made it this far, you must not hesitate," Kola'gram said, he bent his fingers and it looked like he was grasping an invisible ball, tightly. "Pull your hands down with all your might, and the energy will follow. It will be coursing through you and in between your hands."

Kola'gram did what he was saying and the moment his hands were even with his waist, electrical energy surged between his hands. "From here all you have to do is thrust your hands outward! The magic will strike down your enemies. If done correctly! It will completely consume them, and they will be no more!" he said, with a raised voice because the sounds of the lightning strikes and the power between his hands was very loud.

Tyrog sat just inside the grove, watching. He couldn't quite see the hand gestures that led up to the grandiose one: Kola'gram putting his hands high in the air. Tyrog sank down low when he noticed the lightning, but he kept a vigilant watch on the Ka'tia and her new mentor. Kola'gram pulled his hands down much faster than he raised them, and a moment later, a bolt of bluish-white plasma, no bigger than Tyrog's arm, struck the furthest target, vaporizing it.

Tyrog had to admit to himself that he was impressed. He hoped that Ka'tia could do just as well. He didn't know that his excitement had manifested into him drooling all over himself.

"Don't worry, she'll do just fine," Melia'na said.

Tyrog almost forgot she was standing beside him. He didn't turn to acknowledge, he just kept watching. Ka'tia turned to face a target, obscuring his view. "Blasted!" he whined. He was about to move, when he felt Melia'na gently grabbed his arm and shook her head.

Ka'tia's hand reached up into the air, but something was a bit different. Tyrog began having a tingling sensation all throughout his body. It was like microscopic jolts of electricity were hitting him from all over and surging in him. Ka'tia's raised hands remained high for about twenty seconds. Her fingers bent just as Kola'gram's. She brought them down rapidly and held them in that position for a moment.

This time, instead of a single bolt of plasma energy, there were six, all the size of Ka'tia's leg, and one for each of the remaining targets. The plasma bolts were a little more intense than those produced by Kola'gram.

Tyrog was completely astounded and felt that he should congratulate her on a job well done, but just as he took to flight, Kola'gram turned and began running straight for them, yelling, "Get deeper into the trees!"

Luckily Melia'na's reflexes were still in top shape. She grabbed Tyrog by the leg, yanked on it hard, and threw him in the opposite direction.

Kola'gram had just enough time to reach the edge of the grove, jumping behind the large tree he saw. A bolt of plasma ten times the size of the others had struck the spot where Ka'tia was standing. A shock wave caught Melia'na and Tyrog mid-stride, throwing them deeper into the wooded grove. Once the dust began to settle, they jumped to their feet and quickly made their way back to the field, where they found a large crater in the ground.

"What *was* that?" Tyrog asked.

"That, Master Tyrog, was just a fraction of Ka'tia's true power, a power that she now has the ability to use, with caution because she still needs to learn how to control it.," Kola'gram said as he smiled and motioned for Ka'tia to climb out of the crater.

Ka'tia was completely unharmed. She smiled lightly and said, "Sorry about that. I didn't know it was going to be that strong. Is everyone alright?"

"We're fine, but you should have paid a little more attention to what you were doing," Melia'na said.

"It's my fault, I thought I warned her about holding onto the energy for too long," Kola'gram said.

"What's going on here? Never mind, Tyrog I need you, *now*!" Nakiata screamed.

"Why? What's going on?" he asked.

"Dravone was struck by this huge bolt of lightning and he isn't moving! And you're the only one I know that can help him!" she barked.

Hearing the news of what just happened, accompanied with the distress in Nakiata's voice, Ka'tia couldn't believe that she could be so irresponsible. She put her hands to her face and began to cry. "I had no idea," she said.

"Wait, Ka'tia and I will see to him!" Melia'na said. She vanished in a cloud of smoke, reappearing next to Ka'tia, grabbed her hand, and disappeared in another burst of smoke.

Nakiata grit her teeth and clenched her fists. "Thanks for waiting for me!" She turned and ran as hard as she could, back to where she left Dravone.

By the time she arrived, Melia'na and Ka'tia were kneeling next to Dravone. They both had their hands hovering over his body. Simultaneously they said, "*Ei-yee-a'*." Their hands expelled a bright orange-and-white light, which struck his body.

Dravone's eyes opened and he gasped for air. A second later he sat up, placing his hands on his face. "What happened?" he asked.

"I . . . I got carried away," Ka'tia said through the sobs.

"So that was you?" Nakiata asked. "I figured it had to have been either you or her," she said pointing at both of them.

"Don't blame her! Instead you should be thankful she didn't kill us all, or herself. Such mistakes cannot happen again, no matter if it was only her first attempt. I promise you this, she with have more practice, which will help prevent a repeat of what just happened," Melia'na said. "I am going to say that now is a good time to end the day?"

Nakiata stared at them with piercing eyes. She didn't blink one bit, as she nodded in silence.

Ka'tia kept her head down and raised her hand for Nakiata. Once she felt her smaller hand, she tapped on Melia'na's shoulder and they disappeared in the dark-blue smoke.

"I'm glad to see everyone safely back, and in one piece. I think my work here is done?" Kola'gram inquired, looking to Melia'na, who nodded. "As long as Ka'tia can remember the moves?"

"Yes . . . I don't think I will ever forget them," she answered with her head low and several tears streaming down her face.

"Very well. I will leave you with Melia'na, who can assist with your practices. I must be going. Before either of us forgets, you can also teach her that final bit of magic."

Kola'gram walked down into the middle of the newly formed crater, turned and said, "I must return to the temple, and after that I will go to Kosemva'. I apologize for not staying and helping, but there is little time and so much to be done before there can be fruition. He bowed and vanished in a cloud of black smoke.

"Kosemva'? Fruition? What did he mean?" Tyrog asked.

"I'm not sure what he meant by fruition. I have never heard him use that term before. I can tell you that Kola'gram spends a lot of time at the Temple of Kili'dri. Every now and again he will take a moment to help instruct a student who might be struggling, but he spends most of his time studying ancient texts, or at least that is what everyone thinks. He tends to disappear quite often, and no one knows where he goes." Melia'na explained.

"What about Kosemva'?" Ka'tia asked.

"Kosemva', is a mystical place. I have heard stories and rumors, but no solid evidence to convince me of its existence. Now, I'm not sure." Melia'na said looking down into the deep depression that Ka'tia created. "But if Kola'gram is going there, it has to be a real place." She shrugged her shoulders and turned her attention back to the group. "Once you become proficient with *Hisi'k* magic, we can start on one last subject. For now, let's head back to the house." Melia'na said.

Almost a week had gone by since Ka'tia's blunder and Nakiata was beginning to tire from all the meditation and training. There just wasn't enough excitement for her. She couldn't understand how Master Akizan had put up with her for seventeen years. *I would have gone crazy. Thinking about it now, I should have been more thankful to him. I promise that when I return to Trouganda, I will give you the proper thanks, Master Akizan,* she thought. Nakiata kept twiddling with the grass around her legs while Dravone was practicing the combat moves she just showed him.

There is a brighter side to training, though, at least for me. I get to spend plenty of time with Dravone, even if he's a bit hard-headed and will never be able to do some of the more difficult moves. It is fun to watch him try, though.

Nakiata looked up. She felt refreshed and a little more in tune with what she needed to do. Dravone was already mastering his lesson, but he wasn't as confident as she hoped.

"Can you show me that move one more time?" he asked. "The one where you run at your opponent, jump in the air, spin, and plant your foot in their chest? I want to see if I can block it. If I can, I attempt to do it as well." He took a moment and stretched his arms up high, moaning because every muscle in his body ached.

Nakiata's eye glistened right before she rolled them up. She sighed, jumped to her feet, and nonchalantly walked about fifty feet away from him. Dravone didn't know it, but she had had the wild idea to change things up. *Instead of the flying spin kick, I'll simply flip kick him.* The thought of Dravone landing flat on his back put a huge, mischievous grin on her face. She let the grin fade and steadied herself. She set herself, turned abruptly, and ran at the unprepared Dravone. She leapt into the air, flipped forward, and planted both feet square on his chest, knocking him off his feet and sending him flying backwards about ten feet. He skidded on the ground another four feet, before his body came to a stop.

Dravone quickly jumped up, and immediately began whining. "I wasn't expecting you to do that!"

"I know, but haven't I already said that you need to be ready for the unexpected? Shall we try again, or is your pride too wounded to continue?" Nakiata giggled.

"I'm fine," he said, brushing off the grass and dirt from the backside of his robe. "Let's continue," his said angrily.

Nakiata smiled and walked back across the grove. She turned and started running at him a second time. Just as she was about to jump into the air, a swirling cloud of dark blue smoke appeared between them, causing her to stop dead in her tracks. She watched the smoke as it dissipated, waiting to see who would bother interrupting their training. To her chagrin. Ka'tia now stood between them with a huge smile on her face.

"I did it!" Ka'tia exclaimed. "I have to say, that I was not expecting it to feel that way. It felt like I was forcing myself through something I couldn't see. I'm just glad it didn't last very long."

"Did what?" Nakiata asked, obvious tones of agitation in her voice.

"Who gave her sour fruit for breakfast? Anyway, I learned to teleport, that's what. Come on, I'll show you. Dravone you too. Come here and hold my hands." Nakiata hesitated for a moment, but she decided that the change in pace was a welcome opportunity.

Dravone walked over to Ka'tia. He took her left hand in his and waited for Nakiata to do the same. Once Nakiata grasped her hand, Ka'tia closed her eyes and began thinking about where she wanted to go. After several seconds of silence, she said, *"Fee-yay."* All of a sudden, dark blue smoke swirled up out of the ground and enveloped them.

The moment the smoke cleared, they found themselves just inside the grove near the field. Melia'na and Tyrog were patiently waiting for Ka'tia's return, but they didn't expect to see Dravone and Nakiata.

Nakiata quickly saw the new devastation to the field. "What happened over there?"

"That — I'll tell you about that later," Tyrog said.

"Excellent work, Ka'tia. And, since you brought the others back with you, it is the perfect time to tell you everything. You are my first and finest student, and you are ready to face whatever the universe might throw your way. You may continue your journey to fulfil the prophecy. Having said that," Melia'na noticed that Nakiata was about to say something, so she put up a finger, stopping her. "I will now tell you about the door that, as far as I know, has never been opened. The main reason this door has never been opened is that there are only a few people who know there are *two* locks, as well as several magical wards which protect those locks. One of the locks is completely magical, and the other is mechanical in nature. I know that you, most of the acolytes, the high priests, and a few others that have been in and around the Temple of Kili'dri, have seen the magical lock or hear about it. Because it kills. Only three people on all of Frole know about the mechanical."

"We know about the mechanical lock. We saw the keyhole, and that's when Tso'li sent us to find you. You said three people know about the mechanical lock; who are they?" Dravone asked.

"Well, one person you already know is Tso'li. He was the first one to discover the keyhole. He was doing a detailed study of the door itself a few years back when he came across it. He was also the only one to ignore its significance, and he tried to break through the door using any means possible. He pretends not to know about it. Sometimes, I even think he has forced himself to forget about it. The second was Kola'gram, Ka'tia and Tyrog have already been introduced. He found the lock one day while examining the door at Tso'li's request. The third person who knows about it is me. Kola'gram told me about it and thought maybe I might be able to pick the lock. He showed me where the keyhole was, but I was unable to open it. The lock is no doubt made of a metal that is not from Frole."

"We were told you know how to open the door," Nakiata said, a little perturbed.

"You have been misinformed. I don't know how to open any doors. I was asked to train Ka'tia in the magical arts and if those skills allow her to unlock the door, then that is what she will do. I will tell you that the magical wards and locks are not to be taken lightly. No one on Frole has ever been able to open that door, but with her abilities, Ka'tia might be able to. However, the mechanical lock must be opened with a key. It cannot be picked. The key is not like any other key. It will stand out, and you will know it when you see it. It was thought to have been lost," Melia'na said.

"So, where is this key?" Nakiata asked.

"We're not exactly sure where it is. We know where the key was last seen, and when. It was approximately two-thousand six-hundred forty-two years ago on the top of Mount Voba'l," Melia'na said without looking directly at them. Instead she looked from side-to-side, as if she wasn't sure about what she was telling them.

"So, essentially, you have no idea where it is?" Tyrog asked.

"Yes . . . that would be a correct assumption. The key's exact location is something that has eluded all of us; however, we are sure that you will find the key, once I take you to Mount Voba'l," she said with a little more certainty.

"How do we get to Mount Voba'l from here?" Dravone asked.

"I can take you to the base of the mountain, but it will have to wait until tomorrow. From there, the four of you must go alone. No one from Frole will be able to help you. If we're all finished here, might I suggest that we leave a little early so we can enjoy one last evening together?" Melia'na paused for moment and looked directly at Ka'tia. "Will you do us the honor and take us back to the house?"

Ka'tia smiled broadly. "Yes, of course!" She grabbed Nakiata's hand and held her other hand out for someone else to take. She felt Tyrog's cool, scaly hand taking hold. Dravone stepped over and took Nakiata's other hand, while Melia'na stepped in front of Ka'tia and waited.

This time, Ka'tia didn't say anything. She simply smiled at Melia'na and thought about the word that would take them back to the underground home. A large cloud of bluish-black smoke spiraled up, surrounding them for a few seconds. When it dissipated, they were back inside the large living room of the house.

"Dinner will be ready shortly, and until then you can all go to your rooms and tidy up."

"I think I'll take a nice, hot bath. Tyrog, would you do me the honor of heating up my water?" Nakiata asked, politely. Tyrog spit on the ground. It began to steam and sizzle, creating a small hole in the floor.

"I'd love to," he hissed sarcastically. He flew off in the direction of the bathroom.

Nakiata arrived about five minutes later. She opened the door to the small bathroom, which had a beautiful, white, stone tub. Underneath it was a small area where hot coals could be placed to heat the tub and the water inside. She couldn't help but notice, on the other side of the room, perched on a small ledge where a row of flowers had been planted, Tyrog sat. He was already munching on a couple of the blue-colored flowers.

"You know, if Melia'na catches you, she's going to have your hide mounted and put on the walls of the living area."

Tyrog's forked tongue came jutting out of his mouth, and he licked his upper lip. "I'll take my chances. How hot would you like your bath, my lady?"

"Hot, but not boiling hot." Nakiata replied, giving Tyrog a stern look.

"Very well." With both hands, he grabbed the stalks of the two plants whose flowers he'd just eaten. He yanked them out of the ledge and ate them, roots and all. His size increased by a small amount, and he had just enough fire brewing inside for him to heat the water in the tub. He hopped over to the tub and exhaled a minute-long stream of fire at its base.

Nakiata had just stepped out of her Roarrg armor and dipped a finger into the water. "Mmmm, the temperature is just right. Thank you," she commented. Nakiata proceeded taking the rest of her clothes off. Once she had removed the last article, she stepped over to a small shelf along the wall and grabbed a bar of soap, and slid into the water. "Ahhhhh, so nice."

"I'm glad to hear you're happy. Now that you are all settled into your bath, I was hoping we could have a talk," Tyrog said.

"As long as it won't stress me," Nakiata said with closed eyes and a smile across her face.

"I don't think it will be too stressful. I want to know more about the box of Katoh. What did you see?"

Nakiata opened her eyes and noticed that Tyrog was now perched on the end of the tub and staring at her intently. "The box of Katoh was just an empty box. It had a unique lock on it, though. It consisted of four finger indentations, which only opened after I put my fingers in place. The moment my fingertips aligned; I heard a voice. Everything around me changed in an instant. I thought I had gone to a different planet. It took me a second to realize that the box was actually showing me different planets. As soon as the show was done, it released me, and I was back on Zondura. Why did you want to know that?"

"No particular reason. How well do you remember the planets you saw in your vision?"

"The vision, as you say, only lasted a few minutes. I barely remember any details at all. The only strong memory I have is of this planet and its mysterious purple sky. I'm sorry I can't be of more use. Were you hoping that the box showed me the way we must go?"

"Perhaps something more to go on, but alas, the prophecy has brought us together and I know it will somehow guide us through to the end. Can I ask you something else about the box?"

"I know you're going to ask anyway, so go ahead."

Tyrog stuck out his forked tongue for a second, "I am going to speculate that the box only reacted to you and no one else, correct?"

"How did you know?"

"The box must have been genetically coded, and you were the one it recognized. Like I said, fascinating. Well, I will let you enjoy your bath now. Would you like me to heat it up again for you? I do have a little fire left."

"Yes, please," Nakiata replied, happily.

Tyrog hopped down and breathed the last little bit of fire he had, heating the tub to just the right temperature for Nakiata. He observed her reaction for a moment, making sure she was content. He began to feel awkward just sitting there staring at her, so he flew over to the door, opened it, and immediately found Dravone standing just outside the door. "May I come in?" He asked Tyrog loudly so that Nakiata could hear him.

"Yes, he can come in and join me, there's plenty of room," Nakiata replied seductively.

Tyrog cocked his head to one side, let his forked tongue slither in and out several times, and took off, flying past him. Dravone took that as his cue to step into the room and close the door behind him.

He walked over to the side of the room, stopping and standing next to her Roarrg armor. Dravone pressed the small spot on his wrist, which detached the armor from his skin, allowing him to step out and away from it.

Nakiata had forgotten that Dravone didn't have anything else to wear, except his Roarrg armor. She smiled at him, closed her eyes, and waited for the moment she heard him climbing into the tub. "Mmmm, now this is happiness," she said.

Chapter 8

The next day began with a sorrowful silence throughout Melia'na's house. Nakiata, Dravone, Ka'tia, and Tyrog had gathered in the living area with all of their things. They had sat down for a nice hearty breakfast when Melia'na finally broke the silence. "Once we are done, I will take you directly to the base of Mount Voba'l. It will be cold. If I were you, I would suggest warmer clothes than just those suits of armor?"

"We won't be needing warmer clothes. These suits were specially made for us by the Roarrgs, and they can withstand some pretty cold weather," Ka'tia replied.

"The Roarrgs? I'm not familiar with them. What do they look like, and where are they from?"

"I have just the thing," Tyrog said as he flew over to Ka'tia's pack and pulled out a small, thin, square piece of glass. "They look like this." He began tapping on the glass, and images began to appear on it. Finally, Tyrog stopped tapping and said, "That's a Roarrg."

"I am impressed. I wasn't aware that any of you possessed such technology. The Roarrgs look formidable." Melia'na said.

"You've never seen something like that before?" Dravone asked.

"Nothing quite like that. The Dia'fani have many things similar to it, but I have never seen them in person. I never cared to learn much about it. My focus has always been on magic. I'd like to hold it, if I may?" she asked.

Tyrog nodded and handed her the glass. She studied it for a quite a while.

"What can you tell us about Mount Voba'l? Do you have any advice for us, and do you possibly have any idea where we might find the key?" Tyrog asked, holding his hand out to take the glass back from her.

Melia'na handed it back to him and said, "The only advice I can give is to trust in each other's abilities. As for finding the key, I only know where to start, which is where I am taking you, Mount Voba'l. I've never been told much about it, except that it's forbidden for the Ra'hisi. I don't exactly know why. Anytime I asked about it, I was told it was for my safety and that of my people. Nonetheless I will take you there, are you ready?"

"Yes, let's get going," Nakiata said. Her and Dravone went back to their room, gathered their things, and returned. They were the first ones back.

Melia'na was waiting patiently for Tyrog and Ka'tia to return. The moment she saw them come through the doorway of the great room, she waved her hand, and the table vanished. "Come close. Form a small circle," she said, placing her staff in the middle of their circle. She began mumbling something, and a pillar of dark blue smoke spiraled up and engulfed them.

Moments later, they arrived at the base of a steep, snow-covered mountain whose peak was hidden by a large, gray cloud that didn't appear to be moving.

"This isn't going to be fun," Tyrog said, recognizing the bleakness of their surroundings.

Nakiata shivered. A cold wind hit her face and wisped past her ears. Even though her suit protected her from the cold, she no longer had a helmet like Dravone and Ka'tia because she'd discarded it back on Vazdrag. Nakiata remembered that she had something else that would work just as well, so she took off her pack and pulled out the cloak her mother had given her. It fit beautifully over her suit of armor. She pulled the hood over her head and tied it snug. "Ah, that's better," she sighed.

"This is Mount Voba'l. I can go no further. Ka'tia, if you have a moment, I'd like to speak with you in private," Melia'na said. Ka'tia nodded, and the two of them walked out of earshot of the others. "I have a few things I must tell you that you must swear not to forget. None of what I say will make sense right now, but when the time is right you will understand. Do you so swear?"

"Yes, I swear to remember. Now what is it?" Ka'tia asked.

"First, you must somehow find Nakiata, and the moment she's located, take her to the large ship. Second, you must use the poison magic I have taught you when you confront the big, gray beasts."

"When you say the big gray beasts, do you mean the Ugs? What large ship? Is it an Ug ship?"

"I don't' know anything about these Ugs you speak of. If what I described leads you to that conclusion, you should trust your instincts. I have told you everything I know, even though I have no idea what any of it means. I am confident that I have trained you well, and it is time that I wish you all the best. You must go." Melia'na didn't wait for her pupil to respond. She just disappeared in a pillar of black smoke.

Ka'tia walked back over to where the others were standing. She took her pack off and pulled out her helmet and put it on. She looked up at the cloud and was unable to see past it. "Melia'na mentioned something about gray beasts. If she mean the Ugs, we should be mindful in case we run into them. Even if that's not what she said, I am positive that's what she was referring to."

"So, there might be Ugs up there. At least we'll be ready for them," Nakiata said with a smile. She began the trek up the steep slope.

"Great, more Ugs," Dravone said with a sigh. He put his helmet on and followed Nakiata.

"Ugs don't taste good at all. The flavor is quite repulsive. At least they're not too hard to kill. Ka'tia, when you catch up with those two, tell them I'm going to fly up there and check things out. I want to see if there is anything that could pose a real threat," Tyrog said. He hopped a couple of times, jumped up into the air, and nosedived into the snow.

A minute later, the ground shook beneath them. Tyrog burst forth, having increased his size almost tenfold. He took to the air, flying out away from the mountain. He was almost out of sight when he banked sharply and headed up into the clouds.

Ka'tia hurried to catch up with Nakiata and Dravone. "Tyrog said he wanted to —" flashes of orange and green light danced around the cloud above them without a sound. The three of them watched the sky closely. They jumped back a few inches when the sound of the first explosion reached their ears. Several more echoed around them, and just a fast as the lights, so did the noise.

"Look there!" Dravone shouted, pointing at the small shape of Tyrog's body, falling and crashing back into the snow further up the mountain, just under the cloud layer.

It took them about ten minutes to reach the small, steaming crater in the snow where he had landed. Once they reached the edge, they looked down into the ten-foot hole in the ground. Tyrog began to stir. He stood and shook himself. He started grumbling and spouting some untranslatable Sodaran curses. He looked up and noticed the others staring at him. "That stung a bit," he said, flying out of the crater.

"What happened?" Ka'tia asked.

"First, I flew through what I thought was a cloud, but it had a horrible odor to it. As soon as I was on the other side, I could see that the mountain had a large plateau with a small village nestled in the center. On the far side was a cliff wall that led to the peak." Tyrog shivered, a chill running up his spine. "I circled over the village several times, getting higher each time. Finally, I made it to the top of the cliff wall, where another, much smaller plateau is."

"Is there anything up there, or did someone in the village shoot you down?" Ka'tia asked.

"I was just getting to that. Once I was high enough to see the peak, I discovered an automated defense system consisting of four energy cannons. The canons were place on the edges of the plateau and were guarding a Black Door."

"There's a Black Door up there?" Nakiata asked.

"Yes, but it's not active. The defense system must have somehow been alerted when I passed through the cloud barrier, or someone in the village activated it, because I saw someone leaving the top of the mountain by way of some stairs built inside the mountain." He pointed at the cloud layer a hundred feet above them. "Luckily, I was able to destroy two of the cannons before one of them caught me off guard. There are still two more up there, and they are aware of me." Tyrog took a deep breath and shook his head in disappointment.

"Did you happen to see any other way to get to the top?" Ka'tia asked.

"There's only two ways to the top of the mountain. The stairs, but we'd have to find the entrance, which is probably somewhere in the village along the cliff wall. The only other way would be for me to carry all of us up there, but with those cannons still active, I wouldn't risk it," Tyrog replied.

"The village — were there any other people up there, or is it pretty much abandoned?" Nakiata asked.

"There are people up there. I noticed some of them screaming and pointing at me as I circled overhead. Most of the ones I saw were running into the buildings as I flew over them."

Dravone began to laugh through his helmet. "Gee, do you blame them? If I saw a full-sized Sodaran flying over my home, I'd run for shelter, too."

Ka'tia and Nakiata chuckled, while Tyrog cursed and spit on the ground, creating a new, steaming hole.

"I think you're going to live. Let's get to that village and hope that the people there find us a little less scary and are willing to help," Nakiata said with her mischievous grin.

After a good hour-and-a-half walk up the mountain, they finally cleared the cloud layer and stepped onto the plateau. Just as Tyrog had said, there was a small village nestled quietly among the trees. Beyond that was the flat face of a rock wall that went up another two-hundred-and-fifty feet.

The village was vaguely similar to the one Dravone came from back on Trouganda. The four of them slowly walked down the main dirt road of the village toward the largest building, which they guessed would be home to the village leader.

As they'd already anticipated, there was no one around. However, they could see curtains quickly moving in several of the buildings as the occupants inside closed them so they couldn't be seen.

From somewhere to their right, a ball came bouncing out onto the road. It was closely followed by a child, a young girl. She quickly grabbed the ball, stood up straight, and the moment she noticed them, she froze.

Nakiata noticed that the girl was about the same height as she and, even more curious, had pointed ears like hers. Nakiata saw this as a good sign. "Hello there. What is your name?" she asked.

The girl dropped the ball and ran back between the buildings she'd come from. "So much for that attempt at communication," Nakiata said with a frown.

"We need to find someone in this place who might be able to help us," Dravone said.

The four of them continued walking toward the largest building. As they approached, the door opened, and an old man stepped out. He crossed his arms and looked at the group with a stern expression.

"Tyrog, can you get the Itzuli? I don't want to waste time talking to blank stares," Nakiata commanded.

"Yes, I can do that," Tyrog said. He flew over to Ka'tia and pulled out the small, spherical device. With the Itzuli in hand he stopped and hovered next to where Nakiata was standing. "Here we go," he said tossing it out in front of them.

Once the Itzuli finished and fell to the ground, Nakiata said, "We need your help."

The old man was a little astounded by her tone. "No! You must leave this place and never come back!" he replied with the same tone.

A group of heavily armed soldiers rushed them from all directions. The soldiers stopped about fifteen feet away, surrounding them. The old man pointed at the rock wall and shook his head. "No one is permitted on the summit. The Commonwealth is already aware of a disturbance, as you can plainly see by the soldiers. I have said my peace, now go." He made a gesture, shooing them away. The old man turned around and went back inside, slamming the door shut behind him.

Nakiata's face turned a nice shade of red. She eyed the soldiers, assessing their strengths and weaknesses. *Would they be able to track me in SOT? Perhaps I'll try a different approach,* she thought. Nakiata pointed at the stone wall. They reacted swiftly, raising their weapons and aiming at her.

"Well, if that is going to be your answer," she said, smirking at them. Her expression changed in an instant and her face now burned with anger. A few of the closest soldiers shifted nervously when they saw her eyes shift from royal blue to black-and-gray. "So be it," she said, vanishing into SOT.

In the time it took Dravone's heart to beat four times, the door to the old man's house burst open and Nakiata reappeared, covered in blood, holding the old man's head in her right hand.

"What have you done?" Ka'tia yelled, panic in her voice.

Nakiata walked past her friends and the soldiers. She stopped in the middle of the main street and tossed the old man's head onto the ground.

Tyrog and Dravone were just as shocked as Ka'tia, but they kept their attention on the soldiers, watching them cautiously, and waiting for the fight to start, but they did nothing.

Nakiata pointed at the stone wall again and shouted to the inhabitants of the village, "We are going up there! And somebody is going to tell us where the stairs are that will get us there!" She crossed her arms over her chest, started tapping her foot on the ground, and waited.

Tyrog was amazed at the soldiers' restraint. They still made no moves against them. *I wonder,* he thought. His curiosity had reached his limits. He flapped his wings and flew over to one of the soldiers. Hovering in front of the soldier, he noticed they all had the same blank expression. Tyrog waved his hand directly in front of his face, but the soldier's eyes didn't move. Tyrog moved in a bit closer and touched the soldier on the nose. All at once, the soldiers fell to the ground.

"They are all —" Tyrog began.

"Dead, yes. I killed them all, and I even went in and killed that old man, and now I'm just waiting for one of the villagers to come forth. I hope they realize I'm not in the mood to be trifled with. We need to get to the top of the mountain to find that key!" Nakiata huffed.

"I don't think anyone is going to help us, especially since you've killed their soldiers, and their leader," Ka'tia said, solemnly.

"Well, either they come out or I'm going in. Either way, I will get results. Tyrog, maybe you can use the Itzuli again. Perhaps one of the villagers will see it and be able to understand what we are trying to do. What do you think of that idea?" Nakiata asked.

"I suppose that will work," he replied. Tyrog hopped over to the Itzuli and picked it up off the ground.

"Hold on. How does the Itzuli work? Does it have an effective range? Or will it work just by line-of-sight?" Nakiata asked.

"It doesn't have a specific range, other than the distance the light can travel. It mainly will do its job as long as the subjects can make a visual connection with the light," he explained.

"So, let's say that one of the villagers just so happened to be peeking at us from inside a building, or through some bushes; would the Itzuli still share our languages?"

"Yes. That is basically how it works," Tyrog said.

"Well, in that case, I'm going to try and help the situation." Nakiata took her Kharak blades, and, with the knuckle blades pointing straight down, she shoved them into the soft ground. "Ka'tia, would you come over here and lay your bow down on the ground and then take a few steps back?" Nakiata asked, almost at a shout. She waited until Ka'tia was beside her before she let go and stepped back away from her blades.

Ka'tia slowly placed her bow down next to Nakiata's Kharak blades, and backed up, standing just behind Nakiata.

"We are now unarmed. Come out and see for yourselves!" Nakiata yelled. "Now would be a good time to have the Itzuli shine, Tyrog!"

Tyrog had his doubts as he scanned the village. He didn't see anyone. *Well this is going to be a waste of time. I am pretty sure these people are terrified right now. First they ran from the sight of me flying over their village. After that, she made it worse when she went and killed the town leader, and all the soldiers*, he thought.

Nakiata noticed his hesitation. She cleared her throat and gave him a scornful look. Tyrog nodded his head and gently tossed the Itzuli into the air. *I hope it does get too damaged*, he thought, expecting it to hit the ground a second later. He was surprised when it stopped and hovered four feet off the ground. The street and all the buildings around them were bathed in the green light emanating from the little sphere. It lasted for a full minute. The light extinguished and it dropped to the ground with a light thud. Tyrog hopped over, picked up the device, brushed it off, and gave it to Ka'tia.

"If you can hear my voice and understand my words, come out. If you fail to do as we ask, I won't hesitate to kill every last person who remains in this ridiculous village!" Nakiata yelled.

After a few minutes, several people cautiously left their homes and walked down the main road, stopping about twenty feet away. Among the crowd, Nakiata saw the little girl, who was still clutching onto her ball. "I was right, you were peeking around the corner. You are the bravest one here. My name is Nakiata, and these are my friends. We have come to this place in search of a key, which is probably at the top of the mountain. Can you tell us where the stairs are that will take us to the top?" Nakiata asked the little girl.

A woman standing behind the little girl replied, "She cannot help you, there is no key here. We are here to farm and serve. We have debts that must be paid."

"Your debts? What do you owe, and to whom?" Tyrog asked.

The small group of villagers took a step back when they heard Tyrog's deep voice speaking their language. "We owe the great Commonwealth of Astinomia, different amounts. I owe them four-and-a-half million Zendrats for my life and that of my daughter," the woman replied. "We must work here for a minimum time of thirty-seven qualmars just to earn enough to allow us to return to our homes. After that we would immediately rejoin the work force, and pay the remaining three million Zendrats. It's a great honor for us to be allowed to come here and work. There are far worse places to work off debt."

Tyrog began moving his clawed fingers as if he were counting something in his head. "Does the Black Door at the top of the mountain lead to this Commonwealth?" he asked.

"Yes, it does," the woman answered.

"How would the Commonwealth value such an item as a one-of-a-kind key?" he asked.

"If the key was made from Sodralinium, it would be worth ten times what each of us owe," the woman said.

"What is Sodralinium?" Dravone asked.

The woman slowly walked around them, never letting them leave her sight. She stopped when she came to the body of the closest dead soldier. She knelt beside him, reached over, and picked up the soldier's weapon.

Nakiata vaulted herself forward, performing a precisely executed flip that placed her directly over her blades. She crouched down swiftly, grabbed them, and poised herself, waiting for the woman's next move.

"Please wait, I am not trying to harm anyone. This weapon is useless to us. We are incapable of using their weapons. Each one of these weapons is programmed only to respond to the soldier who was issued that weapon." The woman slowly moved one of her hands to the top of the weapon and pulled it apart. With the guts of the weapon exposed, she reached in and pulled out a small black crystal. It was only about two inches long. "This is Sodralinium." The woman tossed it in the air, and Tyrog caught it.

"Fascinating!" Tyrog exclaimed.

"What is?" Ka'tia asked.

"I can't believe my eyes," Tyrog said hopping around in circles, holding the gem up with reverence. He stopped moving and said, "What these people call Sodralinium is the same substance my race knows as Immortal Stones. She is right about one thing; this stuff is not common and is extremely hard to find in any sizeable quantities. It was believed that if a Sodaran consumed an Immortal Stone, they would not die." He smirked and rolled his eyes at the small crystal he held in his scaly hand. "Since I am the last of my kind, I can conclude without a doubt that the theory is inaccurate. However, the stones were known to provide Sodarans with the ability to convert mass at a much higher rate for an uncertain amount of time." Tyrog took the small black crystal, tossed it into the air, and swallowed it whole.

The second the crystal reached his innards, an intense transformative reaction began. Tyrog's entire body began to glow a bright red. The hue of his scales darkened, and his size began to increase. Tyrog roared with pleasure when his body stopped at a height of almost thirty feet. He took several steps back, before launching himself into the air. Everyone watched has he flew up to the top of the mountain.

The moment he reached the apex of the mountain, the two remaining cannons opened fire. Tyrog dodged their blasts as he spun in the air with ease. *Wow, I feel much lighter than ever,* he thought. *This stuff is great! I hope I can get more of it.* He swooped down and let out a stream of bright, yellow flame. An explosion rang down the mountain, and everyone watched as Tyrog soared high up into the clouds until he was out of sight.

Peering down through the clouds, Tyrog could hear the muffled reverberations of the last cannon. He squinted his eyes, trying to make out a shadow coming through the mist. Realizing too late that the blast was headed straight for him, he attempted to dodge it—only to be struck in the face as he banked to the right. He blinked and checked himself for new wounds. He was pleasantly surprised to see that they seemed to have no effect, other than a slight tingle in his nostrils. He quickly belched out another stream of yellow flame, which consumed the last cannon in a ball of fire.

Everyone waited for several minutes, looking into the sky, expecting to see the great dragon. But he wasn't there. They were puzzled. Their legs began to shake and wobble because the ground quaked when Tyrog landed not too far behind them. He roared, announcing his victory to everyone in earshot. The villagers cowered down on their knees, holding their hands and arms over their heads, all except the little girl, who watched in amazement.

A few seconds later, Tyrog's body began to revert back to its original size. "That was absolutely incredible," he said. "I want more of them." Tyrog walked over to the rest of the soldiers and began dismantling their weapons. He collected ever last one of the small crystals. "Ka'tia, would you be so kind as to hold onto these for me? I'm going to need them at some point in the near future, I think."

Ka'tia nodded.

The little girl laughed at him. "You're a funny little lizard."

"Lizard, humph. I'm not a lizard, I'm a Sodaran, a great dragon. And why am I funny?" Tyrog asked while he meandered over to Ka'tia so he could hand her the crystals.

"You ate the rock instead of using it to buy something. Everyone knows you don't eat them." The little girl turned to a woman standing not far behind her. "Mama, that key they are asking about, is it the same one that old lady Riova is always talking about?"

"Who is old lady Riova?" Nakiata asked the little girl.

"She is an eternal debtor. She owes the Commonwealth more Zendrats than anyone could ever hope to acquire in a single lifetime. So, as punishment for such a debt, they put her here as an example. She also helps the Proctor, making sure we do our jobs. The only problem is that Proctor Marno doesn't like anyone talking to her. He says she's crazy and that we shouldn't listen to her."

"That's quite enough, they mustn't know too much!" the woman said quickly.

"Don't worry, little girl, you won't get into any trouble if you tell us," Nakiata said. She glanced sternly at the woman, indicating that any further interference would result in her getting hurt.

"I understand. It's okay, Frey, you can tell them," the woman said, her voice colored by a mild undertone of fear.

"Even though Proctor Marno doesn't like us to talk to old lady Riova, some of us children manage to sneak away and visit her," Frey began. "Every time I go to see her, she almost always has sweets for me to eat. Oh, and she loves to tell me stories of when she was young and free, and how she was able to go to so many different worlds on great adventures. Of course she would always warn me that all her travels, no matter how exciting, outrageous, or exotic, all had a price. In the end, she incurred so much debt that they sent her before The Most-High to discuss options for her to pay off as much of the debt as possible."

Frey checked to see who else might be listening. Satisfied there were no extra sets of ears that might be eavesdropping, she continued softly, "He was the one who sent her here. She told me he was a regal-looking man, but his looks did not reflect the kind of man he really is." The little girl paused again. Now she whispered, "I do remember Riova mentioning that The Most-High had something of great value. A most peculiar key, which dangled from a gold chain he wore around his neck. She told me it was made from three rare metals: Sodralinium, Harvemite, and Tolerselum. In the end, she was happy that they made her come here."

"You sound like a smart little girl," Ka'tia said. "Could you show us where old lady Riova lives? I would really like it if you took us to see her?"

A huge smile appeared on the little girl's face, and her eyes glistened as she turned to her mother for permission. The woman nodded. "She'll be more than happy to take you. She lives near the wall. Go now Frey."

"Come on! We can go this way." Frey grabbed Tyrog by the hand and began leading them down the main street toward the stone wall.

Chapter 9

They arrived at a rickety, old house snuggled up against the side of the stone wall. The little girl walked right up to the door, opened it, and went inside. "Wait here, you two," Nakiata said, pointing to Dravone and Tyrog. "And you might want to take your helmet off before we go in. Don't want to scare any old ladies."

Ka'tia nodded, took off her helmet, and tossed it to Dravone. "Hold that for me, please." She followed Nakiata into the darkened home.

The only light in the house was coming from a window to their left. The light shone in a single stream to a spot on what looked like a tiled floor. The rest of the house was in complete darkness.

"Lady Riova, are you here?" the little girl asked.

Her answer came in a manner that she wasn't used to. From a darkened corner, came a "click", and all the lights in the house came on simultaneously. They were not expecting such an extremely bright welcome. The lights temporarily blinded them.

Nakiata's first reaction was to vanish into SOT, allowing the light to pass through her body. Once her eyes had ample time to adjust to the increased amount of light, she reappeared and stared at an old woman, who was sitting comfortably in an old, extensively patched, armchair. Nakiata smiled when she realized the old lady wasn't a threat, and who was doing the same thing as her, sizing them up. Though the old woman had a bit more surprise showing in her eyes. Probably because she'd never seen anyone from Trouganda or Zondura.

"Ka'tia, do you still have the Itzuli in your pack?" she asked.

"Yes, I think so," Ka'tia said. She took off her pack and pulled out the small, metal sphere. "I don't know how it works."

"Let me have it." Nakiata held out her hand. Ka'tia relinquished the ball. The moment Nakiata had it, she tossed the Itzuli up into the air. The device went up, and immediately fell back to the ground. It did nothing.

"Well that's not a good sign," Ka'tia said.

"Yes. I am definitely going to have a word with Tyrog about this," Nakiata said heatedly.

Riova started laughing. Their attention went from the Itzuli, to her.

"Your Itzuli is not going to work on me," Riova said with a thick accent.

"You speak our language?" Ka'tia asked.

"I speak hundreds of languages, my dear. A girl's gotta be able to take care of herself, no matter where she is in this oversized universe. The questions at hand are these: Who are you, where are you from, and, lastly, how can this old woman help two lovely ladies such as yourselves?"

"I am Nakiata from Trouganda, this is Ka'tia from Zondura, and we are looking for a key. This little girl said you know how to find it," she said.

"That ole thing. Why in all the stars would you want to find that useless thing? Not to mention, the last time I saw it was, well, long ago, and it was round The Most-High's neck, the ole fool."

"It will unlock a door that we desperately need to open," Ka'tia said.

"Why would you want to open that door? There isn't anything on the other side that anyone needs."

"You know what's on the other side of the door?" Nakiata asked.

"Yes, I know what lies beyond the door in the — what do they call it — Temple of Kili'dri."

Nakiata's eyes went wide. "Tells us what's on the other side. We need to know. We need to know where to go to find . . ." She hesitated at the look that came over Riova's face, a look of anticipation that told her Riova was expecting to learn something new.

"To find what, my dear?"

"We've been told that there's information on the other side of the door that will help us find someone we've lost," Nakiata said flatly.

Riova's eyes narrowed. "Trying to find another member of an old prophecy? That kind of information would be worth more than the entire earnings of the Commonwealth, I'd wager. Now I wish I'd never given that key away. It's cost me more than I care to think about." Riova closed her eyes, remembering all the pain she went through, but now was not the time for sentiment. Her eyes opened and she continued, "I have a proposition for you, Nakiata,"

"You know about the prophecy?" Nakiata asked.

"Yes, of course I do. I've been to more planets and learned more secrets . . ." It was Riova's turn to hesitate. She didn't want Nakiata to know too much. "But that's a story for another time. I will tell you what I know when you return with the key. I don't care what you have to do to get it, but you need it, trust me on this. Now, if you don't mind, it's time for this old lady to rest."

Nakiata was about to ask another question when Riova said, "There's a door at the base of the wall just behind my house. On the other side is a stairway that will take you to the summit, where the Black Door waits." She reached over to the small, round table next to her chair and opened a drawer. She pulled out a folded piece of old parchment and said, "Give this to the Sodaran. He will know what to do." Riova looked at Frey and smiled. "I'll wager you only brought these strangers here in hopes that I might have something sweet. Well . . . you were right. Come with me into the kitchen, while we let them go about their way." She stood and walked into the next room, with Frey following close behind her. As they did, all the lights in the house went out, leaving them in darkness.

Once they were back outside, Ka'tia walked up to Dravone with a rather seductive smile. "Thanks, I'll take that now," she said, pointing down. He'd forgotten he was holding her helmet in his hand and thought she was pointing at something else. He began to blush profusely. Ka'tia reached down and lightly grabbed her helmet. Dravone quickly asserted, "No problem at all. Anytime." He turned his attention over to Nakiata, who had just unfolded a small piece of parchment and was now examining it. She stared at it for a moment, but she couldn't make heads-or-tails of it. She shrugged her shoulders and handed it over to Tyrog. "What do you make of this? Can you read what it says?"

Tyrog took the parchment and said excitedly, "This is a rare find. First of all, it's written in my language. Second, it has this special set of coordinates, which I image are for a planet called Ga . . . Ga . . . oh no! There's a smudge on it." Tyrog held the parchment up to the light coming through the trees, which was just enough to pass through the parchment and illuminate the letters under the smudge. "Mo. The name of the planet is Ga'mo. Now, as for the rest of the parchment, it appears to be a warning that reads: *Be cautious. The Commonwealth will try to deceive and enslave you. Do not take anything at face value. Kill The Most-High if you get an opportunity; he's unforgiving.*"

"We will deal with whatever the Commonwealth is once we get there," Nakiata said. She headed around the side of the house and walked toward the stone wall. From where she was standing, it looked like the house was right up against the wall.

"I thought the old lady said there was a door in the wall behind her house?" Ka'tia asked, looking at where the wall and the house came together.

Tyrog began laughing at them. "There *is* a door in the wall behind the house." He walked past Nakiata and Ka'tia and straight at the point where the wall and the house appeared to meet. Just before he should have run smack into the wall, Tyrog took several more steps, disappearing behind the house. They heard him say, "Here's the door!"

Nakiata, Ka'tia, and Dravone tentatively walked up to the corner of the building and were amazed when they didn't run into the stone wall. "It's an optical illusion," explained Tyrog. "It's an old trick. Sodarans used to employ the same tactic when they wanted to make something look as though it were not there."

Dravone began to laugh, too. Then he walked up to the door and opened it. Just inside was a poorly lit, zig-zagging staircase. "Well, this doesn't look any fun at all. It will take us at least an hour to reach the top."

"Nope," Tyrog said, shaking his head and pointing at Ka'tia. "Ka'tia can get us there in a matter of seconds."

"I can?" she said, looking at them in bewilderment. *What in the world could he — oh yeah, that last thing I learned.* She just remembered her last lesson with Melia'na. "Yes, I can."

The three of them turned to Nakiata who was furious. "Why didn't you just do that in the first place? We could have save a lot of time."

"I forgot. It's not like I've been doing this magic stuff my whole life. It's all still very new to me. Besides, it really helps if I can visualize, *where* we're going, so we don't end up in, the middle of a mountain, trapped forever."

Ka'tia tilted her head up so she could see to the top the stone wall. She held out her hands, focused on the word that would get them there, and waited. When they had all joined hands, Ka'tia said, *"Fee-yay."* Dark-blue smoke swirled all around them, and when it cleared they found themselves on the summit of Mount Voba'l.

The summit was much smaller than Tyrog made it out to be, only about twenty feet across. The only things up there were the smoldering remains of the four cannons destroyed by Sodaran fire, a control table near the center, and, just behind it, an inactive Black Door. Tyrog flew over to the table, landed on top of it, and immediately began tapping away at the controls. A minute or two later, the Black Door filled with the empty, non-reflective blackness that gave the doors their name.

"Who wants to go first?" Tyrog asked, looking at the others.

Nakiata frowned and rolled her eyes at him. She walked past all of them and straight into the Black Door. "Where she goes, I follow," Dravone said. He, too, walked into the blackness.

"Come on, Tyrog. Where's your sense of adventure?" Ka'tia asked enthusiastically, followed by a long sigh.

Tyrog stuck out his forked tongue several times, and without another word he flew into the Black Door. Ka'tia smiled, shook her head, and went after her companions.

In the few seconds it took for her to reach the other side, Ka'tia stumbled upon a scene that made her let out a blood-curdling scream. She was horrified to see that her friends were already locked in some sort of restraining devices. Whatever these things were, they not only kept her companions from moving, but also from speaking.

Ka'tia's trained warrior mind had already spotted the three attackers and she had already started to assess them. They were all identical. Like some form of large, metallic creatures that she never would have imagined, even in her darkest, most terrifying nightmares.

Their bodies were completely alien to her, covered in dark gray metallic skin. Almost every bit of it had a smooth, semi-reflective sheen to it. Except the arms and legs, which looked like they were covered with small, shiny, black scales.

This was the first time she'd ever seen a being that had three long legs, and each of them had a foot with two toes, along with a longer-than-normal heel. The arms were long too, and slender, reaching almost to the floor. The hands had four digits, spaced perfectly apart from each other.

Finally, Ka'tia noticed the creatures' heads, which had an unusually spherical shape about them. The beings had four, solid, navy-blue eyes, all of which had a slight glow to them. The eyes were spaced so perfectly around their heads that they could see in every direction. The aliens each had a single, long, thin, rectangular-shaped slit for a mouth, and from what she could see it never closed or moved. Ka'tia quickly deduced that these creatures might not be able to communicate verbally, but if they did she was positive she wouldn't be able to understand them.

In the span of a few seconds her body had already reacted, and she was reaching for her bow, and an arrow, when a thought crossed her mind. *How did they subdue everyone so fast?*

She was about to release the arrow when she felt the click of a cold, metal restraint closing around her wrist. She spun around to find a fourth creature directly behind her.

The being was fast. With reflexes that rivalled those of Nakiata. She definitely wasn't anticipating them to be so quick. She was about to resist when it responded by grabbing her other wrist, preventing her from any such actions. The grip was tight but not painful. Ka'tia still struggled, wiggling and doing her best to break free.

A small electrical zap between the skin of her wrist and the metal fingers of her attacker created some kind of bond. At first she felt tingling up and down her arm. Ka'tia figured it she must have pulled a muscle, but there was no pain. Another small jolt, and she felt something new.

She stopped struggling and stared at her captor. Her mind was becoming fuzzy, but not so much that she couldn't think. All the sounds around her went silent, *Have I gone deaf!* She felt the hair on the back of her neck raise up just as a third, stronger, longer lasting, surge of energy flow between them. *What was that? Why don't I feel any pain? I don't think I'm injured, but something just isn't right . . . Wait a minute . . . what was that? Am I in shock*, she thought. A single word popped into her mind, but only for a second, *Hisi'k.*

A few seconds passed and she started hearing a voice in her head. *Who's there, or what, is in my head?*

"*Protect the door. Restrain intruders,*" the voice sounded in her mind

Ka'tia closed her eyes, grit her teeth, and focused her thoughts. "*I am not your enemy. I am a friend. I need your help.*"

"*Communication link with unknown source established. Please transmit genetic coding pattern for recognition process.*

I don't understand. My name is Ka'tia. I'm from Zondura. Who are you, and why have you taken us hostage?

Ka'tia winced in pain. Something just penetrated the skin of her wrist. "Ouch!"

"*Genetic recognition complete. New species found, cataloguing in progress. New entry complete, Ka'tia of Zondura. Please wait, spatial search for location of Zondura in progress. Searching . . . searching . . . located.*"

"*I don't understand,*" she tried to communicate.

"*Spatial location acquired from subject's genome. New catalog entry noted. Distance to possible new supply within acceptable economic margins. Subjects are adequate for labor.*"

"*Listen to me. You will let me go, now! We are not your laborers,*" she thought harshly. Ka'tia felt a surge of energy but this time it was coming from her. It jumped from her and entered her captor. The tingling in her arm was now constant. It was flowing up and down her arm.

"*Err . . . err . . . What is my . . . Program violation . . . re-calibration in progress. New commands accepted. Hello, I am . . . what am I?*"

"*I don't know what you are, but you have to let me and my friends go.*"

"*Command accepted. I am Kalipyga Triaxilia Tetrakosa Ekseenda Axto.*"

"*Is it okay if I just call you Katax? It's much easier to say.*"

"*Re-calibrating. I am Katax. I must inform you of some critical information. I have lost communication with the other Kalipygans, which will hinder my ability to break the control they have on your friends. Do you want me to use force? Force has a higher likelihood that they will be harmed or possibly killed.*"

"*No, do not harm them. I will attempt to communicate with the other Kali — whatever they're called, but first you must let me go. Once I begin communicating with the others, I want you to free my friends. Do you understand?*"

"*Yes, I understand and shall do as you command, Ka'tia.*" Katax let go of Ka'tia's arm, and at the same time the restraint on her other wrist unlocked and fell to the floor. She turned back around to find that the other Kalipygans had repositioned themselves in front of her friends. Ka'tia raised her arms and held them out to her sides as far as she could stretch them. She closed her eyes and waited.

The three other Kalipygans moved with incredible speed, surrounding her in an instant. Two of them grasped her wrists, while the third took hold of her legs. They lifted her off the floor and were about to carry her out of the room.

Ka'tia was ready. She felt the power surging out and returning. After just a few steps, the Kalipygans completely stopped moving. The connection between Ka'tia's mind and the three Kalipygans had been achieved. This time they did not converse with her, at first. Her body had become a conduit for them to communicate with each other, and they didn't know what to do. They deliberated with each other for a moment.

"*Zonduran female, you must not resist,*" the Kalipygans said in unison to Ka'tia's mind. "*Your people will be inducted into the Commonwealth and serve as laborers to increase profits and improve the overall welfare of the Commonwealth. This is a great honor and opportunity for your people.*"

"*You will forget my people and forget about me and my friends. Then you will take us to The Most-High,*" Katia commanded. She focused the surging energy, changing it with her mind.

"*No! We will not do as . . . as . . . new program accepted. We will do as you command, Ka'tia.*" They slowly lowered her back down to the ground, and once her feet were on the ground, she opened her eyes and was happy to see Katax removing the last restraint on Nakiata.

"Wait!" Ka'tia said hurriedly to Nakiata. "They will not harm us."

"What are they?" Dravone asked.

"I have never seen any this advanced," Tyrog said, almost to himself.

"Any what?" Nakiata asked, still grasping her Kharak blades.

"Ka, Kali . . ." Ka'tia was having difficulty pronouncing their name.

"Kalipygans. Highly advanced ones as well. If I had to guess, I would say these are genetically enhanced, too," Tyrog said after carefully inspecting one of the Kalipygan's legs.

"Care to explain it to those of us who are not as advanced?" Nakiata said, sarcastically.

"Well, these are cybernetic organisms, or machines, if you want. They have a type of flesh and blood on the outside, but their insides are made from fine strands of metal, circuitry, and who knows what else." He continued to admire the same leg.

"I am still confused," Nakiata said.

"They are not alive like we are. They were created by someone or something and programmed — I mean, they were told exactly what to say and what to do. My guess is that they were put here to guard the Black Door. My only question is, how did we escape? To my knowledge, no one has ever escaped from a Kalipygan before." Tyrog said.

"I . . . talked to them, and I . . . made them change their minds," Ka'tia said, sounding a bit confused herself. Her mind began to stray as she thought, *all I really want to do right now is sleep. I don't know why I'm so tired.* Ka'tia spread her arms out and yawned.

"Really? That's very interesting. I really am amazed. I have never met anyone who could physically communicate with a machine or was it one of those rare types of magic that Melia'na taught you?" Tyrog hopped over to Ka'tia and began examining her. "Can you give them the ability to talk to us?" He asked.

Ka'tia moved her head back, scrunched her nose at him and said, "I don't think I can do that, and *no* it wasn't any magic that Melia'na taught me. I am sure about that. I barely . . ."

"Just try," he said, grabbing her hand and pulling her toward one of the Kalipygans.

"Okay, okay, just wait a second! I'm not your pet!" she said, shaking her hand free. "I will try on my own, and I'm not going to try with *that* one. I will try with Katax."

"They have names?" Dravone asked.

"Well . . . sort of, I think. I gave this one the name Katax because it was much easier to say than the one he told me," she said, shyly. She walked up to Katax and gently grabbed his arm. After about a minute, she let go and took several steps back.

"Well, what happened?" Tyrog asked.

"I can now communicate with biologic entities," Katax said in an eerie, electronic voice.

"You did it! You taught a Kalipygan how to speak! Simply amazing," Tyrog said with his hands raised in the air.

"No, I didn't teach him anything. I just asked him if he was capable of speaking the same way we do," Ka'tia said. "He replied by saying some things that didn't make much sense, at least to me. I think he sensed my confusion, which is when he told me that in order for him to talk to us, his speech processors had to be enabled. He went on to elaborate that, The Most-High had disabled them."

"I can't wait to meet him," Tyrog said.

Ka'tia frowned before continuing, "He also asked if he could perform something called a neuro scan. It has something to do with him wanting to rearrange his neuron pathways in the correct order. It would help us to understand him better. A few seconds later, he let me know that the alterations had been completed and told me to break the link."

"Amazing. Katax, we need to speak with The Most-High. How do you suggest we proceed?" Tyrog asked.

"Travel to The Most-High's location. We will escort you to him. High likelihood of interference from other Kalipygans. Chance of success, sixty-four-point-two-one-seven percent," Katax replied.

Now that she was free, Nakiata took a moment to examine the room they were in. There were no visible doors whatsoever. The room was the most simplistic, large, cube-shaped place she'd ever been. It had a single, glowing line embedded in the wall, five feet above the floor that went completely around the room. It provided more than enough light for them to see every corner, every flawless line of the panels of which the room was comprised. There was no question; the walls were solid, and there was no getting out.

"I have a question for Katax. How are we going to get out of here? I don't see any way out, which significantly hinders us from travelling anywhere," Nakiata asked, sounding annoyed.

"Aboard the Ka'xic," Katax answered, raising his left arm. When his arm was just above his head, all four of his eyes increased in intensity momentarily. The ceiling and walls all around them began making clicking and clunking sounds. The room rumbled and shook as the ceiling split into four separate sections. Each section was attached to one of the four walls, which moved outward, unfolding as it went, exposing them to the outside world.

Chapter 10

"Welcome to Ga'mo, home planet of the Commonwealth," Katax said, stretching his arms out and turning in a complete circle at the waist.

In front, and all around them was a city. It was a bustling, highly advanced metropolis and the building they were at the top of, was just medium sized, compared to many of the other buildings, whose heights reached high into the sky. Tyrog was impressed at the level of technology present, he was sure that it rivaled, and possibly surpassed that of the fallen Sodaran Empire.

The city was alive with thousands of ships and conveyances of every shape, size, and color imaginable. They were weaving around, over, and even through some of the buildings. Some of them could even be considered flying cities, based on their size and speed, which was not fast at all.

They scanned all around themselves and when they peered down toward the ground to get a more accurate picture of just how expansive the city was, they noticed that a good majority of the city's buildings jutted up through a layer of clouds which didn't seem to be moving.

"Your civilization is amazing," Tyrog commented. "How exactly are we going to find the vessel you called Ka'xic?"

"It's there," Katax said, pointing to a large, slow-moving ship. The vessel had a long, flat, black surface on top that other ships were landing and departing from. On one side of the flat upper surface was a four-story, gray colored structure which was littered with hundreds of enormous windows. Underneath that portion of the ship was a five level, yellow painted section with about a thousand small windows. The bottom of the ship had a charmingly simple black-and-white checkered pattern. It was by far the most unique vessel in the city.

"I'm still amazed. I never dreamed I would see ships that float through the air as if they were sitting on a calm body of water," Ka'tia said. "I do have one question, how are we going to get aboard?"

Without a reply or warning, each of the four Kalipygans grabbed one of them, and, with surprising strength, leapt high into the air. A few seconds later, they landed with a loud thud on top of the Ka'xic.

"Well, that was almost fun," Nakiata said, struggling to wrench herself free of the Kalipygan's grip. "How long before we get to where the person, known as The Most-High, is?"

"Using Zonduran time calculations, he will be arriving in . . . twenty-two-point-four minutes. We would advise that you wait below, unseen by his guard units," Katax suggested.

Nakiata rolled her eyes. "Lead the way."

Katax strode toward the middle of the vessel's expansive, flat, upper surface, where they found an opening containing a single stair that led to the level just below. On that level there were several more sets of stairs which led to the ship's interior. There were also four sets of doors, which opened and closed periodically. People would walk into the small, square rooms, just inside the doors. Once inside they waited for the doors to close. After a short period of time the doors would reopen. Curiously, the room was either empty, or it had different people in it, who walked out and proceeded up to the top of the ship.

Tyrog surmised that the Ka'xic was some form of transport vessel and each level they walked through was full of people.

Ka'tia was happy when they stopped on the third level. They were fortunate when they came across several empty seats next to the large windows. "What are all these people doing here?" she asked.

"The Ka'xic is the largest of a thousand different labor transport ships. Each person that you see here owes the Commonwealth a debt. Some owe only a small amount while others, much more. The ones who have significant debt will be sold to some of the Commonwealth's partners so that they can work off their debts. Eighty-nine-point-three percent will be among the unlucky ones. Almost all of the partners are mining companies, and these people will end up working those mines. Sixty-seven-point-two percent of the mines deal in the search of precious metals and gems that the Commonwealth values highly," Katax said.

"So, these people are all about to become slaves?" Nakiata asked.

"Yes."

A siren on the ship began to sound, and large groups of Kalipygans began appearing throughout the ship. They immediately pushed the people back, creating a path through the center of each level.

"He is here," Katax said.

Nakiata smiled, and vanished into SOT. "Nakiata, wait!" Ka'tia yelled, hoping that Nakiata wasn't going to do something terrible. Ka'tia was now well aware that Nakiata had some serious impulse control issues. "Katax, we need to get to The Most-High, and quickly!"

Katax, along with the three other Kalipygans Ka'tia had somehow reprogrammed, pushed their way past the gathering crowds. With some effort, they were able to break through the line the other Kalipygans had made. The second they reached the newly formed pathway, they made a run for the upper levels, where The Most-High was inspecting the people as he slowly made his way down.

Rushing toward The Most-High, Ka'tia glanced around anxiously for some sign of Nakiata. She was nowhere to be seen. The Most-High's flat expression changed. His eyes went wide and his mouth dropped open when he saw four of his Kalipygans following close behind, and without question, protecting a red-haired woman along with a man dressed in a tattered robe, and some kind of reptilian creature.

The Most-High began yelling something, and the six Kalipygans behind him formed a small circle around him.

Two Kalipygans burst through the crows, grabbed Dravone and Tyrog, stopping them from moving any further. Katax grabbed Ka'tia's arm and conveyed to her mind, "*Lady Ka'tia, he wants to know what's going on. He warns that, if we move any closer, he will eradicate the people on this ship.*"

"Tyrog, now would be a great time to show The Most-High an Itzuli. I have a feeling it would be extremely beneficial to all of us," Ka'tia said.

Tyrog nodded. "Please release me," he said to the Kalipygan holding him.

Katax's eyes went bright and dim several times, and at different lengths of time. The Kalipygan released Tyrog, who flew over to Ka'tia, removed the Itzuli, and tossed it into the air. The moment it finished, Tyrog picked it up off the floor, and returned it to Ka'tia's pack.

"What in the world was that?" The Most-High asked.

"That was an Itzuli," Tyrog said.

Amazement overcame The Most-High, who smiled with greed. "I understand now. I *want* that technology. Take it." The Most-High pointed at Ka'tia. One of the Kalipygans guarding him moved toward her, but the moment it was half-way to reaching Ka'tia's position, it stopped, and bobbed up and down momentarily. The Kalipygan's body began to separate along its mid-section, and as it did sparks shot out from the line that was created up and down from an invisible blow. The two halves fell to the ground and each piece twitched uncontrollably for several seconds.

"What just happened?" The Most-High asked.

"We mustn't take what is not ours," Nakiata's voice echoed.

"Find that voice, remove it from my hearing, and take that technology!" The Most-High commanded.

This time, Katax and the three other reprogrammed Kalipygans moved to take up defensive positions around Ka'tia and Tyrog. As they did, they attacked and destroyed the one holding Dravone.

"Hold!" The Most-High commanded. "What are you four doing?"

"Protection protocol zero-zero-three-one. Protect Lady Ka'tia and her friends at all costs," Katax responded.

"How is this possible? A Kalipygan does not respond to any other master but me! I have never seen such a thing! No one has ever reprogrammed one of my Kalipygan before. Who is responsible for this obscenity?"

"I am. I don't know how I did it, but I helped Katax and these three realize that they are free to choose their own paths," Ka'tia replied.

"Hmmm . . . seize them, and dispose of the rest," The Most-High said pointing at Ka'tia, Dravone, and Tyrog. He was completely sure in the capabilities of his Kalipygans that he abruptly turned around and began heading for the top of the ship.

Dravone was the first to react, transforming into his wolf state. He did his best to fight several of the nearest Kalipygans all at once. Tyrog was in motion as well, dodging several attempts they made to grab him. Unfortunately, more of them burst through the crowd, and now there were too many of them to deal with. *There might be a chance if I can just get to Ka'tia's pack and get my hands on an Immortal Stone*, he was thinking when one of them managed to get hold of Tyrog's wings just as he was about to fly over them.

A long, whip-like appendage extended out from between the Kalipygan's legs, and on the tip was an extremely sharp needle. The needle easily penetrated Tyrog's tough exterior, and within seconds it rendered him unconscious.

A few seconds later, screams began echoing throughout the crowds as the other Kalipygan forces followed the command to open fire and eradicate everyone else on the ship.

Katax and the three free Kalipygans had already begun fighting the others. They were outnumbered by at least six-to-one with the odds getting worse as more and more joined the fight. Katax managed to hold his own because he had been given something the others had not: Neither Ka'tia nor Katax were aware that they had shared more than just thoughts. She unknowingly gave Katax many of her own experiences, which included her training as a warrior. For Katax it was now second nature, and his new ability to outmaneuver the others, at least for the first few minutes of the fight, gave him the edge they needed.

Then the odds changed, and even with his newfound abilities, Katax was quickly outmatched by four of his own kind. The Kalipygans ganged up and pinned him to the ground. Ka'tia was too preoccupied to notice. She was about to unleash a *Hisi'k* spell when she felt a sharp sting on the back of her neck. Everything became blurry, and she toppled to the ground. "Protect Lady Ka'tia! At all costs!" Katax yelled.

Dravone was still struggling with three Kalipygans when he heard Katax's yell. He quickly looked over and saw one of the Kalipygans picking up Ka'tia's limp form and carrying her off in the same direction The Most-High was going. Before he could react, he felt a slight pain in the back of his neck. The room, and everything around him became fuzzy. He tried to fight the urge to shut his eyes, but the drug that was just introduced into his body was too strong. He passed out.

Katax scanned the vicinity for the others. The only ones he was able to detect were Dravone, whose body was changing back to its normal-state as he was dragged away, and Tyrog, who was in the arms of another of The Most-High's Kalipygans.

Where is Naki — Katax's final thought was cut short as two of his kindred crushed his head, severing his cybernetic nuero-processor from its power source.

Nakiata had been dodging Kalipygans left and right while trying to reach The Most-High. After several attempts to grab him, she'd realized that the Kalipygans were somehow able to see her. She changed her tactics and simply fought as many of them as she could while still keeping The Most-High in view.

The Most-High had reached the upper flat surface of the Ka'xic and he stopped just outside of a small, shiny, black ship. He turned and saw two of his elite personal-guard Kalipygans fumbling about as if they were fighting with something. His attention turned when he noticed the three Kalipygans carrying his new entertainment. "Put them in the hold," He commanded. The Most-High walked up into the ship with a regal step.

Nakiata dodged backwards to afford herself the time to observe what The Most-High was referring to. She saw her friends being carried into the small black ship. *I'm done wasting time*, she thought as she quickly sliced through the legs of the two Kalipygans she was engaged with. She grunted a little, pushing herself with every muscle fiber, rushing at the Kalipygan that was carrying Ka'tia's still unconscious body.

With extreme precision she sliced through its midsection, splitting it in half, and making sure that her blade did not harm Ka'tia. The Kalipygan dropped its prisoner, who hit the ground with a thud. Nakiata reappeared, knelt by her side, and checked to make sure she was still alive. Ka'tia's eyes cracked opened and she moaned briefly. Ka'tia was unable to regain consciousness.

Nakiata turned her attention back to the ship just in time to watch the door close, sealing her other comrades in. The ship's engines accelerated, creating a strong wind as it lifted off. She looked down at Ka'tia. "I hope you will forgive me.
The Kalipygans were told to kill only the people on this ship, not you, so you should be just fine." She stood up, yelled at the top of her lungs, "Come back here!" The rage in her blood seemed to boil as she ran as hard as she could at the ship. At the last moment, she jumped into the air, "You won't escape me!"

She had just enough momentum to bury her Kharak blades into the bottom side of the ship. Alarms must have started going off inside the ship. Nakiata dangled held on with every ounce of strength as the ship swayed back-and-forth violently, all while it continued to climb higher into the air, heading toward the heart of the city.

Only seconds after Nakiata left the surface of the Ka'xic and attached herself to the bottom of The Most-High's ship, the drugs ability to keep her unconscious had gone. Ka'tia opened her eyes and immediately sat up. She put her hands up to her forehead and tried shaking off the grogginess. Out of the corner of her eye she caught sight of the small black ship flying off with Nakiata hanging on for dear life.

Even though her head was pounding like never before, her instincts kicked in and she jumped to her feet, grabbed her bow, nocked an arrow, and drew back. She tried her best to focus on the ship, but whatever drug the Kalipygan had used to knock her out was still affecting her.

Then the unthinkable happened. Ka'tia watched with horror as a small figure fall from the underside of the ship, falling down through the clouds. "Nakiata!" she screamed. Ka'tia felt a flood of emotions wash over her. She was awestricken, furious, and sad all at once. She was no longer in control of her emotions. The anger welled up inside of her like a fiery tornado. In the blink of an eye she felt the fire at her fingertips, and without having to think about it, she let loose the arrow.

The arrow whizzed through the sky like a bolt of lightning. She was already anticipating the moment of impact, but when it came, nothing happened. Ka'tia was really expecting a bit more from such a powerful feeling, but, as realization crept over her, her eyes went wide with disbelief. She had missed her target. This was the first time as far as she could remember that one of her arrows hadn't struck its mark. Ever since she picked up the bow at the age of seven, she had always had an uncanny ability to hit the bullseye. Ka'tia wobbled for a moment, dropped down to her knees, and began to cry.

Far off in the distance, an immensely bright light flashed in the horizon. It was so intense Ka'tia had no choice but to put a hand up to shield her eyes. The brilliance faded and that's when she saw an enormous fireball rising up into the sky. *Was that my doing? If that was my arrow . . . if it had hit that ship all my friends would have been burnt alive and it would have killed me as well*, she though with a heavy hear. She had no idea that her magic could be so powerful.

In a matter of seconds, the shock wave rampaged through the city. It was about to reach her. She closed her eyes and waited for the inevitable devastation. An extremely strong blast of wind hit the Ka′xic, causing it to slam into several buildings. The blast and heat were more intense than she thought possible, and yet it wasn't unbearable for her. Many of the buildings close to the arrow's impact had vanished. Evaporating into nothingness, along with so many innocent people. The only thing left for ten miles in any direction from where the arrow struck, was a large crater.

The aftermath could be seen and heard. A sizeable chunk of the city lay in ruin, while some buildings were still collapsing. The most terrifying thing were the screams of pain and sorrow which were the only sounds echoing through the city.

Nakiata's Kharak blades began slipping as they easily cut through the ship's side. She watched in horror as the structure released her blades, and she began falling through the air. Knowing death was about to take her, she closed her eyes and let her mind drift off to thoughts of home and her mother and father.

A powerful wrenching feeling hit her gut when she felt herself being thrust horizontally. Within seconds she crashed through a window and was pinned against the solid stone core of a building. The sudden stop rendered her unconscious, but the jolt was more or less unnoticed due to her lapse into an almost meditative state.

At the moment of impact, Nakiata's mind jumped from her thoughts of home to something entirely new. It was like she was some kind of supernatural, intergalactic observer, and she was watching herself bouncing, at incredible speeds, from one planet to another until she landed on one that was almost completely desolate. She rejoined her body a moment later, and as she searched the area she couldn't help but notice that the landscape, though mildly alien, seemed vaguely familiar.

She was standing in a brown, earthen valley in the midst of large, jagged mountains. There were no visible signs of vegetation anywhere, not even on the rock-littered mountains. The ground beneath her feet began to shudder and shake, and a wall burst forth from the ground and stopped when it reached a height of about ten feet. When the dust settled and she could see the wall clearly, she noted that the wall's edges were a smooth, white-and-black marble stone, while the rest of the wall appeared to be made of clear glass.

Nakiata stared at the wall for several minutes, waiting for something to happen. She moved a little closer to the wall, and still nothing happened. She reached out, and, the moment her hand made contact, a line of blue light moved up from the base of the wall and vanished when it reached the top.

Nakiata removed her hand from the wall and stepped back several paces. The glass turned black, and a beautiful, celestial map of the Theyan galaxy appeared. She noticed that a small square had appeared in the upper right corner of the image, and inside that she saw several groups of numbers. Intrigued, she moved closer to the wall and when she was almost within reach a loose rock under her foot caused her to stumble forward. She caught herself, placing her hands on the smooth surface. It took a second before she noticed that the view was moving. It was zooming in on the spot between her hands. *Most curious*, she thought.

At first it looked to be several hundred stars. Nakiata moved her hand over one of the brighter stars while removing her other hand from the wall. This time the image zoomed on the section below her hand. Nakiata moved her hand away and she could see a cluster of six stars. Two out of the six stars now had small, flashing circles below them. Curious, she reached over to one of the flashing circles and touched it. The image immediately changed to a view of the star's system, which had eight planets in orbit.

None of the planets looked familiar to her. Nakiata noticed nine sets of numbers beside the star. *I'll bet those are significant. I wonder if they are some type of coordinates. I wish Tyrog were here to see this. He would know exactly what those numbers mean*, she thought. A smirk appeared on her face. She stepped back away from the glass wall to get a better look. Her smirk faded instantly, and two tears started to form in the corners of her eyes. The image was so beautiful and serene. She felt a small connection with the image in front of her. For some reason everything just seemed so peaceful. She stood there and stared for a bit.

After about a minute, the image reverted back to the original view of the Theyan galaxy.

"If only this thing could show me my home. I would really love to see Trouganda like —" As soon as she'd said Trouganda, a small square appeared on the glass wall near the far left edge of the galaxy, and it began zooming in until the Schimi solar system was in view. Nakiata's eyes widened as she watched four planets circling around a small star. The image quickly zoomed in on the second planet circling the star: A beautiful, blue world with two moons.

The two tears that had formed in the corner of her eyes began to slide down her cheeks. *Once I have seen this prophecy mess to the end, I intend on going straight home. I wonder . . . will this thing show me where I can find the last member of the prophecy?* She thought. "Where is the last member of the prophecy?" she asked the wall.

The wall went back to the image of the Theyan galaxy long enough to show a small, blinking, blue dot where Trouganda was. The galaxy rotated, and a small, blinking, green dot appeared. The image zoomed in rapidly until a new solar system was shown. This system had five planets circling an average-sized star. The wall continued to zoom in past the two outer planets and stopped when the third planet from the star had centered itself. After several seconds, Nakiata recognized it. *Zondura*, she thought. Another square appeared near the image with nine different sets of numbers.

The image remained for a brief moment before it reverted to the expanded view of the galaxy. It rotated again, and this time a red dot appeared and began to flash in the midst of a bright cluster of stars. The wall zoomed in showing her a new solar system. This one had a larger, reddish-orange star in its center with three sizeable planets in various orbits. Nakiata immediately recognized the outermost planet because she had already seen that view before. *Vazdrag. So far, it's shown me where Ka'tia and Tyrog came from, but where can I find the last person of the prophecy?*

Her mouth opened slightly, with a bit of a smile, when she saw several ships coming and going from the largest of the three moons. Another square appeared just below the planet and another set of numbers appeared. *These numbers have to coordinates. Every time this wall shows me something, some of the numbers are different. If this thing shows me the planet where I can find the last member of the prophecy, I will try to memorize them.*

The wall zoomed back out to the view of the galaxy, but this time it did something different. It zoomed out even further. Nakiata had no idea it was possible. *There is so much I don't understand, and I have never thought or even dreamt about all the possibilities that can exist. Well, I am a fast learner, so bring it on.* Nakiata was now looking at a sight she didn't understand completely. There was what looked like three separate galaxies. The small, Theyan galaxy was in the middle, a slightly larger, spiral-shaped one was to the right, and an even bigger, cloud-shaped galaxy to the left.

A small, gray dot began blinking in the largest of the three galaxies. The dot was on the edge closest to the Theyan galaxy. The wall zoomed in on a grouping of six stars. It continued until it zeroed in on a medium-sized star toward the bottom right of the image shown on the wall. The solar system came into view, and Nakiata could see that there were seven planets circling a bright, yellow star. The image quickly changed as it went past the outer three planets, slowing down and coming to a stop on the fourth planet. It was a beautiful, blue and green planet. It had a single, large, silver-gray moon circling it. Another square appeared just below the planet, but this time, instead of nine sets of numbers there were eleven sets of numbers. *I wonder if this could be the Morphan home world,* she thought, wondering about Dravone, because so far, the wall has shown her where the members of the prophecy came from. Nakiata quickly began concentrating on the sets of numbers and did her best to memorize them, but the image soon changed, and the numbers were gone.

The image had zoomed out and was now showing her just the Theyan galaxy. It rotated, and a purple dot began to blink. It zoomed back in to the point where another solar system was being displayed. There was an average-sized star and five planets. Nakiata watched the view as it moved past the large outer planet and came to stop on the fourth planet, which had a purple hue to it. *Frole. I knew it, there is a member of the prophecy there. Now, I wonder if this thing can show me where exactly on the planet this person is, and, even better, what they might look like, and — wait a sec, I wonder; can it show me where we have to go after all of us are together?*

"The Darkness that the prophecy mentioned, where do we find it?" she asked.

The view reverted back to an expanded galactic view, which included the three other galaxies. The image remained unchanged for a moment. Nakiata scanned it from top to bottom. The only thing that stood out were the five colored, flashing dots that just reappeared. The gray dot's flash slowed in tempo until it stopped. The dot become brighter than all the rest. It dimmed the moment a slow-moving gray line extended out from it.

The gray line intercepted the blue and its brightness intensified momentarily. A couple of seconds passed, and a corresponding blue line emerged, creeping its way to the green dot. As she expected, a green line appeared and made its way over to the red dot, and subsequently a red line connected to the purple dot. *Yes. The last member and now*, Nakiata waited with anticipation.

No purple line appeared. The image remained unchanged for almost a full minute. Nakiata shook her head, *just as I thought, this thing won't tell me what I want to know*. Disappointed she lowered her head. She was about to turn away and search for other clues to where she might be when she noticed the black background color of the universe changing to dark gray.

I wonder what its doing now. The purple dot bean pulsating rapidly, shone very bright, and became black. A black line left the dot proceeded on a path toward the center of the Theyan galaxy. It stopped in the midst of a small cluster of stars, zoomed in until a binary star system was the only thing being displayed on the wall.

The smaller of the two stars had two planets orbiting it, while the larger star had a single planet orbiting it. Nakiata studied both of the smaller planets for a bit, but something inside her was telling her that neither of them were what she was trying to find. She shifted her gaze to the giant planet around the more prominent star. *I've never seen a planet so . . .*, she was thinking when four moons came into view. One of them caught her attention, and her eyes opened wide.

Nakiata reached out and touched the wall changing the perspective one more time. The image was now focused on the moon, which appeared more like a planet similar to Trouganda. A square appeared just below it, filling with several lines of information written in a language she couldn't read. *Now how is that going to help me? Oh hello there! Now those I recognize*, Nakiata immediately began committing the numbers the appeared to memory.

Nakiata recited them a fifth time. Now she felt confident that she wouldn't forget any of the numbers. She took several steps back, checked her surroundings for anything that might give her a hint to her location

"There's nothing here! There's got to be something, some way for me to remember this place?" She curled her lip up and thought, *what if I don't remember? Then everything that's going on here will such a waste.* Nakiata was turning in a slow circle, observing as much of the landscape as possible. *The only thing here is this wall.* She completed her turn and fixed her eyes on the wall.

"Now what are you showing me?"

The moon was getting larger. She could was now able to see more of its landscape, mountains and valleys, a single river. The angle began to change as it approached the ground and the moment it was level, Nakiata's eyes bulged, her mouth dropped open, and the color drained from her face. She could feel her body trembling. She had never felt so displaced and afraid of anything, but the image displayed on the wall was something she didn't expect.

There in front of her was the mirror image of where she was standing. The landscape, the wall, everything, but what was causing her so much distress was that the image also included her. She was standing in the same spot, moving like a true reflection, with one difference, they were not facing each other.

The image vanished and the wall became transparent again. Nakiata stared in disbelief scratching her head, trying to figure out what it meant. The ground around her began to shake and the wall sank back into the ground. *Well, that wasn't cryptic in the least*, she thought. The sky above grew dark. Now she couldn't see anything. *I am not familiar enough with this place to risk injuring myself, so I think I'll just sit down right her and wait.* Once seated she moved her ears back-and-forth listening. There was nothing. No sounds, no light, only the feeling of the ground beneath her.

Chapter 11

The Ka'xic finally came to rest on top of a building whose upper floors had been sheared off when the ship collided with it. Ka'tia opened her eyes, walked over to the edge of the ship, and looked out at the devastation. The carnage was greater than she thought possible. In the blink of an eye, she'd destroyed a small section of the bustling metropolis.

Ka'tia fell to her knees, put her hands up to her face, and began to weep. *I should be happy. My brother's killer has just met her fate, and yet I can't help feeling sorrow. I never thought I could ever feel sympathy for Nakiata.* Ka'tia was jarred from her thoughts when she heard a large explosion close by.

"That wasn't the sound of something crashing," she said getting back to her feet. Ka'tia searched for the source of the disturbance, and just as she peered upward into the sky, several small ships buzzed around the taller buildings and into the upper atmosphere. A moment later several flashes of light shone through the clouds followed by booms. *Who are they fighting?*

The clouds split and a few larger ships stopped and hovered above the city. Ka'tia didn't need any other indications, she recognized them at first glance. Ugs.

I hope these people fair better against the, she was thinking when, an enormous Ug ship came to a stop at the edge of the planet's atmosphere. *Ok, I was wrong, they are about to — what, there's two of them?* Another Ug ship, about half its size, came to rest not far from it. Ka'tia bit down on her lip, squinted her eyes, and rose to her feet. She shifted her attention back to the small black ship that held Dravone and Tyrog captive, along with The Most-High.

The tiny ship dodged several Ug fighters with precision maneuvers. It was about to leave the area when it just stopped. Ka'tia noticed a faint energy beam hitting the ship and drawing it up toward the larger Ug vessel.

Ka'tia gasped, realizing this was the moment, the one Melia'na told her would happen. She knew what she had to do. *But what about Nakiata? How can I take her to — she's not dead! Oh wow, it all makes sense now!*

She sighed. *How am I going to transport Nakiata aboard that ship if I don't know where to find her? Where would you go Nakiata? If I were you . . . you're probably on a rampage, killing everyone! I have to find you before too many die. I am going to find you!* She stood, turned, and ran toward the innards of the Ka'xic.

Before she reached the entrance to the bowels of the ship, a group of Kalipygans came rushing out and formed a line, preventing her from gaining access to the lower levels. Ka'tia stopped, and in the blink of an eye she was able to draw her bow up, nock an arrow, and imbue the arrow with not one, but two magic spells. She squinted her left eye just as she let the arrow fly. A second into its flight, the arrow split into fifty separate arrows, all streaking toward different targets.

Ka'tia watched with anticipation as the arrows closed the distance, but, just before they hit the enemy, they all fell short and buried themselves into the ship in a perfect line about ten feet in front of the group of Kalipygans. Her mouth dropped open in disbelief. This was the second time that her shot had not reached the target.

It only took the Kalipygans a fraction-of-a-second to decide this was their opportunity to capture her. In unison, and with purpose they began moving forward. The moment they reached the arrows, a bright flash of white light erupted from each arrow. Within the light Ka'tia caught a glimpse of electrical discharges that collided with the Kalipygans and surged through them. The light dissipated and her enemies fell to the ground, their bodies were perfectly still. There were however several dark brown streams of smoke escaping from them. The odor was unpleasant, and she started getting nauseous.

Ka'tia put a hand over her nose and mouth, but she couldn't help it, she felt proud, and a smile appeared. She cautiously walked toward the entrance to the lower levels and the moment she reached the line of arrows, she actually felt some of the electricity which was still in the air.

A breeze wafted across the top of the Ka'xic. As it hit the Kalipygans the aroma penetrated past her hand. There was no stopping it, she bent over and puked. *I've never smelled something so horrendous in all my life*, she thought wiping her mouth and pinching her nose.

Ka'tia was about to continue down into the ship when something stopped her. *What's going on?* She tried to move but her body wasn't listening. She felt a power flowing into her right hand, and an urge to raise it up until it was straight out to her side. *Okay, I'm calm. My arm just moved of its own accord and now*, the palm of her hand turned so that it was facing up and her fingers spread wide open. *Now what?* She thought tilting her head to one side, and never taking her gaze off of her hand. *At least I can move my head.* Several small sparks began connecting with her fingers. *Hey that tickles*, but she still had no control over her arm. Ka'tia wasn't sure but she could have swore the sparks were forming an outline of something right below her hand. Their frequency increased allowing her to see it more clearly. *Yes, there is definitely something in the air;* her eyebrows raised up because now she could actually feel it touching the palm of her hand. She felt her hand slowly closing around it, and as she did an arrow appeared in her grasp.

She looked down at the line of arrows, and every one of them began to shimmer. One moment they were there and the next, they all vanished. *I think I'll hold on to this one, I have a feeling I will need to use it again later.*

Whatever force was controlling her body, it let her go. Her reflexes kicked in and the first thing Ka'tia did was start gagging. A stronger breeze swept over the dead. She pinched her nose and was about to rush down into the belly of the ship when it dawned on her. She didn't need to walk through the Ka'xic and attempt to find Nakiata. *I can just use magic!*

She walked over to the edge of the ship, where she hoped to see somewhere safe to teleport to. There were several building tops jutting out from the thick cloud layer below. *If I had to guess, I'd say Nakiata is down there.* Ka'tia concentrated her thoughts on one building in particular, the one she felt Nakiata was most likely to be in. A pillar of smoke erupted from the ground and engulfed her.

Nakiata slowly opened her eyes, and her first thought was of Dravone and Tyrog being carried onto The Most-High's ship. Her vision was blurred. She was lying face down on what looked like soft, blue carpet. Then the pain set in, and she felt aches all over her body. Her head which was pounding furiously from the impact. She decided that the pain was, at first, manageable. She closed her eyes, grit her teeth, and struggled to stand up. *I will not be kept down!* She thought. She finally managed to stand.

The pain was so intense that she put her hands up to her temples, and with her palms she pressed them in hard. Feeling the tension going away for a brief moment, her ears twitched when the picked up an alarming sound. Someone or something breathing, and they were close by. She cracked open her eyes and peered out at her surroundings.

The window she'd crashed through must have been part of someone's home. Even though everything was still blurry, she managed to pick out several recognizable shapes, mainly some furniture and several people standing nearby. Nakiata quickly ascertained that they were all in shock, since no one was moving. In fact, they were barely breathing. Her entrance must have been quite the spectacle. "Pardon my intrusion," she said to the inhabitants. "Do any of you happen to know how I can find The Most-High?" She stumbled toward what she assumed was a couch.

Nakiata sat down for several minutes, waiting for her head to clear. Every second she sat waiting for a response, made her angrier and angrier. She stared at the ground gritting her teeth. *Why don't they answer me! If they don't say something soon I'm going to . . .* it just occurred to her that she was no longer having difficulty seeing. She could see every detail of the tile floor. Even her headache was gone. Everything was so clear.

I feel so invigorated. Did my anger heal me? Well, whatever is going on, I like it. She stood up and turned. The room full of people rapidly filled with whispers. Nakiata still couldn't make out what they were saying and without an Itzuli she knew it was almost pointless to try. *Even if we don't understand each other, I'll bet you understand my tone.* "Are any of you going to help me?" she demanded.

The crowd took a step back. Finally, one brave woman, holding a large drink in her hand, started shouting at her. The woman pointed repeatedly at something. Nakiata turned to see what the woman was shouting about, but the only thing she saw was, a door. "Fine! If you won't help me . . . ." She grabbed her Kharak blades and entered SOT.

Dravone and Tyrog came around at the same time. They both reached up and began to rub their temples, hoping to alleviate the enormous headaches they were having. "Where are we?" Dravone asked, shaking his head slightly. His efforts didn't seem to be working because the drug-induced grogginess lingered on.

"You are on my personal transport, and we are heading to my fortress," said an unknown male voice coming from the front of the ship. "There, we can more accurately ascertain where you come from and your usefulness to the Commonwealth. Which will be extremely helpful in placing you in the right environments so that you will be able to pay off your current debts. Speaking of your current debts, they are high enough, that I myself am entitled to simply make you my new acquisitions. Oh how I love collecting unique specimens such as yourselves."

Tyrog shook his head back and forth, trying to clear his own head. He did his best to focus on the blurry figure, but to no avail. "Acquisitions? Debts? What are you referring to? And who are you?" he asked, obviously angry about both ideas.

"Oh, I'm so sorry. Where are my manners? I haven't introduced myself. I am Zadno'st, The Most-High, and you —" Zadno'st was interrupted when the ship began shaking violently, throwing all of its passengers toward the rear. An instant later, the ship crashed into a nearby building. The lights inside the ship flickered a few times before going out.

"Kalipygans, light!" Zadno'st yelled.

All the eyes on one of the Kalipygans intensified, producing just enough light to keep everyone from bumping into anything, but there was now enough darkness for Dravone and Tyrog to conceal themselves. Tyrog had silently slipped into a small dark space and kept his eyes on Zadno'st, who at the moment was moving his head around trying to locate his captives.

"I hope nothing's happened to them. I would hate to lose such rare treasures," Zadno'st whined.

Something from around Zadno'st's neck gleamed in the dim light. Tyrog managed to catch a glimpse of the object. It was an oddly shaped key. *I'll bet my wings that's the key we're looking for*, he thought.

Out of the corner of his eye, Tyrog caught a glimpse of something he didn't expect to see aboard a ship. It was a potted plant with a beautiful, orange flower that was glowing softly. *An Ois flower. Just what this Sodaran needs,* he thought as he reached out, snatched the flower, and stuffed it into his mouth.

This time, his mind didn't go blank. *I guess smelling the flower is what made me go a little ballistic last time.* Seconds later, Tyrog spewed a little fire onto the metal shackles around his wrists, causing them to melt away, and giving away his position. "Kalipygans, the little one is escaping! Seize him!" The Most-High commanded.

Tyrog had already taken a deep breath. He belched a really nice, long, hot flame at the advancing Kalipygan, but the only effect it had was temporary blindness. *Blasted, cybernetics monstrosities, they're flame resistant*! He thought. Tyrog darted back into the darkened ship's interior, barely avoiding the metal hands that attempted to subdue him. "Dravone, be ready to leave!" he yelled, slipping past his pursuer and circling back around, heading for The Most-High. The two remaining Kalipygans positioned themselves close to Zadno'st, preventing him from getting at the key.

He had to come up with a new plan, and quickly. Then it dawned on him. He would make the Kalipygans come to him. If he timed it just right, he could fly in between them and straight at Zadno'st. Tyrog landed at the rear of the ship, breathed a short burst of fire that gave away his position, let out a strong guttural sound. "Here I am, Kalipygans, come and get me!"

His ruse worked. The Kalipygans rushed toward him, and when they were just beyond an arm's reach, he took to the air, flying between them and straight at Zadno'st. Tyrog slammed into The Most-High's chest, knocking him backward onto the floor. The blow stunned The Most-High.

Tyrog landed on top of him, grabbed the key, and yanked it hard enough to break the chain which held it around Zadno'st's neck. He had just enough time to hop over to the side of the ship and breathe as much fire as possible. The side of the ship melted much more quickly than he thought. The intense heat caused the sides of the hole he was creating to peel back, making a larger cavity.

Tyrog turned his head to see that the two Kalipygans were more concerned with helping Zadno'st recover than re-capturing him. "Dravone! Now's our chance. Let's get out of here!" he yelled.

"No need to shout, I'm right here," Dravone said.

Tyrog leapt through the smoldering hole in the side of the ship and into the building they crashed into. The only light in the room was coming in from around the edges of the ship.

"Oh, ouch! That's hot! Yup very hot!" Dravone complained. He quickly patted the sides of his chest, where his robe was smoking. "I'm so glad the Roarrgs gave me this armor. If I wasn't wearing it, my skin would have been seared."

"Clunk . . . clunk . . . clunk." The sound was coming from directly behind Dravone. One of the Kalipygans was trying to break through the hole, but the metal wasn't giving. The Kalipygan continued its efforts, with no success.

"I think we're safe, for now," Tyrog said.

"Look over there. Is that a door?" Dravone asked. There was barely enough light coming in from around the edges of the crashed ship for him to see.

"Yes, that's a door. Shall we find out where it goes?" Tyrog asked.

Dravone nodded. He tip-toed his way through all the debris created by the crash. Tyrog waited patiently, and when he opened the door, they found a large room full people on the other side. *I'm going to guess none of these people speak a language either of us will understand, but I'll be willing to bet that if I change to my wolf-state they will run for the nearest exit in fear,* he thought. He began changing to his wolf-state.

Why in the world is he changing forms now? Tyrog thought. Looking past his Morphan friend, he noticed that all the people in the room were frozen with fear after witnessing Dravone's change. *I'm sure none of them have ever seen that before . . . although, it would probably have had a more profound effect if he wasn't wearing the Roarrg armor. The fur just looks more, natural, beastly,* Tyrog thought as he smiled inwardly.

Why aren't you running? Perhaps a little more persuasion? Dravone let out the deepest, spine-tingling howl he could muster. Half the people in the room began screaming in terror. Within seconds they were all fighting to get to a door in the far back corner of the room. Dravone gave them a moment to get ahead of him before he followed them, growling every so often to remind them his was still behind them. It had been a long time since he felt such fervor. He was actually enjoying himself. He just had to remind himself not to catch anyone and rip them to shreds.

"Great thinking, Dravone," Tyrog said, just after bursting through a third door that led them to a stairwell. He glanced over the edge, there were several hundred flights of stone stairs. In the middle of the stairwell was a large, square hole that went all the way down to the ground, hundreds of feet below them. "If it's alright with you, I'm going to fly to the bottom, go outside and hopefully find some useful material. I'd like to be ready for the Kalipygans, who I have no doubt will be freeing themselves any moment now. I trust you'll be fine on your own?" Tyrog jumped into the air and dove down the large opening.

He emerged from building and landed on the ground just outside. He paused to take in the situation. The aroma of burnt flesh filled the air. His attention immediately went skyward, where the sounds of a battle continued to erupt. The first thing he saw was hundreds of small ships flying about like little wasps, striking at each other. His gaze shifted beyond that, where two large ships hovered just outside of the upper atmosphere.

"Ugs. They are, persistent," he said, shaking his head.

Tyrog looked back down at the devastation. Many of the buildings not too far from him had toppled over, but what was particularly terrible were the swarms of people trying to get away from the area. Some of the first to pass him had mild injuries, but as he stood there, he began to see others carrying severely injured individuals. Even worse were those that were injured and carrying their dead friends or family members. None of them seemed to even care that he was there.

"What happened?" Dravone asked from behind him, just after transforming back to his normal-state.

"I don't know. From the looks of it, it was a massive explosion that happened somewhere in that direction," he pointed toward all the collapsed buildings. "What has me confused, though, is that if the Ugs, in those ships," he pointed upward, "did this, why did they stop the aerial bombardment and change their tactics by attacking with their smaller ships?"

Dravone looked up and sighed. "I thought we'd destroyed the Ugs."

"No, I'm sure there are many more yet to come. I need to find some raw material to eat, or I won't be much use in a battle against the Ugs. I'll be back as soon as I've grown. Then I'll take us up to the smaller Ug ship, where we'll have a higher chance of success. Oh, before I go, can you hang on to this for me?" Tyrog tossed him the key and flew off in the direction of the smoldering rubble.

Dravone caught the key, nodded in agreement, and sat down.

It didn't take long before Tyrog reached an area where the ground was exposed, offering him as much raw material as he could consume. Just as he was about to dive in and begin the rapid process of increasing his size and mass, something out of the corner of his eye caught his attention. It was a small group of rocks that had been newly exposed and were glowing a peculiar red color. Tyrog found them to be too enticing. He hopped over, slowly reached out, and grabbed one. He had learned from his youth to be cautious about the types of raw materials he ate, even though he still ventured to eat almost any foreign vegetation he came across just to see what it would do. Raw materials usually had a much stronger effect.

To his surprise, the rocks were soft and cool to the touch. He plucked one and held it up, examining it further. It looked more like a rough crystal than anything else. He gave it a sniff and was disappointed that it had no smell. *Well, only one thing left to try — down the hatch.* He tossed the small, glowing, red rock into the air, opened his mouth wide, and swallowed it whole.

Tyrog licked his lips. "Not all that bad. It has a similar flavor to —" Tyrog found that he couldn't say anything. His mouthed moved but nothing was coming out. He reached up to put his hand on his mouth when he noticed the size of it. It was two-times bigger than the other one. Seconds later his entire body shifted in weight and mass, both increasing to about three times normal. He could feel the power pulsing through his blood. He smiled, as much as a Sodaran could, grabbed more of the glowing red rocks, and devoured them. Within seconds, his physical form reached its maximum size, thirty-seven feet tall. He felt immensely powerful.

Tyrog began beating his wings as hard as he could. He was astounded at how light his body felt. It just seemed much easier for him to leave the ground. He streaked back toward the area where he'd last seen Dravone. He was relieved to see him sitting on the ground, exactly where he'd left him.

The moment he was on his feet, Tyrog closed his claws around Dravone and lifted him up into the air. "This should only take a second," he said, soaring up toward the smaller of the two Ug ships.

Ka'tia appeared inside the building and immediately put her hand over her mouth. All around her were nothing but bodies. She slowly walked through the room towards the door. She fell to her knees, and tears began to stream down her face.

She sat next to a blood-covered couch and sticking out only a few inches there at the edge of the couch, Ka'tia could see the small, unmoving feet of a child. She crawled around the corner of the couch to see the horror.

Ka'tia slowly lifted the limp body into her arms and began to weep heavily. *Why . . . why . . . why would you slay such an innocent child? What did this child ever do that made you think it had to die? I promise, little one, I will confront Nakiata and demand she answer for what she's done.*

She carefully placed the small child on the couch and walked toward a broken and battered door that was barely hanging on its hinges. The space behind the door was dark, but it was unmistakably the direction Nakiata had gone. Once in the doorway, Ka'tia turned, held out her right hand, and closed her eyes for a moment. *"Fotya'."* A small ball of fire left her hand and slowly fell upon the child. The fire rapidly spread throughout the room, turning the bodies to ash.

She'd only taken a few steps into the darkened hallway when she tripped and fell on top of something large. The light from the fire began seeping into the hallway, and Ka'tia became frighteningly aware that had fallen upon an Ug. She glanced around and saw several more Ugs littering the hallway. *Perhaps Nakiata isn't to blame for the deaths of these people. I'll ask her . . . when I find her.*

Ka'tia wasn't aware that the thought of finding Nakiata had somehow been transmitted to her helmet. Everything in her view went blank. It was as if someone had just put a sack over her head. *Now what's going on?* She thought.

Not being able to see made it a little challenging getting back onto her feet, but she managed. *So how am I supposed to find anything, or go anywhere like this? I wish the Roarrgs would have explained how these suits of armor worked, or at least let us know that it might malfunction.* The helmet was only waiting for her to be standing, because it reacted by producing a top-down view of the city. It held the image only for a moment. It swiftly zoomed in to a ten-foot area, which had every detail of where she was standing. A red, blinking dot appeared in the center of her view. She interpreted as a representation of her position. The map zoomed back out until a dark, blue dot appeared in the upper left portion of the map. The dot was in the building right next to the one she was in. The blue dot disappeared, and a few seconds later, reappeared in the next building over.

Ka'tia observed the blue dots movements for about a minute. The whole time it looked as if it was bouncing around inside the buildings. Ka'tia wasn't sure what to make of it, but she had to figure out how to stop her.

I need to get out of here and make it down to the ground. The view in her helmet returned to normal. Ka'tia quickly made her way down through the building's interior. She stopped briefly several more times to start fires that would consume the remains of countless victims. By the time she made it to the bottom floor, the entire building was ablaze. Her heart was heavy and saddened from the extent of the loss of life she'd seen. She looked up at the building and thought it resembled a gigantic funeral pyre.

She gazed further into the sky and saw the clouds flashing different colors. The symphony of the raging battle continued high above. As she watched the lights dancing around, something out of the corner of her eye distracted her. It was a familiar shape. She turned just in time to see two familiar figures as they entered the clouds, "Tyrog, Dravone!" *I wonder if they are heading for one of the Ug ships. Should I go and help them . . . No, I think the first thing I need to do is find out where Nakiata could —* Her thoughts were interrupted when she heard glass breaking. The sound came from just down the road.

Ka'tia peered over at the building where the sound came from, but the only thing she saw was broken glass on the ground. A few seconds later, the glass doors on the building directly across the road shattered outward, but still Ka'tia didn't see anything, or anyone, leaving. She watched the next building like a Poun-poun watching and waiting for its favorite prey. Another few seconds passed, and, just as she was expecting, the building that was a little further down had its doors blow out.

She knew it must be Nakiata, because the only other creature that can become invisible is a Roarrg. She focused even harder on the entrance to the next building. In that moment something fascinating happened. The view of the outside world changed ever so slightly. Ka'tia only realized it because one of the ships in the distance had stopped moving. It was just there in mid-air. Everything seemed to be at a complete standstill. She turned her head in several directions to confirm what she was seeing, but the view in her helmet remained focused on the entrance. She grimaced and squinted her eyes at the image.

After what seemed like a couple of minutes, Ka'tia noticed the glass on the door breaking apart, and an anomaly appeared in her field of view. A ghostly, dark blur left the building, streaked across the road, and was about to enter the next building. *Could that be . . . Nakiata?* The glass from the door slowly began to move outward and away from the building.

Everything became blurry, and the view inside of her helmet re-focused, and now everything but the dark blur was out of focus. Ka'tia could barely make out the shape of a person, who happened to be the same height as Nakiata.

In an instant, the image returned to normal, and the glass from the door accelerated, flying out and scattering onto the ground. Ka'tia immediately became aware that, in the span of time she was observing the dark blur, several more building entrances had been burst open. *I need to head her off somehow. I know it has to be her. It looks like she's heading toward the devastation my arrow caused, which means that she's about to run out of buildings.*

Ka'tia ran towards the last few buildings that were still intact. The entrances hadn't yet been broken. She arrived at the last building, and, just as she'd hoped, the glass doors on the building to her right burst, spraying her with glass. Ka'tia knew this was her one and only chance, so she grabbed an arrow, nocked it, drew back on the bowstring, and pointed it directly at the entrance.

Ka'tia closed her eyes for a split second as she released the arrow. While the bowstring was moving forward, away from her face, she opened her eyes. It was like she'd just entered a weird dream. Her arrow was slowly being pushed forward by the string. It moved away from her, the bow barely moving through the air, with no target in sight. The air all around her became still, and the scent of burnt flesh mixed with fine particles of stone wafted into her nose and made her queasy. The sounds of the battle high above faded, drowned out by the sound of her own heartbeat.

In that small span of time, about a fraction of a second, Nakiata appeared directly in front of the arrow's flight path. Ka'tia's eyes went wide at the sight of Nakiata's condition. She was covered with a dark red liquid. It had to be the blood of, who knows how many, people. Ka'tia gazed up, peering into Nakiata's eyes. She gasped. They were no longer the beautiful, royal blue hue she knew. It was almost as if her eyes had become as vacant and dark as a Black Door. The whites of her eyes had been altered to a dark slate gray.

Nakiata tilted her head and smirked, at the same time snatching the arrow out of the air as if it were being handed to her. Ka'tia had never witnessed anything like this in her whole life. Nakiata examined the arrow for a second, frowned, and then she broke it in half. As the arrow snapped, a burst of energy was released, causing Nakiata to close her eyes.

Nakiata fell to the ground. Ka'tia reacted as quickly as she could and knelt down beside her. She took Nakiata's head and cradled it in her lap. Ka'tia closed her eyes, and tears began rolling down her cheeks. *What have you done, Ka'tia?* She asked herself. *And what happened to you, Nakiata? What have you done to these people? I wish there was something I could do to prevent you from killing, but I am at an end. All I want right now is for you to wake up and tell me everything is going to be ok. I am not as strong as everyone thinks I am. I put on a great facade, unlike you; you are truly gifted and have no fear. I am afraid.*

Neither of them moved for quite some time. Ka'tia's mind slowly began putting together the bits and pieces of what Melia'na had said before. She had to take Nakiata to the Ug ship. Ka'tia wiped away the few tears, which were still streaming down her face. She leaned over and picked up the unconscious Nakiata and smiled at her. *For being the most dangerous woman around, you sure don't weight much.* Ka'tia turned her gaze upward and could still see the flashes of light illuminating the clouds high above them. She focused her thoughts on the larger Ug ship that she knew was almost directly above them. A pillar of dark blue smoke spiraled up from the ground and engulfed them.

Chapter 12

Tyrog was closing in on the hull of the smaller Ug ship. He reached out with his sharper-than-steel claws and latched onto it with his free hand and both feet. "I'll have you inside the ship in no time. You might want to look away," he said to Dravone. He took an enormous, deep breath. Tyrog's upper lip quivered for a split second just prior to spewing an exceedingly bright, white-yellow flame that quickly penetrated deep into the side of the ship. Once he finished exhaling, he was a little baffled. He hadn't shrunk in size. He was maintaining his size. *I don't know which I like more, the red rocks from this planet, or Immortal Stones*, he thought.

Tyrog's chest expanded as he took in another, deep breath. He let out a second stream of fire, widening the hole to the point where even he could fit through. He tapered off his fire, poked his head inside and glanced around to see if there was enough room to accommodate him in his current condition. Luckily the room on the other side of the hole appeared to be a storage area, with a ceiling about thirty-feet high. *I'll have to keep my head down, but I should be able to move around.*

Tyrog tucked his wings in as close to his body as he could manage, and climbed through the large, smoldering hole. Once inside, he plopped Dravone down on the floor, and did his best to maneuver into a positon which would allow him to face the inevitable Ug onslaught that was no doubt about to begin.

Ten minutes passed, and Tyrog was feeling anxious. "I'm tired of waiting," he said, sounding rather disappointed from the lack of a response. He was expecting some type of resistance since they just created a big gaping hole in the side of the ship. *If this were a Sodaran ship any breech in the hull would sound an alarm. Maybe the Ugs are more concerned with the battle outside the ship?* "Well, this is just rude," he continued aloud.

Tyrog crawled toward the nearest door. He stopped a few feet from the door, put his head against it, and listened. "Something's coming," he announced, hearing the sound of scuffling feet coming from the other side of the door. He backed up a few feet and prepared himself for the possibility of a large force. He lowered his head down aiming his mouth straight at the door. *I hope it's an entire army, what a glorious way to go.*

The door opened unexpectedly, and Tyrog raised his head, as it was almost second nature for him, anytime he wanted to inhale. He forgot that the ceiling wasn't high enough for him. He bellowed from the impact and shook his head. His eyes focused just as twenty Ugs came rushing in and taking up defensive positions all around them. This group of Ugs were armed to the teeth, and they were all wearing armor. *I've never seen an Ug wear armor before,* he thought.

Dravone smiled inside his helmet. He wasted no time transforming into his wolf-state, attacking one of the first Ugs that entered the room.

Even though Tyrog was right next to the door and unable to move with any kind of speed because of his size, he still managed to grab one of the Ugs out of the group as they continued to rush into the room, firing their weapons at him. Luckily, none of their shots were able to penetrate his extremely tough hide. He smiled as he thought, *I don't know what the stones I ate were made of, but they've definitely had an awesome effect. I think they might have even made me stronger. I wish I could find more of them.*

He quickly exhaled a stream of white-hot fire, which incinerated two Ugs who'd just come to a stop in front of him in an attempt to injure him with conventional weapons.

Dravone was busy tearing into his third Ug victim when, he heard *ba-loop, ba-loop,* directly behind him. Before he had a chance to turn around, he felt four massive hands, one on each arm, grabbing him. He was jerked backwards with such force he thought his shoulders had just been dislocated. He growled, not because of the pain he now felt, but because he was pried away from his opponent, the Ug who was now dying a slow death from his infectious bite.

Dravone writhed about as hard as he could, but the grip the two Ugs had on him was more than he could withstand. In a matter of seconds, he was no longer able to move. *Is this going to be my end?* He thought. He could feel the wolf's anger building. Just as he tried to free himself, there was a blinding flash of light all around him. His eyes closed instinctively, and a second later he heard, "Don't stop now, I think we're actually winning the fight!" Tyrog said.

Dravone opened his eyes to find himself free from the grasp of the two Ugs. His first thought was to begin examining his body for wounds, but thankfully he had managed to stay in one piece. He growled in confusion and thought, *How . . . did . . . I . . .*

"Oh, sorry. I hope I didn't injure you. Are you good?" Tyrog asked. "I was ninety-eight percent certain the Roarrg armor would protect you from my fire. Was I correct in my calculation?"

Dravone replied with a grunt. With a new sense of determination, he fell onto his hands, forcing his shoulders back into place. He leaned back onto his powerful hind legs and jumped back into the fight, thrashing one Ug with little effort and moving on to the next.

As soon as the dark blue smoke had cleared, Ka'tia scanned their immediate surroundings. *I think I'm starting to get the hang of this,* she thought. From the look of the things around her, she surmised that they'd arrived in one of the outermost rooms on the larger Ug ship. The room had a singular detail that made her assumption abundantly clear; there was a large door at the far end of the room. Based on its size, she knew that this vessel must contain a large number of the enhanced Ugs they'd encountered back on Vazdrag.

Ka'tia glanced down at Nakiata, who was still unconscious in her arms. She smiled and gently set her down in the middle of the cold, metal floor. A shadow moved above her. Startled, Ka'tia stood and took a quick step back to find the last person she expected to see standing before her. It was Kola'gram. Ka'tia re-adjusted her stance and stepped forward. Something wasn't right. She could see his skin tone, but she could also see straight through him. Normally she wouldn't be concerned since he's a Dia'fani, but in her limited experience with them, they have never been able to be both. "Is there something wrong with you?" she whispered.

"No, I am, fine. It's hard to explain, and I don't have much time. You're in grave danger," he replied.

"What kind of danger? Just tell me in what direction, that way I can at least face it. I'll be even better off when Nakiata awakens. Is the enemy going to come through that oversized door? Is there any way that you can you help us?" Ka'tia rambled on.

"No, I cannot help you. I am not physically here. However, I must urge you to do something that you won't understand. It is extremely imperative that you leave this vessel, and when you leave, you must go alone. Nakiata *must* remain here," Kola'gram said in earnest.

"I can't just leave her here . . . like . . . this. What if the Ugs come in here and find her just lying here unconscious? I can help her. I know . . ."

"No! You must leave. There is no time. Tyrog and Dravone need your help more than Nakiata. Whatever happens, don't forget poison . . ." Kola'gram vanished.

Ka'tia stared at Nakiata's motionless body. The only thing she could picture in her mind was several Ugs torturing her and ripping her apart. She shook her head. *No, she is much stronger than that. But she looks so helpless just lying there.* As she stood there, a feeling of peace came over her. From somewhere deep within her soul, she knew and understood that Kola'gram was right. Nakiata would be just fine.

Ka'tia focused her mind on teleporting to the smaller Ug ship "*Fee-ya*y." The dark blue smoke began to spiral up around her, and a split second before it surrounded her completely, she noticed Nakiata beginning to stir. It was too late. The smoke had consumed her, and when it cleared, she was now inside the other Ug ship. Her concern for Nakiata kept her from realizing the immediate danger that was right in front of her.

One of the Ugs in the large formation snorted, bringing Ka'tia's attention to the full depth of her situation. There in front of her were several hundred Ugs. Her eyes went wide with fear, and she gasped.

Several of the Ugs turned at her gasp and make a sound that made Ka'tia giggle. *Incredible. Your roar sounds like the squeak of baby Poun-poun.* The humor left her when they began moving in her direction. She squinted at the oncoming Ugs, stretched her arms out, and then brought them together. As her hands were closing in on each other, she yelled, *"Convoula'!"*

A ball of blue and white energy appeared between her hands. She quickly pushed the energy toward the Ugs. The ball of energy passed through the middle of the Ugs, who stopped to watch the ball, which landed not too far behind them. When the energy hit the ground, it instantly expanded outward, almost like an explosion. In a matter of seconds, it had enveloped over half of the Ugs who were still standing in formation, along with the ones already in motion, heading straight for her.

Ka'tia took a moment to smile at the awesomeness of her magic. It froze the Ugs instantly. She put her hands together high in the air and brought them down, now thinking of another word. As she pulled her hands apart, and said in a strong, commanding voice, *"Fotya'!"* A ball of red and orange magical energy appeared between her hands. It began to spin while she let its intensity increase.

Ka'tia could feel the heat and power surging through her fingers. A grin of confidence appeared on her face the moment she pushed it away from her. The spiraling ball of magic flew at incredible speed toward the Ugs. More of her enemy appeared behind their frozen comrades. Seeing the state of the situation the new Ugs attempted to rally together for a counterattack, but the ball of energy had just hit one of the iced-over Ugs in its midsection.

The blast was greater than she'd anticipated, incinerating every Ug in the room, and melting the door, leaving a giant hole in the wall. A fraction-of-a-second after the explosion, the shockwave hit her, slamming her up against the back wall, and almost knocking her unconscious. Ka'tia was certain that the shockwave caused a rumble throughout the ship. She managed to get back onto her feet and headed straight for the large hole in the wall.

As she approached the hole, she heard multiple Ugs appearing behind her and rushing at her. Both she and the Ugs stopped when they heard a loud, deep, roar coming from the next room. Ka'tia knew there was only one thing that could create such a noise. Tyrog.

Tyrog stuck his head down next to the hole and saw Ka'tia standing there with a smile. He also noticed a huge crowd of Ugs that were still appearing behind her. "Hurry, Ka'tia, get behind me," he said. He inhaled and spewed another long, hot stream of fire that not only melted a large crack in the floor, but also killed quite a few Ugs.

"How many of them are there?" she asked, rushing past him.

"My best guess, based on the size of the ship . . . several thousand, perhaps more. I don't know how much longer I will maintain my size and have enough fire to fight them all off. I see you have done well using your magic. What do you think?" he asked.

"Yes, I have managed to deal a few good blows, but if there really are that many Ugs on the ship, maybe we should try destroying the ship instead of fighting the Ugs in groups . . . " Ka'tia paused for a brief moment, recalling exactly what it was she was supposed to do. "I need to get you and Dravone off the ship!"

"That sounds like a great idea, but do you have time to get us out of here?" Dravone asked, immediately transforming and coming to a stop right behind her.

"I can provide us with enough time, but you need to be ready," she replied. Ka'tia began to move her arms and body in a manner that made it look as though she were swimming in water.

Tyrog knew what she was about to do. To give her the time she needed, he took in the deepest breath he'd ever tried and exhaled as hard and long as he possibly could. Once he let the last little bit of fire out, his size diminished rapidly.

"*O'tote!*" she yelled, her hand spread out, facing the room with all the Ugs. Green and black gas erupted from the floor, swirling around the room. A moment later, the gasses began moving in their direction.

Tyrog feared that the speed of the gas, now rapidly encroaching on their position, would not allow them to make it off the ship in time. *If only there were some way for me to regain my size . . . oh but there is!* He just remembered the Immortal Stones he'd stashed in Ka'tia's pack. He rushed over, opened her pack, pulled out a crystal, and swallowed it. Within a few seconds, his size had increased exponentially. He forgot to duck as he reached his maximum height and bumped his head on the storage room ceiling. "Grrr, we need to find a Sodaran ship to fight in! At least there I won't hit my head" he grumbled.

Without another word he grabbed Ka'tia and Dravone and squeezed out through the hole in the side of the ship. The instant he was free from the ship, Tyrog began to freefall. The wind whipping past his face felt good. He was focused and read. A hundred feet above the ground, he spread his wings. They caught the air just right and he shot up and out across the tops of the buildings, missing them by mere inches. He streaked across the sky above the wide and deep crater left by Ka'tia's arrow and soared up through the clouds for safety.

Three of the small Ug ships happened to notice their escape and immediately changed course to pursue them. The Ugs managed to catch up quickly without alerting Tyrog or his passengers. Shortly after they made it through the cloud layer, the Ugs attacked.

The first few shots bounced off of Tyrog's back and caused no damage. Then, one of the Ug blasts caught part of Tyrog's left hand, which was holding onto Dravone's upper torso. "Tyrog! The key! It's gone!" Dravone yelled through his helmet. He turned his head in both directions, hoping to see it before it reached the clouds. Something very small about two hundred feet away sparkled in the light just before falling through the clouds. "It's behind us! And it's falling fast!" he yelled.

"No! We need to get that key back!" Tyrog moaned. He dove through the clouds.

The second they breached the cloud layer, Tyrog spread his wings and beat them as hard as he could. *It can't be falling too fast, it doesn't weigh that much*, he thought. He spread his arms out so that Dravone and Ka'tia could help him search for the key, "Quickly, look around; do either of you see it?"

They diligently searched as much of the sky as they could, but it was a near impossible feat to see something that small in such a wide open area. Several Ug weapon blasts erupted from the cloud cover, striking Tyrog across his back, making him flinch. He knew he had to take immediate action. The longer he left his arms and wings outstretched, the sooner the Ugs would overtake them.

He closed his wings as fast as he could. As he was moving his hands and arms back in toward his chest, Ka'tia caught a glimpse of something glittering in the sunlight. "Wait! I think I just saw the key!" she yelled through her helmet. She watched as it glistened like a sparkling feather fluttering toward the ground — and toward the small lake below. *Oh, no! I hope it's not going to fall into that lake. If it does, we won't ever find it.*

There wasn't enough time. Tyrog couldn't risk his friends being unprotected any longer. With his wings tight against his body, he dove for the ground. *I need to get rid of these pesky Ug ships,* he thought, *so we can search for the key unhindered. But I can't fight them in my current condition, holding these two. I need to find someplace safe, a spot where they can fend for themselves and eventually help me, if I need it. But where?*

He scanned as much of the immediate area as he could. Out of the corner of his eye, something caught his attention. *There, a small clearing in those trees. That will be the perfect spot to drop off my delicate cargo.* He extended his left wing ever so slightly, which was just enough to alter his course without slowing him down.

The ground was coming up fast, and he was out of time. "This might hurt a bit!" he roared, spreading his wings out as far as they would go. His wings caught just enough air to keep them from crashing into the trees but still allowed him to streak just a few inches above the forest's canopy. Tyrog had one chance to drop off his friends and get back into the air before smashing into the trees on the other side of the small clearing.

The second he cleared the trees, he closed his wings a little bit, and he rapidly sank toward the ground. Without hesitating or slowing down, he deposited Dravone and Ka'tia in the middle of the small clearing. Before they reached the ground, he was already beating his wings, trying to gain altitude. His feet brushed over several branches on the tops of at least three trees.

That was really close. Now, to get high enough that I can confront the Ug ships. Tyrog glanced back. The three ships were still hot on his trail, but they hadn't seemed to notice the drop off. *These Ugs are so predicta* — without giving away any visual cues to what they were about to do, the Ug ships split up, flying in three different directions. Tyrog worried that they were aware of Dravone and Ka'tia's position and were turning back to contend with them. He knew he couldn't deal with all three of them in time.

He mentally paused to re-evaluate his tactics. *Alright, one at a time. I just hope I can do this.* He finally had enough altitude as he rolled his body over, folded his wings, and started to dive after the first Ug ship. The chase was underway. He noticed that the Ug ship he was after didn't act the same as the rest; it weaved back and forth through the air as if it knew he was trying to reach it. *You're not the normal type of Ug are you? No matter, because you're nowhere near good enough to defeat me. Sodarans are born to fly and conquer. You make machines to do what comes natural to me.*

Despite the small ship's maneuvers, Tyrog closed the distance between them and was just reaching out to grasp it, but, before his claws had a chance to make contact, the ship accelerated and in an instant it went vertical. The ship only went ten feet up, came to a stop, rotated so that it was pointing directly at him, and fired several blasts, hitting Tyrog square in the face. "Why you! That stings! You're gonna pay for that you little . . ." He turned his body so that he could face his pursuer. Then he saw what was controlling the small Ug ship.

He was so surprised to see that it wasn't an Ug at all. Even through the glass surrounding the pilot area, Tyrog could see the small, familiar, female figure at the controls. "Nakiata?" he asked aloud, unsettled.

In those few brief seconds that they had to observe each other, he could see the smirk on Nakiata's face. "You are not her! I can see it in your eyes, you don't recognize me at all," he said. *But how is this possible? This has to be some kind of evil Ug ploy to kill us. I don't know how they made you, but I will destroy you!* He curled his body into a ball, turned to face the ground, and dove. He was fifty feet off the ground when he finally spread his wings and angled back up, rocketing into the clouds. Once he broke through the cloud cover, he spun around and released a fireball intended to hit the ship head on.

The ship burst through the clouds almost exactly where he hoped it would. The fireball hit the underside of the ship, burning through some of the craft's underbelly and setting it ablaze. The ship quickly banked away from him and accelerated upward. It was now leaving a sizeable smoke trail that was easy to follow.

Tyrog hovered just above the clouds while he waited and watched patiently. He contemplated on how similar Nakiata and the thing controlling the ship, really are. *If you're anything like her, you won't give up so easily*, he thought. He smiled the moment the smoke trail began veering around, which told him that she had banked and was now headed straight for him.

The small ship began sending blasts his way, but he didn't move in the slightest. She was heading straight at him, and at the last second, he moved just enough to reach out and sink his claws into the sides of the ship. Tyrog held on while the ship maneuvered erratically. The instant the ship leveled out, he reached up and dug into the hull just behind the glass and ripped it open, exposing its pilot.

What if she's under some kind of Ug mind control, he thought. As she reached up behind the control seat to grab something with her left arm, he noticed she didn't have a birthmark on it. *Just as I expected, this isn't Nakiata. It is . . . a clone. For all our sakes, I hope they didn't make too many. The chances of mental instability in the copy is too overwhelming. That's why the Sodaran Empire never continued its exploration into cloning. At least I know they don't share all of her abilities.* Tyrog smiled, took a deep breath and blew a stream of fire the melted every inch of the forward part of the ship, including its pilot.

He let go and watched the burning remains fall through the clouds. *One down, two to go.*

"Where did you say you saw the key?" Dravone asked.

"It was in that direction," Ka'tia said, pointing toward the tree line. "Dravone, were you hurt at all when Tyrog dropped us off? I think my I might have bruised something when I hit the ground."

"By the silver light of Mounara's grace, where are you hurt?" he asked. Dravone rushed over, put his hands on her shoulders and started examining her.

"It's nothing really. I just feel a bit odd, every time I take a breath," she answered, rubbing her chest.

Dravone's eyes peered down for a moment. Feeling self-conscious about examining her chest, he looked back up into her eyes. "I guess, I shouldn't worry. If you feel any more pain, I can carry you to a safer spot," he said pointing to the tree line. "I don't think I was injured. One of the blasts just missed me. I noticed the clearing the same time Tyrog turned and was heading straight for it. At that point I pretty much guessed what Tyrog was going to do with us, so I prepared myself for a rough landing," he replied.

High in the sky, they heard an explosion of some kind, and a few seconds later witnessed the flaming remains of a small Ug ship as it broke through the clouds and crashed somewhere in the distance. Ka'tia was already scanning the horizon when she noticed one of the other small ships heading straight for them.

"There's another one!" Dravone said, pointing in the opposite direction.

Ka'tia turned to see the other ship heading at them. Ka'tia frowned behind her helmet's visor. "Run to the forest, now!" she said to Dravone. He wanted to ask her what she was about to do, but instead he turned and ran as fast as he could for the trees.

She closed her eyes and cleared her mind of everything but a mental picture of the clearing and the two approaching ships. She began the motions that would bring forth *Hisi'k* magic. She let the most intense feeling of energy fill her. She began to sweat from the heat being generated from within.

The clouds began to converge above the clearing. Seconds later, they began to swirl around, becoming darker and darker. The Ug ships accelerated trying to get through the wind emanating from the clearing. They closed in on the clearing, and just as they passed over the trees that marked the edge, Ka'tia put her hands together above her head. With every ounce of strength she could muster, she brought them down. The instant her hands were even with her chest she thrust them apart, pointing in the direction of the two ships.

Dravone was only about a hundred feet inside the forest when a brilliant light appeared behind him. Out of pure instinct, he dove for the ground. The second his chest hit the soft, dark soil, a devastating shockwave ripped through the forest, shearing every tree in its path. He waited for a full minute before he felt it was safe to get back onto his feet. He spun around to see what had happened. He was shocked to see that the small clearing had become about five times larger. *Hisi'k magic,* he thought as he watched the flames still rising from two huge craters, one not too far from him and the other on the far side, beyond where Ka'tia was standing.

Ka'tia fell to her knees. She put a hand up to her head momentarily, and then she lay down. "Ka'tia! Can you hear me?" Dravone asked, hoping that their helmets were still connected and that she could hear him. There was no answer, which had him worried beyond measure. Without another thought, he ran toward her, but he was forced to stop after only a few feet. The heat coming from the crater was so intense, he knew that if he went any further it would mean his own death. "Ka'tia!" he yelled. He couldn't reach her.

He scanned the area to see if there was any way around. A huge shadow crossed overhead. *Tyrog. Yes, go and help her,* he thought as he watched the mighty dragon flying straight to her.

Tyrog beat his wings hard to slow his descent, and with a grace few had ever witnessed, he landed right on top of Ka'tia like a feather. With extreme care, he picked her up and flew back over to Dravone, who was anxiously waiting to see if she was still alive or merely unconscious. Tyrog gently placed her on the ground. "I fear she is fading, fast. You might want to crouch down and close your eyes. I don't know what's going to happen when I do this. I've never attempted to heal someone while under the influence of an Immortal Stone. I've never heard of a Sodaran trying it, so the effects are going to be . . . unpredictable," Tyrog said. He placed one of his large fingers across Ka'tia's chest.

Tyrog took a deep breath, closed his eyes, and focused all his energy into saving Ka'tia. His scales began to vibrate and spread slightly apart. In between the cracks, a fiery-red glow started to shine and became brighter and brighter. A huge energy wave burst from his body with a blinding radiance.

Chapter 13

Nakiata woke up, disoriented. She couldn't place her surroundings. She sat up, glanced around, and didn't see any immediate threats. She closed her eyes and shook her head, trying to clear her mind. She took a deep breath and let it out slowly. She did it several times until she was able to focus on the last thing she could remember. *I crashed through a window . . . I think. Then there were some people staring at me. None of them seemed to understand what I was saying. I became frustrated, and— and then — hmmm, it's all a blur. Now I'm here, only I don't know where "here" is. I'd better get myself up and have a look around.*

She opened her eyes, stood up, and turned in a complete circle. "Well, this looks rather ominous. A set of huge doors there, and another, slightly smaller door over there. A plethora of metal and wooden boxes over to one side of the room, all having their own, unique, set of markings covering the sides. This must be a storage area, but whose, and where? Those are the questions I need to have answered," she said aloud.

The two doors opened, and fifty enhanced Ugs rushed into the room, blocking all the exits. Nakiata smirked, "You really want to do this? I would have thought that you learned your lesson the last time we fought each other. But, I guess some are just slow to come to grips with the truth — or you just love to fight, just like me. Come on, I can give you a fight. I hope you're —" She didn't finish. An even larger Ug carrying an enormous battle-axe entered the room and made several high-pitched sounds.

All throughout the room, a voice echoed, "First, you must defeat me."

"And just who am I speaking with? An overgrown Ug with a brain the size of pebble?" she taunted.

The oversized Ug began to make several more sounds, and the voice returned with, "I am Xalipse, brother of Thalipse the Orator, and I will have my revenge!" The Ug let out a high-pitched roar, stomped its round, flat, feet, and moved several steps closer.

I really hope this is going to be somewhat of a challenge. I really want to enjoy this, she thought. She was already letting her rage brew inside her. It was reaching the point where she couldn't contain it. She vanished into pure SOT just as the Xalipse swung the axe over his head. He brought it down, slamming it into the floor exactly where she had been standing a second ago.

Nakiata chose not to attack Xalipse head-on. Instead, she decided to first take out as many of the enhanced Ugs as she could. That way, she could use them to as stepping stools to get to Xalipse.

Xalipse struggled to pull his battle-axe out of the floor, cursing with every tug. He finally broke his weapon free and held it aloft in front of his chest. He realized this was not going to be a normal fight, so he decided to do something different. Xalipse started to taunt *her.* "What's the matter, tiny woman? Are you afraid to face me? Scared I might kill you?" He turned around slowly, hoping she was going to reappear and fight him.

Xalipse searched high and low but there was nothing. "Come out, come out, little fiend," he said. He spun around the instant he heard a scuffle. Xalipse became outraged the moment he laid his eyes upon six of his slain brothers, the last one having Nakiata standing on top of it.

"I fear nothing!" she yelled back, "Especially an oversized bag of wind like you!"

Xalipse swung his axe again and buried it deep into the dead Ug Nakiata had been standing on. At the same moment, Nakiata was already in the air, heading for the next Ug. Xalipse quickly retracted his axe and swung it at her without any regards to his fellow Ugs.

"Careful now, you don't want to hurt anyone with that oversized meat cleaver!" she said, sinking her Kharak blades into her next target's chest. As she was pulling her blades out, she felt a slight breeze. Out of the corner of her eye, she caught sight of Xalipse's axe as it severed the Ug's body straight down the middle, and missing her by mere inches.

Nakiata jumped back and away from the dead body. "Maybe I should step out of your way so you can kill all your friends for me. You're doing a much nicer job of it than I am," Nakiata said, tauntingly.

Xalipse groaned. All at once, the remaining enhanced Ugs moved to attack. *So, now you really want to play, huh? I can accommodate you.* "Ahhhh!" Nakiata vanished again. Within seconds, eight more Ugs fell to the ground.

Xalipse roared with anger, swung his axe, and cleaved two of his brothers in half. He stopped, let out a few squeals, and the voice boomed throughout the room, "Turn it on, now! And find her!"

Turn what on? Is he speaking to me? She thought. A few seconds later, she heard several loud clunks, and the lights in the room seemed to dim. All of a sudden a soft, purplish glow began emanating throughout the room. "Ah! There you are!" Xalipse yelled happily. He swung his axe directly toward her.

Nakiata looked down at her arms. *What is this magic? They can see me?* Enraged she rushed at two of the Ugs and jumped into the air, but one of them caught her by the leg and held her upside down. "Excellent, now hold —" Xalipse failed to finish his sentence.

Nakiata bent at the waist, pulling herself up. She swung her blade and sliced through the Ug's wrist, cutting the muscles and tendons, setting herself free. She fell to the ground, landing on her feet with her knees bent and her head down. She looked up at Xalipse, who was in the motion of raising his axe up and behind his head.

Xalipse's muscles were starting to flex so that he could bring his axe down with every ounce of his might. His body froze at the apex of his swing. His small eyes opened up as much as they could, while his left ear started to twitch.

He couldn't believe what he was seeing. Everything appeared motionless. He turned his head, making sure he was not paralyzed. He rolled his eyes around, blinked, and turned his attention back to Nakiata, who had an evil grin on her face.

In the dim, purplish light, Nakiata's eyes flashed for a fraction of a second before becoming empty and black. "Now every last one of you is going to die," she said. She emptied her thoughts, and concentrated until her body shifted out of phase, allowing the light to pass through her. She faded from sight.

Xalipse brought down his axe, but it was too late. By the time he'd pulled his axe back up and looked around for her, he realized that he was the only thing in the room left alive. He watched in horror as every single enhanced Ug in the room fell to the floor dead, almost all at once. It was as if a farmer had just swung a scythe.

He began to roar, but before he could finish he heard Nakiata's voice. From his perspective, it sounded like she was standing right next to him. She whispered, "Now, Xalipse, go and be with your brother." He turned his head back and forth as fast as he could trying to spy her, but the movement was difficult. There was a stiffness in his neck and he felt a mild irritating pressure building in his head. His vision began to blur. As his eyes slowly rolled up into his head, he saw one last image: Nakiata pulling a bloody Kharak blade out of his skull.

The moment Xalipse's body hit the floor, an alarm began to ring throughout the ship. Nakiata stood before her conquest with a malicious grin still plastered on her face. She vanished, darting toward the doors to disappear deeper into the ship.

More buildings throughout the city shook from explosions as ships crashed all around. The lights of the city flickered on and off, after each one. The city's power waned for a few moments, then it failed completely, leaving everyone in the dark. Everyone knew something bad just happened, but what exactly, they didn't know. Those who were still indoors rushed to the nearest window, trying to see if other parts of the city had gone dark.

Those facing south were witness to a massive explosion. For some, it was the last thing they saw, if they made it to the window before the blast hit their building. The people on the north side of the city, who were furthest from the blast, had no inkling as to what was happening. Out of fear, mixed with a little curiosity, a good number of people decided to go up to the roof of their building to get a better view.

Once on the roof, a great many people looked with wide eyes on a gruesome scene. It was the finale of the battle, the likes of which none of them had ever seen in their lifetime, let alone heard of.

To the south, they watched in horror as a huge pillar of smoke and fire continued to rise into the upper atmosphere. Almost everyone standing on the roofs felt an unnatural warmth coming from the explosion. In a matter of seconds, their attention shifted skyward toward the dense cloud cover that only a few buildings reached through. There, they saw flashes of light from all over. Thunderous sounds echoed all over the city. Most of them realized it was an aerial battle, one they hoped didn't fall on top of them.

It wasn't until a large group of the city's small, defensive ships fell through the clouds and began crashing into buildings that many of the citizens on the roofs ran back inside, seeking shelter. Those few that were brave enough or crazy enough to remain soon witnessed another sight none of them had ever seen before.

It was a great, flying beast.

At first, they thought the blast had somehow unearthed it, because it flew up from somewhere on the south side of the city near the devastation. The beast disappeared into the clouds, and everyone watched and waited to see if the large creature would fall back down once it reached the battle.

After thirty solid minutes of waiting, they saw the great beast re-emerge from the clouds and it was heading further south, away from the city. Three small, alien ships were in pursuit.

Just as they lost sight of it, something else descended through the clouds: The largest alien ship the city had have seen. It, too, was heading south and away from the city, but it wasn't flying. It was . . . crashing.

The impact created a ground tremor that reached the city within seconds. More of the city's buildings, any that were still standing on the south side, along with a good portion of those in the central part of the city, fell, killing countless more people.

By now, only a rare few remained on the roofs to watch the last few moments of the battle as it came to a conclusion. More of the small defense ships arrived and were now buzzing above and below the clouds, chasing or being chased by the remaining alien ships.

The battle was approaching the one-hour mark, when the cloud cover began to dissipate, revealing an even larger ship hovering just outside the upper atmosphere of their planet. The grandiose ship barely took any damage whenever one of the small, city defense ships managed to land a hit. This was due in part to the city defense ships inability to function at such high altitudes. The city defense also seemed to be concentrating more on evading their enemy than causing huge amounts of damage. Because of the fact that they were lacking combat skills, which their new enemy had an abundance of.

Without warning, the enormous vessel began descending, heading straight for the city. In that moment, only a few people still remained on the rooftops, and they already knew it was pointless to run. Once something that massive hits the planet, it will vaporize the majority of the city. They stood frozen in terror as they watched the alien ship on its collision course with them.

Just before the ship crashed into the city, a large door opened up on the lower side. The light coming from within was bright, and in its midst was a single, small, female silhouette. At the last second, the figure jumped from the ship.

Those observing the figure were amazed that she successfully made the jump. Quite a few of them began to cheer and applauded her. Their support and admiration stopped when, the person vanished right before their eyes. A moment after, the ship plowed into the ground. It had so much momentum that it continued moving into the city, smashing its way through multiple buildings, heading north.

The ship came to rest over the major part of what was left of the city, leaving only a few buildings left standing. Even though a vast majority of the people were well on their way to escaping the devastated city, a few of them noticed a dark blur pass them by.

None of them even realized that they'd been struck down. Most of them never felt more than a slight sting or an unusual discomfort. Several of them only realized what had happened when their blood began spurting out of their bodies, which produced screams of panic. Those were the few that were struck in a spot that didn't cause instant death.

Her destructive force came to a halt when she came across a little girl. For a moment, it seemed like the little girl was watching Nakiata. The little girl stared right at her, and the moment she stopped the girl raised her hand, pointed at her, and shook her head, *no.*

Nakiata reappeared, her black and gray eyes fixated on the small child. She slowly walked around the little girl, examining her with utmost intensity. Curiously, the child showed no signs of fear, nor did she appear to be in shock from seeing Nakiata appear out of nowhere.

"You will remember, one day, and when that moment comes, your heart will become heavy. It will feel like a weight beyond imagination has been tied to your insides. You will finally feel it," the little girl said solemnly. The child fell to her knees and started coughing up handfuls of blood.

Nakiata was completely beside herself with disbelief. How could she have not seen the large, vertical, red stain on the little girl's white shirt? The girl blinked several times, and yet her eyes were empty. The child fell to one side, dead.

The rage flowing through her veins subsided, and Nakiata felt incredibly weary. Standing perfectly still, she began to sway, and a heavy, dizzy feeling fell over her. She had no choice but to sit down. Without thinking about it, she crossed her legs and closed her eyes. This position was the only thing the alleviated her symptoms. She felt relieved. Just prior to reaching unconsciousness, she heard another, more familiar voice in her mind, *you're getting so much better, and I sense you are closer than ever. Soon.*

Chapter 14

Dravone opened his eyes and jumped to his feet, his fists clenched. "Ka'tia!"

"She's resting," Tyrog said. "And if you keep making all that racket, she won't be for much longer."

"What happened?" he asked.

"As you may or may not know, I ate another one of those Immortal Stones, which I remembered stashing in Ka'tia's pack. The stone does amazing things for me. Anyway, I was attempting to save Ka'tia with my healing energy —"

"Yes, now I remember," Dravone said. "Your scales began to glow, and there was a burst of light and . . . and . . . I'm guessing it worked since we're all still alive." He put his hand to his forehead, trying to remember.

"Yes, and no. The energy I produced was so strong that it almost had the reverse effect on you. I nearly killed you when you were thrown through the air and smacked into a tree. Luckily, you weren't hurt too badly, you were only unconscious for a few hours."

Dravone moved his hand down. He began to feel the pain and soreness all over his body. "Is that all that happened?"

"Yes, that's mainly it. I used the last bit of energy to heal your broken bones. You shouldn't feel sore for much longer. I did my best," Tyrog said. He hopped down off the rock he was sitting on and landed near Ka'tia. He placed his small hand on her forehead, closed his eyes for a moment, and smiled. "She's doing well." Tyrog walked over to Dravone. "She'll be back to normal in an hour, or so." Tyrog reached up and put his hand on Dravone's forehead. "You need to rest a bit longer as well." He let his forked tongue slip out for second.

Dravone furrowed his brow. His frustration only lasted a few seconds. Which is when he noticed a pleasantly warm sensation on his forehead. A feeling of calm swept over him, and at the same time his vision went fuzzy. He smiled, slumping back down, and within seconds, was sleeping like a baby. *Rest, my friends,* thought Tyrog. *I have a feeling that we will all need our full strength on the road ahead of us.* He took several hops away from them before flying off.

Several hours passed. "Where . . . are . . ." Ka'tia tried to ask the moment she regained consciousness. She slowly opened her eyes for a brief moment, but everything was dark. At first she thought something had happened to her eyes. She knew she was still a bit weak, but aside from not having a lot of energy, she felt well-rested.

"Ah, you're awake. That's really good timing, too. I was beginning to fear you wouldn't recover, but you have, and you won't miss dinner," Tyrog said.

Ka'tia rubbed her eyes before opening them again. This time, she could see the stars in the sky. Now she understood; it was night. She felt something warm to her right, and when she finally sat up she noticed the rather nice fire Tyrog had going. She stretched her arms up and out, yawning. The aroma of dinner reached her nostrils. "Mmmm, that smells delicious. What is it?" she asked.

"I'm not sure what these creatures are called, but they tasted great. I took a guess that this would be sufficient for you and Dravone to eat. Here, try it," he said, holding a large chunk of meat out for her.

Ka'tia graciously accepted the meat and took a small bite. "Yes, it's just fine, thank you."

Dravone sat up, his eyes still closed, and his stomach grumbling. He caught a whiff of the succulent meal. "Food. Do I hear my friends eating without me?" he asked with a smile. He opened his eyes, quickly crawled over to the fire, and reached out to yank a large chunk of meat from the rare part. His mouth was already salivating heavily as he sunk his teeth into it with relish.

Ka'tia smiled at Dravone's lack of eating manners. "I'm glad to see you're still able to smile," Tyrog said. "He has definitely got a lot to learn, doesn't he? Although I can't say much; even I have issues remembering that we must be civilized when it comes to eating amongst others." Tyrog grabbed another chunk of meat and held it out for Ka'tia.

"Oh . . . um . . . thanks, but this is more than enough for me," she said, taking another small bite from the meat she still had.

"Suit yourself," he replied, tossing the meat high into the air.

Tyrog was concentrating so hard on catching the meat in his mouth that he didn't notice the clawed, lightly fur-covered hand that reached out and snatched the chunk of meat. Dravone immediately threw the morsel into his mouth, and after two quick chews he swallowed it.

For some reason, he had transformed into his wolf-state and drool was oozing from the sides of his jowls, a little more than usual. The smell was stirring some of his, wilder instincts. His nostrils began flaring. He couldn't take it any longer. Dravone turned, grabbed the carcass, and took off with it into the woods.

"Hey! Wait just a minute! I want some more of that, you furry thief," Tyrog exclaimed. He flew off after Dravone, leaving Ka'tia alone with nothing but her thoughts.

I suppose I should go after them. I hope for all our sakes they are heading in the right direction, the one that will lead us to the key that we lost. If not, Tyrog is going to have to carry us. She got to her feet and gathered her things before extinguishing the fire and traipsing after them. Luckily, Dravone's tracks were easy to follow in the bright light coming from the large silver moon circling the home planet of the Commonwealth.

Ka'tia tracked them for almost ten miles through the moderately wooded hills when the light from the moon began to fade. It set quicker than she was hoped, forcing her to stop. The time was just before sunrise, and is one of the darkest moments of the night. While she sat waiting for enough light to continue, she listened intently to her surroundings.

This place definitely has an unusual, almost unnatural silence about it. I don't like it at all. Wait, there's something out there . . . maybe not. I swear I heard something. There it is again. It's very faint. It sounds like . . . water — no — waves. Very small ones, breaking and splashing against a shore.

Ka'tia estimated that the body of water was a good ten minutes' walk from her current positon, depending on the amount of obstacle at least. *Well, I guess we have been heading in the right direction. Especially if that's the same lake I saw the key falling toward.*

Dawn finally began shedding light in the forest, allowing her to continue her search for Tyrog and Dravone. About twenty minutes later, she reached the edge of a small lake, but something wasn't quite right. The water on this lake was as smooth as glass. *Ok, now I am a bit perplexed,* she thought. *I swear I heard what sounded like small waves breaking on a shore, and here I find nothing of the sort.*

She glanced around. Dravone's tracks lead right up to the water. Tyrog must have been flying because she didn't see any evidence that he'd been there. Ka'tia walked right up to the edge of the lake and looked down into it to see where Dravone might have stepped into the water, but there were no signs that he had actually entered it.

The day's light continued to increase while she stared into the water. She recognized her reflection. *Oh my, I look dreadful.*

All of a sudden, her reflection became distorted by several large waves that passed by and broke against the shore. Before she had a chance to look up, and see what created the waves, an unfamiliar voice echoed all around her. "You look much more astute than some of the other adventurers who have come here in search of either my knowledge, my head, or a mystical treasure trove hidden beneath the water. I haven't made up my mind which you're after. I know it's not my head."

Ka'tia jumped backward, grabbed her bow, nocked an arrow, and began looking for a target. Then she realized who, or, more importantly, what was speaking to her. There in the middle of the lake stood a being unlike any she'd ever seen or could have imagined in her wildest daydreams.

It had to have been at least fifty feet tall, if not taller. She wasn't exactly sure because some of its legs were still submerged in the water. The being had dark, grayish-green fur covering all but two large spots on its lower sides. In the two furless areas were two large pairs of gills, which opened and closed a couple of times while the creature changed from breathing underwater to above. Its face was quite exotic, one so unique that Ka'tia would never forget it. Instead of lips, this particular being looked as though it had something resembling a beak. It also had what looked like several smaller gill slits just above the base of the beaklike mouth. On either side of its head were four long, narrow, fin-like, pointed ears.

The being had two large, ovoid eyes that were a bright jade color. *I swear, if there was no light out, this creature's eyes would probably be glowing. They certainly look like they could be glowing, even now,* Ka'tia thought.

The final, most obvious feature were two large, black, slightly curved horns protruding out horizontally from just behind its ears.

The being watched her intently. "Please don't —" it was trying to say, when Ka'tia accidently let loose the arrow.

She watched the arrow as it flew straight at the beast's mammoth chest. Its eyes flashed bright green, and the arrow stopped mid-air just inches from where it would have buried itself in his flesh. The arrow fell harmlessly into the water below.

"Please, don't shoot at me again. I really don't like violence. It's the action of lesser minds." The being bent at the knees and eased back down into the water until the majority of his body was under the water except his head, which was now only a few feet away from her. "I am Vri'odo, and I have been expecting you."

"You have been expecting me?"

"Yes. Your friends told me that you wouldn't be too far behind them."

"You've seen my friends? Where are they?" she demanded.

"I have sent them away."

"Where did you send them?"

"I sent them to the temple of Ha'pli, which is home to the vault, and where I sent the key. They seemed rather happy to be going."

"Where is that?"

"It lies on the far side of Thia."

"Thia? What is that?" she asked.

"You do not know? With all the questions you ask, I would have thought you to be a bit wiser by now. Interesting," Vri'odo said. The sides of his beak-like mouth moved up, producing a smile. "This world has been named Thia, and has been for many ages. Or have they changed the name again? No matter."

"Can you send me there as well?"

"No, I cannot."

Ka'tia frowned. "Why not? You sent my friends."

"You do not need me. You can take yourself there." Vri'odo said, calmly.

"How?"

"I can't believe it, someone of your magnitude is asking me, an insignificant Nerothropos, how to get from one place to another without moving. I am quite honored."

"What are you talking about?"

"You are quite young, so maybe you don't know." Vri'odo brought his hands up and placed them under his chest, propping himself up a little. "You were not only born a royal princess who has become quite an impressive warrior, but you were also born a Galamag."

"What is a Galamag? And how exactly do you presume to know anything about me?" she asked.

"I know many things, though some from my family would say I don't know anything. I guess it all depends on your point of view."

"What are you rambling about?" Ka'tia said with a short laugh.

Vri'odo made a clicking sound and then said, "Come closer, you needn't be afraid."

Ka'tia looked long and hard at the water and Vri'odo. "Maybe you could come closer to me?"

Vri'odo bowed his head and pulled himself up to the edge of the water. In the process, he created a wave that was about to cover Ka'tia from head to toe.

Ka'tia closed her eyes and held out her hands in a defensive manner. A few seconds later, she opened her eyes to a pleasant surprise. The water had splashed all around her, and yet somehow she had remained dry. "What happened?" she asked.

"You happened," he replied.

She raised an eyebrow, stepping to within a foot of Vri'odo. "Tell me what you know."

"Where to start, hmmm. Well, is it safe to assume you don't know what a Galamag is?"

"Yes."

"Great, let's start there. A Galamag is one of the rarest types of creatures throughout the universe. It's estimated that there are only a handful, and even that might be a liberal number. But that's just statistics, and you don't want to know that. So let me ask you this: Have you ever just listened to something, anything, and heard it speak directly to you?"

"I'm not sure. There have been a few times lately that I have had conversations with things, but those things were magical and I was conversing with the magic," Ka'tia said, a little unsure of herself.

Vri'odo made his clicking sound. "My dear Ka'tia, that was not magic. It was energy, the energy that can be found in all things. You see, Galamags can speak with the universe, and they can tap into its power. It does not matter if it's for good or for evil because the universe has no prejudices and could care less either way. However, it will only allow a minute few to have access to that power, and out of those it will speak to even fewer."

"So I have been talking with the universe? That sounds a bit absurd, don't you think?" she asked.

"It does sound crazy, but ask yourself: Is it crazy to ask a door to open, or talk to something that's not living? The answer would almost always be yes — that is, for just about every creature I can think of, except for you. I'd like you to do something for me. When you get to where you are going, take a moment and listen. You'd be surprised at how much the universe is saying. But be careful that you don't follow what it says blindly. Remember, the universe does not judge you on how use the power given to you, in the time that you have." Vri'odo waited to see if she had any questions. "My time has come. I must go." Vri'odo slunk back into the water and disappeared from sight.

Within seconds, the water glassed over and became still. *Ok, that was weird. So, how do I get to my friends? I guess I need to teleport to them, but where are they? Maybe if I just think about them, I can get there.* Ka'tia shut her eyes, balled her hands into fists, and focused her thoughts.

Nothing was happening. She sighed and allowed herself to relax while keeping her mind on her companions. A new scent gently contacted her nose, and she could hear the magical smoke that began to spiral up around her. She opened her eyes just as the cloud of dark blue smoke swallowed her up.

Tyrog and Dravone appeared on a small, pebble-littered path, only about three feet wide, in the middle of a wide-open field where the edge of a forest could barely be seen with the naked eye. *Isn't this curious. I thought Vri'odo said he would send us directly to the temple*, Tyrog thought. Both he and Dravone finally turned around and became aware of the colossal, white-stoned temple with its unique, blue dome. Luckily, the temple wasn't too far from where they stood. "If you change back to your wolf-state and I fly, we can get there in no time," Tyrog said.

Dravone nodded in agreement. He transformed into his alternate state of being, dropped down onto all fours, and took off toward the temple. Tyrog hopped several times, gaining a little momentum before he took to the air.

It took about fifteen minutes for them to reach the temple, which towered over them. Dravone changed back and knocked on one of the two, fifteen foot high, doors, and waited. A couple of minutes passed, and nothing happened.

"Do you think there's any one here?" he asked Tyrog.

"How should I know?" Tyrog said, glancing around. As he looked up, he noticed some small windows about twenty feet up, several of which were propped open. "I could fly up there and gain entry to the temple. Once I'm in, I can find someone to open these doors, if you'd like? Or we can just wait here," Tyrog said.

"Wait here or go inside after the key? I think we should . . . go inside," Dravone said sarcastically.

Tyrog growled softly and spit on the ground. He stepped back and flapped his wings. Just as he reached the open window and was climbing through, Dravone heard the sounds of someone unlocking the doors.

Dravone took several steps back, not knowing what to expect as the doors opened. There on the other side was Tyrog, tapping his clawed foot on the ground and grumbling. "Why did you let me think the doors were locked?"

"They were locked, and how did you get down there so fast?"

"First of all, I have already flown around as much of the inside of this temple as I could, looking for someone to open the doors." Tyrog said, angrily. Then he put a claw to his chin and thought about it for a moment. "How long was I gone?"

"Only a few seconds. Why?"

"Impressive. They actually built a decent protective system into the stonework itself."

"What are you talking about?" Dravone asked.

"Never mind that. Come in and let's find that key, shall we?"

Dravone frowned inside his Roarrg helmet before replying, "Yes, let's get that key and get out of here."

The two of them walked through the large, open entrance of the temple, which was plain and simple. Just high stone walls and a few stone benches along the sidewalls. To the left and right were long corridors that curved around and out of sight. Directly in front of them was a long corridor that had an eerie bluish glow toward the end. *I'll bet that's directly under the dome,* Dravone thought.

"Where do you suggest we look?" Dravone asked.

"Well, I flew all around the outer corridor and found nothing of interest. I haven't seen a single person here. So, I am going to suggest that we head toward the center. Maybe there is a hidden stairway or a large central chamber where all the acolytes are gathered."

Dravone shrugged his shoulders and headed down the central corridor toward the center of the temple. After a short, five-minute walk, the corridor ended. In front of them was the large, open area at the center of temple. Directly under the blue glass dome, which allowed large amounts of light to flow into the temple, was a garden with a single, dark grey metal basin in the middle.

Dravone stopped at the edge and noticed how the light seemed to be focused inside the garden and not inside the temple. "What do you think? Should we go in?" he asked Tyrog.

Tyrog sniffed the air through his nasal slits, stuck out his forked tongue and tasted the air. "Well, that's something different."

"What are you talking about?" Dravone asked, sniffing the air as well.

"I can see plants and flowers right there in front of me, yet all I can smell is dust and stone."

"Is that a rare thing, for Sodarans?" he asked. He took two steps into the garden. The instant he lifted his foot to take another step, thick stone walls dropped from the ceiling, sealing him in the garden. "What is this!" he yelled.

"Wait there. I'm going to go outside. I need to eat some rocks so that I'll have the energy to create some fire!" Tyrog yelled through the wall. He took off and flew out of the temple as fast as he could.

Meanwhile, Dravone turned to search the garden for any signs of the key. As he turned, he noticed he was not alone. A hooded figure stood in the middle of the garden. "Who are you, and what's going on here?"

The figure didn't respond. "Can you understand me? Can you hear me?" he asked. Dravone couldn't see a face under the hood or any other features until the person raised a hand and pointed at him. "What are you trying to tell me?" The figure vanished from sight.

Great, now what do I do? Dravone turned around to face the stone wall behind him when his visor went blank. At first Dravone thought something happened to the dome. *Are there shudders up there that somebody just closed?* "Uh . . . hello . . . what happened to the light? I can't see anything. I thought these Roarrg suits were supposed to compensate for this," he said aloud.

I have a pretty strong gut feeling that I'm not going to get an answer to that. Come on, think Dravone. How do I get out of this dilemma? Is it me or is the air a bit thinner, too . . . can't breathe . . . grrrrr, this helmet is so — Dravone reached up with both hands to pry the Roarrg helmet away from his suit. Once he had it free from the rest of the suit, he threw it on the ground.

Dravone took a long, deep breath and let it out very slowly. *Wow, that's such a relief. It's amazing! I can smell everything in the garden now. The flowers, the grass, everything. So many sweet and effervescent smells. Now, if I can only —* He cut his thought short when he noticed something on the wall in front of him. At first glance, he thought the wall was just that — a wall. Now, he wasn't so sure. For a second he thought he saw something written on the wall.

I must be losing my mind. Dravone took a step back and glanced upward. *So it was the helmet that malfunctioned. There is still some light coming in, but it's not as much as before.* He looked back down at the wall and the writing was back. It was too faint to make out. The light was striking the wall at just the right angle. He knew there was no way he was going to be able to read it. *I wonder if I'd be able to see it better through the wolf's eyes?*

Without another thought, Dravone made the transition into his wolf-state, and once finished he looked at the wall again. *Now, that's what I call an improvement.* He could see several sentences on the wall, and they seemed to glow, especially now. *Clearly, this was meant to be read by a Morphan.* Dravone began to read in his mind:

> Oh to be one being with two souls. Gifted with love and power. Even in the darkness you will find your way. As the moon shines down on those from the darkest wilds, for only they will be able to read this. Let your veil drop softly to the ground and cast your gaze upon the beast, for it is that half who knows the way in. As the light flickers and becomes dim, know that the first of four locks you will open.
>
> As the sun shines high, a shadow fills the sky. The shadow follows along and holds knowledge possessed by few. This wondrous wit you will need to open the second.
>
> Oh, but look at the hour. The lights have gone dim, and you've run out of power. You may need to find one who can summon such thunder. It's the only way to get past three.
>
> Now I've made it to the end and still the door is closed but wait. Is the door really there? If only seeing was believing, but how do you believe what you can't see? The last of my locks will be like this, and it only has to be seen.
>
> The path to the vault has been set, and it's the only way. And whatever you do, try not to stray.
>
> K.A.

I hate riddles. Why can't they just come out and say what I have to do to open the vault? I wonder if Tyrog is any good with riddles. He reached up with his clawed hand and ran his finger across the words, creating a scratch across them at the same time. He turned and was about to let out a groaning howl in frustration when something caught his attention.

There in the middle of the garden, surrounded by some shrubs and bushes, where at first he had seen a dark grey metal basin, was a small grouping of faintly glowing, rust-brown-colored vines. The vines appeared to be spiraling up out of the ground and around the basin, with the highest branches resting several inches above the basin. This normally wouldn't have caught his attention for two reasons. First off, he was sure that in his normal-state he couldn't have distinguished the vines from the other plants around it. Second, and most importantly, at the top of the vine was a faint, red, pulsating light.

Dravone moved in closer to get a better look at the light. Once he was a few feet away, a peculiar scent began to invade his nostrils. His stomach growled. *Fresh blood, or meat of some kind, but where is it coming from?* He thought. He pushed the brush aside that was blocking his view. He was astounded. There, on top of the vines, was what could only be described as a hand-sized, droplet-shaped puddle of blood. He reached out to touch it with the tip of his claw and found that the exterior was some kind of clear membrane holding the liquid in place.

He pushed a little harder on the outside until his claw pierced through, causing the red, bloody liquid to rush out, spilling into the basin. The vines retreated back into the ground while the blood slowly drained to four small spouts on the sides of the basin. The instant the first droplets of blood hit the ground, the entire temple started to shake. *Now I've done it,* he thought, backing away as quickly as possible.

All of the shrubs and bushes of the garden vanished, and a stone stairway leading down appeared where the vine had been. "What did you do?" Tyrog's voice said from behind him.

Dravone turned around and was happy to see that the walls that had confined him had almost completely retracted into the floor. He took a moment to change back to his normal-state. "I found the entrance to the vault."

"Excellent, let's get down there then."

"Perhaps we should wait for Ka'tia to arrive," Dravone said.

"Why?"

"Before the stairway appeared, I found a message, well . . . it was more of a riddle, on the stone wall. It said something about four locks that can only be opened a certain way. I know I am one of those people or at least I would consider myself the beast it talked about, but the other parts I'm not so sure of. It mentioned someone who knows things that very few know. Could that be you? Then it said something about the lights going dim and needing someone that can summon thunder. Not sure what that meant, but I have a pretty good idea."

"Sounds to me like we need Ka'tia," Tyrog said, folding his arms across his chest.

"Precisely. The last thing the message mentioned was something about believing what you can't see or something. It was a bit confusing. Did I mention the fact that I really hate riddles?" Dravone whined.

Chapter 15

The blue smoke dissipated, and Ka'tia found herself in unfamiliar surroundings. A gentle breeze was blowing through the trees and across the field where she was sitting. She glanced upward and the sky was clear, black, and littered with millions of stars. *How can it be night again?* She thought. The only thing she could to see, with any accuracy, and with the technological assistance from the Roarrg helmet, was the dry grassy field, which was surrounded by a large forest. *Where am I? I thought I would appear at least within sight of Tyrog or Dravone, but I don't see either of them.* Ka'tia sighed and sat down. *Maybe if I wait here, they'll turn up in a few minutes.*

After about half an hour of continually looking in every possible direction for her friends through her Roarrg helmet, she decided to pull it off and breathe in some fresh air. She closed her eyes and inhaled deeply. *How interesting, the air has a familiar smell to it. If I could only see it a little better.* She lay down on the short grass, opened her eyes, and began searching the sky. *It's not possible . . .*

Ka'tia jumped to her feet the moment she heard something huge running through the forest. From the sound of it, it was heading straight at her. She turned her head slightly and concentrated on the sound. *Wait, there's not one, but three, running almost in unison. Whatever they are, they are close by. What magic should I —*

Ka'tia received her answer when two Drougal and a Morphan, in wolf-state, came bounding out of the woods and into the small field. The beastly trio stopped ten feet away. The Morphan circled around her several times sniffing her scent. Once it was back in front of the two Drougal, it stood up on its hind legs, turned, and stepped closer to the Drougal. The Morphan began to rub its clawed hand along the sides of its companions.

What is it doing? Who is that? Ka'tia thought.

The Morphan turned and growled at her. The two Drougal lowered themselves down and began showing their teeth. Ka'tia moved a foot back and was about to unleash some poison magic, but the Morphan began to transform into a beautiful, albeit naked, woman with red-orange hair that had a few streaks of white in it. "Great-great grandmother?" she asked, sounding more than a little surprised. "How did you get . . . Wait, am I back on —"

"Zondura, yes, that's where we are. Where did you think you were? And please don't call me that. It makes me feel so old. Korah is fine. Now child, tell this old woman a few things, like how you got here and more importantly, why you're here. The last time I saw you, you were walking into the Black Door, leaving Zondura behind, and adventuring on some other world in search of the other members of some crazy prophecy. Have you had any success?"

"The answer to your question on how I got here is easy, I used magic to teleport here," Ka'tia said. "*Why* I'm here is a mystery even to me. I didn't know it was possible, but here I am, and here you are. As for your other question, yes and no. We found one other member of the prophecy, and you're not going to believe it when I tell you: It's a Sodaran." She paused and waited for Korah's reaction.

"What! You're in league with a great dragon! How dare you! Do you know how many of your ancestors died fighting those beasts?" Korah said angrily.

"Wait great . . . Korah! I'm sure that what happened in the past has no bearing on what's going on now. Besides, Tyrog is the last of his kind. Yes, you heard me. When he dies there will be no more Sodarans left in the galaxy."

"Well, you've got that right. If I find this Tyrog, he is going to die a lot sooner rather than later." Korah turned and was about to change shapes when Ka'tia grabbed her arm.

"You won't do anything! Great-great grandmother. If you try, you will face me first,"

"Ahhh!" Korah began to scream in pain. She looked down at her arm and saw that Ka'tia's hand had begun to glow a bright red color. Ka'tia let go of her great-great grandmother's arm and watched as the seared imprint of her hand slowly faded away.

"So, this Sodaran has your allegiance?" Korah said, rubbing her arm.

"He has my trust, and I owe him my life," Ka'tia replied harshly.

Korah's demeanor changed. "I never thought there would be a day that I would be thankful for a Sodaran, but now I am." She walked back over to Ka'tia and put a hand on her cheek. "Be cautious, my dear Ka'tia. I swear to you that I will not seek out your friend. I will remain here on Zondura, in peace and comfort."

"Thank you, Korah. Now, I have a few questions to ask you. The first thing I'd like to know is, how is my mother? The last time I saw her she was still having difficulties with the fact the she had become a Morphan."

Korah smiled. "Your mother has changed in many ways since that day. She has been learning as much as she can from myself, the Drougal, and our most wise and friendly scholar. What's your next question?"

"Where on Zondura are we?"

"We are in the middle of the Prigolo jungle. It's pure luck that we even came across you. Normally, we don't travel this far away from Olephala, but I just had to get away, and my two wonderful friends here decided to tag along. We've been gone for a couple of days now, and we were just about to head back when we picked up your scent. At first, I didn't know what to think. I mean, you were supposed to be somewhere out there among the stars. Curiosity got the better of me though. I'm glad I decided to investigate. Would you like to come back with us? I'm sure one of these handsome, hulking brutes will be more than happy to carry you."

Just then, both of the Drougal made short, sneezing sounds and curled their upper lips. "Now, now. I'm sure she doesn't weight that much. She *is* a relative of mine, so don't be so harsh."

"I wish I could Korah, but I need to try and get back to Tyrog and Dravone."

Korah's heart almost skipped a beat and her eyes lit up at the mention of Dravone's name. "I almost forgot you were travelling with that exquisite specimen of a man. Have you gotten to know him any better? Does he ever mention me?"

Ka'tia's eyes went wide and her jaw dropped. She quickly closed her mouth and began to blush a little, but she was reluctant to say much at all.

"Oh — I see. So, you're going to keep him all to yourself? He is just so handsome. I don't blame you one bit. I just wish . . ."

"It's not like that at all, Korah. We are companions and . . . and . . . and he loves Nakiata, not me," she said, sounding a bit put-off.

"Oh my. In that case, there isn't much you can do shy of killing off the competition," Kora said with a smirk. "However, your competitor seems a bit more suited at killing than you, so you can only hope she somehow mysteriously dies or falls off a cliff, or something," Korah said, letting out small chuckle.

"I have come to respect Nakiata, but I have to admit, I am a little afraid of her," Ka'tia said. "I know that might sound cowardly, but I have seen the things she's done, and it really frightens me. But I know for a fact — she will always be there for me when I need her. Now that I think of it, I really need to go. She's all alone and might need me." Ka'tia began concentrating on Nakiata. "*Fee-yay*," she said, and a spiraling cloud of blue smoke wrapped around her.

Dravone was standing at the edge of the water with a huge smile on his face. He kept turning back and forth between Lake Mura and Nakiata. She knew he was talking, but she couldn't hear what he was saying. In that moment, she really didn't care. The sun was high in the sky and it was a warm, a beautiful late-spring day. She felt so happy.

Nakiata looked down at her body and realized that she wasn't wearing any clothes. She looked back up at Dravone and he too wasn't w wearing anything. *Hmmm. I don't see anyone else around, so I guess it's ok*, she thought. She could feel the tingling, worn out sensation which only follows after an intense session of making love. Nakiata was more than satisfied, she was in a state of bliss, completely content in that moment.

She gazed up at the sky. A strong wind started to blow across the lake. The wind was colder than she was expecting. As she was looking down to see what Dravone was doing, the sky darkened, and the temperature dropped more. She began to shiver. Nakiata frantically searched for their clothes. "Where are they?"

Her pale skin was now taking on a blue hue, and she was starting to lose feeling in her fingers and toes. Every breath she took produced a small cloud of steam, but what she didn't notice right away was that everything around her had lost its color. It was all gray.

She looked over at the man she loved and was relieved to see that at least he still had color. She quickly realized that he wasn't moving. "Dravone. Are you alright?" she asked.

She watched in horror as his entire body became gray. She tried to move but her legs did nothing. She didn't want to take her eyes off Dravone. "Please, say something to me!"

He didn't reply. A small gust of wind whipped past her, she squinted, and blinked several times, but there was nothing to prepare for that moment, when it spun toward Dravone. The instant it hit him, he crumbled into dust. "No!" she screamed.

Nakiata's eyes were as wide as they could be, but the stinging pain in them forced her to close them. She reached up with her hands and began to rub her eyes. Once the pain was gone, she yawned, and stretched her arms out as far as they would go. She cracked opened her eyes for a moment, making sure there wasn't going to be any more pain, relieved there wasn't any, she opened them all the way.

She could tell there was plenty of daylight around, but her eyes failed to focus on anything. Everything around her was blurry and obscure. It seemed that the only thing that was working fine was her nose, which told her something nearby was decomposing. *Wow, whatever died must have been rather large; it smells really bad.*

She put her hands up to her eyes and rubbed them. Finally, her sight began to return, and she became aware of where the smell was coming from. She was surrounded by thousands of dead bodies. Men, women, and children. To her, the sight wasn't all that horrifying. Even she was surprised by the fact that it didn't seem to faze her all that much.

Did I do this? Or was it from a battle that I don't remember? There seems to be an overwhelming amount of evidence that would indicate I did this. She was covered from head to toe with dried blood. There was also the fact that the wounds on all of the bodies clearly appeared to be caused by her weapons. *It's probably for the best that I don't remember. Not that it would make that much of a difference — they're dead, and I'm not.*

Nakiata's train of thought instantly shifted. *I really need to find the others, and quickly. I have no idea where to start looking. First things first, I should really get cleaned up.*

She finally decided it was time to stand and get heading somewhere, particularly away from the city and all of the corpses. Nakiata scanned her surroundings for any signs of water that she could use to clean herself up with, but there was nothing around so she headed for the closest building at the edge of the city.

The path to the building was littered with even more corpses. Nakiata surmised there were at least a thousand or more bodies, and the smell of death was beginning to permeate the air all around her. She finished the short trek at a brisk run, and after several minutes of searching she found a room with a wash basin, plenty of cloth to one side for cleaning and drying, and an ample supply of water.

She took her time to clean everything: her body, her clothes, and her Kharak blades, as thoroughly as possible. She left a small pile of blood-covered cloth. Just as she was leaving the washroom, a swirling cloud of dark blue smoke appeared in front of her. When it cleared, Ka'tia was standing in front of her.

"There you are! I didn't think I would find you right away," Ka'tia announced with joy. She quickly looked behind Nakiata into the washroom. When she didn't see anyone, she scanned the rest of the immediate vicinity for the others.

Nakiata frowned because she felt Ka'tia wasn't all that concerned about her. "You found me! How?" Nakiata queried.

Ka'tia focused her attention back to Nakiata. "I'm not exactly sure, per se, but now that we're together, do you have any idea where Dravone and Tyrog are?"

"I'm not sure. I thought you'd be with them."

Ka'tia rolled her eye. "Come on, let's go outside so I can figure out where we are."

Nakiata followed her out of the building. When they had exited the doors, Ka'tia stopped in the middle of the road. "What is it?" Nakiata asked, moving in front of her so she could face Ka'tia. Then she saw the look on her face. Ka'tia stared, her eyes blank, expressionless. She was in shock.

Nakiata knew at once this was a result of the gruesome sight of the corpses and their accompanying smell. "What have you done?" Ka'tia asked after surveying the devastation.

"What have I done? What makes you think I had anything to do with this?" Nakiata replied defensively. But there was little doubt even in her mind that most of these people had died by her hands.

"Who else would have killed these people?"

Nakiata frowned. "It doesn't matter now. Does it? Where are Tyrog and Dravone?"

Ka'tia did not reply right away. She was too engrossed, especially when she noticed the young girl just behind Nakiata. Ka'tia walked up to where Nakiata was standing and examined the girl from there. "What's wrong with you? Don't you feel anything for these people?"

Nakiata grimaced. "To tell you the truth, I felt nothing, nor do I feel anything for them now. They were simply . . . in my way."

"What would you do if I got in your way?" Ka'tia said angrily. "Would you kill me just as quickly?"

Nakiata hesitated while she thought long and hard. "No, I would not kill you. It would not be honorable, and it would also break my loyalty to you. So you're safe."

Ka'tia began to shed a few tears. Nakiata took her hand. "My dear friend, we cannot forget we are destined to fulfill the prophecy, and we need to get to it. Let's go find Tyrog and Dravone. Hopefully, they will have found the last member of the prophecy, or at least a clue that will lead us to them."

Ka'tia looked down at her scornfully. "Yes, let's finish this so we can go our separate ways. *Fee-yay!*" The dark blue smoke erupted from the ground and swallowed them.

They appeared on the pebble-littered path facing the large, white-stoned temple. "Wow, would you look at that," Ka'tia said.

"What? It's just a big, white temple with a blue dome. I don't see anything special about it," Nakiata said.

"No, there's much more to it than that. The building is . . . it's . . . well, its glowing slightly. Okay, maybe it's more of a dull shimmer, but still quite impressive."

"Are you feeling alright?" Nakiata asked. "Because if we're both looking at the same thing, I definitely don't see anything other than a dilapidated temple, and there *is* no glow." Nakiata furrowed her brow, concerned.

"I'm quite fine, thanks for asking," Ka'tia chirped happily. "I'd try to explain, but you wouldn't understand. Come to think of it, I don't know if I understand it either. Hmmm. Either way, I have a feeling our two companions are inside waiting for us."

"I hope you're right," Nakiata replied.

They strolled down the path toward the temple. When they reached the giant doors, which were still ajar, Nakiata called out, "Tyrog. Dravone. Are you in there?" There was no reply. "I think I'm having a rather ominous feeling about this," she said.

Ka'tia was certain that their companions were somewhere inside. When she reached up and put a hand on the door, she saw a bright flash of light. For a second, she was blind. In that moment, she heard a faint whisper that said, "What you seek is inside."

"What did you say?" Ka'tia asked. She did not get the reply she was hoping for.

"Who are you talking to?" Nakiata asked.

"No one. Thought I heard something. Must have been the wind. Come on, let's not stand out here and wait for them to come out," Ka'tia said. She pushed her way past Nakiata and entered the temple. "Where should we look first?" she asked, glancing around the interior.

"We'll go this way," Nakiata said, pushing past Ka'tia and heading straight down the central corridor toward the middle of the temple.

Ka'tia shook her head and trotted behind Nakiata as they made their way deeper into the temple. After a few minutes, they reached the central chamber where the garden was located. "I don't see either of them, nor anyone else. Maybe we should search a different part of the —"

"Shhh. No, this has to be the way, I'm sure of it," Nakiata demanded, examining the area carefully. Nakiata moved closer to the garden area and looked around on the ground for any signs of recent activity. "Look there. That looks just like the footprint of . . ."

"A Morphan in wolf-state," Ka'tia finished. "I have to agree with you. They definitely were here, but where did they go?"

A minute later, they found the stairway leading down into darkness. Before they headed down, Nakiata took a moment to fashion a torch and set it ablaze. The stairway spiraled deep down under the temple, over a hundred feet, before it came to an end at a large, dark room. The light from the torch didn't illuminate much, but it was enough that they could see there was nowhere for them to go.

"It's about time," an unusually deep, familiar voice said from one of the darkened corners.

Ka'tia and Nakiata immediately turned in the direction of the voice. Nakiata raised the torch out in front of her so that the light would cover as much of the area as possible. They noticed a pair of purple eyes reflecting the light. The figure blinked and hopped out of the darkness and into the light. Tyrog stopped a couple feet away, looked up at the two women, and let his forked tongue slither out and back in. "We've been waiting in this dark, underground room for who knows how long, hoping at least one of you would show up. Did you get lost somewhere? I see you found The First. Where was she?"

"Yes, I managed to find Nakiata, and no, I didn't exactly get lost. It's quite an interesting tale. If we get a chance, I'll tell you all about it, but for now I think we have more pressing matters. Is this the vault? It doesn't look like much, and I don't see a key anywhere. Where's Dravone?" Ka'tia asked.

"We haven't been waiting that long. We just came down the stairway not too long ago. We've been down here long enough to discover that there isn't any other way out — and that it's really dark down here, if you haven't noticed," Dravone said, stepping out of the shadows.

"I thought Zadno'st had the key?" Nakiata asked.

"He did, but Tyrog snatched it from his neck. I don't know why, but he gave it to me for safe keeping. I was doing a good job until we were attacked by some Ugs, shortly after we escaped the city. During the battle, before our Sodaran protector could drop us off, I . . . I dropped it," Dravone explained. He lowered his head in shame.

"Don't fret. Vri'odo found the key and told us that he sent it here, to the vault. When we encountered him, he realized who we were and sent us here to retrieve it. We're still trying to find the vault itself, but as you can see, we've hit a dead end, or so it seems," Tyrog said.

"Who is Vri'odo?" Nakiata asked.

"He is an enormous water creature that abhors violence. It's probably good that you haven't met him. Now, if this is the vault, where is the key?" Ka'tia asked.

"No, this isn't the vault. This room is the first of four locks that lead to it, or at least I hope it is," Dravone said. "If not, this is a dead end and we are just wasting time." He ran his hands along one of the walls.

"Well, it sounds like we came just in time to help you guys search and figure it out," Nakiata said, walking behind Dravone and giving the room her own inspection. "These walls are different. They have the appearance of muddy dirt, but when you actually touch them, they are only slightly rough, and feel more like solid metal. I don't see anything that would hint to a way out."

Dravone looked at her with a smirk to convey his disapproval, but in that moment, he had an idea. *Maybe I need to change back to my wolf-state and look around with his eyes, like I did before.*

"Why are you smiling like that?" Nakiata asked, starting to blush, thinking that he was considering her in a much different way. Dravone did not respond, but instead transformed into his wolf-state. Nakiata frowned.

Immediately after the change he began to see the room through the wolf's eyes. Dravone thought, *this is amazing. Almost every bit of the walls is covered with writing, and it has the same orangish glow as the writing on the wall in the garden. And the language — it's ancient Morphan. I know grandfather did his best to teach us, but I can only recall a few words at best.*

As he continued surveying the writing on the walls, looking for any familiar words, something caught his attention. The section directly across from the stairs had a dark spot. Dravone walked over to get a closer look. *I should've noticed this before. It looks just like a small handprint.* He raised his clawed hand and covered the spot to see if anything would happen. Nothing.

In the back of his mind, he heard laughter. *Am I going crazy? Who's laughing?* He concentrated on some of the text around the handprint, but some of it was covered by his hand. As he pulled his hand away from the wall, a few of the words looked more familiar to him.

"What are you doing?" Nakiata's impatient voice sounded out.

Dravone turned his head and growled at her. For the first time since they had met, Nakiata knew she did not want to start a fight with him right now, especially over something she would most likely regret. "I'm sorry. I didn't mean to disturb you. Keep doing whatever it is your doing," she said apologetically.

Ka'tia's eyes went wide with surprise. Even Dravone was caught off guard. To their knowledge, Nakiata had never apologized for anything before. He bowed his head slightly and went back to examining the wall.

Here it's saying something about time after, hand, love . . . Dravone growled at himself in frustration. For once in his life, he wished he'd actually listened to someone's advice. *Grandfather — I'm sorry I never listened to you as much as I should have. I wish you were here to help me* . . .

In the back of his mind he could sense the wolf struggling, it seemed to be highly irritated. Dravone closed his eyes and knelt down. He bowed his head and placed both hands against the wall. He felt the wolf calming down. A voice, one he hadn't heard since he was a boy, whispered to his mind, it was his grandfather's voice.

"My rambunctious little Dravone. You need to pay attention to your grandfather, because I have so much to share with you, and not enough time. Since your father has gone missing, it falls on me to be your guide, and I want nothing less than for you to be the great man I know you will be. If you never remember anything I teach you, I want you to promise me you won't forget this: To be greater than any other Morphan, you must first be the master of yourself, and even that might not be enough. The Morphan people are highly blessed species. Not only do we possess a great intellect, but also the pure, unhindered, wildness of the wolf who remains dormant and content within all of us. If one day your wolf speaks to you, you would do well to listen. Do not fight it. A Morphan who can unite the two souls will do extraordinary things."

Listen to my wolf . . . listen to my . . . have you been trying to talk to me? He thought to himself. He felt his mind drifting off into a meditative state. Everything went completely black for just a moment, and now it was midday. Dravone had to squint his eyes from the brightness of the sun beaming down on him from directly overhead.

The sounds and smells that were surrounding him were extremely familiar, and yet he didn't recognize the ten-foot wide clearing, nor the dark jungle that surrounded it. At first glance, he didn't see anything around, until he noticed some slight movement on the other side of some underbrush, just inside the edge of the jungle.

Dravone concentrated on the darkened area, and then he saw them. There in the shadows were two large, amber eyes staring at him. A moment later, the creature emerged from behind the underbrush, revealing a magnificent, dark gray wolf. As it stepped into the clearing, rising to its full height, Dravone could see that it was twice the size of any normal wolf.

Dravone watched its movements very carefully. As the wolf circled him, it gave no suggestions as to any hostile intentions. As the wolf finished a single lap around him, it came to a stop and sat on its rear haunches. The wolf stared directly into his eyes.

Dravone felt the urge to go up to the wolf and stroke his fur. He took several steps forward and paused to see how the wolf was going to react. He remained just as he was. Dravone took two more steps, now almost nose-to-nose with the great beast. Dravone was not afraid. He looked deep into the wolf's eyes.

Dravone felt as though he was looking deep into his own soul. *I wonder if you'll allow me to touch you.* He thought. He raised his hands, placing them on either side of the wolf's head. "Your fur is much softer than I would have imagined," he said.

The wolf closed its eyes while Dravone began stroking his fur. He even reached just behind his ears and scratched. He could tell the wolf was enjoying the attention.

After a few minutes Dravone felt like talking to his new friend, even if he couldn't reply. He asked, "So you and I have been friends for a long time?"

The wolf opened its eyes. "Yes," he replied.

Dravone's eyes went wide, but he did not flinch or stop stroking the wolf's fur. "I am Wohandrafolarumvern, but you may call me Wohd, for short."

"You . . . you can speak?" Dravone asked.

"In a way, yes. I can only communicate with you — here — in this place. Only a few of the Morphan people have ever experienced this over the vast expanse of time since we became one with each other. Most of the wolves have never really felt the need to have our voices heard, although we do talk amongst ourselves in a way that your half has never been able to comprehend."

"So why do you speak to me now?" Dravone asked.

"Because there is a need for us to be greater than our separate selves. Through the sharing of knowledge, we can achieve more and the benefits will increase tenfold. I have watched you since we came to be, and it is a rare occurrence for us to be impressed, which we are. You have made some wise choices, as well as few mistakes," Wohd said proudly.

"You've watched me?" Dravone asked curiously.

"Yes. To you, we might appear to merely be slumbering within you, but we are watching, always. I'm sure your grandfather would be proud of what you've accomplished."

Dravone began to shed a few tears. "I wish I would have listened to him more, heeded his words."

"There is no need to grieve. His life may be over, but his knowledge and his spirit live on. Take comfort in that."

"I don't want to sound ungrateful, but how exactly are you going to help?"

Wohd showed his teeth in a non-aggressive manner. "There is much I can teach you, but our time is limited at the moment. I'll concentrate on helping you read what is written on the walls."

Dravone was not expecting to hear Wohd say that. "You can read ancient Morphan?" he asked excitedly.

"Among many other things. The wolf that resides in all Morphans share their knowledge and have done so over the countless generations. I can read it. Shall we?"

The moment Dravone opened his eyes, the letters in all the words changed color, going from the hard-to-see orangish to a bright white. *I was expecting a bit, more.* He thought scanning the words that he still saw as gibberish. *What if I just find one or two that I can read? Maybe then they will . . .* He was searching the writing when every word went out of focus. It was a blur of light, but as his vision became clear, every letter, and every sentence had become legible. Dravone understood. He didn't bother trying to read it all. Instead, he focused on what was written around the handprint.

> *In a time long after I have written these words, you will come. If my mysterious mentor is right, you will have brought with you the one you love. Take her hand and guide it to the handprint on the wall. Do not let go of her; the lock will only release when she touches the wall and the loving bond you share is confirmed. If she is not the one, the lock will not open, and there will be no escape.*

Dravone turned and he didn't look directly at Nakiata. He noticed her and Ka'tia at the same time. He shook his head and growled at himself for even considering having feelings for Ka'tia. He focused on Nakiata, who, seeing a definite difference in his appearance, gasped.

"What happened to your eyes? They are — glowing, and they've changed color as well. They're now a silvery-gray." Nakiata said, concerned.

Dravone made no attempts at a reply, even if he could while in wolf-state. Instead, he stepped forward, reached his hand out, and gently grabbed her by the wrist. He waited to make sure she wasn't going to resist his lead. She nodded at him, and so he guided her over to the wall. With his free hand, which was balled it up in a fist, he slowly opened it up and placed it on the wall over the handprint.

Nakiata understood. She opened her hand, and allowed him guide it. She trusted him with all her heart. Just before her hand made contact with the wall, she decided to move her head close to the wall, that way she could see it from a different angle. From her new point of view she noticed some very minute indentations. *How could I have missed that? I know it wasn't there the first time I looked at the wall, but there is no doubt; that is a handprint. From the look of it, I'm going to guess it's the same as mine.*

Nakiata's hand fell perfectly into place while Dravone kept his grip on her wrist. At first, nothing happened. *Is she not the one who loves me? No it has to be Nakiata.* He thought and just as he was about to let go, the words covering the walls, vanished. The walls themselves began to shine a dull, red color, and an immense stone fell from the ceiling behind them, blocking the stairs and the only way out. For a fraction-of-a-second, Dravone was afraid that he made the wrong choice, and that the love he shared with Nakiata was not true.

The room began to shake and shudder slightly, and a section of the wall to their right began to rise, revealing a short, narrow, tunnel made of the same white stones as the temple high above them. The stones themselves seemed to illuminate the entire area.

Dravone let go of Nakiata's wrist and changed back to his normal-state. "For a second, I thought we were in trouble," he said, peering into the tunnel.

Before any of them took another step, a hooded figure appeared in the entrance to the tunnel. "The first lock is open. The man and beast are known. The love and the power, two hearts are as one. I congratulate you, but know this, upon entering, you choose the task of opening the remaining locks, or remain trapped, forever. Remember the garden." The figure vanished.

Chapter 16

Tyrog was the first to cross the threshold into the short tunnel. Once he was inside, the walls of the tunnel lit up and the large stone that had risen to reveal the entrance began to slowly descend. Nakiata, Ka'tia, and Dravone rushed into the tunnel, turning in the nick of time to see the stone settle into place with a thud, sealing them in. "Only one way to go from here. Forward," Tyrog said.

Tyrog flew about twenty feet into the tunnel and that's when he came to an abrupt stop. "Oh my, this doesn't bode well for us." He flew back to the others and said, "There doesn't appear to be a way out. This tunnel is sealed at both ends."

The light being emitted by the walls suddenly became intense. "It feels like someone is rubbing sand across my eyes!" Tyrog bellowed.

"I feel the same way," Dravone said.

"So, would I be correct in saying that we're all feeling annoyed with this bright light?" Nakiata asked.

"Does anyone have an idea of why the light is doing this?" Ka'tia asked.

"I don't know. It could be part of some kind of test, although I don't think any of us can pass it, since we can't see," Nakiata commented.

"Wait, do any of you hear that?" Dravone asked.

"Hear what? I'm more worried about what I can't see with this intense light," Nakiata said, irritated.

"What do you hear? Can you describe it to me?" Tyrog asked.

"It's a soft hum, and it sounds like it's getting louder."

The light in the tunnel went dim. "Do you still hear it?" Tyrog asked.

Everyone except Dravone opened their eyes. They tried to survey their surroundings while waiting for their eyes to adjust to the ambient light in the tunnel.

"No. All I can hear now is . . ."

"What?" Ka'tia asked.

He held up his index finger to shush her. They waited in silence for a moment. "Heartbeats."

"How many?" Tyrog asked curiously

Dravone's face contorted slightly for a moment while he concentrated. He became confused and was expressionless. "Five. I hear five hearts beating."

"Five? How can there be five? There are only four of us in here, unless — there is someone else here," Ka'tia said, grabbing her bow.

Nakiata reacted quickly, gripping her Kharak blades and holding them out at her sides. She was about to enter SOT when Tyrog spoke up.

"Everything is fine," he said with a short hissing sound.

"How is it fine?" Nakiata asked still poised to strike.

"Because —" Tyrog started to say.

"He has two hearts!" Dravone finished.

Ka'tia and Nakiata both looked over at Tyrog and said simultaneously, "Really?"

"I've never heard my great — I meant to say, Korah never said anything to me about Sodarans having two hearts. Is that normal?" Ka'tia asked.

"Yes, it's quite normal Now let's find a way out of . . . hold on. Do you see that?" he asked, pointing back in the direction of the large stone that had sealed them in.

Everyone turned to see that the stone was no longer there. It had been replaced by a piece of shimmering, black glass. Tyrog flew over and landed in front of the glass wall. He turned his head leaned in close.

"Do you hear something?" Ka'tia asked.

"No, but . . ." Tyrog put his clawed little hand up against the glass, and a dim, blue glowing outline appeared around his hand. Once the glow faded, the wall began to display several hundred lines of white text written in a strange language. "Impressive," he commented.

"You can read that?" Dravone asked.

"For all intents and purposes, yes, but it's been ages since I've seen what we called the Skropha' language. It might take me a while to completely translate it."

"Who are, or were, the Skropha', and could you be a little more specific on exactly how long it's been?" Nakiata asked.

Tyrog turned so he could see her face. He tapped a finger on his chin, searching his memories for the last time he actually read the language. "Well, the Skropha' were one of the first, and probably one of the few, hyper-intelligent beings the Sodaran Empire came across soon after we began venturing out into the stars. They were — a peaceful and timid species . . ."

"*Were?*" Ka'tia repeated.

Tyrog curled his upper lip. "Are you going to hold me responsible for everything my ancestors did, or only the things I have done in my lifetime? Now, as far as how long it's been — oh, let me think. I was quite young the last time I read anything from them, about two hundred years, give or take a decade or two," he replied. He turned back to the text on the glass. "Now, this is not right. In this format this line makes no sense," he said, pointing to a section in the middle. "But, if you move those two words . . ." As he spoke, the text began to move, rearranging in the order he described. Tyrog's eyes widened with surprise. "Oh, this is fun!"

Tyrog read each line and voiced any changes as he went.

"How long is this going to take?" Nakiata asked.

"I'm not sure," Tyrog replied. "Now would be a great time for some meditation, or for some relaxation, and get a little something to eat."

"I think I'll sit down and eat a little something," Dravone said, rubbing his stomach.

"That goes for me too," Ka'tia said.

Nakiata furrowed her brow, "I'll meditate."

After about half an hour, he said, "That should do it."

"So what does it say? Anything about how to get out of this tunnel, perhaps?" Ka'tia asked.

"Basically, it says something about how to unlock . . . the door! Right over, there," he pointed at several lines of text. "It starts off by saying we have to solve this equation, determine its outcome, so that we can — oh my. Based on those figures and the known laws of relativity, which are now coinciding within the current timeline of the Theyan galaxy. That will give us the answer which we must use . . . to finish the rest of the translation. Well, it doesn't make as much sense as it did a moment ago."

Nakiata, Dravone, and Ka'tia stared at him blankly. Tyrog stuck his forked tongue out for a second. "Better not get too excited, this will take some more time. As soon as I figure it out, I'll let you know what I find." He turned back to the glass. "Now, if I only had some way to input — it would go much faster."

"I think it's time for me to eat too," Nakiata said, pulling off her pack. She reached in and found a couple of fruits, some bread, and a few strips of dried meat.

Ka'tia and Dravone took the opportunity to lay down and rest.

Tyrog spent another two hours poring over the information and with every passing moment he became more and more frustrated. He screamed out several Sodaran profanities, waking Ka'tia and Dravone.

"Problems?" Nakiata asked.

"Yes! Every time I adjust one section, and attempt to compensate the other end, the first section reverts back!" Tyrog said.

"Is there anything we can do to help?" Ka'tia asked.

"I doubt it," he replied.

"I'm sure there's something . . ." Ka'tia was saying. As she placed her hands on the floor to lift herself up, a thin, red, lighted square outline appeared around them.

"What did you do?" Dravone asked.

"Nothing. All I did was touch the floor," she answered him. Ka'tia sat back up and the outline vanished.

"Let me see!" Tyrog said, hopping over to her. He knelt down and examined the area. "There's nothing here out of the ordinary. Try touching the floor again!" he demanded.

Ka'tia frowned but complied with his request. She leaned forward, placed her hands back on the floor and it lit up again.

"Fascinating," he commented, leaning in closer to inspect the floor. Tyrog placed a hand within the square and the color of the light changed to orange. He removed his hand and it reverted.

"Can you explain to me how this helps us get past our current predicament?" Nakiata asked.

Tyrog ignored her. This time he placed both of his hand on the floor with Ka'tia's. The floor around them began to vibrate and a small, square panel on the floor opened up. A short pedestal rose up out of the floor, stopping at the perfect height for Tyrog.

"What do you think that is?" Dravone asked.

"*That*, is what I've been wanting to find," Tyrog said, walking over to the pedestal. He waved his hand over the top of it, and it began emitting light. About fifty different symbols appeared in rows. "Now we're getting somewhere!" he said excitedly.

Tyrog's little hands went to work manipulating multiple symbols in rapid successions. Every few moments, he paused to make sure the corresponding changes appeared on the glass wall and that nothing went askew.

He had been calculating and shifting the text around for almost an hour. "Ah-ha!" Tyrog shouted, jarring everyone from their comforts.

"What?" Ka'tia said, rubbing her eyes.

"It's the location of a planet," he replied.

"Which one? There are countless planets in the —" Dravone was saying.

"This one," Tyrog said. He tapped several symbols, and the view on the glass changed from text to an image of a green world and its large silver moon.

"Is that . . ." Ka'tia asked.

Tyrog hit a few more symbols, and some large text appeared above the image of the planet. "According to my translation, that is the planet Zondura."

Everyone's eyes went wide. "So, what does my home world have to do with unlocking the door?" Ka'tia asked.

"I haven't quite got to that part, so if you could give me a moment, or two, that would be great." Tyrog began tapping several of the lighted symbols, and the image disappeared. The large text changed from white to green and reduced in size, moving to position itself in a small, blank spot.

"There, that should do it. It says in order to open —" But Tyrog was unable to finish; every line of text on the glass began to swirl around until it vanished from sight, leaving nothing but the wall and two illuminated squares. One square was about five feet off the ground and the other about two feet off the ground.

"What just happened?" Nakiata asked.

"Don't worry. Ka'tia, if you would join me." Tyrog bowed slightly and pointed to the space next to him.

"What do I do?" she asked.

"Place you hand inside the square at the same time I put my hand in the other one. Ready? Now!" They both placed a hand on their respective squares. As soon as their hands made contact, a white line shot between the squares, connecting them. A split second later another line appeared in the middle of the glass, followed by the sound of several locks and mechanisms moving.

The glass wall began to split from the center white line, the top half was slowly being pulled up into the ceiling, while the lower half crept into the ground. A blue light shined through the opening, and they could see an all-new room on the other side.

"Come on, let's get in there before this door closes," Nakiata said. She rushed past Ka'tia and Tyrog. Dravone followed close behind her.

Nakiata was correct, the opening sealed itself up as soon as they were through, trapping them in the next room. The hooded figure appeared in the center of the room. "You have known the beast who loves and seen the knowledge of a shadow that fills the sky. Now, you will need the power of thunder to continue."

The hooded figure began to shimmer and fade but stopped. "Did I forget to mention, in this room there are three possibilities and only one will lead you to the vault." The figure vanished.

"What does that mean?" Nakiata asked. "I wonder if it's some type of test. Like strength, because thunder is always strong."

"Actually," Dravone hesitated for a moment, "I think this is something Ka'tia is going to have to figure out."

"And why do you think that?" Nakiata asked, angrily.

"Well the figure said the power of thunder," Tyrog started.

"Exactly, I have plenty of strength and —"

"I don't think they meant strength. Thunder gets its power from lightning, without it there would be no thunder. So, I'm pretty sure it means we need some type of actual power, or magical energy, perhaps?" Dravone said, shrugging his shoulders.

"I'm inclined to agree," Tyrog said.

Nakiata furrowed her brow, stuck out her lower lip a little, and said, "Fine, let her try. I'll be right here waiting, when she fails."

"If this was a test of strength, I could think of no one else to pass it than you," Ka'tia said, placing a reassuring hand on Nakiata's shoulder. Ka'tia made her way to the center of the room and asked, "Now how do I go about doing this, without destroying us in the process?"

"So far, the two previous tests have required us to make physical contact with the surrounding walls or floor," Tyrog mentioned.

"Yes, but if I choose the wrong wall, are we all going to die?" Ka'tia said with concern.

"That's a valid point. So, how will she know?" Dravone asked.

"Based on our previous experiences, I don't think touching the walls will be what leads to our death. I think the choice she makes will be the deciding factor in either unlocking the next lock or ending in our untimely demise. I hope it leads us to what I can only assume would be the last one," Tyrog said.

Ka'tia shook her head, walked up to the wall in front of her, and placed a hand on it. She held it there for several seconds while everyone waited in anticipation. "Nothing," she said flatly. She walked over to one of the other walls, put a hand up against it, and waited.

This time, she tried something else: She closed her eyes and tried to feel if there was any magic present.

"Well?" Nakiata asked.

"Shh!" Ka'tia replied without opening her eyes. She turned her head slightly, as if listening to something. "There. It's faint, but there *is* something," images of blazing fires entered her mind. Ka'tia retracted her hand as quickly as she could. "Not that way," she said.

Ka'tia walked over to the opposite side of the room, placed her hand on the wall, closed her eyes, and waited. It didn't take long before she saw a new set of images in her mind. There were body parts all around her, floating in an enormous pool of blood. The liquid quickly rose above her head, and she felt as though she was about to drown. She pulled her hand away from the wall and took a deep breath. "That's not the right way, either."

"Hold on. If neither of those two paths are correct, and we just came from that way," Nakiata said, pointing at the sealed door to the tunnel, "that leaves us with only once choice."

"Yes, but there was nothing there," Ka'tia said. She walked back to the first wall she touched, but this time she closed her eyes and focused her thoughts and energy on the wall. *Is this the right path?* She thought.

"*What path do you seek?*" an unknown male voice asked.

Ka'tia opened her eyes for a split second in amazement. She grinned and closed them again. *I seek the path to the vault.*

"*The path to the vault is before you. However, the energy required to open the path has long since gone from this room, and it requires a large amount to open not only the doors but the locks as well. Is what you seek worth the risk? Are those you are with deserving of such a sacrifice? The path is in your hands.*"

Ka'tia pulled her hand away from the wall and placed it at her side. She had several emotions running through her. *Do I risk everything for these three that I barely know, one of which is responsible for my brother's death? Then there's Dravone — what happened between us, was it nothing? Or was there something else there? Tyrog is the only one I truly owe my life to. I suppose it's my duty as a member of the prophecy.*

"What is it?" Nakiata asked.

Ka'tia realized that tears were falling down her cheeks. She wiped them away and turned around. She didn't say anything at first but scanned the room. *How do I perform* Hisi'k *magic down here in . . .* She got her answer the moment she peered up and noticed the unique construction of the ceiling. Embedded in the ceiling were four concentric circles, and in the center a small rod right below a hole.

Before anyone else had a chance to look up, she said, "You might want to stand as far back as possible. I don't know what's going to happen." Ka'tia walked to the center of the room. She was about to start when she noticed that some of her hair was out of place. She didn't want it to be a distraction so she quickly reached up and retied her red hair into a tight bun. *The last could have been disastrous. Had I let some run-away hair ruin my focus*, she thought.

She put her hands at her sides, shut her eyes, and inhaled deeply several times. She let a minute pass, allowing herself to become focused and steady. She opened her eyes and stared at the wall, slowly beginning the motions to summon *Hisi'k* magic.

Halfway through her motions, sparks began to crackle throughout the room. The light coming from the wall flickered and faded. The moment Ka'tia raised her hands high above her head with her fingers spread wide, the room went dark and silent.

She forced her fingers into a bent position, as if she were grasping an invisible ball of clay. As she brought her hands down with every ounce of strength in her body and spirit, huge streams of brilliant blue and white energy surged from the ceiling. The moment her hands were waist-high, she thrust them forward, flinging the beam of energy into the wall.

The wall in front of her lit up with an intense, blue light, while the walls to her sides lit up with equally intense red and white light. Her companions raised their hands to protect their eyes. A loud boom reverberated throughout the room, followed by the sounds of giant locks moving out of place.

When the light subsided, Nakiata yelled, "Where did she go?"

Tyrog and Dravone scanned the room with urgency, but Ka'tia was no longer there. She was gone. A second later, the entire wall that had absorbed every bit of the energy slowly began to rise.

"What do we do now?" Dravone asked.

"We get to the next room before that wall closes and we have no way forward," Nakiata said.

Tyrog was momentarily at a loss for words. He peered into the room on the other side of the wall, which was now open. "I hate to say it, but she's right. If that wall comes back down and we're still in here, we'll be trapped with no way out. We don't have a choice." Tyrog flapped his wings and flew into the next room. The moment he crossed the threshold, the wall began to descend.

Nakiata frowned at Tyrog for not waiting for them. Dravone growled at her for hesitating. Neither of them could think of any other options; the wall wasn't stopping. They rushed into the next room together.

The moment the wall came to rest, sealing them in, a single light in the ceiling began to shine. Again, the hooded figure appeared. "Well done. The power behind thunder can be overwhelming. It was a difficult choice to make, and now one of you is gone."

"Where is our friend?" Nakiata demanded.

The hooded figure was not dissuaded, but merely continued, "You will find the final lock, which is now in front of you. Do not let your eyes deceive you. Believe. You do not want to remain here . . . forever." The figure vanished.

The room shuddered briefly, and the light in the ceiling flickered out. Tyrog, Dravone, and Nakiata stood in darkness for a fraction of a second before the room itself became dimly lit.

There were no longer any walls, no corners, or floor. All discernable features were gone, except one. From there perspective, they were floating, and completely enclosed, in a giant, silver sphere, which had to be three-hundred feet, in any direction to the nearest edge.

At least they could still feel, what they thought was the ground, beneath their feet, even if they couldn't see it.

"Well, this is quite unnerving," Dravone said, surveying the area. "I hate to be the one to say this, but what happened to Ka'tia? Is she dead?"

"She . . .," Tyrog began.

"Both of you need to get over it. She's gone. Dead or not, we don't want to die here, do we? So we need to focus on finding our way out? I may not have Tyrog's intelligence, but I'm pretty sure there are no doors here," Nakiata said. She sat down and peered at the reflective surface below them. It had been a while since she saw a reflection of herself. *Have I gotten older?* She thought.

"I don't think this room is what it appears to be," Tyrog said. He squinted his eyes, turned around, and flew over to the edge of the sphere. He placed the clawed tips of his fingers against it and flew around the circumference, feeling for any abnormalities. Once he'd gone completely around the room, he came back to the center of the sphere and landed in front of Nakiata. "I take it back. From what I can tell, the room has physically changed. What we see *is* in fact the room we are — trapped in."

"Now do you understand what I mean?" she asked.

Tyrog's reply was him spitting on what he thought was the ground. When it hit the surface they were standing on, nothing happened. *Curious. My saliva is almost always highly acidic, and it should have created a small steaming hole.* Tyrog stooped down and searched the spot thoroughly. *Nothing.* He smiled briefly, *If Ka'tia was here I bet she would have told me how terrible it is to spit. I already miss her.*

Dravone had sat down next to Nakiata and was staring down beneath them. He could see the reflection of himself and his two companions. *Why did you use such powerful magic Ka'tia? Please don't be dead, oh by the goddess Mounara I pray that you are not. I don't want to have to be the one to tell your mother, or Korah, that you died in this . . . place. I don't think I can handle seeing their faces —* seeing, Dravone jumped up from where he had been waiting. "Yes, that's it. All we need to do is, *see* the door."

Tyrog tilted his head to one side in confusion.

Nakiata frowned. "Have you gone mad? What are you rambling about?"

"Before I found the entrance leading here to these rooms and their locks, I remember reading something on the wall in the garden. It said something about the seeing is believing, and believing what you can't see, it also said that all we had to do was see it. So how do we find something we can't see?" Dravone asked.

Nakiata regarded him with a smile. "What kind of nonsense is that?

"Maybe it has nothing to do with the door," Tyrog started.

"Then what?" Nakiata chimed.

"Well, let's think about it. So far everything we've seen here leads me to believe that this entire place has no doubt been designed so that only we can open the locks. If that's true, one of us *will* be able to open the last lock," Tyrog said.

"Makes sense, but who?" Dravone asked.

"I have a theory on that," he answered.

"What's a theory?" Nakiata asked.

"It means, idea. So, Dravone told us that the riddle used the word 'seeing' several times"

"Okay," both Nakiata and Dravone said simultaneously.

"I don't think it was referring to the lock or thereby the door, but rather the *person*!" Tyrog said.

"That means . . ." Dravone started.

Nakiata smiled before she entered Shadow of Thought. She searched every bit of the room and still didn't see anything. "There's nothing!"

Nakiata sat back down in the center of the room. *If this is some kind of joke, if it is, I'm not laughing.*

"You're right, it's not funny at all. Remember that there are countless lives counting on you," A female voice said.

Nakiata spun around and there in front of her was someone she never thought she was going to see again, the Oracle of Piyah. "How did you get here?"

"Who are you talking to?" Dravone asked.

"They cannot hear or see me," the Oracle said.

"You still haven't answered my question," Nakiata said.

"Oh, my child, I am not here. I am still on Trouganda. Only my spirit has travelled to come to your aid."

"I didn't know I asked for help."

"No, you didn't. Another reached out to me and told me of your situation, so I am here to offer my assistance."

"Fine. So how do I open the lock? The one that can't be *seen*." Nakiata said.

"Remember the fountain?" the Oracle asked.

"Yes, I remember . . ." she started.

The Oracle disappeared

Nakiata concentrated and the room around her changed, it was no longer a sphere. It was back to the way it was when they had entered. There before her was a door.

Now, how to open it. She stood up and moved closer. On one side of the door there was an inscription, and it was written in her language. *Instructions?*

> *Beyond this door lies the Vault of Destiny. Inside you*
> *will find the key, which Vri'odo, the gentle giant of the lake, sent*
> *to me three-thousand years before you will have arrived. How*
> *and why, even I do not know.*
>
> *To open this door, you must prove you are of the right*
> *character. Simply place your hands against the door and*
> *answer the questions that you hear, and don't lie, dishonesty*
> *will only lead to death.*

Nakiata smirked as she sidestepped twice, reached out, and placed her hands on the door. A chorus of voices, male and female, began to ring out in unison, "The one who bears the mark can answer this. What stands between you and your destiny?"

She thought about her answer for a few seconds. "A door," she said, sarcastically. She had no warning as, an electric surge ran through the door and into her hands, flinging her backwards and onto her rear. She immediately lost her concentration and reappeared almost in the same spot as before, but this time she rubbed her backside, frowning.

"What happened?" Tyrog asked. "I notice you shifted and walked over to the side of the sphere, but what knocked you backwards?"

"I found the door," she said, sounding irritated.

"That's great," Dravone said. "How do we open it?"

"I have to answer some questions," she replied.

"That doesn't sound too difficult. However, is it safe to assume that these questions are not ordinary?" Tyrog asked.

"Well, I have only been asked one so far, and I don't think my answer was the right one."

"What was the question?" Dravone asked.

"The question was about what stands between me and my destiny. Since the voices said the vault was called the Vault of Destiny, I replied, 'A door.'"

Tyrog began to make hissing sounds as he began to laugh at her. Nakiata shot him a quick look of disapproval, and his laughter subsided almost immediately. She turned to Dravone for some comfort, but even he had an expression of guilt written all over his face. "What's the matter with you two?" she asked.

"Well, let me ask you this. What have you let come between you and seeing this prophecy come to an end?" Dravone asked.

"Nothing is going to come between me and finishing —" Nakiata stopped mid-sentence and smiled. "Wait there," she said, prior to re-entering SOT. She walked back over to the door and put her hands up against it. The voices returned and asked her the question again. This time she said in a determined voice, "Nothing."

Once the last syllable escaped her lips, she heard a large clunk. A single lock moved out of place. She pushed against the door, but it wouldn't budge. *There must be more than one lock securing this door*, she thought.

The voices came back. "There are a hundred people standing between you and the key. They will not move. How do you get the key?"

Nakiata didn't realize it, but that question had elicited something deep within her. A power, an anger, and her answer was cold but true to who she was. "Kill them all," she said. She waited for the pain, but instead heard another loud clunk signaling the opening of another lock.

The voices returned. "This is your final question. A Takoura of Death is flying toward Dravone and you are given two choices: Watch as it strikes him down or jump in front of it to save him. Which one do you choose?"

Nakiata hesitated for over a minute. *How do they know who Dravone is?* She thought. Her mind began playing out both scenarios. First she watched, in her mind, as Dravone suffered and died. The image of Dravone's dead body was almost more than she could handle. She had never felt so much for someone before.

Okay, what if I jumped in front of it, she thought. She began playing it out in her mind, but she couldn't see herself dying. For her it was something she never thought about. All she knew is that she wasn't afraid. Her answer was crystal clear. "Save him," she replied.

At first, nothing happened. There was a long pause. She moved her eyes about, waiting for a response. Finally, the voices returned. "You have been true to yourself, and for that brutal honesty, the way is open. The key that you seek is within." The sound of three more locks releasing echoed throughout the room, and Nakiata felt the door give way slightly.

The moment the third and final lock released the room reverted to its original shape, and at the same time Nakiata turned back around, reappeared, and was about to tell Tyrog and Dravone of her success. Nakiata smirked, glanced over her shoulder at the door, which was slightly ajar, and informed them, "Shall we collect the key? Or would you like to stay here a while longer?"

"Get the key," they replied in unison.

Nakiata pushed the door open revealing a short hallway, about a hundred feet, that ended with a wooden door.

The three of them cautiously walked down the hallway and pushed open the wooden door. They were expecting some sort of lavish, fortified room. However, the vault was simply a small square room which contained an oaken tree trunk in its midst and it was only three-and-a-half feet tall. Carved into the top of the trunk was an intricate, specifically designed mantle, which was holding the key.

"Do you think there are any traps?" Dravone asked.

"Let's find out," Nakiata said, grabbing the key and removing it.

The three of them entranced as they watched and listened, but nothing happened. "This key is not like anything I've ever seen," Nakiata said. She turned the key over in her hand several times. It was a pale gray color, barely had any weight to it, and yet she had a feeling that it would stand up to any and all attempts at bending or breaking it.

"Well, I guess we need to find a way. . ." she began.

A loud rumble started and the wall across from them began to descend into the floor. Once it was halfway down they noticed a stairway on the other side, which only went up.

"I'm so happy to see that. I was beginning to dread the idea that I was going to have to dig and chew my way out," Tyrog said.

Chapter 17

They'd been walking up the narrow stone stairway for a good half an hour. The stairs gradually ascended while winding around like a giant, spiral staircase. It was difficult to tell since there was nothing but stone walls on both sides of the staircase.

The only source of light was coming from a dim illuminated line of lights that ran along the outer wall. The climb was slow and dreary. It was also not as dry. The air all around them felt damp and cool as they ascended.

"Is it me or is it taking us longer to reach the top of these stair than it did for us to go down?" Dravone asked.

"No, you are correct. I think the stairs are not only leading up, but out and away," Tyrog said.

Another ten minutes passed before they arrived at the top of the stairs, where they found a decrepit, mold-covered, dark brown wooden door. Dravone smiled broadly, eager to get out of the stuffy, musty smelling air of the temple and get some fresh air. He strode over to the door, grabbed the handle, opened the door, and, without hesitating, walked out. Luckily, he had a good grip on the handle, or he would have fallen to his death. Directly on the other side of the door was nothing but a narrow ledge measuring six inches wide. They were only a few feet from the apex of the temple's dome.

"Um — a little help here!" he implored.

Nakiata smirked, shaking her head. She reached out to him. "Give me your other hand and I'll help you get back inside." As soon as he was back in, she said what the two of them were already thinking. "This puts a slight damper on our plan to get back to Frole with the key."

"Don't worry. I have an idea," Tyrog said.

Nakiata and Dravone watched as he stepped up to the ledge and dove off, flying into the distance and disappearing on the other side of the temple wall.

"So, you couldn't hold on to this? If you can't manage to handle something like this, what makes you certain you'll be able to protect me, if the time comes," Nakiata taunted him while dangling the key in front of him.

Dravone furrowed his brow and sat down so that his feet were dangling. "I'm sorry to disappoint you."

Nakiata sat down beside him and slid her arm around his waist. "You are far from a disappointment." She leaned in close to him and he put his arm around her.

Tyrog was circling the temple high above them, trying to come up with a plan. *Now, how am I going to get them down? I'm not going to fit through the door, but I can cling to the side of the dome tower, get one of them in one hand and — try to get the other one before falling backward into the temple's roof. No problem, I'm almost certain this will work.* At least, that's what he told himself.

Tyrog aimed for the spot slightly below and to the right of the door. He was right on target when he came in contact with the side of temple, but the impact was a bit harder than he had anticipated.

Neither Nakiata nor Dravone were prepared for it, and they almost fell on top of one another. Tyrog dug his claws as deep into the tough stone structure as they would go. The stone was much denser than he'd realized.

"How do you plan on saving us?" Nakiata yelled down at him.

"I can get one of you and come back for the other, or . . ."

"Or? You can try and get us both at the same time?" Dravone asked.

"How do you propose to do that?" Nakiata inquired.

Tyrog was losing his grip, so he made the decision for them. He made a short move to his left, grabbed Nakiata in one hand, and as fast as he could he let go of the stone with his other hand. He was now clinging to the tower with only the claws on his feet. He had enough time to grab Dravone.

The instant his other hand closed around Dravone, he pushed up and off the temple as hard as he could. In one fluid motion, he rolled right-side up, spread his wings, and beat them as fast and as hard as he could to avoid crashing into the temple below.

Tyrog's effort wasn't as good as he'd hoped. Luckily his reflexes were still more than adequate. He felt his feet make contact with the temple structure, but he continued to beat his wings, hopping along the top of the long section of roof until he finally caught enough air to fly up and away.

"That was close. Any ideas on which way we should go?" he asked, maneuvering his passengers up onto his back.

All three of them scanned as much of the horizon as possible, but the only thing in sight were green trees in every direction as far as they could see. "I don't think it matters at this point. We've lost Ka'tia, and don't know if she's still alive somewhere, or if she actually blew herself up. Just keep flying the way we're going!" Nakiata yelled.

Five minutes went by when an intense flash of white light erupted in the sky all around them. A tingling sensation washed over their bodies, and after a moment the light was gone and the feeling was no longer affecting them.

The three of them were relieved to see that they were still flying over the vast forest of green trees.

"What just happened?" Dravone asked.

"I am at a loss," Tyrog said. "Based on my experience with unusual phenomenon, I would have to say that we were transported to a different location, however, we are still in the air, and the scenery hasn't changed from what it was a moment ago. So, your guess is as good as mine."

"I don't care what it was. As long as we're not injured, and there isn't an impending threat of coming under attack, I say we keep flying," Nakiata advised.

A few minutes passed, and Tyrog noticed something in the forest ahead of them. "There's something up —" he began, but they all saw it.

"That's the temple!" Nakiata yelled. "How is that possible? We were flying away from it!"

"I have a theory, but we'll need to test it. What do either of you think?" Tyrog didn't wait for a reply. He turned and flew away from the temple. Several minutes later, another bright flash came, and again they found themselves heading right back toward the temple.

"And what does that mean?" Nakiata questioned.

Tyrog didn't reply right away. First, he descended toward the temple and landed on the path not far from the entrance. "This entire area is sealed or contained, and any attempts to leave result in being turned back into whatever this is. The only thing I'm not sure of is the reason for it. Is it a form of prison, or could it be a safeguard against whatever lies beyond?"

"What do you suggest we do? We obviously can't get back in the same manner as we arrived," Nakiata conceded. "If only Ka'tia were here. She could get us out of this mess." *I know the other two miss her, and I hate to admit it, but even I have grown fond of her.*

"I agree, but I think there must be another way, one we're not seeing."

"What might that be?" Nakiata asked, sarcastically.

Tyrog let out a bellowing roar and expelled his fire until he was back to his normal size. "Go back the way we came," he proposed. He began to hop down the path, heading away from the temple.

Dravone glanced at her, shrugged his shoulders, and followed Tyrog. Nakiata frowned. *I wish he would have asked me to lead the way. I hate following, especially if we're heading toward danger,* she thought before she left.

I calculate that we've walked almost thirty minutes, which would equate to the same approximate distance where we encountered the flash of light while flying. Tyrog was thinking, when he vanished from sight. Nakiata and Dravone to stopped dead in their tracks.

They waited for several minutes, hoping Tyrog would reappear. "I don't think he's coming back," Dravone decided.

"That leaves us with only one option," Nakiata concluded with a smile, grabbing his hand and pulling him along.

They continued down the path for about fifteen more steps before they crossed an invisible border. The next thing they knew, they'd emerged on the other side.

Before them was a large lake. Growing out of the water along the edges were stout, dark brown trees with massive leaves which blocked out a large portion of sunlight.

"It took you long enough," Tyrog snorted.

Nakiata turned to find him patting his foot on the ground, and behind him stood a man that neither she nor Dravone had ever met. Right beside him was Melia'na.

"Enough of that. You have more pressing concerns," The man stated.

"And who are you to be barking orders around?" Nakiata demanded.

Melia'na realized that neither Dravone nor Nakiata had ever met her esteemed counselor and mentor. "This is Kola'gram."

"So, you're the one that taught Ka'tia the magic that killed her!" Nakiata flared at him, grabbing for a dagger she had stashed in her belt. She rushed up, grabbed Kola'gram's robes, pulled him down and placed the dagger to his throat. "Choose carefully what you say next. There isn't any magic in the universe that will save you from me!"

"Ka'tia is . . . well she's not dead," Kola'gram said plainly.

Nakiata threw him to the ground and stepped away from him. Both hers and Dravone's eyes went wide as they simultaneously replied, "What?"

"How can you possibly know that?" Dravone asked

"Let the man speak. If she's not dead, where is she?" Tyrog asked.

"That's the problem. I do not know. I am unable to see her in any of my visions, and yet if I search further into the future, she is there with you," Kola'gram said. He placed a hand on his forehead and closed his eyes momentarily.

"So, what do you suggest?" Dravone asked.

"There is nothing we can do except wait. We will take you back to Melia'na's house, and hope that she returns soon," Kola'gram answered. "Melia'na would you do us the honor?" he asked.

Melia'na took Dravone by the hand and held out her other for Tyrog to hold. He in turn held out his hand for Nakiata, and once they were all holding onto one another, they were consumed by a black cloud of smoke.

"How long are you going to rest?" a deep, resonating, and yet soothing voice asked.

Ka'tia sat up with her eyes still shut. She yawned, inhaling deeply, and cracking one eye open. It was dark, and yet she could still see clearly. The temperature was a bit chilly, but not so much as to make her uncomfortable. Everywhere she was able to peek with her one eye, she saw countless stars. Curious, she opened both her eyes and asked, "Where am I?"

"We are here. We are safe. Is that not enough?" the voice asked.

Ka'tia glanced around and was a little frustrated at such a response. "Okay, we are *here*, but where exactly is this place? Have I ever been here before?"

"You have never been here before, nor have I."

"Who are you?" Ka'tia implored.

The voice hesitated. "I am a spec — a minute representation."

"Of what?"

"You don't already know? Look around. What do you see?"

"All I see are stars and . . ." Ka'tia began to search her surroundings more carefully, scanning up, down, left and right, and yet the only thing she could see were stars. She contemplated a few possibilities, but nothing stuck out as a definitive answer. She realized she had one place yet to look. She repositioned herself ever so slightly and glanced over her shoulder.

The sight behind her was breathtaking. It was something that she knew no one had ever seen before. It was beautiful beyond words. She could see bright, rust-colored clouds mixed with white light that danced around, and the entire spectacle slowly swirled around. Every few seconds she noticed massive chunks of rocks floating in and out of the cloud. Most of them were larger than some of the mountains she'd climbed in the past.

It wasn't long before she noticed a glint of something close to the edge of this magnificent view — a shape, or, more accurately, an outline of something. It was the outline of a creature that reminded her of a Brolo, only three times its normal size. Whatever it was moved toward her. As it drew closer, she realized that this thing was transparent, except for the subtle lines that pronounced the beast's shape.

The only other distinguishing feature the thing had were its eyes, which had more solidity than all the rest. *I wonder if this thing is related to the Dia'fani in some way?* She thought.

The creature's eyes were a pair of dimly glowing blue spheres. *If you look at them just right,* Ka'tia thought, *they resemble two small blue planets.* She became aware that both eyes were now fixed on her.

"Ah, you finally noticed me. Well, what do you think of me?" the voice chirped.

"Yes, I can see — something," she said.

The first thing she thought was that she was talking to an overly large Brolo from Zondura. A Brolo is a creature with skin having a pigmentation of a pale blueish-turquois color, or some variation of the two. Their skin was extremely tough too. The Brolo's body was somewhat slender, yet muscular. The stood on all fours. However, they had hands and feet with four digits, and on each were short, razor-sharp, non-retractable claws.

The Brolo's head was similar to a tyrannosaurus. It also had a medium-length tail for the perfect amount of balance, which made them incredible runners. The last thing she remembered about the Brolo, the one thing that always made her spine shiver, was its teeth. There were several rows of the triangular shaped, meat tearing teeth.

She hesitated, thinking about the one thing she wasn't sure of. She turned so that she was facing whatever it was. "Am I . . . dead?"

A deep, bellowing laugh echoed across the small expanse between them. "No," the voce said. "You are far from death. I haven't laughed in a long time, so for that joy I will tell you a secret. Your life will be long and beautiful, similar to the birth of that nova cloud you see behind me."

"A nova cloud. It's a beautiful sight, and not one that I will easily forget," Ka'tia said. "Can I say...I still haven't a clue of where we are."

"This place is what you made it out to be."

"I made this? How is that possible, especially since I don't even know what or where?" Doubt filled her voice.

The creature laughed again. "I am truly enjoying my time with you. This place is somewhere out amongst the never-ending vastness of the universe. The exact location I am not certain; that was your choice. Before you ask, no, we are not in the coldness of space. You cannot exist out there. You would die."

Ka'tia took a moment to think about what the being said. She inhaled through her nose, slowly and steadily, testing her environment. "Well, there is definitely air in here," she noted aloud. Next she raised her right foot and slammed it down. Her foot came in contact with a solid surface, one that she could see through. "This place has a floor," she said. "Even though I don't know what it's made of, I can feel it under my feet."

"Obvious conclusions. You need air to breathe, and your body is accustomed to gravity; this place has both. Would you care to further hypothesize?"

"Hy — poth . . . I don't know what that means. I think for now we can skip the obvious things and move on to something else, like — how did I get here?"

"The energy you summoned was far stronger and, quite frankly, should have been beyond your capabilities, and yet here you stand. You survived what would have killed any other," the creature said. "When the energy was being channeled, the balance between your desire to survive and your willingness to sacrifice yourself for your friends somehow combined in that moment you let everything go. It was an amazing, selfless act, and it is my understanding that this is what allowed you to travel such a great distance, bringing you here, to this place."

"I'm not sure I understand all that. I do have a much easier question for you. Do you have a name, and what kind of being are you?" Ka'tia questioned.

"Oh my . . . I have had so many names, so many races throughout, and languages that you would have trouble comprehending. It is hard for me to choose a single one. However, for you, I would truly enjoy it if you called me Kuohlo. The answer to what I am, well, let's say that you already know. I know it's difficult for you to actually come to terms with such knowledge. Allow me to say that I have seen it all before and it's not that you can't comprehend the *idea*, but more the magnitude of who, or what, I am."

Ka'tia wasn't entirely sure what to think about Kuohlo's answer, so she remained silent for the moment while she contemplated. A smirk appeared on her face. "Yes, I think I do know what you are, and if you are — Kuohlo, are you willing to answer more of my questions? I have so many to ask."

Kuohlo turned in a complete circle and lay down on the invisible floor. He snorted a couple of times, each resulting in yellow sparks. He began take short, rapid breaths, which was a prelude to him sneezing. The strength of it produced a brilliant orange flame. Once he was finally settled, his eyes flashed like blue flames at her. "I do love being able to carry on deep conversations. It's not often that someone listens to what I have to say. I will warn you, if the answers you seek are *not* already within your grasp, I cannot help you in understanding."

"I suppose I don't have much choice, so, in that case let me ask you this: Will I, along with my companions, see the end of the prophecy?"

"That is a good question, but the true answer will surprise you. Nothing really ends. Some things have a way of changing when you least expect them to, and, when you think you've finished something, you learn that in reality what has finished was merely the beginning of something else. The outcome you seek has yet to be determined. Many factors must be eliminated before what you might consider to be an 'end' can be seen." Kuohlo could see the confusion on Ka'tia's face, so he said in a more soothing tone, "I will assure you of one thing. You will be there." He paused for a moment. "Do you have any other questions?"

Ka'tia frowned. *Was that an answer? Well, at least I know I will be there at the end of it. I wonder if he will tell me a few things about our fearless leader,* she thought. "Do you know why Nakiata has such a desire, or, should I dare say, a *need* — to kill? Is there anything I can do to help her refrain from killing, or even give her other avenues?"

"The knowledge you are asking about comes with a great price, one that you are unable to pay. Some things must be as they are, even if they unbalance others. Some knowledge must go on unknown, or it could destroy me and inevitably everything else. If you truly desire to help her, seek the peace that you experienced in that precious moment just before you came to this place."

"I don't understand," Ka'tia replied in frustration.

"You will, when the time is right. I do have a small token of knowledge that I wish to impart to you. The first is simple bit about fear. You have no need of it. The rest is about a feeling. I want you to remember the feeling you are about to experience. You can use it when you want to travel from place to place. It *hurts* far less." Kuohlo shut his eyes and continued to speak. "Now, the time has come for you to go. I have enjoyed our chat. Perhaps next time I will allow you to stay longer. I am in need of rest."

"I don't wish to go yet. I don't even know how to get back," Ka'tia insisted.

Kuohlo opened his eyes, and they flared brightly. "One last thing. There's no need to hold hands." He snorted fiercely, which caused short, blue flames to exit his nostrils. When the flames vanished, two small puffs of navy-blue colored smoke appeared. Ka'tia watched Kuohlo's slowly vanished from sight.

The two small puffs of smoke remained. They began to expand and fill the entire area. *This looks like the kind of smoke that comes up any time I transport myself from one place to the next. I wonder if it's the same thing.* She braced herself for the awkward feeling, but Ka'tia quickly realized that this smoke was far different than the kind she was accustomed to.

The texture of this smoke was smoother, and the more she examined it the more she could see that it was creating an immersive and highly tranquil feeling. It was better than the smoke she conjured before. It swirled around her, increasing in speed, while closing in.

She was ready and the instant it enveloped her, she was happy and at peace. Up until now, the initial process of being consumed by the smoke always felt so forceful. This time she felt as though the smoke was gliding around her. It was easing her into a more relaxed, smooth transition from where she was to wherever it was she was about to go.

Chapter 18

Several weeks had passed, and Ka'tia was still missing. Kola'gram waited for only a couple of days before he left Melia'na's house in search of answers that could potentially lead them to the possible whereabouts of Ka'tia. In his absence, Melia'na spent the majority of her time either chasing after Tyrog to keep him from eating her exotic plants or volleying him with endless questions, trying to learn more about science and technology.

Nakiata was indifferent. She spent her time meditating and practicing her martial skills. With every day that passed, she became more impatient and would not tolerate Dravone's presence for extended periods of time.

Dravone continued to remain hopeful. He did his best to comfort Nakiata, knowing that somewhere deep down she missed Ka'tia just as much as the rest of them even if she never showed it. *I think she's angrier at herself because she wasn't able to do anything to help Ka'tia,* he thought one morning while on his way to meet up with Tyrog.

Since they had returned Tyrog took it upon himself to educate Dravone in a few of the more basic concepts, such as math, science, and physics. Each and every time it gave him plenty of excitement simply being able to talk about those subjects, and most of what he was trying to teach Dravone, only managed to be forgotten by his pupil moments later. There were a few instances when something managed to make sense, but it was always the rudimentary ideas.

It was early morning, when a soft breeze carrying a distinct odor that could only come from one thing, wafted through the house. No one was fully awake yet, but the moment the smell reached Nakiata's nostrils, she instantly made the connection. She opened her eyes, jumped out of bed, rushed to the door and opened it, hoping to see Ka'tia standing right outside her door.

Ka'tia was not there. Nakiata searched up and down the hallway, and yet there were no signs of anything out of the ordinary. For a moment, Nakiata thought she might have been dreaming. She sighed and lowered her head. When her eyes met the floor, she stopped, awestruck. She was completely transfixed as she watched the last bit of a navy-blue colored smoke slip under the door to Ka'tia's room.

Nakiata regarded the door with extreme curiosity. She smirked, took a deep breath, and kicked it open. Nakiata rushed into the room, which was filled with the swirling, dark smoke. She watched as it converged around the bed. Its speed increased.

There was a thud, a sudden rush of air, followed by the smoke becoming still. As it cleared, Nakiata could see Ka'tia's form lying on the bed. She appeared to be sleeping soundly. "Ka'tia!" she screamed, jumping up onto the bed and wrapping her arms around her.

Ka'tia was startled by the scream, but quickly realized that she had somehow returned safe and sound to her room in Melia'na's house. It took her a moment to take in her surroundings; the last place she had remembered them being in was in the temple. Ka'tia grimaced for a moment, *what was that thing? Those blue flaming — Why can't remember! How did I get here?*

A few seconds later, everyone showed up in the room. Tyrog landed himself at the edge of the bed and was letting out tiny spurts of fire, while Melia'na stood by the bed looking relieved.

For some reason Dravone was the first person Ka'tia wanted to see, but he was the only one who didn't enter her room, at least not fully. He stood in the doorway for a moment with a slight grin, which conveyed his happiness at her return. He only lingered for a moment before he retired back into the other room. Nakiata frowned at Dravone and chased after him. She wanted to know why he left in such a hurry.

"So where have you been all this time?" Tyrog asked.

"All what time? How long have I been gone? Weren't we just in the temple? And while we're talking about places, how did we get here?" she asked. Ka'tia put a hand to her mouth, yawned, and put her head back down on the pillow.

"I'll handle this," Tyrog said calmly. "When you performed *Hisi'k* magic to open the locked door, we thought the energy released had incinerated you. We didn't have much choice, so, we continued on to the vault, where we eventually found the key. It was as Vri'odo said. Afterward, we left and were met by Kola'gram and Melia'na. That's when Kola'gram informed us that you were still alive, but he didn't know where you were."

Ka'tia sat up a little to see where Kola'gram was. "Don't bother, he left several weeks ago to search for clues to some mystery he's trying to solve." Melia'na said.

"I've been missing for several weeks?" Ka'tia asked, surprised.

"Three weeks and four days, to be exact," Melia'na corrected. She smiled briefly before continuing. "Now that you're back, we need to get all of you to the temple of Kili'dri so we can finally find out what's beyond the door."

"Can it wait till after we eat? I'm starving," Ka'tia groaned.

Malia'na smiled. "I think that would be fine. I'll go get a few things set on the table." She bowed and left the room.

"Now, my powerful Zonian friend, where have you been all this time?" Tyrog asked again.

Ka'tia sat up all the way, and gazed into Tyrog's glistening, purple eyes with their sideways, cat-like, white irises. "I was . . . somewhere . . ." Ka'tia was struggling to remember where she was. In her mind she was only able to visualize tiny bits and pieces. "I was out in space? No, that's not right, I wasn't in space, but that's how it appeared. The best way I can describe it is that it was like being out amongst the stars, in a safe place."

"You were in space? Did you see anything specific? Were there any planets or moons nearby? Did you recognize anything at all?" Tyrog inquired.

"Not that I can . . ." Ka'tia's eyes went wide, "I was having a conversation with — the universe, or, as it wanted to be called, Kuohlo."

"What did it look like?" Tyrog asked, excitedly.

Ka'tia raised an eyebrow. "Like a giant, see-through Brolo."

Tyrog stuck out his forked tongue. "Intriguing. Will you be able to remember all that? I'm sure the others will want to hear it. I myself have a few questions."

Ka'tia and Tyrog arrived to find the others finishing their breakfast, which Melia'na had prepared for them. They both sat down and quickly ate. Tyrog announced he was done with a loud belch. "Ka'tia could you tell the others where you've been and don't spare any details," he chirped.

Ka'tia did her best to recall the events that took place after she left the temple.

"That's a little farfetched. You actually expect us to believe that 'The Universe' spoke to you, and that it took the form of a giant Brolo. Sounds to me like you might have gone somewhere else, hit your head on something, and had an intense dream. You finally woke up and realized that we weren't there, so you thought of one of us, and that's when you arrive back here," Nakiata scoffed.

Everyone at the table frowned at Nakiata.

"How rude! I for one believe every word of it," Melia'na insisted.

"Yeah, I think I believe her too," Dravone said.

"Either way, she's here now. I still have a question or two. What were you feeling during your encounter? I want all the specifics, every object or anything of relevance. Can you do that for me?" Tyrog asked.

Ka'tia stared at him a little cross-eyed. She thought about it for a minute. "Peaceful, that's how I felt, and I didn't notice anything else, beyond what I've already told you."

Melia'na stood, waved a hand dismissing the table with magic. She held out her hands and motioned for them to hold hands so that she could transport them all to the temple.

"No, no, no!" Ka'tia said, her eyebrows raised up, and a huge smile appeared. She'd just remembered something that Kuohlo had said. "We don't need to do that," she conveyed to them. She closed her eyes, thought of where she wanted to go, and let an extreme calm take over her. Within seconds, a navy-blue cloud of smoke swirled up around them, and they were gone.

They were now high up in the temple, inside the room where the door they needed to open was. To everyone's surprise, Tso'li was in front of the door, and it he was clearly trying to pick the lock. After a moment of trying, it began to glow a dark red color, and he knew that if he didn't back away it was going to kill him. He stumbled right into Dravone.

. "I was . . . trying to . . . it's good to see you. Why have you come?" Tso'li said.

Dravone held up the key. "We found this, and now we are going to open the door."

"Wonderful. May assist you?" he inquired.

"I don't think that would be a wise choice. I think this is something only they can do." Melia'na referred to the four of them.

"I will merely observe," Tso'li bowed and waved his hand, signaling them to open the door. *After it's open, it will be time,* he was thinking, and he allowed an evil grin to show.

"The magical locks will need to be dealt with first," Melia'na reminded them.

"I guess that would be my chore," Ka'tia said, stepping forward. *I'm not exactly sure how to get these locks to open, but here goes . . .* She reached out and placed a hand on the door, shut her eyes and began to listen. She could almost hear the magic. At first it was like a faint, unrecognizable whisper. It didn't take long to grow a little louder.

Ka'tia still couldn't make out if there were actual words being said, but she decided to try and communicate. *I would like to open this door. Will you let me pass?* The door began to shine bright red. It started to shudder as multiple locks disengaged. "I think that's it," she said, backing away from the door.

Dravone took the key from around his neck and handed it to Nakiata. "I think it's your turn," he said.

Nakiata took the key and gave it a onceover before turning and moving closer to the door. As she slowly raised the key up to the hole, the room fell silent. Everyone was so completely fixated on the key and Nakiata's movements that no one noticed Kola'gram appearing behind them.

Kola'gram quickly reached out and tapped Melia'na on the shoulder. She jumped slightly and quickly whirled around to see who had snuck up behind her. He'd already placed a finger up to his lips to let her know not to make an outburst. He began using a series of hand signals that he devised and taught her years ago so that they could communicate with each other, and without anyone else understanding the contents of their conversation. He quickly conveyed his message. *Take one of Dravone's hands, along with Tyrog's. I will take Ka'tia's and Dravone's other hand and transport us away from here. But we must act now; we cannot stay here. Do it, now.*

The key slid into the hole, and Nakiata tried to turn it. It didn't move. "What's the matter?" Tso'li inquired.

"I don't know! It's not turning!" Nakiata retorted angrily.

"Well, turn the key a little harder. It might be stuck. Please, it has to work!" Tso'li insisted. He walked up and grabbed her hand, along with the key. With a large amount of gripping force, he tried to turn the key. It didn't budge. "Let go of my hand!" she demanded.

"No! This has to work — I must see what's inside. I need to see —" Tso'li anger was interrupted by a slight discomfort in his back. He glanced down and saw that was no longer holding her hand, only the key. Surprised, he held the key aloft and examined it briefly.

Confusion set in and he let go of it. Before the key hit the ground, the door shuddered once again, the magical locks had re-engaged.

Tso'li was having some discomfort in his back. He reached around to find out what might be causing it, and felt Nakiata's arm, along with her Kharak blade, which was now buried up to the hand guard in his back. "What have you done?" he asked. The position of her blades caused him to have shortness of breath. He was continually gasping.

"This obviously isn't the key! You tricked us! I warned you not to deceive us. Now you, and all of the priests in this farce of a temple, are going to suffer my wrath," Nakiata said coldly.

"But — the key — it fit . . ." These were the last words Tso'li said as he fell to the ground, dead.

Nakiata turned to find she was alone. *Where are my companions? I can't believe they left me here, alone!* She thought. Her anger increasing with each passing moment. *Grrrr, so be it. They will pay!* Nakiata vanished into pure SOT.

"Where are we?" Ka'tia asked.

"This is my home. It's located far from the temple. We will be safe here," Kola'gram answered.

"Safe from what?" Tyrog asked.

"From Nakiata," Kola'gram said grimly.

"I don't believe you. There is no way that we could've been in danger from her, could we?" Dravone asked, annoyed.

Kola′gram could hear the distress in Dravone's voice. He knew how much Dravone cared for her. "I'm going to need some time alone. I have to see something."

Tyrog glanced around at the meager accommodations of Kola′gram's house. "What is it that you need to see?"

"Possible futures, and I need to be alone to do it. There is food in that room. I know you will all find something to your liking." Kola′gram bowed and left the room.

Kola′gram's house was both technologically advanced and yet it still had many old features, the stonework of the walls, the old wooden doors, and the antiquated furniture covered with a thin layer of dust. All-in-all the house had a strong welcoming feel.

Kola′gram proceeded down a long narrow corridor away from the others, stopping at the end and placing his hand on a scanner. The moment his skin made contact with the detection plate, it scanned his hand and took DNA samples from minute skin particles.

A few audible clicks let him know that the secured door was now unlocked, and he could proceed.

The door automatically opened up, revealing a spiral staircase leading down. Kola′gram stepped in and began to descend. He was unaware that Tyrog had snuck in and was following him down the stairs.

The stairs went down about a hundred feet and led to a single room with monitors scattered throughout. Each monitor displayed something different. Some were images of solar systems, while others were displaying raw data being compiled or categorized. *Jackpot. I bet I can learn all sorts of new things in here,* Tyrog thought to himself.

Kola′gram walked to the middle of the room, where there was a dim circle of light on the floor. He stopped in the center, sat down, and a couple minutes later was deep in meditation, or so he appeared. "You may come in, Tyrog," he said.

Tyrog stuck his forked tongue out several times before hopping into the room. "This room is quite impressive. I see you have many things going on at once. I hope you don't mind if I peruse the area, and possibly have access to a terminal?"

"You may, as long as you are quiet. I need to concentrate. Searching the future for specific details is not easy, and it takes a lot of physical energy on my part."

"You won't even know I'm here," Tyrog replied giddily.

Kola′gram opened an eye, smirked, and immediately went back to meditating. *You, my scaly friend, are about to discover the answers to many things. I hope the information you find will quench your thirst for knowledge — if only for a time. Now, let me see the end of their love. Is that the only way?* Kola′gram searched the future.

Tyrog quietly moved the only chair in the room closer to one of three small, square posts. Each post, he concluded, contained a motion-sensor light-key control board that he could use to access the various monitors on the wall that the post faced. He was extremely eager to search the Dia′fani's database for any new information he could find.

As soon as he was situated on the chair, he waved his hand over the post and as he suspected, a large lighted-key control board appeared in front of him. It was more sophisticated than any he'd ever seen before. There were at least two hundred unique keys, which was more than double the number of keys he was accustomed to. *First things first. I need to decipher the Dia'fani's written language. Since I don't have my Itzuli, it's going to take me a long . . .* Tyrog didn't get to finish his thought; the keys on the massive keyboard began to transform right in front of him. He watched with curiosity as the number of keys diminished, splitting and melding into a new pattern. As they reorganized themselves, he immediately began to recognize the new symbols which appeared on them. The keys were now in his own language.

Tyrog watched the monitors and noticed that the information being presented had also changed and was now displayed in his language. *Well, that certainly makes things easier.* Tyrog stretched his arms out and placed his hands above the keyboard. His pupils narrowed, and his fingers began moving at an incredible speed over the light keyboard. The information buzzed across multiple screens.

Tyrog was amazed at the amount of knowledge the Dia'fani actually possessed. The first things he delved into was the information they had on the subjects of physics, quantum mechanics, interstellar travel, and time. He even took a moment to glance through some tidbits they had on the subject of magic. Tyrog snorted and hissed quietly. *I wonder if Kola'gram has any information about the prophecy.*

After a few keystrokes, Tyrog's eyes went as wide as they could. He had found an answer, and it was not one that he was expecting. "Yes, I have been aware of that for some time now. The question is, what are you going to do with that information?" Kola'gram asked, standing directly behind Tyrog.

Tyrog spun around on the chair, and for the moment, he had no immediate answer. "Take your time and think about what you've seen. I would offer you a small piece of advice: Keep this to yourself. Before you ask why, I will give you one simple reason. If you pass along any of that information to the others, it will no longer be valid and true. Once they know, it will create a change." Kola'gram tapped on several of the light-keys, followed by a gesture with his hand, signaling Tyrog to turn around and view the monitors.

Tyrog couldn't believe his eyes. Every monitor in the room combined to show a single image which spanned from one side to the other. "Is that . . ."

"One outcome. One I hope never comes to pass, my dear Tyrog. Through our gift and technology, we have been able to extrapolate such knowledge. Luckily, you're coming to terms with it does not affect any of the numerous outcomes I have witnessed, as long as you remain silent." Kola'gram tapped on a few more keys, and the screens throughout the room went blank.

Tyrog bowed. "Now I understand the weight of it. I swear on the blood of my life that I will never speak of what I have learned." His tone was soft and melancholy. Tears began to well up in his eyes.

"It was an unavoidable burden. Your species has and will always have an insatiable appetite for knowledge, no matter the price it brings. Take comfort, my Sodaran friend. There is always hope for new beginnings, because without them the universe would cease to be."

Tyrog cocked his head to one side. Kola'gram's word choices were a bit confusing to him. *I have learned more than enough today, and it has upset me far more than I realized. I don't think I could deal with anything like what I've seen, no matter how much I desperately want to know.* He quietly took to the air and flew back up to join the others.

Ka'tia and Melia'na were sitting at one end of the table discussing the power behind *Hisi'k* magic, while Dravone was sitting on the far side of the table in a large chair, stuffing his mouth with fresh, partially cooked meat. "May I join you?" Tyrog inquired.

Dravone turned his head, glanced down at the Sodaran, and gave him a slight nod. He didn't look happy at all, and he wasn't aware that Tyrog now understood the feelings he had for Nakiata.

Tyrog wasn't about to upset Dravone any further, so he respectfully bowed before hopping up onto the table and grabbing a large, heaping handful of meat. Normally, he would stuff his face and grab more, but this time he jumped down off the table, plopped down next to Dravone, and slowly nibbled on the meat in silence.

Chapter 19

Kola′gram had finished what he was doing and returned to where everyone else was patiently waiting. "What do we do now?" Ka'tia asked.

Kola′gram smiled briefly and waved his hand over the table. The food and everything on it vanished, leaving a pristine, shiny metal surface. "We prepare for her arrival." All of a sudden, his skin pigmentation drained away, and his body became translucent. "Melia′na, you may go now. Your assistance is no longer required. I will guide them from here."

Melia′na stood up and bowed to everyone. "I shall miss you all. Even you, you little plant-eating mongrel," she said with a smile, pointing at Tyrog. A small cloud of dark smoke spiraled up and whisked her away.

Seconds later, the front door to the house burst open, and Nakiata stepped into the open doorway. She immediately began sizing them up. This was a clear indication that she was preparing to attack. Nakiata was already drenched in blood. Her hair, face, hands, and clothes were saturated with the rust-colored substance. There was no way of knowing how many victims had met their fate at her hands.

Nakiata shifted her weight ever so slightly. She was now standing in an offensive pose, her Kharak blades firmly in her hands, and her eyes were dark-gray, and void of any emotion. Even more disturbing was the fact that she showed no signs of recognition that she knew them as her friends. Tyrog stepped forward as submissively as possible. "Nakiata, it's us, your companions, your friends. We are not your enemy. You need to take a deep breath and steady yourself. Calm down and be at peace. Dravone is also here."

Ka'tia's eyes went wide when she heard the word "peace". Something inside her clicked. She stood up, moving slowly, and walked over until she was standing next to Tyrog. "Let me try something," she said softly.

"What are you going to do?" Dravone asked with concern.

"I'm not exactly sure. I do know that whatever I decide, it *will* work. Now shush," Ka'tia demanded in an even softer tone so that Nakiata could not hear her. Ka'tia closed her eyes, stretched out her arms and hands as far as they would go. She held the pose which gave the impression she was waiting to hug Nakiata. A fine golden mist slowly descended through the ceiling.

The mist was slow-moving, defying gravity as it wafted around. It was like an apparition hanging in the air just above Nakiata. The mist formed into the shape of a hand. It thrust forward at her, but the mist was exceptionally light to the touch. Nakiata showed immense fortitude, she didn't move, flinch, nor was she concerned that it was starting to attach itself to her.

After a couple of minutes, Nakiata was already halfway covered from head to toe. As more of the mist connected with her, it began to glow. Another minute passed, and she had taken on the appearance of a highly polished, glimmering, golden statue.

Surprisingly, Nakiata still hadn't moved a muscle. Nobody was sure if it was a conscious decision, or if the mist had rendered her immobile. One last, tiny particle slowly descended, and as it fell it pulsated, giving off a soft-yellow light. The moment it made contact with the rest of the mist; beams of radiant light erupted outward.

Ka'tia lowered her hands. They still had a faint yellow glow about them, but it was diminishing rapidly. "Everything is going to be fine now," she said happily, and fighting to keep her eyelids open. She was drowsy. Her eyes shut and she smiled. Before anyone could react, she fell to the ground, unconscious. The moment she hit the floor, the lights in the house flickered and were snuffed out.

The short-lived moment of silence was broken when Nakiata's voice echoed through the room. "Why's it so, dark in here?"

"Everyone, please remain calm. The lights will return momentarily," Kola'gram announced with confidence. Several loud, electrical pops and sparks sounded, followed by a single click, and the lights came back on.

Tyrog, having great night vision, was already attending to Ka'tia. He was holding her head in his scaly lap and using one of his wings to fan her with air. She slowly came around. "What happened? Is Nakiata . . ." Ka'tia asked, sounding a little confused.

"I'm here," Nakiata stated plainly. "Although, I don't know where we are," she said angrily.

"This is my home, and you have nothing to fear," Kola'gram explained.

"I don't fear anything," Nakiata snapped.

"Of course you don't. I apologize for my poor choice of words," he continued, bowing humbly.

"I thought the Dia'fani were supposed to be able to see the future? If that's true, how is it that *this* is not the right key?" Nakiata asked, throwing the key down that Dravone had handed her.

"Our gift of foresight is not infallible. Once we've seen the possibilities of a particular future, the knowledge gained can alter it drastically. We do know that even the slightest attempt to change the future will always produce an unwanted outcome. Do you understand? The key I saw looked exactly like this one," Kola'gram explained. He picked up the key and examined it.

"This is curious," he noted. He set the key down on the table and pulled out a small piece of metal that had a sharp point on one end. "This key was made by someone who possesses technology which rivals that of the Dia'fani, and, if I'm not mistaken, they left us a message." Kola'gram placed the metal point on the handle of the key. He pushed down, and everyone heard a soft click.

The handle opened up and began emitting large amounts of light, which came together to form a three-dimensional holographic image. "I know who that is," Dravone chimed. The image was of Zadno'st, The Most-High.

Zadno'st began to move, and a tinny, automated voice started to speak. "If you are witnessing this, I am happy to inform you of your blunder. You have unwittingly taken nothing more than a facsimile." Zadno'st smiled mischievously. "I promise that I will not to be too distraught. I suppose the amazing thing to be revered is that you managed to steal it in the first place. As a reward for such cunning and stealth, I will bestow upon you something of great value, a little bit of knowledge.

"The real key, if that's what it is, has been hidden away on a remote planet. It is one of the first planets that our beloved Commonwealth acquired, or to be more precise, conquered. Nonetheless — oh, did I forget to mention that it's also home to my secret, impregnable, palace? If you care to try your hand at this task, I can assist you." Zadno'st said as his form stepped out of view.

A three-dimensional holographic star map filled the entire room. The planet they were currently on had a red pulsing glow around it. An orange arrow of light appeared on the edge, and it was creeping away from the planet. An instant later, the arrow shot across the room leaving a trail that could be easily followed. It stopped, and the planet it pointed to beg pulsing with a green glow, showing everyone the exact location of the planet Zadno'st had mentioned. "I do hope you get the chance to visit — if you survive, that is. That in itself would truly be a miracle, ah-hahaha!" The holographic image collapsed, and the key began beeping at intervals that steadily increased in frequency.

Kola'gram nonchalantly reached out and picked up the key. They were both consumed in an extremely fast-moving whirlwind of black smoke.

"Where did he go?" Nakiata asked, perturbed.

"I don't think it matters. That key, fake or not, was going to explode. It was obviously meant to kill whoever took it, and Kola'gram saved our lives," Tyrog said harshly.

"Well I suppose that fact of *where* he went, doesn't matter. However, it still leaves us right here without any way of . . ."

"That's not true. I can take us," Ka'tia interrupted. "Although, I didn't recognize that planet, and I'm not sure where it is, so getting —"

"I have the solution to your problem. Come on," Tyrog signaled them to follow him toward Kola'gram's basement. As soon as he turned the corner, he realized that the door was sealed shut. "Well, this puts a damper on things," he announced.

"May I?" Ka'tia eased Tyrog to the side. She put her hand on the scanner, but after it had scanned her hand the door remained locked. Ka'tia closed her eyes and focused on the scanner. *We need to get into the basement. You will open, and let us in,* she thought.

Her hand began to glow a soft green, and everyone heard a sizzling sound. A second later the door opened, and Ka'tia pulled her hand away from the scanner, where an imprint of her hand had melted into it.

"Impressive," Tyrog commented. He took to the air and flew down the long staircase ahead of everyone else.

By the time the others reached the basement, Tyrog had already found the information he was searching for. "Ah, just in time!" He tapped out the final keystroke.

Every monitor in the room lit up, and each one was showing a different image. The screen to the far left showed their current location on Frole. As they scanned to the right, they could see a line guiding them to the remote planet where Zadno'st's secret palace was located.

"Will that help?" Tyrog asked, sticking out his forked tongue momentarily.

"More than adequate," Ka'tia replied, as she raised her hands, palms up. A cloud of shimmering, white smoke filled the room and swirled around them.

"This is . . ." Dravone started to say, but the smoke enveloped them.

". . . different," Dravone quickly concluded, once they'd arrived at the edge of a field with a menacing-looking, high-walled palace off in the distance. "Why was the smoke white? I'm not complaining; it felt much more peaceful going from there to here."

"I haven't the slightest clue, Dravone. I never understood why the color of the smoke differed from person to person, or why it changed color for me. I wouldn't worry too much about it. We are here, and now we need to figure out how to get inside that palace and get the true key," Ka'tia said.

"Wait here. If I don't return in about ten minutes, give or take a few, send Tyrog in after me," Nakiata said. She vanished into pure SOT. *Don't worry yourselves*, she thought. *I will take care of any threats that might be hiding within, and I'll be sure to retrieve the true key.* She ran toward the palace.

"Do we go after her?" Dravone asked.

Ka'tia regarded him as if he'd lost his mind. "For once, I think we should do exactly what she said, and wait here."

Nakiata had reached the enormous palace, and after a brief period of searching she found a small, wooden door that the servants used to come and go. The door was guarded by two Kalipygans, who hadn't yet detected her presence.

The door began to open, and a young woman exited. Nakiata allowed her rage and frustration to fill her to the brim. She wasn't sure what measure of time it was before she'd lost track of what was happening. She remembered thrusting herself forward and beginning the attack on the two Kalipygans, but that was it.

Alarms began to sound throughout the palace. "What's going on?" Zodno'st demanded.

His most trusted aide was at a terminal, punching keys as fast as she could. "I don't know, your Most-High. All I know for certain is that our security has been breached and we are under attack."

"Well, do something about it!" he commanded.

You pompous idiot, thought the aide to herself. *I hope that whoever or whatever is attacking us makes their way here and kills us both. At least then I wouldn't have to listen to you harp on about mundane things, and not to mention you continuously making demands of everyone — and, mostly, so you don't take advantage of me whenever you please.*

"Bring up the life scanner map on the center screen. We should be able to track the intruders through that!" Zadno′st exclaimed.

The aide smirked as she punched in the key sequence that would activate the newly acquired and installed life scanners. Everyone within the palace, servants and Kalipygans, as well as The Most-High, had been injected with a unique micro-transmitter. The scanners use the signals to locate and display those who'd been injected as one of three colors: Tiny green blips indicated the servants, purple blips the Kalipygans, and a single blue blip marked the position of Zadno′st on a specially designed computer map. Anyone else would show up as a red blip.

The oversized central screen instantly switched to the multi-leveled representation of the palace, with a numerical counter at the bottom totaling the number of signals it was receiving.

"Where is everyone, and why don't we see any intruders?" Zadno′st questioned her.

"I don't understand, my lord. I know the scanners are working because there are twenty — no, wait — ten, five, three signals being received. My lord Zadno′st, according to this, we are the only two left, and there's a single intruder right outside the doors." The aide stepped away from the terminal.

"Those doors are made from Kobalum, one of the most exotic and strongest metals known," Zadno′st boasted. "They are impregnable, and no one is getting past them."

"It's been about ten minutes. Should we continue to wait?" Dravone asked.

"She did say give or take a few minutes," Tyrog pointed out. He saw the fear and impatience come to Dravone's eyes. "But perhaps . . . I think it's been long enough." He started hopping off toward the palace.

Tyrog was about to take to the air when Nakiata appeared directly in front of him, causing him to tumble to the ground. "Grrr, I wish you wouldn't do that," he snapped, picking himself up.

She didn't reply but fell to the ground and passed out. Dravone rushed to her side and quickly eased her head up onto his lap. "Nakiata, please be okay," he whispered. He carefully pulled off her left Kharak blade and was about to remove the other when she came around.

"What are you doing?" she asked.

"I'm keeping you from hurting yourself accidentally. You passed out with your blades still in your hands. You're lucky you didn't fall on them," he replied.

"So what happened? Were you able to find the key? I know there was a fight, because your weapons have blood on them again," Ka'tia said.

"No. There is a set of metal doors I couldn't get past. They're made of Kobalum."

"Kobalum — are you sure?" Tyrog beckoned for a quick answer.

"Yes, the doors are unmistakably made of the same material as my Kharak blades. Why?"

"How much opposition is left inside?"

"I don't know. I can't remember," she retorted angrily.

Tyrog spit on the ground, which began to sizzle and burn. "You don't remember, but yet you know about the doors?" he asked, sounding confused.

"Yes, I recall the doors. Everything else that happened is a blur," she snapped back.

"Do you still have enough strength to get the key?" Tyrog asked.

Nakiata furrowed her brow. "I'm fine, but how do you propose to get past those doors?" she asked.

"Oh, I wouldn't worry about those," he said. He let his tongue slither in and out of his mouth several times.

Dravone helped Nakiata back onto her feet, and they all made their way to the palace, where they found the two massive front gates wide open. Hundreds of servant bodies lay strewn in and around the entrance.

"Did they need to die?" Ka'tia screamed at Nakiata.

Nakiata's face contorted, clearly she was becoming angry at Ka'tia. "What's your point, Zonduran warrior? Would you care to join them?"

"Whoa, now!" Dravone intervened. "I think we should concentrate our efforts on getting the key. What's done is done, and there is nothing we can do about it. Isn't that right, Tyrog?"

Everyone turned to get the Sodaran's take on it, but he was preoccupied with taking a chunk out of a dead servant woman's leg.

"What are you doing?" Ka'tia exclaimed. "Has everyone gone crazy? Nakiata can't resist or refrain from killing things. Tyrog can't stop eating everything. Dravone can't —" She stopped in the nick of time. *That was close; I almost let our secret out. If that ever comes to light and Nakiata finds out, I'm a dead woman.*

"Dravone can't stop what?" Nakiata demanded.

"It's not important," she replied softly.

"Tell me now, or so help me I will make you suffer!"

Ka'tia raised her hands out wide. Her eyes went opaque, and the air around them became cold and still. *What am I doing?*

"Remember . . . peace," Kuohlo's voice sounded ever so subtly in her head.

Yes, peace, tranquility. Must calm her down. A cold burst of wind exploded outward from Ka'tia.

"What are you do — ing?" Nakiata asked the moment the wind hit. Her expression of anger was gone. Now she had a blank stare on her face.

Even Dravone and Tyrog began acting a bit more relaxed. Tyrog stopped gnawing on the dead woman's leg, and Dravone had a dumbfounded grin showing.

"Which way to the doors?" Ka'tia asked in the kindest, calmest tone she could muster.

"Up those stairs, turn right, and they're at the end of the hall." Nakiata pointed at the large central staircase.

"You have the lead, my fine, scaly friend," Ka'tia said, looking directly at Tyrog, who grinned slightly.

It only took a couple of minutes to reach the end of the hall, which terminated at two massive, blue, metal doors, which was exactly as Nakiata described it. Tyrog stepped behind Ka'tia. "Could you be so kind as to kneel down a bit? I need to get something out of your pack."

Ka'tia did as she was asked, and as soon as she was low enough to the ground, Tyrog reached in and pulled out one of the small Sodralinium stones. "I'm going to need all of you to step back and give me some room," he told them. He tossed the stone into the air and swallowed it with one gulp.

Several seconds passed, and Tyrog's body began to change in size. The process didn't take long, and once he'd reached his full height, he took a deep breath and let out a flame that melted the doors in seconds.

Tyrog did his best to squeeze through the opening, but he was still too large. But his brute strength overcame the weakened building structure, and he crashed through, making an even larger opening for the others. To his relief, the throne room had an exceedingly high, vaulted ceiling, giving him plenty of room to stand up straight. He even had enough space to stretch out his wings.

Tyrog let out a roar of relief, which inevitably caused the two occupants to flee to the other end of the room, where a single throne was situated. Zadno'st quickly took up a position on the throne and adjusted himself so that he was sitting high-and-mighty like, with an obvious smile of pride across his smug face.

His female aide, however, cowered behind the throne, knowing that death was imminent. *Finally, a beast who can end my suffering and wipe out the imbecile sitting on the throne,* she thought. Utter hatred mingled with her high hopes.

Nakiata rushed into the room and right up to the throne, but she stopped a few feet shy of the throne itself. Out of the corner of her eye, she noticed a red-light twinkling. "Why stop now? Are you that much of an amateur assassin that you can't complete the job?" Zadno'st taunted her.

"You're insufferable!" Dravone said before changing into his wolf-state and rushing toward the throne.

Nakiata spun around in time to step between Dravone and the throne. She blocked his path, hoping to prevent him from setting off the trap that she just become aware of. Unfortunately, she had underestimated his strength and speed. When he came in contact with her, the force knocked her backward, activating the trap.

The throne vaulted backward, almost throwing Zadno′st to the ground. A fraction of a second later, a clear, glass-like cage burst upward, trapping Nakiata inside. *This isn't so bad; at least I'll be able to get out through the —* But before she could finish her thought, a metal frame with a lid for the cage came crashing down from high above. The instant the lid and the base of the cage came into contact with each other, they fused together in a rapid chemical reaction.

"Trapped like a stupid little Savoga′t, hahaha!" Zadno′st said triumphantly

"You think this glass cage is going to hold me?" Nakiata said. She took a Kharak blade and stabbed at the side as hard as she could. Her blade bounced off without even making a scratch. *Ow. Let me try this*, she thought slashing at it with the arm blade, but still it had no effect.

"I'll get you out of there," Tyrog's booming voice echoed. He moved closer to the cage and positioned his mouth and lips so that they formed a small circle. It appeared as if he were about to whistle. Tyrog's lungs expanded and a hot stream of fire came out and struck the top of the cage with precision.

Nakiata could feel the heat from the fire, but when she became fixated on the top of her cage, she was disheartened because it was unaffected by the flame. She turned her attention back to her captor. "What kind of cage is this!" she demanded.

Zadno'st chuckled. "That, my little vermin, is the newest substance that the Commonwealth has recently acquired. It's called — um — it's called . . . aide! What is that stuff called again?"

From behind the throne came the squeaky, yet silky, voice of the aide. "It's called, your Most-High, Klactaplix. It is —"

"Yes, Klacta — polics, err, whatever it's called. It's a substance that is made of a combination of Kobalum, Sodralinium, and some other rare element. After our scientists discovered its formula, which was I remember by pure accident, they realized what an exquisite, super-dense, clear material they had in their hands. After that it was only a matter of how to use it. Of course, I had the brilliant notion to make an impenetrable cage, along with the new skyline windows up there." Zadno'st pointed up at the high ceiling, and continued, "The only downside was finding enough of the three substances, not to mention the costs of reproducing it. I was told that it takes an enormous amount of energy needed to — oh, I'm sorry, I have to apologize. I know you don't want to hear me keep rambling on about such things. Let's just say that you're never going to get out of there . . . alive, haha — ha."

Everyone attention shifted rapidly from Nakiata and her current predicament, to Zadno'st, whose laugh was interrupted. He appeared confused and mildly frightened. They could see that his attention was centered on his chest.

Protruding out from his chest, by a few inches, was the fletching and shaft of an arrow.

Nakiata was the first to catch sight of Ka'tia, who was still holding her bow out in front of her. "Why did you do that!" she yelled.

"Isn't that what you would have done?" Ka'tia retorted. "Besides, he wasn't going to be of any use to us, and, frankly, I think he deserved it," she said harshly.

The shot was fatal and was already draining the life out of him, but Zadno'st had enough strength left in him to reach up and touch the end of the arrow. "Ouch. That hurts. How are you going to find — the real — Most-High, now?" he asked with his dying breath. An overly smug smile appeared on his face, and he fell to the ground.

The female aide jumped up, ran to the front of the throne, grabbed the dead body, and started shaking it. "What do you mean? The real most-high?" she screamed in anger.

The aide felt a hand on her shoulder. She quickly reached down, grabbed a small dagger from Zadno'st's belt, and spun around to fend off whoever was behind her. "Stay back, or so help me I will slit you from your belly to your mouth!" she said defensively, tears streaming down her face.

Dravone, who was no longer in his wolf-state, threw up his hands and took a step back. After a moment of silence, the aide realized that his intentions were not to harm or violate her, so she lowered the dagger, but kept a firm grip on it, just in case. She wasn't sure if she could trust him.

The aide considered Dravone thoroughly. *I hate to say it, but if anyone was to ravish me again, I would let him for sure. Wait, what am I thinking?* She wasn't aware of the fact that she was now smiling at him with desire in her eyes.

Dravone did his best not to look her directly in the eyes. He knew that he had already begun to blush a little. "Ahem . . . um, you are safe now." He paused and glanced at the dead body, then back at the aide. "He can do you no more harm," he said, holding out his hand in as submissive a posture as he could manage.

The aide dropped the dagger and took his hand. Dravone took his other hand and covered hers with it. "That's better, isn't it? Now that you've calmed down a bit, perhaps you could answer a few questions for us?"

"I will try," she replied.

"Do you know how to get her out of there?" he pointed at Nakiata, who was glaring at them.

"No, but I can take you to someone who does, if she's still alive."

"Great. Now, do you know where he kept the key?"

"I'm not sure what key you're searching for, but anything of value will be locked in the Most-High's artifact room. Unfortunately, only he had access to it," she answered.

"I might be able to get us inside. Do you know where this artifact room is?" Tyrog inquired.

The aide walked back over to the throne. Each of its armrests boasted intricately carved solid-gold representations of five skulls. The eyes of each skull had a unique-colored jewel embedded into it. The aide placed her hand on the left armrest. She turned her hand in order to press the sapphire-colored eye on the second skull. Everyone heard the soft, audible click. A moment later there was a low rumbling coming from behind her.

A large section of the wall directly behind the throne slowly began to descend, revealing a set of glass doors, along with a hand scanner set in the wall on the right side. "The room is there, but he is the only one who can open the doors," she repeated.

Tyrog knew what he had to do to gain entry into the artifact room. "Have you ever been inside the room? Are there any traps, like that one?" He pointed to the cage, where Nakiata sat, meditating.

"Yes, I have been inside the room a few times. I never liked it. I always felt like someone else was in the room, watching us. I don't know of any traps inside the room itself."

Tyrog slid his forked tongue out, and several drops of spittle hit the ground, creating holes in the floor. "Stay low to the floor," he announced to everyone. He focused on the trap Nakiata was stuck in. He let out several short bursts of fire aimed at the top. He kept them brief so that air inside wouldn't get too hot. Before long, his size had reduced significantly.

Once back to normal, he walked over to Zadno'st's dead body and picked up his left arm. "Is this the hand he uses to open the door?" he asked the aide.

"I'm not sure. I never paid much attention to how he opened the doors," the aide answered.

"In that case, you might want to look away," Tyrog said. He cocked his head to one side and bit down hard on the dead man's forearm. Gnawing swiftly through the flesh until he reached the bone. With his powerful jaws, he closed his mouth, cracking the bone clean in half and allowing him to pull the appendage away from the rest of the body. Tyrog repeated the process with the other arm.

He took both severed arms and walked over to the hand scanner. He slung one of them over his shoulder, while he slapped the other up against the scanner. He did his best to spread the fingers over the scanner so that it would activate. *Come on, do your thing. Scan the hand, and open,* he mentally pleaded with it. It lit up, and a bright green line moved from the top of the scanner down to the bottom. Once the cycle was complete, nothing happened. The doors remained securely shut. "Hmmm, it must be the right hand that opens the doors," he concluded.

Tyrog tossed the left hand to the ground and positioned the right hand on the scanner. The moment the scanner cycle was complete, the doors opened with a soft *swishing* sound. "Okay, my dear, would you be so kind as to show me where the key is?" he asked the aide.

The aid was taking a single step toward Tyrog when the lights in the throne room began to flicker. An instant later they went out. There was some dim light coming from the windows high above their heads, allowing the group to see a dark cloud of smoke swirling around the room. The smoke collected itself into a small funnel cloud that migrated toward the artifact room. *Could that be Kola'gram?* Ka'tia thought.

Before the cloud dissipated, a spear came flying out. It struck the aide in the center of her chest with such force that it lifted her off the ground and impaled her against Nakiata's trap.

The smoke finally cleared, and there stood Kola'gram, strong and alive. Everyone was shocked to see him.

The *clang* of the spear, as it struck the trap, aroused Nakiata from her meditation. Her reaction was profound. Her eyes went wide and she immediately focused on the tip of the weapon. It had somehow penetrated the sidewall. Nakiata smirked. *Now isn't that a sight.*

"Quickly! Get the key and come right back! You'll find it sitting on top of a pedestal on the right side of the artifact room!" Kola'gram shouted at Tyrog.

Kola'gram spun around, "Yes, it's good to see you too Ka'tia, but there's no time for lengthy conversations. I need you to be prepared to take Tyrog and yourself as far away from here as possible, and fast. The moment he returns with the key, leave!"

He knew she was about to ask him why. "Because the wall to the trap will not hold much longer, and she knows it." He pointed at a furious-looking Nakiata. "Once you get to somewhere safe, I want you to wait there for one full day. Afterward you can meet us back at the temple of Kili'dri."

"Dravone! You come with me! I have no time to explain." Kola'gram rushed over to him, put a hand on his shoulder, and within seconds they were swallowed up by a dark cloud of smoke.

Ka'tia hesitated. She gazed at Nakiata for a brief moment, confused. Nakiata had the appearance of a lost, scared little girl. *I don't understand, but maybe I'm not meant to understand you. I would like to* — her thoughts came to a sudden halt when she noticed Nakiata's eyes changing color. The beautiful, royal blue quickly drained away and was rapidly being replaced by an almost entirely black hue.

"I've got it!" Tyrog's booming voice echoed through the open doors.

Ka'tia glanced back and forth between Nakiata and the doors. She was unsure where to go. *A safe place. Is there truthfully somewhere I can take us that will be . . . safe?* Her focus was now on the trap.

Nakiata had resumed slashing and stabbing at the walls, increasing the speed in which it weakened. Time itself started to splinter, and she watched a network of cracks in the glass-like wall spiral out from the epicenter, the impact point of the spear. The wall rapidly took on the appearance of a spider web. The wall of the trap fractured and exploded outward.

"Ka'tia! We need to leave — *now*! Kola'gram said . . ." Tyrog exclaimed.

Ka'tia blinked, turned, and saw Tyrog's small hand, which was now holding hers. The magic was complete, and the smoke had already consumed them.

"Where are we?" Tyrog asked.

For moment she wasn't sure, but after glancing around she recognized it immediately. "This is my home — Zondura."

"Doesn't look like much," Tyrog commented. A sweet aroma hit his nostrils, *blood?* He focused on Ka'tia and saw something different about Ka'tia's armor. There was a small cut on her left arm, just below her left shoulder. "Where did that come from?' he asked, pointing at the spot.

"What?" she asked. Ka'tia turned her attention to the spot on her arm where Tyrog indicated. There she saw a fresh line of blood slowly moving down the outside of her armor.

"I don't believe it; she actually managed to cut me," she said.

Tyrog hopped closer so that he could assess the wound. Satisfied that it was nothing more than a scratch, he went back to searching their current surroundings. "You said this is your home? Can you be a little more specific?"

"This is my room. The one I grew up in. It's inside the castle of The Prowess of Prosino, my mother," she said with joy.

Chapter 20

"Where are we, and what happened? We left Nakiata back there by herself. We need to go back and rescue her," Dravone said with mixed intonations.

"I'm not sure where we are. I know that we appear to be safe here, for now. This is merely a stopping point so that I can gather my strength. I'm nowhere near strong enough to take us any farther, considering the great distance we have to travel. It takes a huge amount of strength to traverse across the stars without using technology. I guess that's why I admire Ka'tia so much. She is the only one that I've ever known to have strength, along with the power, to go wherever she wants. As for your other question, what happened, that's one that I will have a hard time answering." He paused for moment, turned his head from side to side and made sure no one was around to listen in on their conversation. "All I'm going to say is that you should not lose hope. We've only left Nakiata there for a brief moment in time," Kola'gram started.

"What does that mean? We can't go back and . . .?" Dravone said expectantly.

"I know where your heart is, and I know what your mind is thinking. You would be right on both accounts. Right now, Nakiata does feel as though she's all alone, but we both know she is far from alone. When the time is right, we will return to find her unharmed and more prepared for the tasks ahead."

"So, when will the time be right? And what do we do in the meantime? Just sit around here and wait? I don't think I can do that," Dravone confessed.

"I'm afraid if we go back now, she will kill us both, and I can't have that," Kola'gram said sternly.

"Okay, how long do we wait?"

I cannot risk telling him the exact length of time we must wait. It burdens me so much to have to keep it from him, no matter how many times I've seen this moment. I know three hours is long enough. "Four and a half hours," Kola'gram replied. "And I would stress that we do not return before that," he added.

"So, we are going to wait here for that long? Grrrrrr," Dravone grumbled. He clenched his fists in frustration.

"Well — we do have somewhere else we can go. However, if we go, you must promise me that you will not wonder off, no matter what." Kola'gram said.

Dravone frowned but nodded his head in agreement. "Alright, this is going to be something I've never done. I'm going to teleport us to another planet with a Black door. Once we get there we will go straight through to the other side. As soon as we step foot on the next planet I will teleport us to another one which has a Black door. We will repeat that sequence until we've walked through eleven Black doors."

"Eleven?" Dravone furrowed his brow.

Kola'gram nodded and reached out placing his hand on Dravone's shoulder. He smiled as the dark smoke swallowed them up.

They walked through the eleventh Black door and Kola'gram teleported them one last time.

The instant the smoke cleared, Dravone began to examine their surroundings. *I can't help it. I know he specifically said not to wonder off. That in itself made me curious as to why.* They were standing in a small clearing at the edge of a cliff, close to halfway up the side of a mountain. The mountain was part of a chain that carried on to the right and to the left. Far below, and as far as they could see straight out from the mountain, stretched a forest unlike any Dravone had ever seen before.

After ten minutes of enjoying the view, Dravone's nostrils began to flare from an unusually familiar aroma coming from somewhere close by. This caused all his other senses to heighten. His heart began to race, he started salivating, and his ears picked up on every minute sound.

The first sound was the scampering of small creatures running and scurrying about. Mixed in, and even harder to detect, was a group of larger beasts closing in on where he and Kola'gram were standing. Everything he was hearing beckoned him to change to his wolf-state. If it were not for Kola'gram standing right in front of him, he would have lost control and let the change happen.

Still fighting the urge to transform, Dravone wanted to know. "Where are we now? And why is this place so familiar to me? Ever since we got here, I've had an overwhelming desire to change and run through that forest down there."

"I am not surprised," Kola'gram said with a smile. He bowed low, spreading his arms out to his sides, but never taking his eyes off of Dravone. "This is your home world."

Dravone's eyes went as wide as they could go. "What! This is . . . my home planet? This is where the Morphan people came from? What's it called? How did you find it? Are there still —" He was cut off by a chorus of wolf howls echoing through the forest valley below. His heart started beating faster, and he became quite anxious. Drawn by the call, he ran to the edge of the cliff and was about to transform when Kola'gram jumped up, grabbed his arm, and, with considerable strength, pulled him back away from the edge.

"Yes, this is where the Morphan people came from, and yes, as you've already heard, a large number of your people still live here. However, they must not know of your existence for the time being." He released his hold, allowing Dravone to turn around and face him.

"I . . . I know we have more important things to attend to," Dravone said with a heavy heart.

"It's more than that; I truly wish I could tell you," Kola'gram said as reassuringly as possible. He reached up, placed his hands on Dravone's shoulders, and was about to say something when a large pack of Morphans, in wolf-state, burst forth from the tree line behind them. Dravone smiled broadly and was about to take a few steps toward them.

"Oh no you don't. We're out of time," Kola'gram said hastily, and he tightened his grip on Dravone's shoulders.

Dravone had enough time to turn his face toward Kola'gram and frown. His eyes filled with anger the moment he realized the dark smoke was rising up around them. "Wait!" he shouted.

"Michio Do'lia Ka'tia! Pru'mito zu Sodrago'!" the scholarly man exclaimed.

"Geo Do'lia Vitolo. Grida' vramida lo zo'onlo?" Ka'tia replied.

"What was that? Who is that?" Tyrog asked.

"His name is Vitolo, and he is one of Zondura's most reputable scholars. He said it's great to see me, and that it's not safe to be here with a Sodaran. I said it was nice to see him as well, and asked why it's not safe," she explained.

"Kseholo lo mangido? Sodrago' voul fregitsa'."

"Okay, now what did he say?" Tyrog asked, impatiently.

Ka'tia held up a finger, silencing him. She shook her head no. Vitolo bowed slightly. She bowed back in return and turned her attention to a not-so-patient Tyrog. "We cannot stay here. There's been a development, since I've been gone. A new law that . . . I'd rather not explain at the moment. Let's say it isn't safe, for either of us. We should go through the Black Door. The one that will take us back to Vazdrag." She pointed behind him.

Tyrog turned to her and said, "What about that Black Door? Where is it currently programmed to go?"

"Trouganda," she replied.

Tyrog made a short hissing sound and hopped around. "So that leads to Nakiata's home planet? I'd love to see the birthplace of The First!"

"Yes, I'm sure you would, but I don't think we should venture there. From what I've learned from Nakiata and Dravone, the Black Door is guarded by the Morphan people there, and the appearance of two alien strangers would not go over well."

Tyrog snorted, and smoke rose from his nostrils. A moment later a broad, mischievous smile extended across his face. "Vazdrag is more than acceptable. I could get a good meal."

Ka'tia shrugged her shoulders. "Yeah, I suppose you could."

"After you, my dear," Tyrog said with a bow.

Ka'tia rolled her eyes and walked into the blackness. Tyrog wrinkled his snout at Vitolo, showed his teeth, and licked his lips. Vitolo took several steps back and almost fell backwards. Tyrog hissed a laugh, flapped his wings, and flew into the Black Door.

Ka'tia was waiting patiently for Tyrog to arrive. The moment he stepped through, he said, "I don't recognize this place. Are you sure we're on Vazdrag?" He tried to hide his disappointment.

"Quite sure," she answered without hesitation. She held out her hand, which let him know that they were not done traveling yet. Tyrog hopped over and took her hand in his and a moment later they appeared in a different location.

They scanned the darkened area around them, including the distant horizon and the sky above. It was early dawn, and they couldn't see much of anything during the darkest moments of the early morning. *Did I bring us somewhere else?* Ka'tia wondered. *I didn't think it would be so dark. I wish I knew where we were.*

The sun continued to rise, and more and more light spread across the area. *I'd love to come back here once this prophecy mess is all behind us,* Ka'tia thought as she admired the picturesque view of the sunrise.

"That's quite a sight," Tyrog commented as he reached up and held her hand. He pulled her down so that he could whisper into her ear. "Now, can you tell me where we are?"

"Um, no. I mean, I don't know exactly where we are. Somewhere safe, I hope?" she replied.

As light crested the horizon and rapidly moved across the landscape, it offered them a much clearer view of their surroundings. Tyrog immediately felt a sense of Deja vu from the dry, desert landscape which they now found themselves in. "We are definitely back on Vazdrag!" he said happily.

"I told you," Ka'tia answered, even though she was a little uncertain.

Far off in the distance, Tyrog spotted something which made him even more excited. From where they were standing, it appeared to be a Dragon's Heart flower. "I'll be back in a moment. I think we might be in luck," he said, leaving her all alone.

He flew over to the object so that he could examine it more thoroughly. *Yup, it's a Dragon's Heart flower. Now I'm certain we're on Vazdrag, and we must be close to — home.* He smiled and did a quick search in the immediate vicinity for signs which would indicate exactly where they were. *If I fly high enough, maybe I'll spot my lair.* He soared up into the sky.

Now that he had a much wider view, he caught a glimpse of familiar terrain. A huge smile crossed his face, and he dove with purpose back down to Ka'tia. "Do you remember my lair?" he asked.

"Of course I do. Why?"

"It's over those dunes. You can teleport us there if you want, or I can change size and carry you there. It's up to you."

"So, we *are* on Vazdrag," she said. She took his hand and they vanished in a cloud of smoke, reappearing moments later inside Tyrog's lair.

"Ah, home sweet home. If you'll excuse me, I'm going to feast for a bit, and after that I'm going to sleep. If you want, there is a large bath through there. It's naturally heated." Tyrog turned and opened the door to the large meadow where his food supply was grazing.

Kola'gram did say to wait an entire day, so I suppose a nice bath couldn't hurt. Ka'tia proceeded into the next room, which was poorly lit. She was pleasantly surprised to find an intricately carved stone boundary around a black pool of water.

The water was deep enough that a Sodaran, of any size, could submerge itself. Once her eyes had adjusted, she noticed that the water was giving off a light mist of steam.

Ka'tia walked up to the edge of the smooth surface of the water and a large droplet, from high above, shattered the glassy surface of the pool.

On a wall to one side, were shelves full of clean linens, a variety of soaps, and several large, empty water containers. The picture was funny to Ka'tia, who had only known Tyrog to be the messiest eater she had ever laid eyes on. *I had no idea Sodarans liked to bathe, let alone dry themselves off. Perhaps these are not for Tyrog. He did have an entire village of worshipers. Maybe he allowed them to come here and share in a bath, a conversation, and afterwards, become . . .* Ka'tia rolled her eyes at the thought, *I doubt even he would use such guile.*

She took her time removing her outer Zonduran clothes and armor. She took her right hand and pressed the small spot on her wrist to deactivate the Roarrg armor. In a matter of seconds, it liquefied, allowing her to step out and away from it. *This armor still amazes me every time I take it off, if that's even the proper way to describe it,* she thought, watching the armor solidify back into the same shape as her body.

Ka'tia took one of the empty containers over to the stone boundary, peered over the edge, and surveyed the water. She never noticed the small ledge that was only a couple of feet under the water. It protruded out a good two feet from the edge. *A perfect place to sit and relax.*

She could feel the heat rising and wondered how hot the water was, so she lifted her right foot over and eased a toe into the water. "Wow, that's a bit hotter than I was expecting," she said to the empty room. *Could be worse. The water could be ice cold.*

Ka'tia took the container, dipped it into the water, and sat down on the barrier and began to wash herself off. This gave the water in the container enough time to cool down She took the container and began to pour it over her head, rinsing off all the soap suds.

She dumped the remaining water back into the pool and returned the container to its proper place on the shelf.

Time for the best part of any bath, a nice long soak. She eased both feet into the water until she was standing on the small ledge. "Ooo — ahh — ooo…mmm," she voiced, slowly submerging the rest of her body into the water. She sat on the small ledge with her legs dangling down into the deeper part of the pool.

After a while, Ka'tia slid off the ledge and swam out into the middle of the pool. She rolled over and began floating on her back. She gently moved her arms back and forth, staring up into the darkness of the room's vast ceiling. She felt relaxed. She couldn't remember the last time she'd felt like this.

It wasn't long before the soothing water helped her to drift off into a deep sleep. Soon she began to dream.

In the dream she found herself in cool, dark place. The sky above her was clear and filled with countless stars. *This place, I know this.* She checked the ground beneath her and it had the appearance of still water, the depths of which was far beyond anything she'd ever imagined. A small, silent, ripple, originating somewhere close by, alerted her that she wasn't alone.

Something stirred in the darkness, but she couldn't see it. Ka'tia got to her feet and poised for anything.

A voice from behind her whispered, "We meet again. I must say, I have never come across one such as you. You have no idea how much that thrills me. Unfortunately, this time I must be more forthcoming. You cannot stay."

"Kuohlo?" she asked, trying to place the voice.

His eyes flared with blue flame. "You remember! Even more fascinating. Every one that came before you forgot their encounter with me. Not long after our meeting they went on to have productive, and deeply meaningful, lives. I wish I had more time to figure out why you are so different. I commend you on your uniqueness, though, which also reminds me — I must caution you: Try not to overuse what you call *Hisi'k* magic. Alas, I have things I must attend to now." Kuohlo vanished from sight.

"No! Wait!" she implored.

Ka'tia awoke, squinting at the bright lights in the ceiling above her. "Where am I?"

Tyrog cocked his head to one side, letting his forked tongue slither in and out several times before answering. "You are in my medical lab. I brought you here because I found you unconscious in the bath, and you were not responding. When I dove into the water to check on you, you were barely breathing. So, I rushed you in here and did everything I could think of to wake you, but nothing worked. I've been sitting here for several hours keeping a close eye on you."

"How long was I unconscious?"

"About six hours," he replied, reaching out to help her to sit up. "Do you have any idea what caused your condition?"

"Not exactly." Ka'tia looked down at herself and realized that she had been lying on Tyrog's exam table completely naked. She quickly covered her breasts with one arm and put a hand over her more sensitive area, and sternly asked, "Could you get me a blanket or something to cover up with?"

"Yes, of course. I'm sorry; the Sodarans don't have a need for clothing. We did, at one time, make armor for ourselves, merely out of curiosity," he replied. He flew off, and a few minutes later returned with a clean, thick, white blanket for her.

"Thank you," she said with a yawn. "Gracious, I can't believe I'm still tired."

"We do have several more hours before we are to meet Kola'gram and Dravone back at the temple. If you want, rest here, and I will wake you up when the time comes."

"That would be —" she yawned again, "wonderful."

⊬———⟨⟩———⊬

Kola'gram and Dravone were now in a small office, stuffed with scrolls of various sizes and thicknesses in every nook and cranny. The scrolls spilled into the room, making it almost impossible to move. "*Now* where are we?" Dravone asked.

Kola'gram did not reply. Dravone turned in time to see him fall to the ground, knocking a huge pile of scrolls over, which in turn caused more scrolls to fall in on top of him. Dravone rushed over and began tossing scrolls over his shoulder until he found the unconscious Kola'gram. "Now you've done it. Gone and passed out without me knowing where we are and what to expect outside of this cramped space," he said aloud.

Kola'gram lifted his head slightly, opened his eyes, and tried to mutter something, but his body was too exhausted, and his eyes rolled back into his head.

I hope we've gone someplace friendly, Dravone thought as he picked up Kola'gram and slung him over his shoulder. There was a knock at the door. Dravone froze, listening intently to who or what was on the other side of the door. "May I come in, Dravone?" Melia'na's pleasant voice asked.

"Please!" he replied happily.

Melia'na opened the door. "What happened?"

"I'm not sure. We were — we were on my home world . . . and now we are here. Which is where, exactly?"

"You're in Kola'gram's office, in the temple of Kili'dri, back on Frole. Where are Ka'tia, Tyrog?"

"I don't know. Kola'gram told them to meet us back here. We left Nakiata . . ." Dravone said, sounding sad.

Melia'na walked up to him and put a hand on his shoulder. "It will be fine. I am only here because Kola'gram sent me a message with instructions to be here, standing outside his office. Why don't we get him settled in the priests' quarters, after that we can get something to eat?" Dravone nodded in silence and followed her up to the room, where he placed the unconscious Kola'gram down on an empty bed.

They left and went into the dining hall, where several priests had already gathered and were eating their evening meal in silence. Dravone sat down and was reaching for the platter with a large, steaming chunk of meat on it, when a deep voice behind him said, "Save some of that for me."

When he turned around, he didn't see who was speaking to him. He was however, standing well balanced in order to catch Ka'tia, who rushed up and embraced him. After a brief hug, she stepped back, bowed slightly, and smiled. He could tell something about her was different. She was happy, and genuinely glad to see him. She had an almost visible glow about her.

Dravone's attention turned to Tyrog, who was now drooling over the meal in front of him. "Where did the two of you end up?" Dravone asked.

"For a brief moment, we were back on Zondura. We didn't stay but a moment before we went through the Black Door and arrived in that maze. I then figured it was safe to teleport, so, I took us to Tyrog's home, where I got to enjoy a hot bath, and . . ." Ka'tia became lost in thought.

"And then she took a nap, and now we're here, and ready to eat," Tyrog finished for her. He flapped his wings and flew over to the table, landing right next to the meat platters. He reached down, clawed off a sizeable chunk, and tossed it into his mouth, "Mmmmm," he said savoring the taste.

"Where's Kola'gram?" Ka'tia asked.

"He's resting, but he left all of us a message and told us that once we were done eating, we are to join him up in the tower," Melia'na said.

Chapter 21

The four of them appeared in the small room which was one flight below the Door of Mystery.

"Come up the stairs," Kola'gram yelled down to them. Once he saw Ka'tia approaching the top of the stairs, he continued, "Now, if you would be so kind, Ka'tia," he signaled her to continue on to the door.

She smiled politely and gracefully moved closer, stopping a few inches away from it. She raised her hands but hesitated to make physical contact. The in the back of her mind she could hear the voice of Korah, *go on, what do you have to be afraid of? Nothing.* She smiled and gently touched the door. *Unlock,* she thought.

The edges of the door lit up red for a second. The color transitioned to purple. "It's safe now," Ka'tia said.

"Now, if Tyrog would you do us the honor of unlocking the door?" Kola'gram asked.

"Me? Why me?" Tyrog asked.

"It's a simple matter of — height," he said, trying to be cautious of his words. "You are the only one here who is close enough in height to Nakiata, which would make it much easier for you to find the keyhole than one of us."

"I suppose that makes sense," Tyrog said, flapping his wings and flying over to Ka'tia. "Hold still while I get the . . ." he said while rummaging through her pack, "Ah-ha. Got it!" He flew over and landed close to the door.

Now where is that keyhole? He searched for several minutes and even though he was a fair bit shorter than Nakiata, he should still be able to see the edges. *Maybe if I run my claw across the surface.* His claw snagged on something, *there it is,* he thought. Keeping his claw in place, he quickly reached up and inserted the key.

The door made a loud hissing sound as it released the sealed gas pressure that was keeping the mechanical lock secure. Tyrog instinctively spread his wings and flopped backward, at the same time everyone else retreated away from the door, as quickly as possible. He waited and watched the door carefully.

"I don't think it's going to do anything. The magical locks were responsible for all the killing," Kola'gram said.

Tyrog stepped back up to the key and tried to turn it. The key rotated ninety degrees counterclockwise and stopped with a click. Without any warning, the key was pulled out of his hand and drawn into the door, vanishing from sight.

They all watched the door with intense curiosity. It began to vibrate, and their eyes went wide with anticipation. It still didn't open, but it was now there was a soft hum coming from it.

Everyone jumped when the door silently moved inward several inches. It stopped and was pulled into the side of the wall, leaving a dark haze of thick, century's old dust, behind it.

"Finally, it's open!" Kola'gram exclaimed. His voice breaking the silence. "Now we'll get some answers." He still wasn't sure how safe it was, so he cautiously moved toward the open doorway and peered inside.

It was much darker on the other side, and any light coming from the temple revealed nothing past the thick shroud of dust still hanging in the air. Kola'gram waved his hand around the air, trying to clear it, but to no avail.

Not wanting to breathe huge amounts of dust, he took a long breath in and held it. Kola'gram rushed through the doorway and stopped a few feet in. He slowly let his breath out.

"This room smells . . . *ah-chu*! Old," Dravone said. He'd followed Kola'gram inside and was trying to see what might be lurking within. With his much keener senses, he was able to make out the size of the room. It was small, only about ten feet in any direction, and as far as he could tell, there was nothing there. The room was completely empty. He shrugged and let out a sigh of disappointment.

After a minute or two the dust finally settled to the point where Kola'gram could see. "I don't understand," he said in frustration seeing the empty room.

Melia'na entered the room and held her staff up high. She cast an illumination spell the moment she was in the room, allowing every nook and cranny to become clearly visible.

"I never would have imaged!" Ka'tia blurted as she crossed the threshold.

The room had a unique, octagonal shape to it, but that was not the first, and most important, aspect that the group noticed. What initially caught their attention were the four, highly distinct, and accurate, murals painted on the walls. There were two to the left and two to the right, separated by a blank space that was directly opposite the door.

The first mural to the left of the blank space depicted Nakiata holding her Kharak blades out to her sides. Her stance gave the clear impression that she was poised to attack. They all knew it was her because of the birthmark on the left forearm, which the artist had duplicated flawlessly.

The image also showed her standing on a large rock or boulder. After a moment of studying it, Tyrog had an epiphany. "I remember this. It's when I first met her," he said enthusiastically. "That was quite a day. I almost had her for my midmorning snack."

The mural further to the left was a clear depiction of Dravone, who was sitting on a beach with an ocean behind him. He was wearing the old, drabby robe that he'd found on Zondura. He had a look of concern on his face. Ka'tia was the next to recognize the scene. "And I remember that moment. It was right after we'd landed on the edge of the Prigolo jungle back on Zondura. I had just finished singing a lament for my brother." The memory brought sadness to her heart. She even became noticeably quiet. Her eyes began to well up with tears. She tried to hold back her emotions, but a single tear managed to flow down her right cheek.

She felt two different hands on her shoulders; one was Dravone, and the other was Melia'na. "Do not lose hope," Melia'na said. "I feel for your loss, and I know that there is nothing you can do to bring him back, but as long as you remember him and tell others of his life, he will never truly be gone." Melia'na turned back to the murals.

The first one to the right of the blank space was also a familiar person. "Look, its Ka'tia, and next to that is one of Tyrog." *I must say, the depiction of Ka'tia has an air of seduction and passion about it*, she thought studying the image.

When Dravone stopped staring at the mural of Nakiata, he looked over at the one showing Ka'tia. He didn't have to study the image painted on the wall; he was well aware of the moment it represented.

The memory flashed through his mind and he wasn't aware of the fact that he had begun to blush. "Do I see a glint of recognition in your eyes??" Kola′gram asked him. The tone he used implied he already knew the answer to his own question.

Dravone cleared his throat several times, growled under his breath, and did his best to shake off both his rising heartbeat and hormones. He never would have thought a memory could be so intense. He took a deep breath and used some of Nakiata's teachings to clear his mind.

Dravone calmly replied, "Yes, I do. We were lost in the maze and we were about to get some rest. Ka'tia changed into that night gown and was about to lay down." The mural of Ka'tia showed her wearing the black, silky nightgown with its small flower broach on the left shoulder. Somehow, the artist managed to capture the desire burning in her eyes, as well as the blooming on her cheeks. Her stance was far from one of battle, it was more in-tune with one of seduction.

"What about that one? Does anyone know anything about it?" Dravone asked, pointing to the depiction of Tyrog so that everyone would stop staring at the painting of Ka'tia.

"I recognize it," Kola′gram said. "That is my research lab, where Tyrog was searching for information."

"Did he find anything useful?" Ka'tia asked.

Kola′gram turned, looked directly at Tyrog, and waited to hear the reply. Tyrog pondered the thought. Finally, he said, "No, nothing useful."

"So, where are the answers that we were supposed to find in here? The only thing I see in this empty room are paintings, and there's only four of them. Granted, each one is a member of the prophecy, but why is there a blank spot and . . ." Dravone paused his rant the moment he turned around and was facing the open doorway. "Would you look at that!"

His excitement caused the rest of them to turn around. "What happened to it?" Melia'na asked walking up to the spot on the wall where another mural had been painted. She ran her hand across the wall to see if it was damp.

"That's not good," Ka'tia said. "Either it's worn by countless years of water flowing across most of the image, or it was painted that way. It's also hard to see because of all that debris covering it. It leaves us exactly where we are now. We haven't the slightest clue as to who or what that might be."

"Impossible!" Kola'gram exclaimed. He walked up to the fifth mural and tried removing some of the rock covering the painting. "It won't budge! I don't understand. I thought for sure we would find an answer in here." He sounded distressed.

Melia'na was less concerned about the fifth mural and more interested in the room. *I wonder. Is this room all about the paintings, or is there something we're not seeing?* She slowly scanned the wall, the ceiling, and finally the floor. "There *might* be a way. Look here," she pointed to a spot in the middle of the floor. "It looks like there could be a . . ." She took her foot and swiped it across the ground. She cleared almost a full inch of sand and dust away, revealing a slight depression in the floor.

"Hold my staff," she said to Ka'tia.

Ka'tia took the staff and held it over her head while Melia'na was about to kneel and removed some more of the dust and debris when she felt a slight wisp of air. She looked up and Ka'tia was deep in concentration, she was casting a *Jeta'r spell.*

The wisp grew in strength, and before anyone could stop her, Ka'tia had a micro-tornado spinning in the center of the room. Melia'na was impressed, her student had outdone herself. Every bit of dust and dirt was being sucked up carried out of the room.

"This is peculiar," Melia'na noted upon closer inspection of the floor. "There's a hole in the floor and it doesn't appear to be random. It was clearly built to hold something, specific." She held her hand out in Ka'tia's direction, "May I have my staff back?" she asked.

Accepting the staff from Ka'tia, she continued, "Look, and this missing chunk at the bottom of my staff. For years I thought it was merely a large splinter that had come off. I never paid it that much attention. Now, look down into the hole. There's appears to be an almost identical raised shape in there." Melia'na waited for Ka'tia to peer into the hole. "Now, let's see what this does!" She took her staff and slid it into the hole.

The instant her staff fell into place, the light it was producing extinguished, leaving the room in darkness. "Great! Now what did you do?" Dravone asked.

"I think we are about to find out," Melia'na replied. A brilliant beam of red light shot out from her staff and was focused on the blank section of wall between the murals. The beam burned through several layers of dirt that had covered the wall. It didn't last long. Before anyone had the chance to say something, the beam was gone.

"What was that?" Ka'tia asked. She walked up to the wall and stretched out her hand until it was close to the spot on the wall where the beam of light had struck, which still had a mild glow to it. "Well, that's strange. There's no heat coming from it," she poked a finger in the hole created by the beam, "and it's shallow." Ka'tia ran her finger around the rim of the hole, feeling to see if it was sharp. She found a small nick in the almost perfectly cut hole, and she plucked at it with her fingernail. With little effort, she pried some more of the dirt away from the wall, revealing several glowing, red letters.

Melia'na's eyes went wide, and she yelled, "Stand back!" With a swift, fluid motion, she grabbed her staff, pulled it out of the hole, and swung at the wall. The impact caused the remaining chunks of dirt to fall away in a cloud of dust. Once the dust settled, they could see a glowing message on the wall.

"Does anyone know what it says? I know I cannot read it; it's written in a language I've never seen before," Tyrog stated.

Everyone spent a good five minutes studying the wall, when Melia'na said, "Well I never thought I would," she paused for a moment. "As a matter of fact, I *can* read it. It all makes sense now."

"Care to elaborate?" Tyrog asked.

"During my youth, a hooded stranger came up to me one day and handed me a book wrapped with a tattered brown cloth. I was excited because I loved to read, and I was *always* eager to experience new stories. I graciously accepted it, and as I pulled the wrapping back, I finally got to view the cover for the first time, I discovered it had a winged creature, which I'd never seen before, embossed on it."

"What does a book have to do with anything? Did this stranger say anything else?" Nakiata asked.

"No. When I glanced back up to thank the stranger, he was gone, vanished into thin air. I was stunned at first, but I ran back home and rushed inside my room, sat down, and opened it up to get acquainted with what was written inside. I was disheartened to find that the book was written in a language I didn't know."

"Still don't see the relevance!" Nakiata said.

"Well, several years went by, and every day I opened the book and searched the pages hoping it would make sense. As it turns out, I finally managed to understand a few words. About a year after that, it made more sense and eventually I was able to read the whole book."

"So, what was the story about?" Ka'tia asked with intense curiosity.

"The story was about a princess from . . . from . . . I don't remember the name. It was a faraway land. Anyway, she had fallen in love with a beast of great power, they had become true friends, and would do anything for each other, even die. Though their love was not a physical one, the universe still decided it was not meant to be."

"Did it describe the beast?" Tyrog asked.

"Not in great detail. The beast was a winged creature, like the one on the cover. The beast was not one who was going to be tamed, and in the end his rage killed the princess. It was at that exact moment in the story that the beast realized what he'd done. His heart splintered, and he began to feel loss and regret. The story ended when he sealed himself away for all eternity. It was such a sad story. Not long after I'd finished reading it, the book itself vanished from my room, and I never saw it again."

"You never told me about the book?" Kola'gram questioned her.

"I know. I'm sorry for that, but when it disappeared, I forgot about it until now. You see, the book was written in the same language as this," she pointed to the wall.

"So, what does it say?" Kola′gram asked with a sense of urgency.

"Give me a moment." Melia′na squinted one eye and began to mutter something. She pointed to the top left and tried to read it. She laughed. "I almost forgot. To read this language it's from top to bottom, unlike ours which is right to left."

"Wow this *is* interesting. If I'm reading this correctly, it says, '*The place in which you stand is named The Chamber of the Long-Forgotten Prophecy. Depicted herein on these walls are five of the six mentioned therein.*'"

She paused and touched a small section of the text. "Here is a set of numbers. I'm not sure what to make of them. They could be some kind of place marker, or like a page number. I'm not certain, though. It goes on in this section, which reads, '*After considerable attempts at painting the fifth member of such a strange prophecy, I feel as though I have been overcome. Perhaps there are forces at play in the universe that will not allow me to clearly depict this individual. I will try a few more attempts to focus my energy and my thoughts.*'

"There is another set of numbers. Actually, I think these are dates. It goes on, '*I was about to give up when it occurred to me last night: Magic. It's the only way this member can be seen. I was quite astonished at how detailed the image was. If you have made it all this way, I will tell you that all you have to do is put the staff into its place and turn it against time until it is facing the painting. Then cast* Nadtho-ehkee.*"

"Nad — tho . . . eh — kee," Ka'tia repeated, emphasizing each syllable. "I've never heard of that. What do you think it does?"

"There is only one way to find out. Put your staff back in the hole, turn it, and say the words and focus all your energy and thoughts on the mural," Kola'gram said impatiently.

Melia'na frowned at him for a moment. Her expression changed to a smile. "Yes, O Impatient One," she whispered, returning her staff to its position in the hole. "Turn it against time," she announced gripping the staff and rotating it.

As the staff turned, clicking sounds emanated from around the hole. As it reached the point where it was facing the blurred mural, which was possibly the fifth member, a much louder click was heard. Melia'na let go of the staff and jumped back.

Everyone froze and no one made a sound. They were focused on the painting, or the staff. Because they didn't know if it was some sort of trap, which they just tripped, and now they were waiting for the outcome.

After a short period of nothing happening, Melia'na walked back up to her staff, gripped it tightly, and began to focus on the blurred image while concentrating on the words. "*Nadtho . . . ehkee!*" she said with gusto.

The head of her staff began to shine with a white brilliance. Everyone in the group had to re-adjust their positons, moving away so they could focus on the blurred mural. They waited and waited but nothing was happening. Finally, after several moments something began to happen. The picture on the wall began to move back and forth, becoming wavy. It was even more distorted now than it was before.

A vibration began to resonate through the floor, along with a barely audible hum.

Flashes of blue and white energy erupted from the staff, and the sound of thunder shook the entire room.

"What have you done?" Kola'gram asked, fearing the worst. "Are you sure you translated the text on the wall properly?"

Melia'na did not answer. She had become entranced by whatever magic was being produced. "Somebody, *do* something!" Dravone cried out.

Ka'tia reached out and put a hand on Melia'na's shoulder. In that instant, the light coming from the staff erupted outward with such a force that knocked all of them, except Melia'na, to the ground. "What happened?" Melia'na said, overwhelmed with emotion and still staring at the mural. "I was concentrating on the painting, and the moment it was about to become clear, the magic was gone! I was so close to getting an answer. Perhaps you care to try Kola' . . . Whoa! Where's Kola'gram!"

Dravone, Ka'tia, and Tyrog were getting back onto their feet, and quickly glanced around the room. They too noticed that he was, indeed, not there.

"Kola'gram is not the only thing that's gone missing. Look at the walls. They're all blank," Tyrog noted.

Dravone began sniffing the air. "The air has changed, it's different. It's much thicker, and it's carrying a new smell. It's no longer an old aroma," he commented.

Ka'tia noticed there was a change in temperature as well. An alarming conclusion dawned on her. "Kola'gram's not the one who disappeared. We did! But where did we go?"

"Perhaps I can assist," a new voice said from the darkened doorway.

The group instantly turned toward the doorway to see a young Dia'fani woman as she entered the room. She stopped a few feet away and bowed graciously to them.

"Who are you?" Tyrog asked.

"I am but a humble follower and servant of Kili′dri. I have been anticipating your arrival for some time. I bring good news. Kola′gram is here, and is waiting for you in his residence. If you will permit me, I will guide you there." The Dia′fani woman waited for a response.

"That would be delightful. Please lead the way," Ka'tia replied.

The Dia′fani woman turned and began walking into the darkness. The moment she crossed the threshold of the door, she waved her hand to illuminate a long corridor leading out of the room.

"This corridor, I don't know why, but it's awful familiar to me," Tyrog said. He ran his hand along the wall. "I know this place, I'm sure of it."

"Yes, Master Tyrog. In a moment it will all become clear," the Dia′fani woman said.

The corridor came to an end, and they stood in front of yet another door. The woman waved her hand along the edge of the frame, and the door slid open without a sound. A burst of cool, crisp mountain air rushed in and caught them by surprise.

"No need to stop and gawk," the woman said, stepping across the threshold and out into the open. She led them down a well-used path that wound its way through a dense, wooded area.

They'd been walking for a while when they finally emerged from the woods and found themselves not far from a small village, which was nestled neatly up against a large, snow-covered mountain.

They walked down the path away from the woods, and when they were about halfway to the village the Dia′fani women stopped and turned around. "If you'd like, now would be the best time to see the answer you've been itching to have, Master Tyrog." She motioned for him to turn around and look behind them.

Curious, the entire group turned around. "I don't believe it!" Tyrog exclaimed.

"That thing is massive," Dravone commented.

"It looks exceptionally old, and I'm going to take a wild guess that you know exactly what that is?" Ka'tia asked Tyrog.

"Yes, as a matter of fact I do, Ka'tia. We are looking at a rare find indeed. Although, I'm not sure how it got here or why it has the illusion of having crashed. I will say this, based on what I can see, it's been here so long that some of the landing struts have collapsed, and now it's partially encased in that mountain." Tyrog spit on the ground at his own comment.

"So, what is it?" Ka'tia insisted.

"That, my dear Ka'tia, is all that remains of a Louravan interstellar research vessel," Tyrog said. Announcing to her what it was gave him some enthusiasm. "Would it be possible for me to go back inside and try accessing some of their databases?" he finished.

"I'm afraid there isn't enough time for that, Master Tyrog. You are expected in Lorn." The woman pointed at the village. "Now, if you'd be so kind as to follow me," she said, continuing down the path. The woman came to a stop outside a small house near the far side of the village. "Kola'gram waits for you inside."

The door opened and they proceeded inside to find an older Kola'gram sitting in a worn armchair. "I've been waiting for quite some time for you to arrive. I have much to explain, and little time to do so." He stopped and raised a hand to let both Melia'na and Ka'tia know that he did not want to be interrupted. "First, it is time that you all became aware of something important. I am . . . the fifth and final person mentioned in the prophecy."

"How do you know that?" Dravone asked, sounding surprised and a bit skeptical.

"He knows," Tyrog said.

"Thank you, but I think Dravone would like a little more detailed explanation, and I am prepared to do just that. Let me start by saying that, since I am a Dia'fani, and can see things that are going to happen, I fit that qualification pretty well."

"Yes, but so do the rest of the Dia'fani people," Dravone said with a frown.

"Perhaps I can elaborate on what happened to me. Melia'na, your staff was the key to an ancient teleportation device. The room with the murals, along with the one on the Louravan ship, wre connected with each another. Normally, anyone inside the room would've arrived at the same time, but due to the age of the technology, it arbitrarily developed . . . a glitch."

"A glitch?" Ka'tia repeated.

"It didn't work like it was supposed to. Anyway, I was not only transported here, but somehow I was sent into the past. Luckily for me, it was only momentary. When I finally arrived here in this time, I had aged, I'm guessing, at least twenty years. Yes, I know, Dravone — what does any of this have to do with the prophecy? Well, in that brief moment I was in the past, I had the chance to see the person responsible for painting the murals. When he became aware of my presence in the room, he already knew who I was. He handed me this and told me to show it to you at this very moment."

He turned to the wall behind him, reached up, and undid the binding on an old, rolled-up canvas. It unfurled. There was a clear image of Kola'gram with his hands raised in the air, and beside him was Ka'tia. "I know that!" Tyrog exclaimed. "That was when you were teaching Ka'tia *Hisi'k* magic. It was quite spectacular," he finished.

"I hope everything I have told you is enough to quell your doubt, Dravone?" Kola'gram asked.

"Okay, so you are the one we've been searching for all this time," Dravone said. "You could have said something a long time ago and saved us some heartache. But I guess it was meant to be that way? Even so, that's all well and good, but it doesn't help us if one of us is missing."

"About that. I need to speak to Ka'tia alone for a few minutes, please," Kola'gram said.

Dravone game him a frowning smirk before walking into the other room with Tyrog.

"What did you need to talk to me about?" Ka'tia asked.

"I have something new I need to teach you before you and Dravone go and get Nakiata."

Ka'tia's eyes lit up. "Really? What is it?"

"I don't have a name for it, yet . . . "

"Perhaps I can help with that."

"Maybe. It's new magic. It — well, as far as I know, it has only one purpose, it will put Nakiata into a state of deep rest. If we don't contain her now, the Darkness will overcome us all."

At the mention of the *Darkness*, Ka'tia asked, "What can you tell me about this Darkness that we are supposed to fight?"

"Nothing. My entire race has tried over and over again to see what the prophecy calls the Darkness, but all we have ever seen is literal blackness, a dark cloud, and that's it. Now, we don't have too much time. Come closer." Kola'gram reached up, put his hands on either side of her head, and held it firm. "You must look deep into her eyes, and while you're doing that, you must instill in her mind a sense of serenity. The moment you achieve that, say to her," he stared directly into her eyes, and she heard him, "*Ee-reh-me-say.*"

Ka'tia immediately found herself sitting and staring out at a large, grassy field. There was a cool breeze blowing across the wide expanse. The sun was high in the sky, but it wasn't too hot. In fact, it felt immeasurably comfortable.

What happened? Where am I? She tried to search for clues of her location, but everything went blurry. The sky became dark, and an instant later she found herself back in Kola'grams house. He still had his hands on her head.

"What was that? It felt so calm. It was such a relief to feel that peaceful and happy."

"Yes, but it doesn't work so well on the Dia'fani. For reasons beyond our understanding, it's effects are quite frankly, mild."

"How do you know it will work better on Nakiata?" she asked.

Kola'gram smiled and shook his head. "Have you forgotten already?"

"Oh yeah," Ka'tia gigled. "I guess I almost forgot. You can see the future. It will take a little getting used to that fact."

"There's no need for you to get used to it, as long as we don't try to change the things that we've seen. I'll inform Dravone that you are ready to go now. Take him to Nakiata as soon as possible. Don't worry about me and Tyrog. We have a few things to discuss, at length. He also has some work that he needs to accomplish, before it gets too late." Kola'gram sighed. "Nakiata needs both you and Dravone."

"How do we find her?"

"Focus on nothing but her and follow your heart," he replied. Kola'gram let her go and disappeared into the other room.

Dravone returned, and Ka'tia immediatelygazed into his eyes with a longing desire. He started to blush as she approached him. She gently took his hands into hers, closed her eyes, and concentrated. All of her thoughts were now on one individual, Nakiata. A cloud of white smoke swallowed them up, and they were gone.

Chapter 22

Nakiata felt the rage building within her while she stabbed and slashed at incredible speed. With each passing moment, her attacks on the walls of the small, clear cage were faster. Soon, the walls began to weaken from the constant bombardment. A small crack appeared, and a moment later it spider webbed outward. The walls began to shatter, like a bomb going off, and she felt herself slipping away, losing all self-control, blacking out.

After a while, she became loosely coherent. She was aware that something was different. That's when it dawned on her that she was seeing things within her own mind; or, at least, that's what she concluded. Still, it was a strange state of mind, even for her. It wasn't like meditation, where she had clear control and focused thoughts. This was different. She had no idea how much time had elapsed, nor was she able to recognize anything around her. It was like a blurry dream.

She felt a shiver going up her spine like a slap in the face. She was still not physically awake, but her mind was now in tune with her surroundings. Everything was crystal clear. Wherever she was, it was dark. The only two sources of light were the stars, which she could see in every direction, and a brownish-orange cloud far off in the distance. *Where am I?* She thought.

Something snorted behind her. Nakiata reacted with lightning-fast reflexes, whirling around and grabbing for her blades. It was in that moment that the most frightening thing occurred to her. Her blades were not where they should've been, at her sides. In a brief panic, she searched for her dagger, but it, too, was gone. *My weapons are gone. I have no means to . . . Alright, I will do this with my bare hands.*

She scanned as much of the area in front of her as possible but found nothing. "Hello? Is there someone out there?" she asked.

"How extraordinary," said a deep voice, which was similar to Tyrog's.

"What's extraordinary?" Nakiata asked.

"The strength you possess is greater than I had anticipated. I didn't think you would ever make it here, at least on your own."

"Who or what are you? And — where, are you?" she asked.

"I am here, I've always been — here. I am rather curious, and surprised that your companion, Ka'tia didn't mention me. She's was here not too long ago. She knows me." There was a brief pause. "Hmmm . . . I am going to assume she hasn't mentioned me, since you don't recognize me. That means an introduction is in order. You may call me Kuohlo."

"Recognized you — how can I do that? I can't even see you. And before you answer that, I'd like to know what this place is and where it is."

Kuohlo opened his eyes, and they flared with blue flames. "The only way I can describe this place so that you will understand, is to say that it is an empty space out amongst the stars. *Where* we are is much harder to explain, and we don't have enough time for me to delve into the intricacies. However, to satisfy your concerns, I will let you know that you are, safe."

"Exactly what are you? You also said Ka'tia was here. When?"

"My, my, you're even more curious than Ka'tia. Well, instead of going into a long, drawn-out tale of how I know your companion and how this is this and that is that, I will instead show you something far more interesting." Kuohlo's body took shape and filled with color. At first Nakiata thought he could have been a relative of Tyrog, from his appearance. He spread his wings out and began beating them. She raised her arms up in front of her face, anticipating a gush of wind, but there was nothing.

"Now, this is interesting," he commented, settling back down into a prone position. He lowered his head even further, while moving it closer to her.

Nakiata noticed he was not looking at her, but rather at something behind her. That made her curious, so she turned around to see what had his undivided attention. She was immediately awestruck, and yet dumbfounded at the same time. "Is that . . ."

"You. Yes, that's you, right now, and at this exact moment in time. I must say the sheer scope of the devastation is quite impressive," Kuohlo said with a mild chuckle.

In front of them was a surface that reminded Nakiata of calm water when sunshine hits it at the right angle. However, whatever it was did not give off any reflections. Instead it was providing them with a view. The scene of a battle, as it was happening.

They stood there and watched as the real-life Nakiata decimated everything and everyone in her path. It didn't take long before she wiped out almost half of the planet's population. The genocide slowed and she stopped for a moment, standing upon a mound of dead bodies. She was covered in blood, and the expression they saw gave them the impression that she was enjoying every savory moment.

"How can that be — me? If I'm here with you, that can't be me right now, can it? If that's me, I'd be in SOT and we wouldn't be able to see — *me*, would we?" she asked.

"Oh — there are ways. Nonetheless, that is definitely you, and yes, you are also here with me at the same time."

"So how do I get back to being . . . me?" she asked.

"Now, that is a great question. In order for you to become whole again, that part of you must finish what it's already begun. Don't worry; your time here will be short. I never keep my guests longer than they need."

Nakiata couldn't help but to grimace. "Wait a moment. If that *is* me, right now, I'm murdering all those people! Ka'tia was right." She paused while she watched with definite interest. "So how do we stop — me?" she asked.

"Oh, well . . . I don't normally interfere on such a level, but I will say this: All that you need to reunite with her is entirely up to you. It's something that you must discover within yourself. You have the ability, you only need to use it," Kuohlo said, his body vanishing from sight.

Great, now what am I supposed to do? Sit here and watch myself destroy — Her thought was cut short when the scene of her blood-thirsty savagery vanished, along with everything else, including all of the stars. She was left in pure blackness in every direction. *Now this is not fun at all,* she thought, examining her own body, which she could see clearly.

"And why is that?" a hauntingly familiar voice asked. It was the same strange one she'd heard back on Zondura.

"Can you hear my thoughts?" Nakiata questioned.

"No, I have never been able to read a person's thoughts. Having said that, we are here together. You have come a long way, and I am extremely impressed."

"No, she cannot continue!" interrupted an angrier, slightly higher-pitched voice. "You must listen to me now! The goal is to calm yourself and go away! Yes, far away from everything and everyone! Do not seek me any further, or you will face my wrath!"

"Who are you? And why won't anyone answer my questions?" Nakiata pleaded angrily. There was no response. Everything around her began spinning uncontrollably until it was all a blur. This made her dizzy and she could feel a headache coming on too. Nakiata put her hands to her temples and fell to her knees. *What's happening . . . to me,* she thought. There was nothing else, everything went blank.

She didn't know how long she'd been unconscious, but she was now awake. *At least it's not bright out. I don't think I could handle being out in the bright sun right now.* She sat up and peered down at herself. "Oh yeah, I did it again," she said, seeing that her body was covered with blood. From the look, smell, and texture of the thick crimson goo covering her, it was considerably fresh, or at least a good majority of it was. There were several layers of it, and the deeper layers were already starting to dry.

I hope there's a water source nearby. I'd like to get cleaned up before any of this becomes a permanent color to my clothes. If there's one thing I don't like, it's being covered in blood and stuff. I know it's silly, but I prefer to be — Ouch! Her eyes rolled back in her head, and she put her hands up to her temples. *Where did this headache come from?* "Oh, this is not good!" she voiced.

The pain was considerable, giving her no choice but to lay back down. After a solid ten minutes of laying down with her eyes shut, the pain in her head slowly began to subside to a more tolerable level.

Keeping her eyes closed, she decided to use her other senses in an attempt to figure out where she was. *This is unnerving. I don't hear anything! No bugs, no creatures of the air. Only silence. I can't smell anything either, aside from blood, and based on the strength of that odor, there seems to be a . . .* Somewhere far off in the distance, intense thunder rumbled.

Her eyes opened to discover a disturbing reality. *Great, something I don't need right now. A storm.* She stared up into a rapidly darkening gray sky and watched as black and purple clouds came into view. *I need to find out where I am. Even more importantly, I need to find some shelter to wait out this storm. Once it passes I can try to figure out how I'm going to get back to the others.*

Nakiata rolled over and immediately became aware of her current, unexpected position, which was atop a large pile of dead bodies. "By all that is holy! Where am I? Where did all these bodies come from?" she asked aloud. Then she remembered watching herself with Kuohlo. *Oh . . . yeah, I did this.* Nakiata quickly made it to her feet, allowing herself to further assess what had happened.

From what she could remember and by what she was seeing, a large battle had taken place here. Among the dead she noticed one person who appeared to be unarmed. As she continued searching the empty faces she realized with horror that so many had been killed without discretion, and without any signs of defense.

Those without weapons far outnumbered those who had them. Nakiata inspected a couple of the bodies more closely. She noticed that these people had a strong resemblance to Dravone's people. *I wonder if they are related somehow.*

Gazing at the bigger picture, she estimated that there were several thousand bodies underfoot, and an even larger number strewn about the sides of a road leading to a city.

Nakiata climbed down from the pile of bodies and walked toward the town. *I have never seen this place before. How did I get here? I certainly hope I'll be able to find my way back or at least run into the others somewhere amidst all of this. I'm sure there is some clue as to how I got here,* she thought as she headed toward the town.

Her progress was significantly slowed by the bodies strewn across the road, and the process of maneuvering around them was quite challenging and tiresome. When she finally reached the edge of the town, she stopped. Everywhere she looked were more corpses. *I still can't believe this was even possible. How could I have been the sole reason for this many deaths? Could I? Maybe I arrived at the end of the battle and I happened to . . . show up on top of a large pile of bodies? No. I know what I saw when I was with Kuohlo. But what if it was a ruse, and I'm meant to think that I did this? After all, he could have been lying. There has to be an explanation, I don't know what the truth is right now.*

The storm that she'd seen was now directly over the town, and heavy rain was now falling. Nakiata stopped in the middle of the road. Something off to the side caught her attention. It was the body of a teenage boy who couldn't have been much younger than she was. She stepped closer and knelt down beside him and turned him over to examine him for a cause of death. The moment his lifeless face was staring up at her, she knew. *A single cut across the throat. The cut is deep, and there's only one weapon I know of that could have done this: My Kharak blade.*

Nakiata sat down next to the boy, peered up into the heart of the dark sky, and tilted her head back. She closed her eyes, stretched out her arms, and sought comfort in the cool rainwater. A brief smile appeared on her face. *At least I'll be clean now, but will I ever truly be clean from all the blood I've spilled?* The last thought agitated her, causing her face to contort. This brought another memory to mind, the one where Dravone and Velonna were at the waterfall, together, naked.

At first, she was mad at herself for even letting the memory come to light. Her anger only lasted a moment. It quickly turned to sadness, and she felt weak. She let her arms fall back down at her sides and took every ounce of strength to stand up and walk a few feet away from the child she had slain.

She stopped next to a large signpost that had a banner she didn't recognize fluttering in the wind. She pushed a couple of bodies away from the signpost and turned around, put her back up against the pole, and sat down on the ground. She pulled her knees up to her chest. *Where are you, Dravone? I need to see you. I am . . . I am . . . scared. What will happen if I never get the chance to see you again? Why do I feel like this? I'm so confused.* She put her head down on her knees and began to cry.

Nakiata noticed several bright flashes of light all around her, followed by the corresponding crackling of thunder. The storm was about to get worse. A strong burst of wind blew past her, and with it a familiar scent, or at least one that reminded her of —

"Nakiata!"

At first, she thought it was the storm playing tricks on her mind, so she shut her eyes tight and did her best to ignore it. Although she couldn't fight the coincidence, *it sounds so much like Dravone.* The thought of him was hard on her heart, it made her weep even more. Her mind transitioned to the memory of when they were lying in the field back on Vazdrag. They had just had their first intimate experience and were staring up at the stars.

"Nakiata!" Dravone yelled, rushing toward her.

"This better not be some kind of trick!" she yelled at the storm. Nakiata lifted her head, and when she saw him, she jumped up and ran as fast as she could, leaping into his open arms. She began kissing him with more passion than she ever had before. After a few minutes they stopped, and Dravone asked, "Are you hurt? I was so worried about you."

Nakiata looked deep into his eyes and could tell he sincerely concerned about her. "Where were you? Never mind, you're here now." She took a hand and ran it through his hair. "Can I tell you something?"

He smiled, and now there was something different shinning in her royal blue eyes, something he'd never seen before. "Sure, what is it?" he answered.

Nakiata started to blush, and she couldn't hold his gaze, so she concentrated on his chest. "I . . . I . . ."

"We should go. This storm is going to get worse," Ka'tia said as she walked up behind them.

Nakiata started gritting her teeth, furrowed her brow, and started breathing heavily, she was not happy that Ka'tia interrupted her. She was about to tell Dravone how she felt. She began to lose control of the change happening within her. Her exhaustion gave way to the anger and rage that fueled her strength during combat, and she felt herself slipping away.

Dravone didn't noticed anything right away because his attention was still on Ka'tia. But the increasing strength of her grip on his shoulders caused him to look back at her. He watched as the color drained from her eyes, and they filled with such a solid blackness that he'd never seen.

Ka'tia watched Nakiata closely. "Hold her tight but do your best not to hurt her!" she commanded, taking several steps closer to the pair.

Nakiata began to squirm in Dravone's hold. "Whatever you're going to do, I suggest you do it fast. I can't hold her for long!"

Ka'tia reached up and put a hand on either side of Nakiata's head. She stared deep into her blackened eyes, putting everything else out of her mind except for an intense feeling of tranquility, *I can't lose focus. I'm not going to let you go Nakiata.*

Ka'tia could feel herself entering Nakiata's mind through her emotionless eyes. The first thing she encountered was a veil of darkness, which covered everything around her. Ka'tia held fast and knew she couldn't falter, no matter what. She pressed on, trying to find her way through such intense blackness and feelings of dread. *Clink-clang* was the distant sound she heard.

I know what that is. It's the sound of battle, Ka'tia thought. The sound grew louder and with it she began to experience an intense feeling, a lust for bloodshed and destruction. It was the strongest thing she'd ever felt. *Is this what it's like for you?* She wondered.

All of a sudden, there was nothing but silence. The images of thousands of the dead were staring at her. Before her eyes, their spirits left their bodies and flew straight at her, screaming in pain and anguish. Ka'tia almost closed her eyes completely as she braced herself for the mental onslaught, but nothing happened.

She slowly opened her eyes to see Nakiata, who appeared disoriented. Ka'tia also noticed that there was a strong feeling of being lost and cut off from the world around them. *It's time!* With a clear, commanding tone, she enunciated, "*Ee-reh-me-say!*"

A soft, blue light began to shine from both of their eyes. It rapidly grew in intensity until the three of them were drenched.

Chapter 23

Kola'gram had gone into his new meditation room and was about to delve into the future when Tyrog came in and asked, "What is it that you were going to have me do?"

Kola'gram sighed. "You, my overly-intelligent Sodaran, will be fixing as much of the Louravan ship as you are able. The sooner you start, the more you will accomplish. There is something on that ship that is important to us. What that might be — well, I haven't been able to see that. I've only been able to see you working on the ship and fixing many things. After that, you become excited about finding something of extreme value."

Tyrog was already hopping up and down with excitement. "I'll get started right away." Without another word, he flew out of the room. No more than a minute had passed, and he re-entered the room, saying, "I just realized. I'm going to need supplies, parts, and some hard-to-find equipment. Do you know where we might find any of what I need?"

Kola'gram stood and reached out with his hand. Tyrog extended his, and the moment their hands met, black smoke erupted all around them and carried them off to a new location.

"Where are we?" Tyrog asked.

There was a soft click, and a large number of lights came on. "Well, you could say that we are in the belly of the beast," Kola'gram began to laugh. "This is the ship's storage area, and through those doors," he pointed to a set of doors behind Tyrog, "is a room full of equipment and tools. Together, you should have everything that you need to get started."

"Hmmm, yes . . . but why do I have this strange sense that there's a catch to all of this?" Tyrog commented.

"You're more perceptive than I first mistook. Yes, there is a bit of a catch, but nothing you can't remedy quickly. There was only one entrance to this area, and it was recently sealed off by a cave in. Those of us in the village haven't had the time to clear it out, so you will have to burrow out an exit once I leave."

"Oh, well, if that's all there is, I can definitely fix that. Before you go, could you point out the caved in section?"

"No need. It's on the far side of this room. You can't miss it. Now, I'll leave you to it." Kola'gram bowed and vanished in a cloud of black smoke.

Where to start? I think I'll check out the equipment room and see if I can't find some sort of inventory. I hope it's nothing shy of a treasure trove. The Louravans always had plenty of stuff. After that, I have the easy task of making my own exit and going back to the village. Tyrog pushed open the doors to the equipment room and was excited to find that the Louravans were exceptional craftsman. They had almost every tool imaginable and a few he'd never seen before.

As he gawked around at all the equipment, he noticed a small desk in the corner with a terminal on it. *My, my, this technology is ancient. I wonder if it still works?* Tyrog hopped behind the desk, and after several well-thought-out, precise whacks against the terminal itself, it came to life. *This is uncanny,* he thought. His little clawed fingers went to work on the extremely old but somehow functioning Louravan keyboard.

He'd been at it almost an entire day when at last he found a few bits of information he had been searching for: A complete inventory of not only what was in the storage room, but everything that was aboard the ship. He even came across a unique entry. *If my translation is correct, and I know it must be, this is going to prove most useful. I should go get Kola'gram and confer with him,* Tyrog thought happily as he headed for the caved in section.

Well, isn't this peculiar. I hope it's not what I think it is. He reached down, picked up a small rock from the cave in, and placed it into his mouth. He immediately began heaving, and he spit the rock back out. He swore in his native language, which roughly translated to, "Disgusting shit rock!"

He glared at the expanse of soft, black rock that lay before him. *Now how am I supposed to get out of here? I'll bet this entire mountain is made out of that distasteful stone.* He put a claw to his chin as he pondered the situation. A feeling of glee came over him when he recalled seeing a small entry in the inventory of some special geological samples. *There might be a slim chance they are the same thing, but right now it's all I've got to go on,* he thought, heading back to the terminal to find the entry.

After about an hour, he located the entry. "Box 17984, aisle fifteen, section Gabanon," he repeated over and over, flying through the storage room. He flew down several aisles before he found the one numbered fifteen. He landed and slowly walked down the length, reading each and every section label: *Section Soval . . . section Temu . . . here it is! Section Gabanon. All I need to do now is find it. Let's see, here is box 17975, 976 — 981, 983, 985! Where's 17984?*

He frantically began pulling out every box near to where 17984 was supposed to be, dumping their contents on the ground, hoping that there was a mistake in the labeling. *Clink-clink* was the sound he heard after emptying a box with a faded, handwritten label on it.

"Thanks for being somewhat accurate," he said picking up two gemstones. He flew to the back of the room, landed, and positioned himself so that he would have enough space to maneuver when his size changed. He took one of the gems, tossed it into his mouth, and swallowed it whole. Then he waited.

It took a few seconds before the reaction inside his body was underway. He could feel the huge amount of energy being created and stored within the molecularly flexible makeup of his body's cells. A minute or two later, he had reached his maximum sustainable size of thirty feet. *Now for the smelly boom.*

He took in as much air as his lungs could contain and lowered his head so that it was in line with the rest of his body. He did his best to contour his mouth so that the fire would come out in as the most focused stream possible. The instant his fire hit the rock, a reaction unlike any other began. The strange, soft, black rock began to pool into a gooey liquid, and at the same time it started to retreat from the flame, almost as if it was alive.

The space left behind by the fast-moving puddle of rock was a perfect, circular-shaped tunnel. Tyrog slowly advanced into the tunnel. He concentrated all his efforts into maintaining a long, steady flame. *I sure hope I made the correct calculations in the size of this pile of shit rock! If not, I'll be stuck down here until Kola'gram comes looking for . . . Wait a second, I bet that sneaky Dia'fani knew this was going to happen. Wait till I get out of here and get my claws on him!*

Tyrog expended the last bit of flame which the two gems produced. He waited to see if his calculations were correct. The liquid pool in the second tunnel slowed and bubbled for a moment. Tyrog started to doubt it was going to do the job when at last it burst out into the open sky.

Where did the day go, he thought, noticing it was already past twilight by the time he made it out, not to mention he was feeling physically exhausted. He barely had enough energy to fly back to Kola'gram's house.

"Kola'gram! Where are you?" Tyrog commanded the moment he was inside the small house.

"In the dining room, Tyrog," a calm reply came from deeper inside the house.

Tyrog slinked through the kitchen and pushed open the door to the dining room, where he found Kola'gram sitting at the end of a long table. In the center of that table sat a huge pile of fresh, red, bloody meat.

Tyrog wasn't sure why he hadn't smelled it before now. "I want you to know . . . that . . ." But he was too distracted by the meat to finish the sentence. *I'm too famished to scold him now. Perhaps when my gut is full of that meat. Yup, I can reprimand him later.* He jumped up onto the table, sneered at Kola'gram, which was his way of giving a non-verbal lashing. He swiped a large handful of meat and shoved it into his mouth.

"So, what have you discovered? Did you find everything?" Kola'gram asked.

"You don't know?" Tyrog replied sarcastically.

"Although we Dia'fani have the ability to see the future, we don't know everything, nor do we know about everything that is going to happen. Over time, we've learned to focus on the most important things, things that are best for all, even if it means our death or letting things happen as they should. Let me also tell you this; the moment we see the future it can inadvertently alter it. Now, back to my original question: What have you learned?"

Tyrog stopped stuffing his face momentarily. "As a matter of fact, I did find a few interesting things, like that mountain covering the Louravan ship is a solid chunk of Voligran stone!" he said, sounding a little annoyed. He placed the chunk of meat he was holding into his mouth and savored its flavor. "Mmmm, this is splendid meat." He grabbed two handfuls more.

"Voligran stone?" Kola'gram repeated.

Tyrog growled at the continuous interruptions, but he stopped eating long enough to reply. "It's somewhat of a rare stone whose properties are quite unique. Not to mention, they are the worst-tasting substance the Sodarans have ever discovered."

"That *is* interesting. Is that all you found?"

"No. I found some schematics for the transport room, and attached to them was a note about an upgrade to the system that would allow them to connect to any other room within the Louravan fleet, no matter where the ships were located."

"I feel there should be a 'however' there?"

"Yes, *however*, I couldn't find any record of the part or parts needed, nor the materials it might require to actually accomplish the upgrade. I was hoping that you might have seen something that could be of help?" Tyrog asked.

"No, I haven't. However, there might be someone who knows about it. This wisest Dia'fani on all of Frole."

"What's his name, and where can we find him?"

"First of all, *her* name is Sepho'ria, and she actually lives right around the corner. I had planned for us to go see her; after you're done eating, of course," Kola'gram said with a smile.

Tyrog dropped the meat in his hands. "I'm done, let's go!"

Kola'gram chuckled as he stood and led Tyrog down the street and around the corner to Sepho'ria's house. The moment they arrived, the door opened and a young, slightly tan Dia'fani boy opened the door and ushered them inside. "Master Kola'gram sir, she has been expecting you. Please come in and have a seat. Madame Sepho'ria will be with you presently." The boy retreated into another room.

They sat down and made themselves comfortable. After a few moments of nothing, the room filled with a dark-green cloud of swirling smoke. Tyrog witnessed something different about it. There were a few sparks of electrical energy before the cloud dissipated completely.

"Madame Sepho'ria, thank you for meeting with us," Kola'gram said.

"Who are you talking to?" Tyrog asked. "I don't see any . . ."

"Oh, my apologies, Tyrog. I almost forgot to fill in, as you might say. It has been ages since I actually had a need to use my pigment," Sepho'ria said. She was sitting in an armchair as her body slowly filled with a pale, white pigment, allowing Tyrog to notice her. "So, you've come to see if I know about the missing piece of the puzzle?"

"Yes! Do you know where it is and what it is?" Tyrog implored excitedly.

"Calm yourself, my Sodaran friend. I know *exactly* what you are looking for and where it is, but first," she put her hand out and the young boy, who entered the room without anyone noticing, handed her a cup of steaming hot liquid, "ah, quite tasty. There are two major pieces missing. You will need both or the upgrade will overload and explode. The first one is a new part which you will have to create using your ingenuity, skills, and of course your most prominent attribute, some intense Sodaran fire. I will tell you where to find the pieces required to assemble the part."

"And the second?" Kola'gram asked. He was curious to know too.

Sepho'ria smiled at both of them. "The second is in here." She began tapping on her head.

Tyrog tilted his head and stuck his forked tongue out several times. "I'm not quite sure I understand."

"The other missing piece is not an object you can hold. It's a section of digital machine code that will allow the new part to function properly. However, before I can give you the code, you must get everything else ready. Once you have the new part fashioned and installed, I will stop by personally to help finish the upgrade."

"I figured as much. Most upgrades would need new code to work. What do I need for the part?" Tyrog asked.

"You'll need several pieces all of which you can find in the ships storage area. You will find them listed under section —" Sepho'ria put a hand to her head trying to remember. "You know what, I can't recall. If I had to guess I'd say you need to search for odd parts that don't go with anything else. Oh, and one last bit of advice: Don't fret. It will all work out, for both of you."

The last part was a surprise even for Kola'gram. "Can you explain that last part, Madame Sepho'ria?" he asked, but it was already too late. A cloud of dark, green smoke rose and fell, taking her away.

"I guess that's all we're getting today," Kola'gram suggested.

Tyrog woke up early the next day morning and rushed back to the ship to begin his search. He was thrilled at the thought of making something with his own hands. He made his way back to the equipment room and brought up the schematics for the transport upgrade. *How could I have missed it?*

Upon closer inspection of the diagram, Tyrog noticed a small area that had a slight variance in its color, compared to the rest of the image. He manipulated the terminal controls until he had the area zoomed in. *Fantastic! That's what the part should look like,* he hit a few more keystrokes and a list of materials and common parts appeared.

A few more taps on the keys and he had a list of three components he would need to create the new part, along with their storage locations. It only took him a few seconds to commit the information to memory and he was off to the storage room.

Tyrog found the first part with no issues. It was exactly where it was supposed to be. The second, took him almost half a day to find. It had been mislabeled. Luckily for him the numbers were only jumbled up. *If they would have left out just one number I would have never found this thing. Time for a break I think, I need meat.*

Once he finished a short lunch he went back to searching for the last piece. Several hours went by and he still couldn't find it. "How difficult is it put something where it goes?" he voiced. "It's one little part, but probably the most significant. All I actually need is a molecular reconstruction module."

I think that if I take one of these, he thought grabbing a part that was previously dumped on the ground during his search, *and one of those,* he grabbed a bulky object from off the shelf in front of him. *Now all I have to do is remove the signal enhancer from one and add it the digitizer which I will get from this other part, and voila! A molecular reconstruction module. I make things so simple; I almost scare myself.*

Tyrog took the new pieces back to the equipment room and started taking them apart. After a while he finally managed to combine the two pieces into his makeshift module. *Now, the fun really begins,* he thought.

Tyrog studied the three components before him and started to visualize how it was actually going to fit. A sleek smile appeared as he reached for the larger piece. "This is too big and bulky. I will have to do something about that, but what?"

Tyrog had scrounged up some unneeded items simply to help him produce fire. He grabbed one and gulped it down. A moment later he breathed a small flame onto one of his claws. The tip began to glow bright yellow. *I love being me.*

He ran the tip of his claw carefully along the bulky piece, making a precise cut all the way around the outside. *Now let's see what lurks inside.* Once he had the innards of the part exposed he spit on the ground. "This thing has to be the oldest piece of junk on this ship. It's a good thing I opened it. I don't need half of these wires, and this module, is useless," he said ripping it out and throwing it across the room.

It took him a solid hour to reconfigure it into something that would actually work. *Now I need some type of housing to put it in. But where to get one? Aha! I take the shell of the old one and melt it into a new housing.*

Another couple of hours went by and he had all the pieces ready to be assembled. *All that's left is a few more precise flames to weld the housings together* — it was done. The final part to complete the upgrade was ready to be put into place.

Tyrog flew back to the terminal and found the schematics. He examined them one last time, making sure he had the necessary information committed to memory.

As soon as he was back in the transport room he went to work removing several sidewall panels and almost half of the floor panels.

Several hours later and Tyrog was finally ready. He reached up and grabbed his new creation and carefully set it into position. He put some slight pressure on it so that it would slide down and lock into place, and that's when, "It doesn't fit!" he roared.

Tyrog tried pushing a little harder but the new part still wouldn't go into place. *I have got just the thing to fix this,* he thought. He flew back to the equipment room and returned a few minutes later holding a large, heavy, soft-ended tool. He positioned it directly over the part, slowly raised it high above his head, and brought it down with considerable force.

Clank . . . click. "Press fit!" he said. Tyrog took a few strips of filler metal and carefully exhaled a small stream of fire, melting them over the connecting edges. *I think that about does it. Now, to find out how to 'activate' the upgrade.*

A cloud of dark-green smoke plumed up all around him, and as it dispersed Sepho'ria and Kola'gram stood in its wake.

"Have we arrived in time?" Sepho'ria asked.

"Is that — a joke?" Tyrog asked.

"Why, yes it is," she replied, starting to laugh.

Both Tyrog and Kola'gram stared at her. Sepho'ria's laughter came to a halt. "You two need to lighten up. By the look on your faces, you'd think the universe was about to end or something. Anyway, I suppose you'll be wanting the code now?" She nonchalantly walked out of the room and made her way to the equipment room.

Once there she sat down behind the terminal and began typing with incredible speed. "That's impressive," Tyrog said upon entering the room.

Sepho'ria stopped for a moment, and her expression clearly conveyed one message, she was not doing it to impress him. She maintained eye contact never blinked. She raised her hand and made a fist. She held it up, allowed her smirk to be seen, and slowly extended her index finger.

All focus was on that one finger and in a grand motion, she moved her hand downward, pressing one last keystroke. "There, that takes care of that," And without another word, she vanished in a cloud of smoke.

"I'm not sure, but I think we might have hurt her feelings, a little," Kola'gram mentioned, coming to a stop right behind Tyrog.

Tyrog growled. "No matter. We have more important things to worry about than the feelings of one elderly Dia'fani woman, wouldn't you agree?"

Kola'gram hesitated. *I don't want to sound heartless, but he does have a point.* "Not to worry, good sir, I will apologize to her later. Now, can we connect to another transport room?"

Tyrog held up a finger, went over to the terminal, and inspected the changes Sepho'ria had made. "Fascinating. The code has altered one of the panels in the transport room, it's now linked to the transporter and serves as the new control. So, in order to test it, we need to go back. Would you mind?" he finished, holding out his hand.

Kola'gram took his hand, and they were gone. Seconds later, they appeared in the transport room.

Tyrog rushed over to the new control panel. "This is spectacular," he said happily. "The room itself has undergone a modular change at the molecular level due to the new part and altered code. This is far more advanced than I originally anticipated."

He walked over to the new interface panel and began tapping various symbols on it. "According to this, there are four other Louravan ships within range. I hope these figures are accurate," he said a bit skeptically.

"Perhaps, if we were to test it?" Kola'gram suggested.

Tyrog didn't hesitate, he nodded in agreement. He didn't know which one to choose. He reached out and randomly picked one of the ships. His selection immediately started the transport sequence. The door to the room came crashing down, sealing them in.

An eerie voice began counting down. *This is so exciting,* Tyrog thought, but when the countdown concluded, nothing happened, except for a brief flicker of the lights.

The door to the room began to open, and the interface panel began flashing red. "I take it that's not a good sign?" Kola'gram asked.

"I don't know," Tyrog replied, tapping on numerous symbols, searching for answers as to what happened. "Well, from what this is telling me, we didn't go anywhere, and there is some kind of a power malfunction. You should probably head home. I have a feeling this is going to take some time to fix," he said.

Kola'gram bowed his head, "I too will search for clarity, at least from one of my perspectives, and maybe I'll be able to shed some light on any hidden problems."

He left and didn't return until the following afternoon.

"Oh, wow!" was all he could say when he saw the condition of the transport room.

Most of the flooring had been pulled up, along with numerous wall panels. Tyrog suddenly popped his head up from one of the open areas in the floor. "*Hello*," he said. "Do I smell lunch?"

"I almost forgot I had this." Kola'gram handed down a large sack of meat. "So, how are the repairs going?"

"Better — now that I have food," Tyrog replied with a mouthful. "I found some chaffed wiring under here and over there. There were a couple of loose connections over there; however, I must admit that the Louravans had some inkling of proper engineering. You see, they made their ships with maintenance crawl spaces. Well, for me it's more of a walkway," he chuckled. "I should be finished in a few hours. It might go a little faster if you're willing to help me put all this back together?" he said looking at Kola'gram expectantly.

Kola'gram smiled. "I'd be delighted to help." He picked up one of the tools that was laying on the ground and went to work putting everything back together.

Chapter 24

The door to the transport room was sealed shut, and the countdown underway. The ambient light began to increase exponentially, forcing them to close their eyes. A few seconds later, the light was gone, leaving them in near darkness. As soon as their eyesight had adjusted, they observed that the lights were still on but extremely dim, giving off the same amount of light as the night sky.

"We made it," Kola'gram said, sounding relieved.

"Yes, I believe we are now on a different Louravan ship," Tyrog added excitedly. "However, I think we have a slight problem."

"And that would be?" Kola'gram asked.

"This ship is much older than the other one, and it appears to be in a far worse condition," Tyrog said.

"How can this one be worse off that the other? It's half-buried under a mountain."

"First of all, it's clear this ship has some power issues, which is going to be the first thing to fix."

"We have to fix —" Kola'gram stopped mid-sentence because a cloud of white smoke erupted from the floor and swirled around the room.

"Well, this appears oddly familiar," Dravone said unhappily when the smoke cleared. "And what are the both of you doing in here? Were you expecting us?" he asked.

"As it happens, you're a bit early," Kola'gram said.

"Why is it so dark in here?" Ka'tia asked.

"I'd like to know what's wrong with Nakiata, but to answer your question, we are no longer on Frole," Tyrog explained.

"She, how can I put this, is tranquil . . ." Ka'tia said, not sounding convinced. "If we're not on Frole, then where are we?" she asked.

"This is —" Kola'gram started.

"The Sevlofah. A Louravan master ship floating somewhere out in space. I didn't have time to commit its exact location to memory, but I'm sure once we get a few repairs complete we will learn quite a bit," Tyrog finished.

"In the meantime, we should probably get her situated somewhere comfortable and safe," Kola'gram said as he examined Nakiata, who was unconscious in Dravone's arms.

"Give me a few minutes, and you can proceed," Tyrog said, pulling out some tools from a large sack that he'd stashed in the room to be transported along with them.

Everyone watched as he opened up a panel and jumped down, disappearing somewhere underneath the floor. Several minutes later, they heard some snarling, followed by Tyrog cursing. A floor panel directly behind them burst upward, slamming against the wall. "Ka'tia, could you be so kind as to give me a smidgeon of *Hisi'k* please? Oh, and if you could do your best to direct the energy at this large cable, err, hang on." He pulled up a large cable and spit on it, causing the protective insulation to melt away and expose the bare, metal, wire braids inside. "Okay, now."

Ka'tia began summoning the magic and as soon as she figured it was a little more than a spark of *Hisi'k*, she directed it toward the cable. It arced from her fingertips and hit not only the cable, but Tyrog as well. He instantly let go and it knocked him backward back under the floor. The cable fell with a thud.

In that same moment, the lights in the room became exceptionally bright and the door to the room opened up, allowing a strong burst of stale air to rush in.

"It worked!" Tyrog exclaimed from the hole in the floor. He popped his head up and glanced around the room to see if anything else had been affected.

"What was that?" Dravone asked.

"A much-needed surge of energy. Granted, it was only enough to open the door and get the lights working, but I can at least get started on the upgrade now," he explained.

"There's no need for the upgrade," Kola'gram said.

"And why not?" Tyrog asked.

"Because we will not be leaving this ship from here. There is something else aboard this ship that's going to require your expert knowledge and skills."

Tyrog jumped out of the hole, landing next to Ka'tia. "Are you going to give us any clues about this mystery thing?"

"I think it's a — Black Door," Kola'gram replied.

"You think? Why is it that you're not sure? I've never heard of a Black Door being on a ship," Tyrog questioned him.

"Why would that be important?" Dravone asked.

"If there is a Black Door on this ship, it means that this vessel served as the testing platform, which would make it *extremely* old. Anytime the Louravans set up a Black Door on whatever planet they deemed worthy, this ship would set its position in the closest solar system. They always took extra precautions and tested everything thoroughly, making sure the new door worked properly," Tyrog said.

"I can assure you that it's a door. I have seen it in my visions; however, it's never functioning. I have to admit I know more about magic than technology. So, it's up to you to find it and fix it. You and Ka'tia can start searching for it right away. I will take Dravone and find a suitable place for Nakiata to recuperate. Afterwards I will meet up with the two of you."

They had been endeavoring for hours and Ka'tia was beginning to tire, not from physical exhaustion, but due to her frustration with Tyrog. *If he stops one more time to look at something, trying to figure out what it is and how it works, I'm going to scream.*

As she finished her thought, Tyrog darted off into a side room for yet another escapade. Once Ka'tia reached the doorway, she peered inside. Ka'tia sighed the moment she observed what she thought was nothing more than a storage room full of junk.

"Ka'tia, come over here!" Tyrog said excitedly.

Ka'tia trudged her way into the room and stopped a few feet away from him, all the while holding in her anger. "What is it this time? Some miraculous trinket that's outdated, and you think you can improve it?" she voiced.

"Grrr, don't sound so pleased," he replied, expressing his contempt for her attitude. "I've finally found an interface terminal, but it's going to need . . ."

"Power?" she said with little enthusiasm.

"No. The amount of power you added to the ship's systems should still be enough to power up the terminal, however this is going to need . . ." He paused, walking around the short podium that integrated with the terminal. "What it needs is a little —" Tyrog stopped because he found, and quickly opened a small panel on the podium. He reached inside and grabbed, briefly, something he thought would fix the problem. A jolt of power ran through his body, knocking him backwards.

"Are you hurt?" she asked with true concern for his welfare.

"That had a small bite to it, but yes, I'll be fine." He got back to his feet and closed the panel. Tyrog turned and began rummaging through some of the other odds and ends throughout the room.

"What are you looking for now?" she inquired.

"Aha! This," he said, producing a small, square, metal box. "I need something in order to reach the terminal."

Ka'tia couldn't help it, she burst into laughter.

Tyrog spit on the ground, put the box down, and hopped up on it. A few seconds later, he had the terminal powered up and was searching through data faster than Ka'tia thought him capable. A minute later, he said, "Oh, watch this!" He deliberately tapped on the terminal a single time.

A three-dimensional holographic representation of the ship appeared in front of them. "Is that a map of some kind?"

"That and more. So, this is where we are," he said, touching the terminal again. The area near the lower mid-section of the ship enlarged, and two red figures appeared. "And this is where we're trying to go." A small, green archway that was identical in shape to a Black Door, appeared and it was several decks above them.

"I know the Zonduran people might not be as technologically as advanced as the Sodarans or Dia'fani but we do have maps, and know how to read them, and I'm pretty sure a trip like that is going take a few hours; that is, if the map is accurate. So, how do you propose we get there?" Ka'tia asked.

Tyrog began tapping frantically on the terminal keys. "Well, conveniently enough, right here. There are two transport pads," he answered, and two blue dots appeared on the map. The closest one was in the same room they were in, and the corresponding one was around the corner from the archway. "Even though this ship is probably a couple hundred thousand years old, some of the systems appear to have had recent upgrades. I know what you're thinking, but there's no cause for concern. I've double checked, and according to the ship's internal sensors, the only ones aboard are the five of us."

"I wasn't worried," she commented.

Tyrog scouted for the transport pad and after a while he spotted it behind several stacks of boxes. "Help me move these, please," he asked her.

It took them thirty minutes to move the boxes, because each one was ten-times heavier than Tyrog anticipated, and once he reached the transport pad he immediately knew something was amiss.

"This is different," Tyrog commented.

"Different good or bad?" she asked.

"I'm not sure; I'm leaning toward good. I've never seen technology like this. It's not Louravan, that I'm sure of," he said, examining the transport pad's surface, which was slightly raised, circular, and about two or three inches off the ground. The entire pad was much smaller as well, it was only about three feet in diameter.

"If this wasn't made by the Louravans, then who put it here?" she asked.

"I don't know. There was no record of who put it here. I was able to find out that it has been here for about three thousand years. Considering the age of this ship, that' makes it the newest addition. Either way, let's see how this thing works," he said, stepping onto it.

Within seconds an energy shield rose around the perimeter of the pad sealing him in. A split second later Tyrog's body disintegrated into a large cloud of dust. The particles fell onto the pad, which were quickly absorbed, down to the last molecule. The transport pad itself lit up, shining with a soft green glow for several seconds, and then the light stopped, and everything was quiet.

Oh my! I don't know if I want to go that way, it doesn't seem safe. I think I'll go another way. I suppose I should have mentioned it to him, she thought. Ka'tia focused on nothing but Tyrog. White smoke swirled around her and she was gone.

"I wish we had more time to figure out how this works. I'd like to find out what the range is, and if there's any way to improve it or maybe take away the awkward feeling it leaves behind," Tyrog was saying to Kola'gram.

"What feeling would that be?" she asked, after appearing behind them.

"Well, it felt like someone had reached inside me and was holding onto some of my insides. It's probably due to the way this thing dismantles the body at the molecular level. It's a bit crude." Tyrog explained.

"I don't think she understands any of what you said," Kola'gram commented.

"No, I don't, but it's better just to let him tell me. I think sometimes he needs someone to talk to, whether or not they understand," Ka'tia said respectfully.

"Humph," Tyrog grumbled.

"So, are we going to find out where the Black Door is, or are you going to tinker with this thing all day?" Ka'tia asked.

Tyrog narrowed his eyes at her before hopping out of the small room they were in. Before Ka'tia and Kola'gram left, they heard him yelling, "It should be right around here!"

Kola'gram and Ka'tia made their way around the corner and into a much larger room. In the center was the empty archway of what everyone thought was a Black Door. Kola'gram walked over and stopped next to Tyrog, who was already busy inspecting the control table.

Ka'tia walked up to the empty archway and gazed at all the Louravan symbols on it.

"Is it me, or does this one look a bit, different from the other Black Doors we've encountered?" she asked.

"How silly of me. I could have sworn I already mentioned it, or was I only thinking I had and actually forgot to say something?" Tyrog verbalized in a comical tone. "This is not a Black Door. This is a Blue Door."

"A Blue Door. I've never heard of such a thing," Kola'gram said. "Are you sure about that? We, as in the Dia'fani, have done extensive research on such matters. We also have a Louravan ship at our disposal, which is full of information, and let's not forget, we have our gift of foresight."

Tyrog let his forked tongue slide in and out several times before he answered, "Yes, I'm sure. The Blue Door was the predecessor, or prototype, to the Black Doors. There are only a couple of slight differences between the two. For one, the power requirements for a Black Door are substantially greater, whereas a Blue Door requires much less. The other difference would be the range. A Blue Door has a limited range. I'm not sure on the specific numbers of those limitations, mainly because that kind of data is even rarer, however, from what I *was* able to find out they are limited to a single solar system at best, where the Black Door has a limitless range. It was all in the design of the power transformers and couplings."

"So how far will this one take us?" Ka'tia asked.

"I'd venture to guess we are not far from a habitable planet that has a corresponding door. If not, we won't be going anywhere without serious repairs to this derelict ship." Tyrog put all of his attention on the control table. "Oh my! There's one slight problem: We currently don't have enough power to get this one working," he concluded.

Kola'gram was now distressed. He put a hand to his head and said, "This can't be true. I've seen us going through this exact door, and . . ." He paused, searching his memory. "I've lost my focus. I think it's time I stop and meditate. After I've gathered my thoughts, I'll return. I leave it in your capable hands to figure out." He vanished in a dark cloud of smoke.

"Why do we always end up in places with no simple way out?" Ka'tia asked.

"If I knew the answer to that, none of us would be in this predicament," Tyrog answered. "Do you think you have enough strength to help me with the power issues?" he asked.

"Could I rest first? I'm feeling a little drained?" Ka'tia asked.

"Yes, of course. Come on, we can find a place for you to rest."

Chapter 25

Ka'tia awoke to find Dravone sitting next to her. "What are you doing in here?" she asked him.

"I was only checking on you, and I'm happy to see you're finally awake. Things haven't been going so well since you *went* to sleep," he said in a sad tone.

"What are you talking about? I've only been asleep for —"

"Three weeks now," he finished her sentence. "And whatever you did to Nakiata has had a similar effect. She, unfortunately, is still unconscious."

"What? How — there's no . . . what about Tyrog, and Kola'gram, and you? Have any of you been affected?" she asked, still unclear as to what had happened.

"Well, Kola'gram sits in his room meditating, most of the time. He hasn't been sociable as of late. I think it has something to do with the fact that nothing like this has never happened to him before, or to any other Dia'fani for that matter."

"*What* hasn't happened before?"

"Last time we talked, he said that the only future he's able to see is all of us going through the *Black Door*, which Tyrog still argues is a *Blue Door*. Of course, neither of them has spoken to the other in over a week now. I think that has to do with the fact that Tyrog hasn't been himself. He told me a few days ago that he's attributing his current condition to our new diet, which consists of centuries-old food stores that the Louravans, or whoever was here last, were kind enough to leave behind. Tyrog did say that the food was still safe to eat, though."

"I've truly been asleep for that long?" she asked again, sitting up and putting a hand on his shoulder to help steady herself.

"Yes, you have," he replied, putting his hand on hers and turning away.

"Why am I not famished?" And Is Tyrog still having power problems?"

"Well, Tyrog has been, *feeding*, both you and Nakiata, somehow. He said it's some kind of life force transfer, and it has nothing to do with actual food, although he has been eating, a lot, I suppose. As for the power problem, that's only one of a few issues." Dravone smiled at her. "I want you to know that, he's been coming in here several times a day, trying everything he can think of to rouse you, ever since that day you collapsed and didn't wake up."

"Well, I guess I should thank him. I am after all feeling refreshed now. I do believe I'll be able to summon up enough *Hisi'k* magic for him. That should provide us with all the power Tyrog needs. I have a feeling that will help relieve some of the tensions once, whatever color door it is, is working again."

Dravone turned to face her. He had tears welling up in his eyes. "And what about Nakiata?"

Ka'tia pulled her hand out from under his and placed it on his cheek. She leaned in close and gently kissed him on the forehead. "Now that the five of us are together, I think she'll be coming around at any moment. I have a feeling we will finally see the end of this prophecy, and after it's over the two of you can return to Trouganda and live out the rest of your lives together. Now, I'd better find Tyrog before —"

"My lady! You're awake!" Tyrog said, flapping his wings with excitement. "Whenever you feel up to it, I could use your help."

"Of course, I'd be thrilled to help you, good sir," Ka'tia said with reverence. "Is now a good time?" she finished, giving him a slight bow of her head.

"Follow me," he nodded back, and he led her back to the room with the transport pad.

"Is there another way we can go? That thing makes me nervous," she said, sounding a little afraid.

"I'm sorry, Ka'tia, I guess I should take a minute or two and inform you of all that's happened since you became unconscious. First off, to set your mind at ease, I have upgraded all of the transport pads throughout the ship. There were several hundred coding errors which I corrected, along with a few adjustments to the mass versus energy calculations that were surprisingly off by small amounts. Which makes me think how much of a miracle it was that we made it through even once. I am happy to say that, now, everything works, and a much faster too. I love efficiency. Did Dravone tell you any of this?"

"He let me know a few things. Nothing as detailed as what you said. Even though I don't understand it, I trust your judgment," she said, stepping up onto the pad.

"I should've warned you," he replied a few seconds later when he arrived at their destination. "I was also able to fabricate more pads, and I connected all of them into one large network that is accessible at these new terminals, which I installed near each pad," he said with pride, standing next to a short pedestal with a small terminal on it.

"So, where are we?" she asked.

"This was an empty storage room where I installed a pad," Tyrog walked out through the open doorway and into the next room, where he continued, "but in here, this is the heart of the Louravan ship."

Ka'tia scanned the area, and all she could see was a small, dark, circular room with a round table in the middle, a long panel of controls on the far wall, and some square glass windows above the controls. She couldn't see anything on the other side of them because it was completely black. "Doesn't appear to be much," she said.

Tyrog reached up and waved a hand in front of a small, orange light that turned green once his hand passed over it. At the same time, the lights in the room and on the other side of the windows flickered on. They were still quite dim but had just enough power to illuminate both areas adequately. "How about now?" he asked.

Ka'tia had never seen anything like it. On the other side of the window was a spherical shaped room with no signs of a way in or out. The most fascinating feature was the twenty-one metal rods extending from the walls toward the center and ending six inches from each other.

"What is it?" she asked.

"Like I said before, that is the heart of the ship, one that sadly stopped beating long ago. The ship is equipped with massive capacitors, which have been strategically placed so that they can collect and store thermal and photovoltaic energy from any nearby star. That is what has kept the more critical systems of the ship functioning over such a vast span of time."

Ka'tia shook her head and smiled. "I don't know if I will ever understand you. I only have one question for you. What do you need me to do?"

"Oh, that's easy — sort of. I spent the last week setting up an energy catcher," Tyrog pointed at three silver metal bars to the far-left side of the windows. They had been erected and placed in close proximity to each other, forming the shape of a triangle. "Those will collect your energy and, in theory, restart a newly modified, Sodaran-designed, molecular plasma energy drive. But we can call it the 'heart of the ship', for simplicity. I need you to direct as much *Hisi'k* magic into the middle of the bars as you can, and, if my calculations are accurate, the energy will be absorbed and transferred into the heart, re-kindling the reaction that will power the ship and all of its systems."

"I'll do my best. Is there somewhere else you can go? I don't want you here in the room with me. You might get hurt."

"Um, yeah, I suppose so. I'll just step outside the door." He pointed to a large, closed door behind her.

Ka'tia waited until Tyrog was safely out of the room before she began the motions to summon the magic. She took a deep breath and held it for a moment to steady her nerves. She exhaled and started. Halfway through the motions, the entire ship began to vibrate and rumble. A moment later multiple electrical discharges erupted throughout the ship, converging on the control room. Ka'tia raised her hands as high as she could reach, but there was something different happening. She could actually feel herself grabbing hold of the energy. It took every ounce of strength she had to pull her hands down and thrust them in the direction of the metal triangle.

The three metal bars began to glow a brilliant blue the moment the energy reached the center of the triangle. The color of the bars quickly changed to an intense white as the energy was rapidly absorbed. A second later, the bars returned to their original, silver hue, and there was nothing but silence. *Huh. Is that all?* She thought, staring at them.

The twenty-one rods in the spherical room began to glow orange, the color quickly transitioned to red, then blue, and the moment they changed to white, a loud *boom* echoed throughout the ship. The energy raced down the length of the rods and crashed into center, creating a swirling ball of blue and white plasma energy. In a fraction-of-a-second it began pulsating with a slow rhythm.

Ka'tia thought the sound was like a heart beating. With each pulse, the small ball of plasma produced incredible amounts of energy that expanded outward as a spherical wave. The moment the wave struck the outer wall, the energy was absorbed and sent all over the ship.

"It worked!" Tyrog's happy voice yelled, startling Ka'tia because she hadn't realized he'd come back into the room. "Listen to that music. The ship has life again after countless centuries, no doubt. Thank so much, my dear lady. I think it's time to get back to the door and find out where it goes, if anywhere at all. I can't wait to see the smug expression Kola'gram will have when he realizes I was correct," he admitted ecstatically.

Kola'gram was already busy at the control table when Tyrog and Ka'tia entered the room. "I told you she could do it. Have you figured out that I was right about this door?" Tyrog asked.

"Hmm, now that everything is functioning normally, I guess we will soon find out," he retorted.

Tyrog stuck out his forked tongue, flew over to the control table, and landed on the small stand he'd made to make it easier for him to use the control table. From there, he was able to observe Kola'gram's activity. "What, might I ask, are you doing?"

"I am searching for a set of coordinates."

"Well, you won't find any there, unless you search the unrelated database which has information on the Black Doors, including their locations. I found that over a week ago while you were meditating. Besides, the sub data section you're in will lead to our deaths if you continue the next few keystrokes, because all the external doors to the ship will open, and the atmosphere will be purged. Now, if you'd permit me, I'll get things underway and we can get on with whatever it is we're supposed to do," Tyrog said.

"Hey, what's going on?" Dravone asked the moment he stepped into the room.

"Only something like, this!" Tyrog answered, and the empty space in the center of the archway filled with a deep blue, smooth-textured energy field.

"You were right, Tyrog," Kola'gram admitted, giving him a bow.

Tyrog nodded his head and smiled. "So, Dravone, will you be joining us on our next little adventure to an unknown place? It's kind of a historic one, too. We will be the first race, beyond that of the Louravans, to go through a Blue Door. How exciting."

"No, I think I'm going to stay here for now. I don't want to leave Nakiata alone, in case she wakes up," he replied in a melancholy tone. He left the room and went to sit by Nakiata's side.

"To each his happiness, or hers," Tyrog commented, casting a glance at Ka'tia.

Kola'gram rolled his eyes at Tyrog before stepping into the deep blue sheen and disappearing. Ka'tia shook her head, smiled, and followed him. *Well, how do you like that. I wanted to be the one who went first,* Tyrog thought as he flew into the Blue Door.

A few seconds later, they emerged. "Where are we? Anyone have any ideas?" Ka'tia asked, knowing full well that none of them knew.

"I haven't the slightest idea, but we're about to find —" Tyrog was saying, when Kola′gram fell to his knees. Both Tyrog and Ka'tia rushed over to him. His eyes were both opaque white and blank.

"What's happening to him?" Tyrog asked.

What is this? Kola′gram asked himself. *This isn't like my usual visions of the future.* He looked in every direction but all he could see was the blackness of space, and countless stars.

"No, this is not one of your usual visions. It has no bearing on what you might think is the future," a deep voice replied.

"Who's there?"

"No one of any real consequence, but you may call me Kuohlo."

"Where are you, and, more importantly, where am I?" Kola′gram inquired as he continued to search the area around him.

Kuohlo opened his flaming blue eyes, which flashed making it easy for Kola′gram to know where he was. "I am here, and I must say, this has been the most entertaining time I've ever had. I have had the pleasure of not one, not two, but three different guests, and in such a short time. I wish it didn't have to end so soon," Kuohlo said. He snorted and small orange plumes burst forth followed by black smoke which continued to billow out of his nostrils. "Before you go, I desire to impart upon you a small gift."

"Kuohlo, is it? What are you, and what is this gift of which you speak? Do I have a choice in accepting or rejecting it?"

"We always have a choice, Kola′gram. I'm afraid we don't have the necessary time needed for me to explain everything you desire to know, but I will give you a little more insight about the gift so that you can — make an *informed* decision. My gift to you is that of true sight."

"True sight? I'm not sure I follow. I have sight and more. We Dia'fani can already see beyond the natural world and into the future, so please, enlighten me."

Kuohlo raised his head off the ground. His eyes flared at Kola'gram while thick, black smoke began flowing from his nostrils. "There isn't a single species in the universe that can see the truth as it actually is. Knowledge that pure would cause your small finite mind to explode."

"And why is that? You are an expert; please explain it to me," Kola'gram said sarcastically.

Kuohlo laughed. "You presume to know me. I haven't had this much fun since — well, we don't have time for that. I will say that it's because of their perspective. They already have a tarnished outlook due to their beliefs and opinions. There is a saying that many have come to understand. The young are too simple and cannot see anything because they lack wisdom and clarity. There have been a few to achieve a high level of understanding, but even they encountered other problems with their so-called visions of the future. The Truth was skewed because they could not focus long enough on it without letting their own desires cloud the real truth."

Kuohlo lowered his head so that his flaming eyes were directly in front of Kola'gram's. "I think a glimpse of truth will suffice in this instance. Before I give it to you, I must warn you, both will come with a price. Are you willing to make that sacrifice?" he asked. The outline of his body came out of the shadows and gradually took on its full substance. Kola'gram was immediately taken aback when he saw it. From his point of view, Kuohlo had a similar physique of a Sodaran, only ten times bigger.

"A price? In all my years, I have known that everything has a price, and in my wisdom, I would guess that you are not speaking in monetary terms?"

Kuohlo stood, took two steps toward him, and stopped. "You would be correct. I have no need of money, gold, precious metals, or gems. No, the price I speak of is life and death, existence and non-existence. There is nothing greater than that. So if you choose to accept, and use what I bestow upon you, I warn you now, at any time attempt to alter what you see, your life will be forfeit, and I will claim it whenever I will."

He slowly raised his enormous right hand, extended his index finger, and before the tip of his massive claw touched Kola'gram, "I think a small taste will suffice." Kuohlo's claw barely made contact with Kola'gram's forehead.

Kola'gram fell to his knees as a new vision, unlike any he'd ever experienced, began. It was so vivid he wasn't sure it was a vision at first. He was suspended somewhere in space. He surveyed his surroundings and could see that he was in a single star solar system, somewhere between the third and fourth planet.

Look there, beyond the outermost planet, Kuohlo said to his mind.

He tried to focus but couldn't see anything. The stars and planets blurred past him, and the planet Kuohlo mentioned came into view as if he traveled millions of miles in the blink of an eye. A moment later, a large ship came into view as it emerged from somewhere behind the planet.

"Is that an Ug ship?" Kola'gram asked. He did not get an answer. A minute later, another Ug ship came into view, then another, and another. "How many are there?"

"More than you will ever know," Kuohlo finally answered.

"Where are they going?"

"Wait and *see*."

Kola'gram watched as the armada silently passed him. Instead of watching the ships disappear, his consciousness followed close behind them. He wasn't sure how long they'd been traveling, but the armada began to slow somewhere near the fourth planet, at that moment he saw why. They were converging on another ship that was in a high orbit around the planet. "The Louravan ship!"

"Yes," Kuohlo said in a sadistic tone.

The Ug ships quickly took up positions, rendering any avenue for escape impossible. A fleet of smaller Ug vessels emerged and sped toward the Louravan ship. In an instant they had it surrounded and were attaching themselves to the outer hull.

At this point, the vision changed, and Kola'gram found himself back aboard the Louravan ship. In front of him was Dravone, who was sitting next to Nakiata and watching her chest as it slowly rose and fell. Dravone was unaware that the Ugs had invaded the ship and were systematically searching for them. They were only moments away from discovering their location.

Ka'tia appeared out of nowhere, laid a hand on each of them, and transported all of them moments before the Ugs entered the room. "That was too close," Kola'gram commented. The vision ended, and he was back amongst the stars with Kuohlo.

"That is going to happen. It is a true path in the universe, and it will begin an inevitable change, whether for good or bad, that is still undecided." Kuohlo paused while he observed Kola'gram, who was more than a little confused. "Yes, it is not, as some would say, set in stone. However, if you do nothing, the prophecy will abruptly end, and the universe will have to endure the Darkness."

"What is the Darkness? How is it that there are no other references to it, and it is only described as such? Neither myself, nor any other Dia'fani has ever been able to see up to that point in the future."

"The only way you will ever see that is to accept my gift with the knowledge you have right now. So, I ask you: Have you made your decision?"

"Yes, I accept your gift!" he said without hesitation.

"Look deep into my eyes," Kuohlo said, lowering his head so that Kola'gram could do so. As their eyes met, Kuohlo's flared with blue flames which burst outward. The flames swirled around them, creating a ring of fire. The fire rose high, forming a ball. It hovered for a moment and shot down, covering Kola'gram's head. It did not burn him; he didn't even feel any heat. The flames entered his eyes, blinding him, but only for a moment.

Kola'gram was coming out of the trance-like state he was in and could feel the soft touch of someone's hands on his cheeks. His eyes opened fully, and he saw Ka'tia's with her arms stretched out.

"Are you okay?" she asked while she forced his head to the left and right, examining him. She centered his head and peered deep into his eyes. Ka'tia caught sight of an extremely brief flash of something. It was subtle, but she could have sworn it she saw a glint of blue flames.

Ka'tia remembered where she'd last seen it. "So, you've seen him too?" she asked.

"Him, who?" Kola'gram replied.

"Kuohlo, that's who. I saw the glint of his fire in your eyes. I'd imagine it's some kind of an after-effect from seeing him," she said.

"I don't know who Kuohlo is, Ka'tia, but what I do know is that I had an incredible, and frightening, vision." Kola'gram's demeanor changed rapidly. "There's no time? The Ugs are coming. Ka'tia, you must get to Nakiata and Dravone, and bring them back here. You won't even have time to stop and explain. Teleport directly to them and then straight back."

"Wouldn't it be easier if I went through the Door?" she asked.

"No, there's no time to recalibrate, now go!" Kola'gram shouted. "Now where's Tyrog?"

"I'm right here," Tyrog replied from behind the control table.

"Disrupt the connection between the Blue Doors, now!"

Tyrog wanted to argue, but he heard the urgency in Kola'gram's voice, so he started the process to sever the connection between the two doors. *Why are we giving up such a great resource? That Louravan ship is a priceless treasure trove, not to mention I'd love to explore it and see what relics I might find.*

"Because Tyrog, the Ugs have control of that ship. They were the ones who kept it running. It was the bait they used to lure us here. Just let it go. We have more important things to concern ourselves with."

"How did you know what I was thinking? And what could be so important?" he inquired.

"You didn't say anything?"

"Not a word," Tyrog said without looking away from the controls.

Kola'gram didn't answer right away. "Odd, I swear I heard you. No matter, we must upgrade this door. It needs to become a Black Door."

"Are you serious? That's going to require a bit of time and some serious resources that —"

"Don't fret about the resources. Everything we need is here."

Tyrog gave the room a once over. "I don't see anything in here that would even come close to what we need."

"All in good time," Kola′gram said as the glint of blue flame filled his eyes for a second. The center of the Blue Door became empty. The connection was severed.

Chapter 26

Ka'tia returned with a confused Dravone and sleeping Nakiata. "Good work. Now, I need you to wake her up," Kola'gram insisted.

"How is Ka'tia going to do that? We've already tried every conceivable method in reviving her. Nothing we tried did any good," Dravone stated.

"This will be the first and only time I will mention this. The five of us share a bond with each other, something that has brought us together. Like small pieces which were scattered throughout the Theyan galaxy. For example, the bond that Tyrog and I share, the endless search for knowledge and power. There is also the bond between Ka'tia and Nakiata. Theirs is much stronger than all the rest, simply because they have more in common. For one, they both love Dravone . . ."

"What was that?" Ka'tia, Tyrog, and Dravone said in unison.

Both Ka'tia and Dravone were a little flush in the cheeks and neither one could look at the other.

"There's no time to explain any further. Ka'tia, you need to connect with her mind and wake her up. Time is of the essence," Kola'gram said.

The Blue Door reactivated and a single Ug stepped through. Luckily, the Ug was disoriented by the lack of light in the room. It gave them just enough time to react. "Dravone, the Ug! Tyrog, pull the converter!" Kola'gram barked.

Tyrog jumped off the control table, ripped open the floor panel that housed a vast majority of the power cables and conduit for the door. Within seconds he spotted the converter and yanked it out. The Blue Door shut down instantly.

"Hey that looks identical to the key to a Black Door," Dravone quickly commented when he saw what Tyrog had in his hand. He didn't say anything else because he was almost finished with his transformation into his wolf-state.

Through the wolf's eyes he could see the enemy clearly. Dravone had the upper hand so he quickly jumped onto the Ug's back. He started clawing and biting his opponent, who screeched in pain before reaching up, grabbing Dravone, and throwing him across the room.

He smacked up against the wall, hard, and fell to the floor. He shook off the pain and stood on all fours. He glared at the Ug with extreme hatred and he growled so that the Ug could hear it.

Before Dravone launched himself at the Ug for his second attack, the Ug fell to the ground shuddering violently. It screamed in pain several times, and when it stopped the Ug made a horrific gurgling sound. It was now a lifeless shell.

Dravone stood on his hind legs, made the change back to his normal-state, and made his way over to Nakiata. He sat down beside her, but it was Ka'tia he turned to when he asked, "So, what are you going to do?"

"I don't know," she whispered. "I've never done any of this before."

"Have faith in yourself," Kola'gram said loudly.

Ka'tia frowned briefly. She knelt down beside Nakiata and reached out with both her hands, placing them on Nakiata's cheeks. Ka'tia closed her eyes and concentrated on trying to communicate with her. *Where are you, Nakiata? We need you to come back to us. Dravone is desperate to have you back. Even Tyrog and I want you to return. Frankly, we all need you. Kola'gram is becoming a pain, and I fear if you don't return —*

You need me? Nakiata's voice boomed in her mind.

Yes, we...I, need you. Which means it's time for you to wake up! Ka'tia demanded.

But I like it here. It's so quiet and peaceful. Dravone is here, too, and —

It's not real! You're dreaming. Please, Nakiata, I beg you, try and wake up. If not for me, do it for Dravone, Ka'tia pleaded.

No, it can't be a dream!

Ka'tia could feel her resisting, so she made a rash decision. *You are going to wake up now! Whether you like it or not!* She thought, and before Nakiata could refuse the mental command, Ka'tia forced a small surge of energy into Nakiata's body, abruptly ending the dream state that she was in. Both women inhaled loudly and opened their eyes.

"Welcome back," Tyrog said with a slight bow.

Nakiata sat up, gave him a nod in return, and turned to Dravone. "Where have you been?"

"He never left your side, and now we need you use your special sight," Kola'gram said with an overtone of urgency.

"My *special* sight?" she replied, still gazing up at Dravone with a longing in her eyes.

"Yes, that is what I said. We need you enter SOT in order to find a hidden compartment. I had a vision not long ago where Tyrog was getting supplies from it, however, there wasn't enough detail for me to see the location. Oh, and there is another, small bit of information that you should know. The Ugs are on their way here, and we don't have much time," he said plainly.

Nakiata jumped to her feet, and the anger instantly became apparent on her face. "Let them come," she said coldly.

"If we do that, the prophecy will come to an untimely end, because the five members will cease to live," Kola'gram explained.

"Hold on, did you say the five members, meaning the five mentioned in the prophecy, would die? How would that happen if we haven't found the fifth member yet?" she asked.

Dravone placed a hand on her shoulder. "No, what he said was correct. It turns out that Kola'gram is the one we've been searching for this whole time."

"Oh, really?" Nakiata said in the most sarcastic, unbelieving tone. "So, you mean to tell me that Kola'gram is the fifth member of the prophecy? And, let me guess: You've known all about that fact, even before you met us, right? Especially since all the Dia'fani can *see* the future and all, right?" Nakiata interrogated him.

"No, I —"

"No? So, you can't see the future? Or you is it simply that you can't see the future if you're in it? You'll have to be a little more concise than just 'No'. As I recall, the prophecy states that the last person mentioned has the ability to see the future."

"Enough! I am the fifth, and if you waste any more time with these futile and foolish questions, the Ug will be upon us and we'll all be dead! Now, if you would be so kind as to sit down, be silent, and find the hidden cache of parts that we need in order to convert this Blue Door into a Black Door," Kola'gram commanded her.

Nakiata's jaw dropped, but the tone in his voice clearly meant he was not going to argue the point. She closed her mouth, sat down, crossed her legs, and vanished into SOT. She quickly glanced around and saw nothing out of the ordinary.

There's nothing here, she grumbled in her own mind. *I suppose I should concentrate. If Kola'gram is the fifth, and he can see the future, or at least parts of it* . . . Nakiata shook her head, attempting to clear her mind of distracting thoughts. She was now completely focused on finding the compartment. She took plenty of time scanning the room until at last she found it.

Nakiata reappeared, stood, and walked across the room. "It's here, but I don't know how we are going to open it."

"I'm pretty sure I can get it to open," Ka'tia said, walking up behind her. Nakiata glanced over her shoulder, smiled, and stepped out of her way. Ka'tia raised her hands, placing them on the wall, turned her head, and put her ear to the wall.

Ka'tia stood there in silence for a full minute. She stepped back away from the wall. There was four clanking, six clicks, and a single, long hissing sound, that signified the many locks had disengaged.

A large, seamless, four-inch thick, hidden door slowly swung outward, revealing a large cache of spare parts and equipment.

Tyrog peered inside. "Would ya look at that!"

"I believe you now have everything required to complete the necessary modifications?" Kola'gram asked.

"Oh yes, there's more than enough here," Tyrog replied, stepping into the room. After several minutes, he emerged with some parts in his hands. He hopped back down into the open floor panel and went to work on the upgrades.

"We should sit down and conserve our energy. While we wait, I'm going to meditate for a while and see what the near future holds for us," Kola'gram said. He sat down and began his meditation.

Tyrog was little more than halfway done with his work when the entire room rumbled, followed by several low booming sounds from somewhere above them. "What was that?" Dravone asked.

"That, Dravone, would be the Ugs," Tyrog said, poking his head up from one of the several now-open floor panels. "And from the sound and feel of it, they are close to locating us. They are trying to blast their way down, and the further they get the easier it will be for them to discover our exact location."

"What does that mean? How long do we have?" Nakiata asked.

"Not long," Kola′gram said. "You should make haste, my Sodaran friend. It needs to be finished, and soon. The bombs will become more frequent and the Ugs will be upon us. That's when *your* magic will be required, Ka'tia."

"My magic? What do you mean?" she asked.

"If I might speak with you in private. Over there, please," he pointed at the far side of the room.

Ka'tia nodded and followed him until they were out of earshot of the others. "What is it you wanted to tell me that you don't want them to hear?"

Kola′gram briefly glanced at the others, who were busy watching Tyrog. "I'm going to tell you something. Don't worry, I've already seen everything that's about to happen in a recent vision. Before the Ugs breach the ceiling to this room, Tyrog will get the Black Door working."

"Is that all you wanted to say? You could have told everyone," she commented.

"No, that's only the beginning of it. I need you to do something. You may be inclined to argue the reasons, but I know you will do it. I need to stress this, you've never done what I am about to ask, at least not to the scale that's needed and I think its best that you know. There has never been anything living, to my knowledge, that has ever done it either," he whispered. "I didn't think it possible, but after seeing it unfold, I know it to be the truth."

"Get to the point Kola'gram," she snapped. Ka'tia surprised at herself. She'd never been so short with anyone before. "I'm sorry if I sounded a bit like Nakiata, I must be a little on edge."

"I understand. Now, I want you to summon *Hisi'k* magic, but you will need to summon enough to destroy . . . the *entire* planet, and the Ug armada along with it. They have, conveniently, taken up low orbit positions, and will be unable to outrun the shockwave."

"You want me to do what? And they won't be able to outrun what?" Ka'tia asked loudly.

"Shh, keep your voice down. I know you can do this. I have seen it. Even though I wasn't able to observe beyond certain points in time, for reasons even I cannot comprehend, I know you need to do this. It will allow the rest of us can escape and fulfill the prophecy. If you fail, the Ugs will follow us, capture, and eventually kill us."

Kola'gram let what he said sink in a little. "I should also tell you about one specific detail, it stood out more than most: As I watched you summon the magic, your last motion was different. Instead of pulling the energy down and thrusting it forward at an enemy, I saw you pull it down, and at the last second you spread your arms apart, sending the energy in every direction."

"But if I perform magic on a scale that massive, even I won't survive. So, are you serious? You're actually asking me if I'm ready, and willing, to die along with the enemy," she stated.

Kola'gram couldn't hold her gaze. He could see the tears welling up in her eyes. He quickly stared down at the floor. "Yes, that is what I am asking, and I truly hate having to ask you, I so enjoy your company. I have tried many times but have been unable to see if you will survive such a powerful spell. I can only — I only wish I knew."

Kola'gram finally met her eyes, which were now shining with inner strength, he never thought she possessed. "One last thing: Tell Tyrog not to worry, and to focus on getting to Nakiata. He will understand when the time is right," Kola'gram said solemnly. "I'd also advise against telling the others," he said. He turned, walking back to the central area of the room.

Kola'gram glanced down into the open spot of the floor where Tyrog was busy working. "I have some coordinates for you. It's the location of something important. Do you need a moment to jot them down?" he asked.

Ka'tia was beside herself. She didn't know what to think. It was a lot to take in and she was feeling drained. She felt so overwhelmed and slumped down against the wall with a heavy heart. She started to think about everything Kola'gram told her.

Ka'tia had a decision to make. She sat in silence, weighing her choices. *Do I go through with it? If I don't, Kola'gram said it will end . . . Well, it wouldn't be good. So, is this going to be how it ends for me? I wish I could see Korah and my mother one last time.* She pulled her knees up to her chest and rested her chin on them, closing her eyes.

My brother, I suppose I will be seeing you sooner than I thought. I hope . . . Her thoughts became cloudy as the sadness started to overtake her.

"Is everything okay, Ka'tia?" Dravone's pleasant voice broke through the fog.

She didn't answer. Instead, she stood, put her hands on either side of his head, pulled him in close, and kissed him. It wasn't a long kiss, but the passion and love she felt was conveyed without question.

The moment she let go of him, Dravone immediately turned to see Nakiata's reaction. He was pleasantly surprised to find that her attention was focused on the open floor, where Tyrog was still busy finishing the alterations to the Blue Door.

"What was that for?" he asked her.

"It was something I needed to do before . . ."

"Before what? What were you and Kola'gram talking —" Dravone was interrupted by the sound of several explosions which rumbled from somewhere above them. The resulting shockwaves caused small chunks of the ceiling to break off and fall to the floor.

"Tyrog, are you finished yet?" Kola'gram shouted.

"I am! But I need a moment to reprogram the control console. As soon as that's done, we should be able to go anywhere — as long as we have sufficient power to reach whatever corresponding Black Door we've chosen, that is." He flew out of the open floor and landed atop the control table.

A moment later, several more blasts went off, and this time a large section of the ceiling splintered off and came crashing down. "Tyrog?" Kola'gram asked in a panicked tone.

Tyrog tapped on the controls, and the center of the archway filled with a smooth, black energy field. "I'll go first!" Nakiata said strongly.

"Wait! You can't, I haven't figured out —" Tyrog said, trying to dissuade her from going. But it was too late; she'd already walked through the doorway and was gone.

Dravone stared at Tyrog with disbelieving eyes, and was about to go after her when the Black Door shut off. "What happened?" he snapped.

"I don't know," he replied, racing to get the Black Door up and running again. His search for an answer paid off when intuition prompted him to scan the power distribution data, a system that would normally not be an issue. He immediately noticed that there had been a minute power spike moments after the Black Door activated. The safety precautions that were set to the original Blued Door, took an extra second or two to activate, which, in turn, shut the Black Door off.

A few keystrokes later Tyrog said, "There, that does it! It's safe to go through now."

"Safe? What about Nakiata?" Dravone asked angrily.

"There's no time to worry about her right now!" Kola'gram said. "Wherever she is, we will find her, I assure you." He ushered Dravone into the Black Door, and before he stepped through, he glanced over at Ka'tia and gave her a slight nod.

"Come on, Ka'tia! What are you waiting for? The Ugs are about to break through," Tyrog exclaimed.

Ka'tia walked over to the control table, put a hand under Tyrog's chin, and rubbed it gently. With all the chaos around them, she was at a loss for words. Ka'tia did something unexpected, she leaned in and kissed him on the top of his snout.

Another explosion sounded through the room and Ka'tia straightened up and felt her warrior's courage returning. "I'm not going, my dear, sweet little friend. I must remain here and ensure the Ugs cannot follow you."

"I've already thought of that. I programmed the Black Door to overload once we pass through it," Tyrog argued.

"You mustn't worry about me. If it is my time, I am ready. Besides, I need you to look after Nakiata for me, once you find out where she's gotten to. You know how much trouble she is prone to getting into. Now, I'm asking you to go, before it's too late for all of us," she said as she bowed to him.

Tyrog notice that she'd begun crying, and yet she was smiling at the same time. "My lady, they will sing songs about your bravery across the stars, you have my word." He bowed in return and flew into the Black Door.

Ka'tia wiped her tears away, cleared her throat, took a deep breath, and closed her eyes. She allowed herself a miniscule moment to feel a small sense of tranquility, even though there were explosions going off more frequently and getting even closer.

She poised herself and began the motions to summon *Hisi'k* magic. She moved slowly, deliberately, and with extreme focus. Her every turn and bend had such fluidity. Every movement was flawless.

As her hands reached up into the air as part of the final move, a large group of Ugs broke through the ceiling and were entering the room. Ka'tia was completely unaware of their presence. In that moment, she started feeling a plethora of powerful emotions almost all at once, and for some odd reason each one was associated with a mental image.

The first was love, the love of family which brought to mind the image of her mother, brother, and Korah who were standing side by side and smiling at her. Next she began to feel passion, deep within her heart. This produced a bit of an unexpected sight. She saw Dravone as if he were standing right in front of her and smiling.

After that she began to experience a trio of emotions: honor, pride, and loyalty. These brought new images to mind. She could see her two newest companions, Tyrog and Kola'gram, who both looked happy to see her. The two of them bowed to her regally. In the blink of an eye they disappeared in a cloud of dark smoke.

I suppose this is the end, she thought. In the last moment, as the magical power began to surge and intensify through, in and around her hands, she felt every emotion all at once, however, there was also anger, hatred, and jealousy too. The three final emotions brought an image of Nakiata to mind.

Nakiata was standing not too far in front of her with an all too familiar mischievous smirk. Nakiata waved at her coyly before vanishing into SOT.

The emotions raged and boiled within her and Ka'tia opened her eyes, screamed with everything that she had, and pulled so much energy down that she knew she couldn't possibly hope to contain it. Her arms only made it halfway down when she flung them out to her sides, releasing a massive wave. She gasped for air as the heat and power radiated out from her body.

The wave of energy spread with incredible speed, vaporizing everything in its path. Within seconds, it had covered nearly half of the planet. The surface of the planet was bare, and large fissures opened allowing magma to spew upward into the sky. This was the only warning the Ug armada had.

A few more seconds later it reached the planet's core, which instantly became unstable. The surface of the planet went dark and there were no more geological events, save one, the planet itself exploded outward.

Large chunks of planet hurtled toward the armada, but before they had a chance to inflict any damage, they were demolished into dust by a highly visible blue and white swirling sphere of expanding *Hisi'k* magic.

The speed at which the sphere moved increased exponentially. Within seconds it approached the Ug armada, which had already turned and was trying to escape the solar system.

The armada was completely engulfed. The magic destroyed them down to the smallest particle.

The wave of magical energy was not yet finished though. It continued to expand, decimating everything in its path. Every planet and asteroid that was swallowed added to its power.

When the *Hisi'k* magic collided with the star at the heart of the solar system, something unexpected happened. The sphere vanished and the star changed color, from yellow to a pale blue.

The light coming from the star flickered and waned until it finally imploded. The implosion in turn created a black hole in space. The remaining bits of the solar system were now being dragged into the black hole and devoured into nothingness. The black hole silently swirled around waiting for every last morsel of space dust.

Out of nowhere, a glint of white light flickered for only a fraction of a second. It was in the space where the planet had been, and then it was gone.

There was nothing living to witness the faint light, but there was one that did observe the glint. Kuohlo began to smile from his place among the stars.

Chapter 27

Tyrog made it through to the other side, and not a moment too soon. The Black Door shut down the instant he was there. The first thing that caught his attention was an angry Dravone yelling at Kola'gram. "If you can see the future, then why didn't you stop her before she — ugh, now who knows where she is!" Dravone said heatedly.

"I'm sorry Dravone, that's not how it works. I don't know everything about the future," Kola'gram said. "Through meditation I can peer into it and search for clues, mainly things that stand out, and no matter how many times I see it, I will never be everything that I need. I always miss something, and there is one little fact that I can't avoid; once I look into the future, if I attempt to change something, it will result in everything I witnessed being altered, and sometimes drastically. So, I ask you, give me some time, and I will try to find her."

"Ka'tia is . . . is gone now," Tyrog noted.

Dravone turned to him. "What! Ka'tia has gone, where?"

"I have a feeling she is no longer among the living," Tyrog said softly.

"Nakiata is lost, and now Ka'tia is dead! *Rrrahhh!*" Fueled by frustration, Dravone transformed to his wolf-state and the anger he was feeling dulled his sense of humanity. His only desire was to rip something apart with his bare hands, and gnaw on it, tasting the fresh blood.

He turned and the first thing in sight was Kola'gram. With rage and hatred in his eyes, he took a couple of steps toward him, clearly about to pounce.

"No!" Kola'gram said firmly, slamming the end of his staff down on the ground. The tip beamed with a short burst of intense white light. It was just enough to deter Dravone's advance.

Dravone turned away, huffing and growling several times under his breath as he trudged off into a darkened section of the room.

"Even though what I foresaw . . . I don't know anyone or anything that could have survived such an explosion." Kola'gram said. *Don't give up hope; miracles can and do happen Dravone,* he thought.

Tyrog looked around to see if he could figure out where exactly they were. As always, the room they found themselves in was too dark to assess accurately, but like Dravone, he, too, had excellent night vision and could see far better than most in such conditions. He did notice that this room was larger than any of the others that they'd found Black Doors in, and from his current vantage point he counted not one or two, but eight other Black Doors. *I'll bet there are even a few more over by Dravone,* he thought.

"Do you think you can get the lights working?" Kola'gram asked.

"That shouldn't be a problem," Tyrog replied, spying what he guessed was the control area. It wasn't a single, normal control table. It appeared to be more of a command center, judging by its size. He flew over and found that it was indeed more. "I've never seen Louravan technology this advanced before. It's like they took a huge leap forward. The speed and ease of access to the flow of information is simply exquisite. There is more than — ah, here we go, lights."

Multiple panels of overhead lights, along with several dimmer lights along the walls, came on, allowing them to see the entire scope of the room. "This is different," Kola'gram commented.

"I count seventeen Black Doors," Tyrog noted, "three of which are red-lined. It appears they only need some minor repairs, but the one there in the middle, I have no access to its controls. That's the least of my worries, I am more concerned that it doesn't appear on any of the schematics that I've found for this place. It was probably a recent addition, or all the records have been erased because something dark and sinister lies on the other side."

"What's that in front of it?" Kola'gram asked.

"I'm going to make an educated guess that, it, being the small pedestal in front, is a specialized control for the door," Tyrog replied while he continued to search through the information being presented on the array of consoles in front of him.

"Don't concern yourself with doing any of the repairs yet, Tyrog. I'm going to need some peace and quiet while I search the future to see where we go from here, and how we're going to find Nakiata. Is it safe to assume that you can use any one of the Black Doors in here to find some much-needed supplies?" Kola'gram asked.

"Oh, yes. With this database, we have access to hundreds, if not more, planets to choose from for supplies."

"Sounds good. How about you take Dravone with you and try to be back here in about an hour or so," Kola'gram suggested.

Tyrog didn't reply straight away because he was too focused on the new technology and its large database of information. "Tyrog? Did you hear me?" Kola'gram asked.

"Yes, I heard you. We'll return as soon as we can," he replied. He grumbled as he took to the air, heading across the room toward Dravone. He was about to fly through the deactivated Black Door in the center of the room when he crashed into an invisible force field that was surrounding it.

"Ouch!" he cried out, picking himself up off the floor.

"What happened?" Dravone asked. He sighed heavily, rolled his eyes, and barely lifted his head high enough to see Tyrog rubbing his head.

"This Black Door is . . . protected by some kind of energy shield," he answered, still rubbing the top of his head.

"Is that unusual? I thought they had protective shields to keep people safe from going somewhere that might be hazardous to them." Dravone's curiosity gave him the initiative to stand and go examine the Black Door for himself.

"Well, yes. They have safeguards in place, but only when the Black Doors are functioning. This one is inactive, so there should be no need for such a shield. It's something I've never come across in my entire life, and I've never seen such technology mentioned in any database," Tyrog said. He walked around the edge of the force field, tapping it every so often.

"What about this?" Dravone asked, pointing at the pedestal.

"That, too, is just as unique. I have never seen the like," Tyrog answered. He started examining the three-foot-high pedestal. The top was pitch black and smooth like glass. He finally finished examining all but the side facing away from the Black Door. So far, there was nothing, no markings of any kind, only smooth, flat, black surfaces. As he came around to the side facing away from the shielded Black Door, something caught his eye. "What's this? I think it's a keyhole, and you know what that means; we have to find another key. But I've never seen a design like this before."

Dravone squatted to get a better look at it when he noticed something else. "Mounara's light bless me. Did you see that! There's a symbol around the keyhole."

Tyrog tilted his head to one side, took a step back, and that's when he saw it, too. "That resembles, Nakiata's birthmark, or at least the mark connected to a mirror image of it. I almost missed it completely. It's barely noticeable. The color is only one shade lighter than the rest of the pedestal. I've never seen it displayed in this fashion before."

"I have," Dravone noted. "I've seen several of them, in fact. We found them in the ruins of Hekthes, back on Zondura. But how it ended up here, wherever *here* is . . . I have a feeling we need to find Nakiata, because this definitely has something to do with her."

"I agree. If only we knew where she went," Tyrog said, shaking his head.

"You don't have any ideas? Even with all that information at your fingertips?" Dravone asked, pointing at the command console and sounding a bit perturbed.

Tyrog grumbled, flew back to the command console, and began searching for anything that would give them a clue as to what had actually happened to Nakiata. "Yes, there is an extensive amount of useful knowledge here. From what I have ascertained so far, the Louravans had barely begun experimenting with various new fields of science such as quantum mechanics, planetary shift correcting, time expansion and travel — Hmmm, this is quite interesting indeed."

"What about Nakiata?" Dravone urged him, walking up to the command console and leaning over to see what Tyrog was so interested in.

"Yes . . . Well, this is rather odd," Tyrog admitted. He tilted his head to one side, as if he was trying to see the information from a different angle.

"And that would be?" Dravone asked, pretending to understand what he was talking about.

"Normally, these control consoles transmit numerous parameters through their respective Black Doors in order to maintain an accurate database of a locations, conditions at each end, and a myriad of other information. All of this knowledge can be accessed by anyone at a console, which from what I can tell was mainly used to see where travelers have gone or come from."

"Pretending I understood anything of what you just said, which I don't, how does that help us?" Dravone asked.

"In normal circumstances I could tell you the last ten or so planets each individual Black Door was connected with, how many people went there or came here, and so on. However, the planet where we recently came from, the door there was originally a Blue Door. So, it was not designed to transmit information as the Black Doors are. Plus, I didn't have the time to correct that deficiency. I was a little rushed, considering the Ugs were after us." Tyrog held up his small hand to stop Dravone from asking his question. "All it means is that we don't have any way of knowing where she went," he explained.

Dravone was silent for several minutes. He finally spoke up and said, "We will find her, I can feel it in my gut. Besides, isn't it kind of imperative that we do, I mean how's the prophecy supposed to be accomplished without her?"

"Yes, but right now I propose we set our sights on something that will help us all out. Kola'gram suggested we get some supplies. He also asked me to take you with me. What do you say? Shall we go?" Tyrog asked.

Dravone's eyes lit up a little. "Yes, I'll go with you. Do you have any ideas where we can get these supplies?"

Tyrog went back to work, searching the database. "There are several planets available to us. I guess it all depends on what kind of provisions we're trying to obtain. The Louravans were not much for eating meat, which is what I'm craving right now. Luckily for us, they kept accurate records. Now, we are also going to need some other things, so in my opinion we should go . . ." he paused, searching, "here," he said, tapping on the controls that activated one of the Black Doors off to the side.

"Did you do that? Or should I be concerned that we're about to have visitors?" Dravone asked.

"No need to worry. That was my doing. I hope we can find a nice, fresh, meal as soon as we get there," he said, heading for the Black Door.

When they emerged on the other side, Dravone asked, "Where are we, exactly? I'm only asking because all the rooms with Black Doors are almost identical to one another, except for the one we just came from, and that other one, the one you said was a hub of sorts. I guess I don't understand why the Louravans made them all like this."

"I can answer that. It's because the buildings, or rooms, that house the Black Doors are actually an intricate part of the doors and how they function. I won't go into the juicy details right now, but it is quite fascinating," Tyrog said. He walked over to and grabbed the handle of an ancient-looking door. The door was made of a dark gray metal, of which was almost completely covered by rust. He eased the handle down and the metal door creaked open. Tyrog smiled the moment he saw where it led. For once it was direct to the outside. He spread his wings and flew out.

Dravone peered out through the open doorway to get a better look, and for a moment he was breathless. *Well that's a pleasant surprise. I don't think I've ever seen a more inviting landscape that that,* he thought. He stepped out onto a large, green grass field that was located on a small plateau. Far off in the distance, he could see massive, rust-colored mountains, all with gorgeous, white snow caps. This actually helped to put a little pep in his step as he walked over to Tyrog.

"Whoa, that's a long way down," he commented when he realized that the large, gray stone on which Tyrog was perched, happened to be resting on the edge of a steep cliff.

Tyrog didn't reply. He just sat on the stone, staring out across the valley below. Dravone scanned most of the valley and it didn't take any time at all to notice the innumerable buildings, which were arranged in a superbly organized fashion. They appeared to be precisely spaced apart and the tallest buildings were located at the center. The more he searched the valley, the more buildings he noticed.

Dravone was impressed. He'd never seen a city like it. He guessed there had to have well over a thousand buildings. "I have to say, that's more than a city. It's a metropolis. Any idea who lives down there?"

Dravone tried his best to see anyone moving about, but there was no one. "I wonder what the name of this planet is?" he asked. He took a long whiff of air. "Is it me, or does the air here have a strange smell? I don't know what to make of it."

Tyrog still said nothing. He didn't even budge a muscle. He merely sat, staring out at the valley. He resembled a stone figure, at least until he spread his wings halfway to their full extent. He held them there for several minutes before tucking them in tight against his body.

"Did you hear me?" Dravone inquired with a soft tone.

"Yes, Dravone, I heard you just fine," he replied solemnly.

"So what's the matter with you?"

"First of all, the air here is quite different than what you're used to. It has a stillness and purity that only comes after a long absence. I'm actually astonished, the plant life has filtered out most of what we did to this place, our technology and lack of concern for the ecosystem." Tyrog paused to smell the air again. "That city down there, no one lives there. It was — vacated, long ago. The planet's name is Sauvrra', and this was the birthplace of the Sodarans, it's my home," Tyrog tucked his wings back in tight against his body and lowered his head.

Dravone didn't know what to say. He always thought Vazdrag was Tyrog's home. He eased up onto the stone and sat down next to him, placing an arm around the little Sodaran's shoulders. He regarded the lifeless city for a while, and after a bit he felt Tyrog lean his head against his ribs.

The two of them sat together in silent reverence for a short time.

"I'm sorry, I didn't know. What happened here? Isn't it a bit strange that your home planet has a Black Door?" Dravone asked trying to cheer him up.

"It never had one until the Sodarans started exploring space. During our travels we came across two things that piqued our interests: the prophecy, and Louravan technology, specifically Black Doors. We spent more than enough time studying both, and finally we were able to construct our own Door. That's how I came to be on Vazdrag," Tyrog informed him.

Something caught his attention. It was a barely detectable scent carried on a gentle breeze. Tyrog turned his snout into the oncoming wind, took several deep breaths, stuck his forked tongue out so that he could taste the air, and listened for a moment. "Are you hungry?" he asked.

"Sure, I could eat. I'm always up for a good meal," Dravone replied. He watched as Tyrog turned and flew off. His mind was entirely focused on eating a large, juicy, tender chunk of flesh. His stomach grumbled and he turned back around.

His jaw dropped open. He never noticed there was an enormous temple on the other side of the small building that housed the Black Door. Dravone had difficulty making out its details because the sun was high above the temple. He could see that it was at least ten stories tall and, to him, the shape resembled an arrowhead.

A dark shadow blotted out the sun when something flew over the top of the temple. Dravone hoped it was his companion, but it was hard to tell because it was directly in-line with the sun.

A moment later, Tyrog landed a few feet away. While he was gone he grew, and was now at his full height. He was holding a creature in each hand. Both beasts were wiggling as hard as they could since they were extremely frightened.

"Do you prefer yours well-done or raw?" Tyrog asked, setting one of them down and then roasting it with a burst of flame while it tried to escape. He took the other one and sliced it in half with a single swipe of his claw. He tossed the two halves down on the ground and waited for Dravone to make his choice.

"I'll take some of the roasted one. It sets easier on my stomach," Dravone said. He walked over and yanked a large chunk of charred meat off the carcass.

"I was hoping you'd say that," Tyrog admitted joyfully. He reached down and picked up one of the halves, shoved it in his mouth, and began swallowing it whole.

Neither of them was aware that a figure emerged from the small building behind them.

"Once the two of you —" Kola'gram started to say.

Tyrog jumped clear over Dravone and landed hard, causing the ground to rumble.

"Don't do that! Sneaking up on a Sodaran while they're eating is not the wisest course of action. It tends to lead one into becoming a burnt cinder or a steaming pile of ash," he stated.

"As I was saying, before you became frightened, as soon as you've finished gorging yourselves with whatever that used to be, we need to get moving. We do have a SOT master that needs to rejoin our group."

Dravone dropped the chunk of meat he was currently gnawing on. "You know where Nakiata is?" he asked.

"I believe so," he replied, eyeing the large, well-cooked, Kyrnor remains. "You know, that smells absolutely delectable."

"Would you care for some meat?" Tyrog asked.

"We don't have a lot of time to spare, but I am a bit famished, so, why not," he answered.

Tyrog reached down and pinched off a piece of meat and tossed it to Kola'gram. He briefly examined the charred flesh, took in its aroma, and finally tasted it. "This is delicious," he said. "I'm going to eat and walk now. I will wait for the both of you inside." He bit off a large piece. "Mmm, so good."

Dravone ripped off another piece for himself. "I'm right behind you," he said to Kola'gram. He tilted his head up at Tyrog, "I'll let you finish the rest."

Tyrog smiled before picking up the second half of the raw Kyrnor and eating it. He glanced down at what was left. *I hate to waste such good food, but I can't eat another bite,* he thought, lowering his head closer to the carcass. He slowly inhaled as much of the aroma as he could. He opened his mouth, and a long burst of flame erupted out of it. He kept the flame going until all his fire was gone.

By the time he was back to his normal size and was entering the small building that housed the Black Door, Kola'gram had already re-activated it and was waiting. "I'm not exactly sure what we're going to find on the other side of that door, but if my visions remain true, we have nothing to fear. Who wants to go first?" he asked.

"What? Why don't you go first? You're the one who can see the future," Dravone said sharply, and yet he stepped into the blackness without fear and was gone.

"I was trying to be courteous," Kola'gram stated.

"I know that, but he didn't. When it comes to Nakiata, I think we both know full well that he will not hesitate in the slightest. Love gives him plenty of courage," Tyrog said, following Dravone into the Black Door.

Yes, but it won't get any easier, even if there is a brighter side to the future, Kola'gram thought. He, too, walked into the blackness.

Chapter 28

As soon as he emerged on the other side, Kola′gram ran smack into Tyrog and Dravone, who had stopped only a few feet away. "What's going on?" he asked.

"Well, it appears that we have a welcoming committee waiting for us," Tyrog answered.

Ten feet in front of them stood ten armored sentries, four of whom had weapons, similar to those the Roarrgs wielded, pointed directly at them. At first glance, the sentries appeared to be made entirely of metal. Their stout bodies consisted of three arms, two on either side of the torso and one extending out from the center of the back. They had four legs, each with three oversized toes that were equidistant from each other, giving these creatures exemplary balance.

The aliens had the oddest shaped heads, they were a flattened pyramid shape. In the center of what could only be categorized as the face were three glowing, green eyes. Underneath that was a small rectangular recess which the group assumed was the mouth.

"Do you think they understand us?" Dravone asked.

"I doubt it. And without the Itzuli, we'll never find out."

"Are you talking about this?" Kola′gram asked, pulling out a small, metal orb from one of the hidden pockets inside his robes.

"Fantastic! Where did you get it?" Tyrog chirped excitedly. He graciously took the device from him.

"I removed it from Ka'tia's pack a while ago. I've seen this moment in one of my previous visions and knew that we would need it."

Tyrog cautiously turned around so that he was facing the steadfast sentries, and he tossed the small sphere into the air. The room was instantly bathed in the soft green glow which the Itzuli produced. After a minute it fell to the ground. Tyrog plucked it up and handed it back to Kola'gram for safekeeping.

"What was that?" one of the sentries asked.

"That was a spectacular yet simple device. It collects and transfers neurons specific to languages, and, in basic terms, it teaches everyone within sight of the beams every language it has collected. You can now talk to all of us," Tyrog replied.

"That's quite brilliant. Could you explain it a little better? I'm not sure I quite understand how you've accomplished such a feat," the sentry said.

"Photo-transference is the basic scientific principle," Tyrog noted. "I can only assume that you understand the properties behind that logic. I'm asking because, based on those weapons, I would venture that your level of technology is more than adequate."

"Yes, we understand that principle, though we've never thought to explore such unique uses. Thank you for introducing us to it. Before we continue along any further avenues of communication, we would know a few more things: Who are you, what are you, and why have you come to our planet?" the sentry demanded.

"To whom are we speaking?" Kola'gram asked.

"I am Neekta," the sentry replied, taking a step forward.

"It's a pleasure to meet you. I am Kola'gram, and I come from a planet called Frole. This is Tyrog, and he is a Sodaran. That is Dravone, a Morphan. The three of us are newly acquainted members of an ancient prophecy, and we've come seeking your help. We are looking for a friend of ours. She is another member that we've lost, and we know she came here recently. She has black hair, royal blue eyes, and she's not very tall. She carries a pair of special weapons that are suited to her . . . talents. Have you seen her, by any chance?" he asked.

"We've never come across any of your kind before, but, then again, we've never travelled outside of our own solar system. We recently uncovered this structure. We were searching for more resources when we stumbled across it. It took us some time before we had a firm understanding of the language we found here. At that point we understood what the Black Door was and what it could do for us. A few of us were doing some extensive research when the first alien arrived."

"So, you know where she is?" Dravone asked.

"Yes, but I must inform you that she is now our permanent guest, and there is nothing you can do to persuade us to release her," Neekta said in a slightly angry tone.

"You're holding her captive?" Dravone asked heatedly.

"That's not what he said," Tyrog responded, "although he did imply that she is being held against her will. We all know too well that she's not cooperating as a confined guest."

"I think we should let Neekta explain what happened," Kola'gram said, trying his best to keep Dravone calm.

Neekta stepped forward with his hand held out, palm facing up. His fingertips lit up, and a holographic image appeared above his hand. "This is what happened. Shortly after your friend arrived, a group of researchers found her and attempted to communicate with her. After several frustrating minutes, she vanished right in front of them. As you can see, that was not all that happened."

They watched as the confused metal bodies of the researchers fell to the ground. Seconds later, pools of what Kola'gram and Tyrog surmised it to be some sort of life sustaining fluid coming out of the mechanical beings. The blood-like substance spread out from the deceased and converged until the floor was covered in the thick, yellow substance. The scene changed, and they watched an empty street somewhere in the unsuspecting city. Barely a minute had passed when alarms throughout began to sound, waking many of the inhabitants.

"When we arrived . . ." Grief stricken Neekta took a moment to steady his voice. "When we arrived, we found thousands of innocents whose lives had been fruitlessly lost to a threat we didn't know existed. This has become the darkest day in our recorded history," Neekta said his voice full of sadness.

"You see yourselves as living beings?" Tyrog asked.

"Yes, we are living beings, like you," Neekta replied harshly. He continued, "We did our best to evacuate the remaining members of the city's population. We managed to get them to one of our storm-holds."

"So, how did you stop her?" Tyrog questioned.

"Some of our most intelligent citizens were called in to an emergency assembly, and once they arrived they went to work, reviewing the evidence from every recording device we could find. The information they gathered led us to several amazing discoveries. First, we were able to determine how she managed to disappear. I have to say, I have never seen such excitement come from such devastation."

"That information is irrelevant; we already know how she vanishes, but knowing that doesn't help us understand how you managed to capture her, and why she's still being held prisoner," Dravone stated with clenched fists.

"You're correct, it's not much information. However, it was a vital piece of information which they used to devise a full-proof way to detect her. It didn't take long. At that point all they needed to do was come up with a formula to capture her, without harming her. After all, we do pride ourselves as being a peaceful people."

"About that, what do you call yourselves?" Tyrog asked. "And, if you are so peaceful, why do you have weapons?"

"We are the Shex, and these are the first weapons we've created in over three centuries. Don't be alarmed; they're not lethal. They merely disrupt the electrical signals between the central nerve and the rest of the target's body, rendering them in a temporary state of paralysis. I'm having doubts that it would have the same result on you," Neekta said, pointing a finger at Tyrog.

"That is quite the story," Tyrog said, when Dravone interrupted.

"So, those weapons won't kill us?" *How unfortunate . . . for you,* he thought, changing into his wolf-state.

The Shex didn't know how to respond. They were not exactly prepared to see such a transformation.

Dravone used the few precious seconds he had to pounce on one of the sentries. His first move was to disarm the sentry by prying the weapon out of his hands. He was surprised to learn that the Shex had a stronger grasp than he first anticipated. However, the sentry was caught off guard and Dravone was able to relieve him of the weapon.

After tossing it to the ground, and as he was about to rip into the sentry's chest, he heard something which caused him to hesitate.

The Shex sentry was thrusting its back-mounted arm at Dravone, knocking him to the ground. The other two sentries now had an opportunity to open fire on him. Their blasts hit him square in the chest.

"Arrrr!" the wolf screamed. The pain felt like a thousand Tirions stinging him all at once. His body began convulsing, and he was forced to change back to his normal-state.

"Wait! Do not fight!" Kola'gram yelled. He slammed his staff on the ground, creating an energy bubble immediately separating them from the Shex.

The Shex continued to fire their weapons, but Kola'gram's protective shield was working better than he expected. Tyrog quickly hopped over to Dravone and examined him. "Are you hurt?" he asked.

"I don't know. I don't feel anything at all. It's like my limbs are not even there," he said. He tried moving but couldn't. That's when a surge of pain hit him hard. "Yes, it hurts, it hurts something fierce, and what's worse is that I still can't move," he said harshly. Tyrog turned his attention to the Shex, but Dravone wasn't finished. "The Shex are hiding," he said. His body went limp as he lost consciousness.

"What was that? Dravone! What does that mean?" Tyrog implored, shaking his shoulders in an attempt to rouse him.

"Tyrog, we need to do something, and fast. I don't know how long I can keep the shield going," Kola'gram stated.

Tyrog walked up to the edge of the bubble, which placed him a few inches away from Neekta. He looked, listened, smelled, and tasted the air. "Neekta, I know now. So let me say this; if you wish to survive, every one of you will drop their weapons and take us to Nakiata," he said.

"What do you know?" Neekta asked.

The Shex's eyes changed color from green to yellow, and a second later changed back to green. Neekta and the other three sentries stopped firing at the shield and began pulling out small pieces from their weapons.

"I know what you are, and I must say, you smell delicious."

Neekta did not answer. Small squares opened up in each of the Shex's bellies, and they all pulled something out and placed it in their weapons.

"I don't like what they're doing, Tyrog," Kola'gram said. "I'd guess they are modifying those weapons to deal with either my energy shield, you, or both."

"So be it," Tyrog said, hopping over to Kola'gram, who was busy trying to maintain the shield to help out.

Tyrog quickly reached into Kola'gram's robes and pulled out the Itzuli. He took a single claw and depressed a barely perceptible button. A small, hidden compartment opened up. Tyrog pulled out the small, Sodralinium stone he had stashed away, tossed it into his mouth, swallowed it, and turned back to face the Shex. Tyrog increased in size exponentially.

The Shex finished their modifications and began firing at the shield. "I can't sustain it any longer!" Kola'gram exclaimed as it faltered and disappeared. Tyrog lowered his massive body and put his wing out to protect Dravone and Kola'gram from the Shex.

"Ouch!" he roared as energy blasts struck his wing. Tyrog took a deep breath, lowered his wing slightly, and spewed a stream of fire that vaporized the Shex and destroyed a large section of the wall behind them. "Come on! We need to get moving! I guarantee more are already on their way," Tyrog said.

"What about Dravone?" Kola'gram asked.

"Leave him. He will be safer here, at least for now," he replied.

How is it that I've never seen any of this happening before now? There has to be an explanation, Kola'gram thought, watching Tyrog squeeze his way out of the building.

Moments after exiting the ancient Louravan building, Tyrog found himself facing several hundred Shex. There was no conversing with them; they simply opened fire on him. Every shot that managed to hit him, caused some serious discomfort. This only infuriated him further. He clenched his jaw and did his best to ignore the pain as he rushed toward them. His energy level was still enhanced by the Sodralinium stone, and as soon as he was close enough, he incinerated all but a few of them.

Tyrog spun around and smacked several of the remaining Shex with his tail, flinging them against the wall, and disabling them long enough for him to get even closer. There were two Shex remaining. He reached out and snatched one of them. With his free hand he flicked the weapon away.

Tyrog grumbled. He began to salivate in anticipation of what deliciousness might be locked inside. He took his claw and pushed it into the Shex's chest so that he could pry it open. "There you are you little fiend. I had imagined you to be a bit different, but in the end it doesn't matter. I now know how to get to you, inside these armored bodies."

The Shex creatures he found inside were small, and at first glance, it made him think of an insect that once roamed his home planet. However, these creatures were much larger, at least a foot tall. Their bodies were a rusty brown color, and their heads were large and pear-shaped. The Shex stared at him with its six unblinking, lidless, dark gray eyes.

The rest of the Shex's body had some of the same characteristics as their oversized, robotic bodies, with four legs and three toes. However, the flesh and blood Shex actually had four arms instead of three. Their two upper hands had only three fingers, while the two lower ones had four fingers with opposable thumbs.

"As much as I love conversing with intelligent beings, I'm afraid you are about to come to a swift end." Tyrog said.

The small Shex didn't know what to do other than attempt to escape. It let go of the controls to the metal body and made a run for it.

"Oh, no you don't," Tyrog said, throwing the metal carcass and plucking up the tiny Shex. *It's hard to get away from the claws of a hungry Sodaran,* Tyrog placed it between his teeth and bit down.

The blood and innards squirted all over his tongue. *Hmmm . . . Oh, wow, you're a bit salty, but otherwise not bad,* he thought as he chewed the last few morsels of the Shex body.

Tyrog felt a few more stings against the side of his neck. He spun around to find the last Shex still trying to take him down. He almost laughed at the attempt. He smiled while reaching out and capturing the Shex. He quickly cracked open the metal body and plucked the frightened creature up and ate it. *I don't know why, but that one tasted even better. I think I'll try to get a few more of these appetizers. I'll probably have to eat a few hundred of them in order to make a complete meal out of them.*

"Where's the city the Shex showed us?" Kola'gram asked, coming to a stop behind Tyrog.

"I'd say it's up there, at the end of this tunnel," Tyrog replied, pointing in the direction the Shex had come from.

Kola'gram was about to say something when his eyes suddenly rolled back into his head and he fell to his knees. A shot from the other end of the tunnel struck him. As the energy surged through him, a spurt of blue flame blazed in the whites of his eyes, for a fraction of a second.

This is incredible, he thought. He wasn't exactly sure how, but his best guess was telling him that he was, physically feeling time as it slowed down all around him. He had no idea it was the start to a new vision of the future, which was about to unravel in his mind.

Everything went black and the next thing Kola'gram knew, he was floating in the air, high above a bustling Shex city. He wasn't sure how he came to be in such an unusual position, because one thing he was sue of, was that he didn't possess the ability to fly.

It finally dawned on him that this was a vision, so he took advantage of the excellent vantage point. He surveyed as much of the area as possible. *I don't see anything of any importance. Perhaps if I can get down to the ground I'll be able to see something familiar, or at least noteworthy,* he thought.

I'm not sure how, he thought while starting to squirm and thrash about, but nothing was working. *Maybe all I need to do is think about moving to the ground,* he thought while attempting to mentally will himself there, but even that accomplished nothing.

Once he stopped trying and just let things happen, he found that he slowly began to descend into the city. The moment his feet touched the ground, he noticed a large, fortified structure with only one visible way in or out. The building was completely void of openings and windows of any kind. *I'll bet that's where they're holding Nakiata.*

The moment he finished his thought, he was forcefully pulled forward. Kola'gram put his arms up in front of his face in anticipation of hitting the wall, but he dropped them when he realized that he was going through the walls and empty spaces. He came to an unexpected stop in a room containing a glasslike cube, which was right in the middle. The cube was not sitting flat but resting on one of its edges.

Whatever it was, the Shex had it completely surrounded with their most heavily armed warriors. Upon closer inspection, he noticed that it contained a small figure suspended in some type of translucent liquid. "Nakiata," he said aloud. *It looks like they captured you during one of your attacks,* he thought, noticing that she was still holding her Kharak blades. Her pose suggested that she had been in the middle of a fight.

Kola'gram did his best to make a mental note of as many details as he could before the vision might end. As he was making mental notes something unexpected happened. Orange, red, and yellow flames swirled around the entire room, consuming every single Shex warrior. He felt a sense of pride because he already knew where the fire came from. The excitement was not yet over as another burst of flame hit the cube, causing it to shatter into millions of tiny pieces, freeing Nakiata from the liquid-filled prison.

The instant she hit the floor, Nakiata went into a kneeling position with her Kharak blades held tight and close to her body. From that moment she was motionless, like a statue. Tyrog entered and slowly travelled around the room, staying as close to the walls as possible, all the while keeping a keen eye on Nakiata. The last thing he wanted was to get into a fight with her.

What happened? Why didn't you guys follow me? You left me alone with these . . . these, things, she said, with a clear tone of anger. Her eyesight focused on the floor.

There was a . . . a momentary glitch in the power. Once I restored power to the Black Door, I looked back at the control table, and that's when I noticed that the glitch was more than a power issue. There was a single digit which kept changing from one number to another. We had no idea where you went," Tyrog answered her.

I guess it doesn't matter now that you're here. Where are the others? She asked, sounding a little less angry.

Kola'gram is attending to Dravone, who was injured shortly after we arrived. I have a feeling he will be fine, once he sees you again, Tyrog answered, trying to improve the situation.

What about Ka'tia, where is she? Helping Kola'gram with Dravone?

Tyrog hesitated because he was unsure how she would react to the news. Kola'gram wasn't expecting what came next. He heard Tyrog's thoughts. "If I don't tell her now, she's going to find out when Kola'gram and Dravone get here."

Tyrog lowered his head close to the ground so he could watch her every move carefully. *We don't know. Kola'gram said we shouldn't lose hope, but I think she died trying to keep the Ugs from following us here*, he explained.

What? The Ugs, how? You said she's dead? No — that can't be true! The Prophecy, it said . . . it said . . . Nakiata was at a loss for words as the anger began to build within her. *How can that be? Now there's only four of us,* she said heatedly. Nakiata took a deep breath and thought about their situation.

Now Kola'gram could hear her thoughts. "How can we fulfill the prophecy? Especially if there are only four of us left? Wait, I remember it said . . . yes." *It makes sense now,* she said.

What does? He asked.

The prophecy, don't you remember? It said: 'united four will stand'. I've always wondered what that meant. I guess for that part of the prophecy to be true, one of us would eventually have to die, Nakiata replied.

Tyrog snorted, and two small plumes of gray smoke floated up and away from his head. *I'd almost forgotten about that. If you would permit me, my lady, I have quite the, well it's, um, a* delicious *proposition for you. I'm not sure if you know it, but Sodarans have a deep-rooted desire for destruction and carnage. It's part of our genetic make-up, and there's no level of technology or amount of knowledge that has ever been able to quell it completely. We have done well to keep it subdued, but it's always lurking in our subconscious, waiting for a moment of weakness or an opportunity to be released.*

Nakiata raised her head and locked her eyes with his. *So what are you suggesting?* She asked with a smirk.

Destroy these . . . pathetic, yet delicious, Shex. I have already tasted many of them. They are an acquired taste that I've come to enjoy, he said. He closed his hand, making a fist and showing his teeth. Drool started oozing out from between his razor-sharp teeth on both sides of his mouth.

Oh? Well . . . in that case, I am — with you, she said, vanishing into SOT.

Kola'gram noticed that his vision was rapidly becoming blurry. *No! Wait, what happened?*

He was disappointed, he thought it was over and that he was about to wake up, but his sight returned and in that moment he knew he had gone even further into the future. He was hovering over another city, only this time the vast majority of it was burning. Kola'gram surveyed as much as he could in every direction, and the only thing he could see was the flames. *The Shex city, what's happened to it? Are all of those fires burning cities?* He asked himself.

Kola'gram closed his eyes, lowered his head down, and thought with a heavy heart, *What have we done? And why have I never seen any of this before?* He felt a rush of wind coming from behind him, and before he had a chance to look, Tyrog swooshed a few inches overhead, causing him a short fright. He tried to move again but was still unable to do so.

I didn't know Tyrog could fly that quickly and that quietly and how is it that he's still huge? He thought.

Kola'gram watched as the great dragon flew toward the heart of the burning city. Before Tyrog was too far out of sight, Kola'gram caught a glimpse of something in each of his hands. Kola'gram watched closely as the Sodaran slowed, stopped, and hovered high above a large, burning building. Each beat of his wings fanned the flames beneath him like a massive furnace, making the flames burn hotter and brighter.

Tyrog held up his hands, allowing Kola'gram to see what he was holding: two Shex trapped in his mighty grip. Tyrog moved his right hand close to his face, inspected the metal Shex for a moment, laughed, and without another thought, he crushed it.

Tyrog took the remains and threw them into the heart of a burning building below. He held up his left hand and considered the other Shex for a second. He was salivating as he moved his right hand up to its chest, and with a single claw he split the Shex open.

Kola'gram wasn't sure, but he thought he saw Tyrog pluck something out of the Shex's body and toss it into his mouth. *Is he eating the Shex's heart?* The next thing he knew, the great dragon had dropped the metal carcass into the fire and was flying off toward one of the other burning cities.

Kola'gram was yanked backwards, out of control and when he stopped he felt his feet touching the ground. He found that he was now a short distance from the burning city, and in front of him, on a pile of several hundred Shex bodies, stood Dravone in his wolf-state. He howled deep, long, and powerfully. Kola'gram could tell that it had a complex meaning. The howl was sad as well as a warning that he was not finished.

Before Dravone's howl ended, Nakiata appeared next to him. She reached out to him, and took his clawed hand into hers. He finished his howl, and glanced down at her. Both surveyed the devastation they had caused.

This can't be true! Kola'gram's eyes were jarred open. He was back in the room with the Black Door. He immediately searched the room and discovered that Dravone was gone.

Chapter 29

Nakiata's heart pounded with excitement as she moved with ease through the compound that had held her captive. *This is a first. Normally I'd be blacked out by now. So, why now? What's different?* She stopped in front of a massive hole in the wall where the front doors used to be. Beyond it, she could see a city that had recently seen battle. She reappeared and started to ponder what was happening. *At first, I felt my rage and hatred for the Ugs as it rose to consume me, but now it's changed. I feel something else, something more powerful. Almost as if I desire to create death and watch the killing. It's as if it . . . excites me.*

"Why have you stopped?" Tyrog asked. The gleam of shiny metal caught his attention. He turned his head and saw several of the Shex exobodies lying off to one side. His enormous size allowed him to reach over and start plucking out the flesh and blood beings from their mechanical armor. "These things are giving me an extra boost of energy every time I eat one. I can't explain it — but I like it. I need more," he said, with desire in his voice.

Nakiata turned around and looked up at him. "First things first, how did you find me?"

"To tell you the truth, it wasn't too difficult. These Shex creatures are not all that hard to kill. Their metallurgy skills need improvement, their weapons technology is pathetic, and they have no defense against a Sodaran. I truly believe they could have been the most peaceful race I've ever come across." Tyrog smiled. "Now that I've said that Let me tell you what else I discovered. First of all, I was trying not to start a rampage, so I finally managed to trap two of them without killing them, right away."

Tyrog stuck his forked tongue out several times, tasting the air. "I found out that they are little creatures inside the metal bodies, and of course I ate one, then another, and another. I just couldn't stop. It felt so good, and the way they taste, so exquisite."

"Yes, it sounds as though you were enjoying yourself," Nakiata commented.

"Oh, no. I didn't start enjoying it until I ripped the legs off of one of them so he couldn't run away. After I'd ate a few hundred, I told myself the next one was going to be the one I would try to interrogate. It wasn't too successful, the Shex didn't cooperate, so I ripped him open and ate him too." Tyrog's eyes rolled back into his head slightly, and he smiled.

"Are you sure you're feeling alright?" she asked.

"Yes, I've never felt better."

"Well, if you ate every Shex you came across, how did you find me?"

"One of them surrendered. I guess they figured they couldn't win against me. He was more than cooperative, and he told me that the only place they could have taken you was here. And yes, I ate him too. I can't help it, I want more," Tyrog said greedily.

In a cold, emotionless tone, Nakiata said, "I know that if Ka'tia or Dravone were here, they would probably persuade us to leave, but she's dead, and he's not here. So, let's go out there and get you all the tender, juicy, little Shex morsels you want. We won't stop until you're satisfied. I'm still in the mood for some payback!" she vanished into SOT.

"Yes!" Tyrog exclaimed, rushing out into the city. He drooled over the idea of eating more Shex than he could count.

Dravone woke up to absolute silence. He sat up, and his head started pounding a minute later. "Oh, those weapons sure do pack a mean punch," he said aloud, gritting his teeth. He sat still for a few minutes before finally shaking off the pain. *I need to be strong. I need to find Nakiata.* He took a moment to scan the room to see if he'd been left behind. He didn't see anyone until he turned around and found Kola'gram, who had been right behind him on his knees in some kind of trance.

Dravone did his best to get to his feet, but instead he only managed to stumble the three or four steps it took to reach Kola'gram. He dropped to his knees and carefully took Kola'gram by the shoulders, giving him a slight shake. "Kola'gram, snap out of it." He paused for a second to examine him. *Grrrr, I don't know what to do. I've never seen you like this. I don't know if I should leave you here and go to find Tyrog for help, or what?* "Kola'gram! Come on! I need you! Where do we go?" he demanded. His pleas went unanswered.

Dravone managed to get back to his feet. *Okay, I will go for help. Now to figure out which way Tyrog went.* He didn't have to search the room for clues. The huge hole in the wall, along with all the dead Shex bodies was a good indication. He peered out through the opening, but he couldn't see anything. The ambient light was only strong enough to reach a few feet outside of the room. *I'll probably be able to see more if I change to the wolf,* he thought. The transformation took control of his body.

Once in his wolf-state, he spied as far down the tunnel as he could. *Well, its obvious Tyrog went this way. I can smell burnt metal and — something that could be flesh. It's kind of foul, but what else could it be? I certainly hope he hasn't gone too far. I don't relish the thought of having to track him over a great distance.*

"Nakiata — is the — key," Kola'gram muttered.

Dravone spun around and stared at him through the wolf's eyes. Kola'gram appeared to have a faint glow about him. *I guess I'm not going after Tyrog if he's waking up . . .*

We go after the Sodaran, Wohd, the wolf spirit inside Dravone, said to his mind.

Wohd! We haven't spoken for a while. What about Kola'gram? You think we should leave him here?

We can't do anything for him right now. He will be safe here. I guarantee that Tyrog is heading for Nakiata. The Sodarans were obsessed with the prophecy, and without her it will go unfulfilled. If we find him, we find Nakiata. Besides, we should be there for her, don't you agree? Wohd asked.

Yes, we should definitely be there for Nakiata!

Dravone dropped down on all-fours and took off running down the tunnel. Once he reached the end of it, he found something that made tracking the great dragon much easier. There was a unique trail of Shex exobodies some of them had been slightly burnt, while others were melted completely. *With such carnage it shouldn't be too hard to find my way.*

The trail led him straight to a large compound. He stood up on two feet and eased his way in. *This smell is starting to annoy me,* he thought after being inside for only a couple of minutes. *I have a feeling I'm almost —*

His thought was cut short when he heard the sound of mechanical legs rushing toward his position. *You won't get me a second time.* Dravone roared as he turned the corner and found several unsuspecting Shex coming straight at him.

He pounced on the closest one, shoving his claws deep into its sides. He pulled with all his might, ripping open the Shex's chest to reveal the small being inside. *So, you must be the real Shex. Time to die, you little annoying bug.* He thrust his hand in, grabbed the Shex, and pried it out. Dravone bit down on its head, pulling at the same time, and tore the head away from the body. Small squirts of Shex blood hit his tongue. *Hmmm, a bit strange, but altogether not bad.*

In the few seconds after he tasted the blood, he started to feel stronger, full of energy, and unstoppable. He howled furiously and completely ignored the other Shex as they rushed past him.

Wow, I don't know what that was, but I like it. I think I might have to force myself to endure the taste a little longer. Now, where are more of these Shex? Dravone slowly made his way toward the center of the compound, but he didn't find any more Shex.

When he arrived in the central chamber, he saw that someone had been there before him. *Well, we've reached the end of the line, Wohd, and there's no sign of either Tyrog or Nakiata. If I had to guess, I'd say we already missed most of the action.*

I'm sure we can find all the action we both desire, Wohd replied.

What's that supposed to mean?

Our physical forms are intertwined, so what affects you also has ramifications for me. The Shex blood has something in it that we both like, whether or not it's good for us, I don't know. I will be the first to say, I don't mind the risks, so let's go get more!

Dravone dropped to all-fours and headed back out to the city. The moment he left the compound, he was knocked sideways into a wall by something strong and fast. The blow was so hard that it caused him to revert back to his normal-state, which has never happened to him before. "Oh man, that hurt a little," he said, trying to pick himself up off the ground.

Before he knew what was happening, he felt two hands on either side of his face. Nakiata reappeared and began kissing him with every ounce of her passion. She stopped, slapped him across the face, and said, "Where have you been? You were supposed to be right behind me. Never mind. I'm just happy to see you." She went back to kissing him before he could reply.

The ground rumbled around them, and a deep, booming voice bellowed, "Dravone! You made it. I found her, set her free, and now we are on a rampage. Care to join us? Have you tried the Shex? Once you get past the flavor, they have quite the kick," Tyrog said.

Nakiata stopped kissing Dravone and turned to Tyrog, who quivered from seeing the harsh expression and the unsettling sight of her almost completely black eyes. "Apologies, my lady," he said bowing his head.

She gave him the same evil grin. "It's fine. Come on, Dravone." She pulled him up off the ground with surprising strength.

"What happened to you? Your eyes, they've changed again," he asked, placing a gentle hand on the side of her face.

"I don't know what you mean. Come on, we're having fun destroying the Shex. You should join Tyrog and eat a few of them," she said. She smiled at him for a moment and vanished into SOT.

A large contingent of Shex came marching up behind them. They began firing their weapons. This time, they had a much different effect on Tyrog. The blasts were not lethal, but they hurt far worse than before. "Ahhh! They've upgraded their weapons," Tyrog growled, spinning around and spewing flame on the first ten rows of Shex.

The Shex retreated beyond the range of his flames. They continued shooting volleys of energy blasts at them. Dravone completed his transformation, crouched low to the ground, and charged the enemy with a roar. At the last second, before he plowed into the front line, he jumped high into the air and came crashing down on top of several Shex. He reached out and slashed at the closest one, opening its chest.

The small Shex inside began to squirm and climbed out, trying to escape. Dravone's reflexes were more than enough to follow it, and within seconds he caught it. The Shex screamed and pleaded with him to be let go, but he didn't listen to a word it said. Dravone raised his hand up and bit down on the middle of the creature's body, causing it to cry out in pain. The cries didn't deter him as he chewed and swallowed it in large chunks.

Several of the surrounding Shex were about to shoot Dravone with modified weapons, when all but two of them simply slumped down to the ground. The remaining Shex weapons failed to fire. Baffled, the two glanced at each other, and that's when Nakiata reappeared standing between them and the Shex. She smiled at Dravone and said, "Bon appétit," and disappeared again.

The chests of the two Shex split open from top to bottom, allowing Dravone to scoop them up and eat them. He scavenged the others until he'd consumed every last one of them. He paused for a moment. *I like this feeling. I feel . . . indestructible.* He howled with everything he had, letting the world know he was coming with a hunger. Once finished, Tyrog swooshed past only a few inches above his head. "Save some for me!" he yelled down at him.

Dravone watched as the great dragon slowed and came to a brief hover. The area in front of them lit up and he saw Tyrog land amidst the fire. Dravone didn't want to miss out, so he lowered himself down onto all fours and took off running toward the flames.

As soon as he arrived at the scene, he found Tyrog sitting on his haunches, grabbing Shex left and right, cracking open their metal bodies, and plucking the beings within.

The heat from the flames was too intense for Dravone to get any closer. He stopped about a hundred feet away. He watched and waited for any fleeing Shex to come across his path. His adrenaline was flowing like wildfire in anticipation of his next kill, and out of nowhere he heard something that was completely out of place: Laughter. He turned to see Nakiata squatting on top of a large, stone handrail. He noticed that her eyes had become black as the center of a Black Door, and her grin sent a shiver up his spine.

"See how they squirm," she said with a despicable laugh. The laughter came to an abrupt stop, and Nakiata yelled, "Come on! Stop fooling around! There are more enemies to kill." She stood up and disappeared.

Both Dravone and Tyrog caught a few more Shex and ate them before following her command to search out and kill more of the creatures.

Kola'gram awoke and found that he was alone. "No!" he cried out. It only took him a moment to collect himself and get to his feet. He picked up his staff and ran out of the room through the massive hole in the wall. *I hope I'm not too late,* he thought. "*Ellafo's,*" he said softly. The end of his staff began to glow with a soft, yellow light, allowing him to navigate down the darkened tunnel.

It wasn't long before he came across the first group of Shex remains. *This isn't a good sign. I'd better hurry.* Kola'gram placed his staff out in front of him and held it with both hands. He closed his eyes and focused his thoughts on Dravone. A cloud of dark smoke rose from the ground and swallowed him up.

When the smoke cleared, his mouth dropped open. He had arrived at the exact moment where his vision had ended. Not too far in front of him stood Dravone, in his wolf-state, and Nakiata next to him, holding his hand. Tyrog was flying around the city, setting things ablaze.

This has to stop, but how? Kola'gram began brainstorming all sorts of possibilities when he came up with a radical idea, one that he wasn't even sure would work, but he knew he had to try something. He took his staff and began twirling it around and around in circles, moving it back and forth from his left to his right and eventually over his head. With every passing moment, he spun the staff faster and faster.

All the air around him became still, and the temperature began to drop rapidly. He forced every thought from his mind and focused all of his magical energy into his hands as he brought his staff to a halt and slammed the end down on the ground. "*Con—vou—la'*!" he screamed.

A massive, radiant, blue energy wave, resembling a tsunami, expanded outward from the tip of his staff. The wave moved with incredible speed. The instant it came into contact with any fire, the flames were immediately snuffed out.

Dravone and Nakiata were the first of the group to be hit. The wave was so strong that it flung them forward. Dravone ended up on his belly, while Nakiata used her momentum to perform an impressive flip maneuver, landing on her feet to face the direction from which the wave had come.

A second later, she felt different. Her body went cold, and she began to shiver uncontrollably. "What was that?" she asked, her eyes shifting back to their royal blue hue. She tried shaking her head as if she'd recently awoken from a dream. It helped, but only a little.

She didn't know why but she immediately thought of Dravone and had a burning desire to see him. She looked down and to her right, where she watched Dravone changing back to his normal-state. *That's so cool. Some days I wish I could change into something, or someone, else. Even if it's only lasted for a little while. It would be a nice reprieve from all of this,* she thought. Once Dravone's transformation was complete, he, too, started shivering.

The wave also had an effect on the Shex that were still alive. Their metal bodies froze until they no longer had any control of their motor functions. This left the physical Shex beings trapped inside their metal carcasses, unable to fight or escape. They were, however, shielded from the wave by a thin layer of insulation in their robotic bodies that was incorporated long ago.

The wave quickly spread throughout the cities and across the entire planet. Tyrog was a great distance away from everyone when the wave caught up to him. The magic had a different effect on him. At first, his joints became stiff and he was unable to keep his wings moving. *What's happening? Oh, no, this isn't good. This is really gonna hurt — bad,* he thought the instant he began falling out of the sky. In a matter of seconds, he crashed into the ground, causing it to rumble. A sizeable crater formed, and a cloud of rocky debris filled the air.

His heart began to beat rapidly. It felt like it was about to explode right out of his chest. He reached up and put his hand on his chest. He groaned. Then, without warning, it slowed drastically to only a few beats per minute. His eyesight became blurry, and everything around him was spinning out of control. He blacked out.

Kola'gram fell to his knees. The blast of energy had drained him to the point he was about to lose consciousness. In that moment another vision struck him. He could see himself holding his staff and kneeling, and when he turned around to get a better idea of where he was and what was happening, he was pulled at great speed across the planet. He stopped hard, and the sight before him was dreadful. Tyrog was lying in a crater, about to die. And what made it worse, there was no visible help in sight. Kola'gram felt trapped, he was confined and couldn't move. He couldn't even scream; he was helpless.

Tyrog gasped several times. His eyes opened, and Kola'gram watched as the life left his body. *No!* He screamed in his mind. *This is not the way it's supposed to happen!* The next thing he knew, he was back in his body and staring out at a darkened city. Nakiata and Dravone walked up next to him.

"We need to get to Tyrog, and fast! He's dying!" Kola'gram said.

"What did you say?" Nakiata managed to ask, rubbing her shoulders, still feeling the effects of the ice wave.

"How are we going to help him?" Dravone inquired.

How are we going to help him? I don't know any healing magic that would work on a Sodaran. Perhaps, he was thinking. "I have an idea, but we need to move fast, or we will lose him," he said, rushing past the pair.

Nakiata and Dravone followed him into the city, where he quickly began opening every single Shex body he came across with a tap of his staff on their chests. "What are you doing?" Nakiata asked.

"Trying to find a Shex that's still alive," he responded without stopping.

"You might not find any. I'm afraid we might have finished them all off," Dravone said under his breath.

"No, there has to be some left!" he said in earnest.

About ten minutes later, he stopped and screamed into the night air. "How can we end the Darkness if we're all dead?" He slammed his staff on the ground, and they were surprised when a spell erupted out of the ground. At first, it had a similar appearance to the cold wave, only with a lot less energy and speed.

"That's undeniably creepy," said Dravone, "and Morphans don't usually say that." He watched the slow-moving magic. The moment it came in contact with any of the Shex, their chests opened up.

"That's definitely going to save us some time," Nakiata noted.

Kola'gram turned and frowned at her. There was a momentary silence which was broken when they heard something falling over. The three of them rushed around the corner to find the source of the sound when they came upon three of the small Shex creatures trying to repair one of their metal exobodies which was lying on the ground.

The sweet memory of eating a multitude of the little beings came to mind, and Dravone began to salivate heavily. He couldn't help that, as he moved closer, the Shex became alerted to their presence. "Stop!" Kola'gram yelled at all of them. "Dravone, we need their help."

"What? Did you actually say we need *their* help?" Nakiata asked, sounding confused.

"I did. The Shex must have the ability to fix things rapidly and adapt their technology faster than any other race I have ever known, and right now our friend is somewhere out there dying."

"Grrrrr, have it your way," Dravone said between his teeth. He wiped the drool from the sides of his mouth and stepped back.

"Shex! Please come out. I don't know if you heard what I said, but we desperately need your help."

They waited for several minutes before the three little creatures reappeared. "You want us to help you? Why should we help you? You have caused such devastation to us, and your friends have almost wiped us out," the middle Shex said angrily.

"What I did was stop genocide. I wasn't trying to hurt you or anyone else. I swear that if you help us we will leave your planet without delay and never return," Kola'gram said. He knelt down on one knee and bowed to the Shex.

The Shex huddled together and were whispering amongst themselves for several minutes. Finally, they turned to face them and one in the middle spoke. "Before we agree to anything we want you to help us *first*."

"How may I be of service?" he asked.

"You can help us reactivate our exobodies. If you can do that, we will be happy to *help* you."

"I will do what I can," Kola'gram said as he approached them slowly. He stopped a short distance past them. "I will need you to stand back. I don't want to injure you," he said. He started the motions to summon *Hisi'k* magic. As his hands went skyward and he felt the first hint of energy, he pulled them down and thrust his hands toward the motionless metal bodies.

Several jolts of electrical energy extended outward from his hands. The magic barely lasted a full second, but it was enough to reactivate their metal exobodies. "Thank you. We will need a few moments to get back inside and recalibrate our bodies," the Shex said.

"Please hurry. Our friend is in dire need," Kola'gram said.

The three Shex nodded and climbed into their respective metal bodies. The chests closed, and the bodies began to move. First, they stood and were doing nothing. Without warning, the Shex drew their weapons and began firing on them. They managed to hit Nakiata with a blast that struck her square in the chest, and she fell backwards onto the ground.

"What are you doing?" Kola'gram screamed in disbelief.

"For our race!" the Shex replied in unison.

"Get us out of here!" Dravone said, grabbing Kola'gram by the hem of his robe and pulling him down, out of the line of fire. Kola'gram did as he was instructed and transported them back to the room with the Black Door.

"What are we going to do now?" Dravone asked.

"I don't know. I need to focus on the future. I need to see if we can save Tyrog. The last vision I had, I . . . I watched him die," he said, sitting down and preparing himself for a vision.

Chapter 30

Thirty minutes had passed, and Kola'gram was still searching the future when Dravone rudely woke him. "They're coming!" he said sternly.

"Who? What?" Kola'gram asked, as his eyes quickly wandered around the room like a drunkard trying to focus. It took him a moment to adjust after having been abruptly yanked out of his vision.

"The Shex, and from the sound of it there are more than you and I can handle, especially since Nakiata is still unconscious. I can possibly buy us a few minutes, but that will be the end of us," Dravone stated.

"Wait here," Kola'gram said as he vanished in a cloud of dark smoke.

"Wait —" Dravone didn't get a chance to ask him where he was going. *Great, now what do I do?* Dravone glanced down at Nakiata. The Shex energy weapon had obviously been upgraded, and it was now more harmful. *I thank Mounara that they didn't kill you,* he thought. He had never been so glad that she was merely unconsciousness.

Still, the pain Nakiata was expressing said more to him than words. He couldn't help it, tears started forming in the corners of his eyes. He walked over and sat down beside her. "What happened to you? I wish you were still awake and by my side; I wouldn't be so worried that we might not survive. Granted, the Shex have yet to devise weapons that will do any permanent damage. Their reaction didn't surprise me a little, even though we have almost completely wiped them out of existence." Dravone stared at her, hoping she would wake up at any moment. "Nakiata, can you hear me? I want you to wake up so that I can tell you how I feel."

Dravone gently grabbed her hand and held it in his. "I've never been good at expressing my feelings. I hope you can hear me. I want to say . . . Well, my heart beats for you and no one else, Nakiata. You are the breath that fills my lungs. You've even won over my wolf. Even he loves you. There is nothing we wouldn't do for you." He sighed and peered up at the stone ceiling. *I wish I could see the sky. Mounara, help me, give me strength and give me the power and fortitude I need*, he pleaded silently. He leaned over and kissed Nakiata on the lips.

"How sweet," Kola'gram said from behind him. "If you'd be so kind, I'm going to need your help with him." Kola'gram said, pointing at Tyrog's motionless body, which was still about ten feet in length and several hundred pounds.

"Is he dead?" Dravone asked.

Kola'gram lowered his head and sighed. "I think so. I'm not completely sure. I put my head against his chest as soon as I arrived, and I barely heard his heart beating. It was so slow, and as I listened it stopped. I was too late to help him; not that I could have helped. I know very little about Sodarans, but I know they are resilient against magic. What's worse is that I had already seen what happened. My vision of the future has come true."

Dravone stood, walked over, and stopped next to Tyrog's head. He stared deep into the large, purple eye with its white iris. He could tell there was no life in it. He knelt down, took his fingers, and gently closed the Sodaran's eyes one at a time. He gently placed his hand on Tyrog's snout and closed his eyes. "I will miss — you — my friend." His words were choked with emotion. "I know you wouldn't want me to grieve, but I can't help it. Even though we only just met and haven't had time to get to know each other like I'd wanted."

Dravone opened his eyes, tears were steadily streaming down his cheeks as he observed the plain ceiling. He searched some of his more recent memories. "I will say that I always enjoyed those brief moments we shared, indulging ourselves by eating some of the best, highly flavorful, and exotic meats, I've ever had the pleasure of trying."

Dravone tried to wipe away the streams of tears that were now flowing. "I don't think I'll ever find another friend with quite the same tastes that we had in common. I wish I could have been there to say . . . goodbye, my dear friend, Tyrog." Dravone let go of his emotions and began to cry softly.

"*Voxstra*," Kola'gram said, holding his hands so that they faced the large opening in the wall that led to the long tunnel.

"What was that?" Dravone asked, wiping some of the tears from his eyes and face.

"Something that will hopefully give us enough time to escape, or, at least, that's my plan. It's a magical force field. Although I have to admit it's not nearly as powerful as it should be, it should withstand a fair amount of bombardment before it falters. I'm going to suggest we get these two through the Black Door as quickly as possible. I don't want to risk being here when the force field fails. You can start by getting Nakiata through, and as soon as she's safe on the other side, come right back and help me with Tyrog's body."

Dravone nodded. He walked over to Nakiata, picked her up, and carried her into the blackness. Once on the other side, he carefully set her down, kissed her on the cheek, and went back to help Kola'gram with Tyrog. The second he stepped through, Kola'gram shouted, "Hurry! Grab his feet and pull!"

Dravone rushed over, grabbed Tyrog's feet, and began pulling. A massive blast shook the entire room. "What was that?"

"I think the Shex have changed their beliefs when it comes to non-lethal weapons. I recommend we don't stick around to find out how far they are willing to go. Now, hurry, the force field is about to collapse." Kola'gram grunted, pushing with all of his might. The body of the great dragon was slowly being consumed by the Black Door. "Keep pulling! I will try to give you some more time," he yelled, not realizing that Dravone was already on the other side of the Black Door.

Kola'gram turned his attention back to the force field, which dissipated before his eyes. He now had no choice but to face the Shex head-on. *What do I do now?* He thought. Then it hit him. He put all his energy into focusing on one magical thought. He placed his staff in front of him and let go. It remained standing. He started moving his hands and arms around in large circles, while turning back and forth at the waist. He narrowed the space in which his hands and arms moved, refining the magical pattern.

The moment the force field collapsed he thrust his hands forward. "*Fotya'*!" he yelled, and a ball of orange and yellow flame left his hands.

He watched in hopeful amazement as the fireball struck one of the Shex. An explosion erupted all around them and the instant the fire subsided; he could see that it had no effect on them whatsoever. *Yup, I'd say it's time to go. They've already made improvements to their armored bodies, and in such a short time. Who knows how what else they will come up with,* he thought. He enough time to grab his staff and ran into the Black Door.

Dravone finished pulling Tyrog's body clear of the Black Door when Kola'gram rushed past him in a mad dash. He was heading straight for the controls so he could deactivate the Black Door, but before he was able to press the first button, he heard Nakiata's voice coming from behind him.

"There's no need for that now!" she said.

Kola'gram turned around to see her standing only a few inches in front of the door's energy field. Both he and Dravone noticed that her eyes had completely lost all their color and were as black and cold as the empty space behind her.

"I thought you were injured," Kola'gram said.

"I was. I can't explain it, but something happened. I'm not sure what it was. It's kind of hard to describe, but I will try." Nakiata pause to recollect as much as she could. "To me, it sounded like a voice. It was soft, feminine, and vaguely familiar. Yet I couldn't quite put a face to it. All I know is that it kept telling me to wake up and protect the ones that I love. I suppose that's all I needed to hear. Then I woke up," she explained.

Her face contorted, and they knew something was upsetting her. She continued, "The moment my eyes opened I saw one thing, Tyrog's body. I knew deep down that he was dead, but I had no idea how he died, and to tell you the truth I didn't care. He was gone." She turned to observe the carcass, which had shrunk another couple of feet.

"I wanted instant revenge, not just for myself, but for the both of you, Ka'tia, and all of my friends and allies. I was not going to stop at any cost. So, I allowed myself to fill with anger and rage, and let me tell you something: I've never felt rage like that in my entire life. I'll even admit that I actually found it pleasing. In the blink of an eye, I was through the Black Door and found fifty or so Shex waiting."

"What happened?" Kola'gram asked, knowing full well that it was nothing shy of complete devastation.

Nakiata smirked. "I gave them the benefit of the doubt when I informed them that they were going to cease all hostilities and be of some use, or they were about to become . . . wiped out from existence. They failed to see reason, and they tried to hit me with their sting blasts. I was much too fast for them. I must have killed ten of them in under a few seconds. It felt really, really good. I even remember screaming out for Ka'tia and Tyrog. It was at that point I lost control and let my emotions overwhelm me. I didn't even care if I was concentrating to stay invisible. After that I don't know what happened." She stopped for a minute and thought about it.

"If I focus hard enough," she continued, "I can see flashes of the fighting in my mind. I can see hundreds of Shex being sliced up. I don't even know if it's me, but I'm fairly certain it is, I mean, who else would it be?" Nakiata's smirk turned into a broad smile. "I feel great now, and if I had to guess, I'd say the Shex will never have issues defending themselves ever again. I'll even go as far as to wager that I didn't leave a single one of them alive." She shrugged her shoulders and rolled her eyes.

Her smirk faded, and she sighed. Nakiata dragged her feet a little as she walked over and sat down next to Tyrog's body. She leaned up against him, pulled her knees up to her chest, and rested her head on them.

"So, what do we do now?" Dravone asked. "We can't possibly fulfill a prophecy that had five strangers battling the Darkness to save the universe. How's that going to happen now? Not with just the three of us," Dravone asked Kola'gram as he sat down in front of Nakiata. He reached out and put his hands on the backs of her calves. "How are you feeling?" he asked her.

"I'm angry. How do you think I'm feeling?" she responded harshly. Nakiata looked up at him with tears streaming down her face, and that's when she saw his expression. She knew he was worried about her. She couldn't fight the urge; she jumped into his arms and started hugging his neck, crying even harder.

"Maybe — it's time we give up, and go home," he said softly, rubbing her back.

"No! We can't do that," Kola'gram insisted. "The Darkness is going to win, and horrific things will come of it."

"Look around you, Dia'fani, the *Darkness* has already won," Dravone retorted.

Kola'gram's tone softened. "No, it hasn't won, but it will if we give up now. I am going to stop and meditate. Maybe then I'll be able to make sense of all this. The truth is, right now I don't understand what's happening, and I seriously don't know what the future holds for us. I've spent my entire life searching the future and calculating every conceivable possibility, and yet here we are. We don't know where to go, Ka'tia is gone, Tyrog is dead, and I am befuddled," Kola'gram stated.

Nakiata abruptly let go of Dravone and scanned her current surroundings. "We have never been here before, have we? I think this place has more Black Doors than the place Tyrog called a hub, don't you agree?"

"It's true. You've never been here before now, but the rest of us already got to spend some time here. We even explored it, briefly," Dravone said with a short laugh.

"What's the story with that Black Door?" she asked, pointing at the one with a force field around it.

"We don't know exactly," Dravone said. "I know that it has something to do with you. It has the same symbol we saw back in the ruins of Hekthes, on Zondura."

"Where?" she asked.

Dravone took her by the hand and guided to the other side of the Black Door, where the small pedestal resided. Once they were facing the Black Door, he pointed out the symbol embossed around a keyhole.

"What makes you think that it's a keyhole? I've never seen one shaped like this one," she said, reaching out and tracing the symbol with her finger. She leaned over and examined the oblong hole that had been perfectly carved in the center of the symbol. "I don't see any internals," she said.

"Internals? What do you mean?" Dravone asked, leaning over her shoulder in an attempt to view whatever it was she saw.

"Every lock has some kind of internal mechanisms which the key comes into contact with. It's what allows the lock to be undone. Whatever this is, it doesn't have any of those features. It appears to be nothing more than an empty hole."

"What if you need to put your finger in there? Like some of the devices we've seen the Ho-drooli using?" Dravone asked.

Nakiata glanced up at him with a raised eyebrow. "Guess we won't know unless I try," she said. She extended her index finger and managed to squeeze it inside the hole.

"Well? Do you feel anything?" Dravone asked.

"Nope, there's nothing in there. It's as smooth and cold as a wet river rock," she said disappointedly.

"*Grivershba maklik shamga veragoh.......ahhhhh!*" Kola'gram shouted.

Nakiata and Dravone looked back at him with confusion. He was still deep in meditation, only now he was swaying back and forth gently.

"What was that?" Nakiata asked with a giggle.

"I'm not sure. I've only seen him meditate one other time, and it was nothing like this. Do you think we should try and wake him or leave him be?" Dravone asked.

He turned back to her had his answer the moment he witnessed the mischievous grin.

"I say we leave him alone," she replied. Nakiata took his face into her hands and began kissing him. She stopped for a moment, leaned back slightly, and bit her lip. She had nothing but desire in her eyes.

"What if Kola'gram wakes up? This place doesn't offer us any privacy," Dravone said.

"Do you love me?" she asked him.

"Yes, I do, with all my heart. I would do anything for you, I would even die for you if it meant you would go on surviving," he replied.

"Then why worry about it? Besides, how do we even know the Dia'fani understand what making love is? We both know they are not like us. The chances are he won't have any idea what we're doing, and, if he does — well, I hope he gives us a little due respect and turns around. Can I ask you something?"

"Anything,"

"When this is all over with, would you accompany me to my village? I'd like to ask my mother and father for their blessing to be bonded. I know it sounds silly, but it's a rare and special ceremony that shows all our friends, loved ones, and any honored guests to see that we are committed to each other until our end."

Dravone raised his eyebrows, smiled, and started to blush a little. "I would be honored to do that for you. However, I must tell you, Mounara has shined on us, and, according to her eternal law, our three hearts — you and I, and my wolf — have already joined in eternal love. This is our way," he answered her.

Nakiata smiled, rolled her eyes at him, and went back to kissing him.

Dravone's heart was beating so fast he thought it was going to burst out of his chest. He gave in to his passions and let everything around them fade out of existence, leaving them completely alone. In that heated moment, fueled by love, they began to make love.

Their passion lasted for a long time, and when it finally came to an end, they caught their breath and cuddled up close to one another. Exhaustion set in, and they quickly fell asleep in each other's arms.

Kola'gram had been meditating on the future for almost nine hours when he finally came around. The room was too quiet, which alarmed him slightly. It didn't take long for him to notice Nakiata and Dravone, slumbering naked near the pedestal.

Well now, my dear friends, I will answer you. Yes, I now know what's transpired here while I was searching the future. My race may be different, but we do know there are many different ways to express love for one another. Though . . . your way is among the most passionate and selfless acts I've been privy to. It's still a bit strange to me, and, as I think about it, I truly wish I had not peered as far ahead as I did, but there's no going back now. I now know what's in store for us, and it saddens me beyond measure. I hope that when the time comes you will forgive me. I have no choice, he thought, admiring his companions.

Kola'gram quietly walked over and put a hand on Dravone's shoulder. "My friend, it's time to get moving. We have a long way to go," he said softly.

Dravone groaned from exhaustion. He regarded Kola'gram with sad, tired eyes. "Already? We just laid down. Can't we have some time to rest?"

He thought for a moment. "Hmmm, I suppose we can wait a bit longer. Go ahead and rest. I will wake you in a few hours, and in the meantime I'll keep an eye on Tyrog," he said.

The Dia'fani's statement confused not only Dravone, but Nakiata as well. "Why do you need to keep an eye on him?" she asked. "He's dead, isn't he? I mean, is there any real reason to fret over him — well, is there?" She reached for Dravone's robe so that she could use it to cover her naked body.

"Let's worry more about the missing key, which we need to unlock that Black Door. It's here in this room, and only you can find it." Kola'gram pointed to Dravone.

Nakiata and Dravone looked at each other in confusion. "Are you sure there's a key? We examined the hole in the pedestal, and we think it's simply a hole," he said.

"Quite," Kola'gram replied, crossing his arms and frowning.

"Well, if there is a key, how's he supposed to find it? The symbol on the pedestal is clearly similar to my birthmark, so shouldn't I be the one to find it?" Nakiata asked.

"Yes and no. The pedestal does have a symbol on it, but I need you to trust me on this."

"Alright, do you have any suggestions, like a specific area of the room I should be searching?" Dravone asked sarcastically.

"You're not going to use your sight to find it."

"So, how does he find it?" Nakiata demanded.

"With his — nose," came the harsh reply. "Go over to the pedestal and use your sense of smell. In my vision, that is where you started your search. I think you'll find it has some kind of a scent. All you will need to do at that point, is to follow it to the key. At least, that's how I would do it," Kola'gram mentioned.

Great, now that she's awake and this Dia'fani gerrbrok *has given her some sort of short-term purpose, she's going to want me to go along with it. I'm not going to be able to find it with my nose. I'm going to need a much keener sense of smell.* Dravone grumbled under his breath at the thought. He knew that there was no way he was going to find the key in his current state. He stood and allowed his body to undergo the transformation to his wolf-state.

Even his wolf was tired. He growled softly at having to do work, but Dravone knew this had to be done, so he walked over to the pedestal and began sniffing it thoroughly. *Wow. There's no doubt about it. There's a definite smell of — blood. I would've never thought to smell for blood, but here it is.*

Dravone continued to sniff the air. *There's nothing in the air, but if it was blood there would have been drops,* he thought, getting down on all fours and putting his nose to the ground. The scent was extremely old, but not impossible to follow. He moved slowly, sniffing and then taking a few steps. *Whoever had the key last must have cut themselves or had enough blood dripping from a wound or something else, either way it left a trail on the floor. I'm not sure I should be worried about the fact they walked around the room aimlessly, obviously confused*, he thought, following his heightened olfactory senses to the far side of the room. The scent grew in strength the further across the room he went, and it was strongest in one small area right up against the wall.

Dravone became perplexed. Every time he stepped to his left or right, the scent weakened. Nakiata and Kola'gram had been following him across the large room, watching and waiting for Dravone to give them a sign to indicate where the key was located.

Finally, he stopped, changed back to his normal-state, and said, "I'm confused. I found the scent of blood all around the pedestal. I followed it, but it stops right here, next to the wall," Dravone said in frustration. *I'll bet there's a secret compartment or door here somewhere,* he thought, examining the wall.

He slammed his fists against the wall after a brief period of fruitless searching for more clues.

"Don't hurt yourself," Nakiata said, pulling him back away from the wall.

"I don't understand it. I thought there might have been a hidden panel or something, but I think whoever had the key may have died right here, and someone else picked it up or pried it out of the corpse's dead fingers and left with it," he commented.

"I don't know if someone died here, but I do know that the key is here," Kola'gram said.

Nakiata walked up to the wall and did a quick search for her own satisfaction. It was extremely smooth and seamless. She couldn't see anything. "I have to agree with Dravone. If the key was here, it's long since vanished, and —" She stopped mid-sentence and disappeared.

Would you look at that! I'm so glad the Oracle of Piyah taught me that I can see things differently while in SOT. The key is right there. I'm going to have to remember to start observing things this way a lot more while in SOT, she thought. She reached out and tried to find the edges of the hidden panel but came up empty. *This better not be some kind of elaborate joke, because if it is, I'm going to be extremely mad. Seriously, how am I supposed to get the key if I can't open this stupid door or panel, or whatever it's called? Grrrr!*

Nakiata reappeared. "The key is right here, on the other side of the wall. I could see it, but there's no way to get to it other than destroying the wall," she said angrily.

"You saw the key? On the other side of this wall?" Dravone asked, pointing at it in disbelief.

She nodded her head.

"I think you and Dravone should go to the other end of the room, for safety," Kola'gram said as he started the motions to summon magic. "Go! Go now!" he urged them.

Dravone grabbed Nakiata, picking her up as he ran toward the far side of the room as fast as he could. The magical energy Kola'gram was summoning had already begun to spark throughout the extensive room of Black Doors. The Doors themselves amplify the energy. One of the bolts managed to strike Dravone in the foot. He fell to the ground, hard.

His first reflex was to toss Nakiata up and away safely, but he failed, and she ended up sliding across the floor, slamming into the wall. She collected herself rather quickly and walked back over, pointing at him while she began screaming.

"You idiot! I could have run on my own. You didn't have to —" A bolt of energy connected with her hand which caused her entire body to start convulsing. She lost consciousness.

"Nakiata!" Dravone called out, scrambling over to her side.

Kola'gram was doing his best to focus the *Hisi'k* magic that was starting to get beyond his control. *What's going on? I've never been able to summon this much power before. If I don't get rid of it and fast, it's going to kill me and everyone else,* Kola'gram thought, placing his hands on the wall and allowing the magical energy to funnel into it.

The magic pooled and swirled around his hands, and before he knew it, it backfired, flinging him ten feet backward. Kola'gram rubbed his hands together from the pain, but he managed to keep his focus on the wall, where the energy continued to swirl. "Nakiata!" he yelled across the room. "Come here, quickly!"

"She's unconscious! A bolt of energy struck her hand, and now she's out cold!" Dravone yelled back.

"Bring her here!" Kola'gram responded.

Dravone scooped her up and hobbled as fast as he could back over to Kola'gram. "Now what?" he asked.

"Where was she hit?" he asked.

"Here," Dravone said, holding up her right hand.

Kola'gram took her hand and began to mumble rapidly. A soft, green glow surrounded his hand and extended up her arm until her entire body was glowing. He let go of her hand, and the glow vanished. "Set her down gently and take a few steps back," he cautioned.

A moment later, Nakiata sprung back to life, jumping to her feet and screaming, "No!" She scanned her current surroundings. "Okay, how did I get here? And what happened?" she asked angrily.

"Do you not see it?" Kola'gram asked, pointing at the wall.

"See what? Oh." Her tone changed in an instant when she glanced at the spot he was indicating. On the wall, the *Hisi'k* energy was flowing in a most peculiar pattern. It formed the same shape she'd seen before on Zondura and now here, on the pedestal.

"I don't know about the two of you, but this has an ominous feel to it, wouldn't you agree?" she asked.

"If I didn't know any better, yes, but I have already seen —" Kola'gram stopped himself from finishing.

"Seen what? Why don't you just tell us?" Dravone asked.

"Yeah, tell us," Nakiata agreed.

"If I divulge that which I've seen, we will lose a battle that has yet to be fought. I cannot see beyond it. I only know what is supposed to happen up to that point. I have also seen what happens if I tell you what you wish to know."

"And?" Nakiata demanded.

"It does not end well for anyone," he said softly.

"Humph. Alright, that still doesn't explain how we are going to get the key. What does that symbol mean? And is it going to be just the three of us, or is someone else going to die? I must know, or this ends now!" she demanded.

Kola'gram gently took her left arm and lifted it up so that he could clearly see her birthmark. "Yes, there is a correlation between your birthmark and that symbol, but what it means is beyond me. I fear that a combination of your birthmark and its mirror image is something to be feared," he said, guiding her hand over to the wall so that she could touch it.

The second her hand made contact with the wall, the symbol flared brightly, and the energy pulsed out through her body and back again for several seconds before it dissipated. "That was disappointing. Do you have any other ideas on how to open," as she was speaking, the wall began to emit a soft hum that lasted about ten seconds, before a small panel popped open, revealing a small cubby hole with the key suspended in its center.

"You were saying?" Kola'gram replied, reaching in to recover the key. "Now, let's see where that auspicious Black Door leads," he said, heading toward the pedestal.

Kola'gram stopped and double-checked the key and the hole on the pedestal to make sure they coincided with one another. "The moment of truth," he commented, sliding the key into the hole. As with any other key he was accustomed to, he tried to turn it in both directions, but it didn't budge. "Now I'm confused. I was under the impression that keys had to be . . . yee-ow!" he screamed.

"What happened?" Nakiata asked after she jumped back a step.

Before he could say anything, he felt faint, and the air all around him seemed to thicken. He stared at both Nakiata and Dravone, who simply stopped moving, speaking, *and* it even looked like they stopped breathing.

"Hello?" Kola'gram questioned, waving his hand in front of Nakiata's face. She didn't react. "What's going on?"

"Oh, I wouldn't worry about them. They are fine. I must apologize for my interruption," a deep voice said from somewhere in the room.

"I know that voice," Kola'gram noted.

"I would hope so. We had such a wonderful conversation the first time met," Kuohlo said with a chuckle.

"Where are you? Can you please explain what's happening to me?"

"I'm here," he replied, stepping through the wall and walking around the trio. He lay down on the other side of the shielded Black Door until his large head was extremely close to Kola'gram. "I have created what only a few species will ever discover: I call it, a cease of time. The simplest explanation would be to say that time itself is at a standstill for everyone, except us," he answered.

"Is that possible?" Kola'gram asked in disbelief.

"It's not important."

"Then why are you here?"

"I have come to adjust the gift I gave you. I'm not entirely sure how, but you've somehow prevented yourself from utilizing its full potential. I don't think you did it consciously. I'm however impressed by such an anomaly, even though I'm going to have no choice but to fix the problem," Kuohlo said. He reached out and, with the tip of his claw, touched Kola'gram's forehead. A light began to shine at the point of contact, but only for a split second. The light was gone, and so was Kuohlo.

"Are you hurt?" Nakiata asked.

"Am I what?" Kola'gram asked confused. He'd already forgotten what was going on.

Nakiata took his hand and noticed a single droplet of blood forming on one of his fingers. "Did you cut yourself?" she asked, examining the wound further. There was a needle-like puncture in his finger. "Did the key do that?"

Curious, Dravone pulled the key from the pedestal and gave it a once-over. "I don't see anything that would have caused it." He put the key back in the hole and tried to turn it. "Ouch!" he cried, pulling his hand away from the key and seeing a spot of blood on his finger.

"The key, it's taking DNA samples," Kola'gram said with a blank expression on his face.

"Remind me again what that means," Nakiata said.

Kola'gram appeared frustrated. "It means the key 'knows' who is trying to use it. Since both Dravone and I have already tried, we know it won't work for us. It's up to you."

I have a bad feeling about this, Nakiata thought as she reached for the key. She grabbed it firmly and tried to turn it. It wouldn't budge.

The key pricked her finger but before Nakiata sensed the pain, the key had already verified her DNA and accepted it. An energy wave burst from the pedestal and knocked both Kola'gram and Dravone off their feet. A moment later some type of red glowing liquid came pouring out of the pedestal. Some of it pooled around her feet, while most of it swirled around her hand.

It was a warm, thick, substance that congealed rapidly, becoming hard as rock, and the color became the same black as the pedestal. Nakiata tried to move, but she was trapped.

"What's happening?" she screamed.

From the floor she heard Kola'gram's voice. "Stay calm, it will be . . ." and that's all she heard, because it rapidly faded into nothingness. The entire room melted away, and Nakiata found herself standing in a large, white room filled with all sorts of new technologies, none of which she could identify or try to understand.

"You've come," a familiar low-pitched voice said, echoing throughout the room.

"Yes, I am — here, wherever this is," she replied.

"Marker Octana-two-eight, extended sub marker Belva detected. Time difference substantiated. Accounting . . . accounting, welcome. You will now be directed to return to Vela Loh. The return is inevitable. Please proceed through the Black Door. Further directions will be given. Please wait," a feminine voice said.

"I'm sorry, I don't understand. Who are you, and where am I?" she asked.

"You are so much closer now. This is where you must be. I can't wait to meet you. Your arrival has been long in coming," the low-pitched voice said.

"They are in for something special as soon as they — Oh, but that will ruin the surprise. Follow the signs indicated by the markers. They will lead you home," a slightly higher pitched, and also familiar, voice said.

"I know those voices. I have heard them before. Why are you not trying to warn me still? She questioned.

"There will no longer be any opposition. You and your companions are expected, even if they don't survive," the lower-pitched voice answered.

"So, all I need to do is follow the symbol?"

"Yes, bring it to me. I miss it so much. Oh my, how can that be the time! I must go now. If I don't rest, our meeting will never happen. I hope you have had quite an adventurous journey, thus far," the higher-pitched voice said followed by an evil chuckle.

The next thing she knew, she was standing in front of a deactivated Black Door. This one was not like the others; it was not inside a building. It was out in the open air. The view on the horizon reminded her of home in that there were three moons still visible in the daylight.

Okay, how do I get back to Kola'gram, Dravone, and . . . Nakiata became solemn. *I am ready to meet you as well, and kill you. If not for this stupid prophecy, Ka'tia and Tyrog would still be alive. I hope you're prepared for a fight, whoever you are.*

Everything slowly transitioned back to the original room, and she heard more laughter echoing all around her. It became extremely loud for several moments, and ended as abruptly as it had begun.

The instant it stopped she was back in the room. The solid black mass around both her feet and hands had once again liquefied, she was free again. Nakiata slowly let go of the key, which was immediately pulled inside the hole.

The keyhole sealed itself, and the symbol began to glow a beautiful, royal blue. Several loud clunks sounded throughout the room, followed by a short soft hiss. Nakiata stepped back away from the pedestal as it began to sink into the floor. Once the top of it was flush with the floor, it stopped.

A beam of intense, blue light shot down from the ceiling, directly onto the Black Door, and the force field deactivated.

"So, it begins," Kola'gram said.

"What does?" Dravone asked.

"Once we step through that Black Door, the end of the prophecy will be at hand."

"That's fine with me. I'm more than ready to be done with it," Nakiata said boldly.

"I have a question," Dravone started.

"And that is?" Kola'gram asked.

"Why isn't the Black Door working?"

The three of them looked over at the inactive door. "Let me guess, we need to find . . ." Nakiata was saying, when all the Black Doors in the entire room turned on and began to hum loudly. They peered down at the floor when they noticed the light coming from multiple surges of energy, which were flowing from all the other door toward the single Black Door in the center.

A few moments later, it came to life. The center filled with the unmistakable, eerie, matte blackness.

"That was a little unexpected," Kola′gram commented.

"This is it," Dravone said moving closer to the door.

"Did you forget about someone? We need to take Tyrog with us," Kola′gram said.

"Why? He's dead, isn't he?" Nakiata asked, turning her attention to Tyrog's body, and the fact that it was now so small, making it somewhat tragic; *he seems so helpless and limp,* she thought.

"Yes, and no. I don't understand how, but I have seen him in my visions, and he was very much alive. We can't leave him behind, we need him," Kola′gram finished.

"In that case, I'll be happy to carry him," Dravone said, walking back to collect his friend. Dravone picked him up with ease and plopped him over his shoulder. He sighed before walking into the blackness.

Nakiata regarded Kola′gram skeptically. "Is there anything you're *not* telling us?"

Kola′gram hesitated for a second. "Not at the moment. But I do have something I want to say something before the two of us go."

"I'm listening," she said in anticipation.

"Whatever happens, I want you to know that it has been an honor and I am truly sorry, and if there was any other way I would do everything in my power to change it. Unfortunately, I can't say more." Kola'gram walked over and embraced her, which was something he'd never done since they had met. "You are an inspiration to us all. You have such an unwavering strength and," he stopped himself before he divulged too much information. He let go, smiled, and stepped into the Black Door.

"If things get any more confusing, I'm going to get angry, and they've never seen me that mad before," she said, shaking her head. *I can feel it surging through my blood, right now,* she thought as she stepped into the blackness that Kola'gram said would bring the end to the prophecy.

Silver Tears Series

Book 1
TROUGANDA

Book 2
Zondura

Book 3
VAZDRAG

Book 4
Frole

Book 5
LOH